February 1942: With national paranoia about Japanese spies rampant, President Roosevelt signs Executive Order No. 9066. Almost immediately some 110,000 Japanese-Americans—many of them U.S. citizens—are served evacuation orders. Given forty-eight hours to dispose of their businesses, homes, and furniture, they are relocated to internment camps, where they are held behind barbed wire and under armed guard. *(Culver Pictures, Inc.)*

May 1942: Secretary of War Henry L. Stimson authorizes the formation of a Women's Auxiliary Corps. Joined by their sisters, the Navy WAVES, the Coast Guard SPARS, and Women Marines, the WACS will serve as airplane mechanics, typists, truck drivers, and pilots. By the end of World War II, some 300,000 women will have served. *(Culver Pictures, Inc.)*

December 1942: A young singer named Frank Sinatra makes his solo debut at the Paramount Theater in New York City. Discovered singing in a New Jersey roadhouse a few short years before, Sinatra becomes an overnight hit with bobby-soxers, who form 2,000 Sinatra fan clubs across the country and write the star some 5,000 letters a week. *(Culver Pictures, Inc.)*

December 1943: Postmaster General Frank C. Walker revokes second-class mailing privileges from *Esquire* in a moral furor over the magazine's girlie pictures. Pinups such as Rita Hayworth decorate military lockers and Quonset huts from Europe to the Pacific Islands, and American G.I.s complain that such pictures are one of the few comforts of life in the field. *(Culver Pictures, Inc.)*

June 1944: As Allied forces in England prepare for a full-scale invasion of Europe, General Dwight D. Eisenhower sends a message to his troops: "The year is 1944! The tide has turned! The free men of the world are marching together to victory!" The next morning, D-Day, some 176,000 armed infantrymen land on the beaches of France. *(Culver Pictures, Inc.)*

October 1945: Jackie Robinson is signed by Brooklyn Dodgers president Branch Rickey to play for the Brooklyn farm team. Two years later he will be brought up from the minors to play for Brooklyn—the first African-American ever to play major league baseball. *(Culver Pictures, Inc.)*

The American Chronicles by Robert Vaughan
Ask your bookseller for the books you have missed

DAWN OF THE CENTURY
OVER THERE
THE LOST GENERATION
HARD TIMES

THE AMERICAN CHRONICLES

VOLUME FIVE

PORTALS OF HELL

ROBERT VAUGHAN

BANTAM BOOKS

NEW YORK • TORONTO • LONDON • SYDNEY • AUCKLAND

PORTALS OF HELL

A Bantam Domain Book / December 1993

DOMAIN and the portrayal of a boxed "d" are trademarks of Bantam Books, a division of Bantam Doubleday Dell Publishing Group, Inc.

ISBN 0-553-29276-5

Published simultaneously in the United States and Canada

Bantam Books are published by Bantam Books, a division of Bantam Doubleday Dell Publishing Group, Inc. Its trademark, consisting of the words "Bantam Books" and the portrayal of a rooster, is Registered in U.S. Patent and Trademark Office and in other countries. Marca Registrada. Bantam Books, 1540 Broadway, New York, New York 10036.

PRINTED IN THE UNITED STATES OF AMERICA

OPM   0 9 8 7 6 5 4 3 2 1

**THIS BOOK IS DEDICATED TO MY WIFE,
RUTH ELLEN**
"Do you?"

The Evolution of Man

In his most graphic dreams,
He encounters a recurring theme:
Violence.
His sleep is besieged with screaming silence
Issuing from myriad precursors of modern man—
Australopithecus
And *Homo sapiens*, Neanderthal and Cro-Magnon—
Executing grotesque acts of homicide
By ripping invaders *and* tribesmen
Limb from hirsute limb
And viciously dismembering fingers, toes,
Heads, testicles, and breasts
With premeditated, sadistic bestiality.

In this cave-pocked desolation,
Creatured by these genocidal beasts
Systematically cannibalizing their own species,
Carnivores of the basest kind,
He recognizes sinister signs of malignance
Infiltrating the existing order.
He spies a pictograph,
Certainly informed by a higher intellect,
Scraped across the face of a limestone cliff,
Consisting of two intersecting lines,
One end of each thrusting left, the other right:
A swastika,
Not yet assigned its place in the evolution of Man.

—LOUIS DANIEL BRODSKY

CHAPTER ONE

JUNE 3, 1940, SAIGON, FRENCH INDOCHINA

When the port engine on the twin-engine Grumman flying boat exploded, a jagged piece of metal smashed through the left side window, then out the windshield. Something—either the piece of metal or a shard of glass—slashed a deep cut in Jimmy Blake's forehead, and blood started streaming down his face. The fire that followed immediately lit up the inside of the cockpit with a wavering orange glow.

"Shit!" Jimmy shouted.

He looked out the shattered left window and saw flames shooting out the front of the engine and curling back around the nacelle. Oily, black smoke billowed out behind the fire, already so heavy that the wingtip was obscured. Jimmy put the airplane into a severe right crab so that the windstream would blow the fire on the left wing away from the cabin. He also shut off the fuel and feathered the still-spinning propeller. The propeller wobbled to a halt, then sagged slightly downward as the crankshaft began to melt and warp under the intense heat.

1

"Are we going to crash?" the young Japanese woman seated beside him asked. Although her voice was calm, her hand was shaking as she put a handkerchief to the cut on Jimmy's forehead and held it there.

"Not, by God, if I can help it," Jimmy replied, his blue-gray eyes narrowing resolutely. "I'm only thirty years old; I'm not prepared to die just yet." He hit the red fire extinguisher button for the number-one engine, and a thick white foam began oozing out from the front of the engine. Within seconds the foam did its job, and the fire subsided. "Yeah!" Jimmy shouted, grinning. "Yeah, I got it! I put the son of a bitch out!"

By the time Jimmy corrected the crabbing angle and leveled off his rapidly descending airplane, he was no more than twenty-five feet above the Saigon River, a very busy trade thoroughfare whose surface was dotted with scores of ships, barges, and boats of every size and description. Jimmy knew that hundreds, if not thousands, of people would be on those vessels or standing alongside the river, watching the crippled plane come down. Some might even be hoping to see a crash, but he had no intenion of providing them with that show.

He lowered the flaps and hauled the blunt, boat-shaped nose of the Grumman up, slowing it down so that it was hovering just on the point of a stall. Nevertheless, the flying boat still hit the river very hard and sprayed up sheets of water onto the windshield, momentarily obscuring his vision. All the while the young woman held the handkerchief to Jimmy's face, helping somewhat to stem the flow of blood. When the water fell away a second later, the airplane was speeding across the surface of the river, headed for an unwanted rendezvous with a big wooden boat that glared back through the large red eyes painted on its bow. The occupants of the boat—an old man, an old woman, and a young child—unable to do anything to prevent the impending collision, stood on the deck, transfixed by fear, watching the airplane race toward them.

Steering with the water rudder and his one good engine, Jimmy managed at the last minute to swerve away from the boat and head toward the seaplane pier that protruded out into the river from the foot of Tu Do Street. By the time he reached the docking area, his speed had gradually decreased to the point that he had everything under control and was even able to hold the handkerchief himself. He killed the engine and allowed the airplane to float gently for the last few feet until it bumped lightly against the wooden pier, where an Annamese dockworker stood holding a rope, ready to make the plane fast. Not until his aircraft was secured did Jimmy let out a long sigh of relief, running a hand through his sweat-soaked sandy hair, and allow himself to look through the window at the damaged engine.

It was misshapen and twisted; a big, jagged hole gaped in the nacelle; and the propeller dangled uselessly, canted at a bizarre angle. The sheet-aluminum covering of the underside of the wing was scorched by fire, and the fabric of the control surfaces was burned away, exposing the bare ribs underneath. Just on the other side of the blackened wing was a fuel tank—and if the fire had reached it, the plane would have gone up in one huge explosion. Jimmy breathed a prayer of relief that the thin-gauge aluminum skin had proven strong enough to impede the fire.

It was only then that Jimmy thought of the young Japanese woman beside him, a passenger he had brought to Saigon from Port St. Jacques. She was sitting quietly, not having uttered a sound since asking if they were about to crash.

"Thanks for the first aid, Miss Amano," he said. "Are you all right?"

"Yes, thank you," Yukari Amano answered in a tiny voice. Her eyes were fixed straight ahead, staring through the windshield, and she gripped her Western-style purse tightly, one hand stained with Jimmy's blood.

Jimmy unsnapped his seat belt and harness. "Well, it's over with. We can get out now."

"Yes, thank you," Yukari replied again in the same small manner. She made no effort to move.

Jimmy looked at her curiously. "Are you *sure* you're all right?"

"I . . . I seem quite unable to move," Yukari admitted.

Jimmy chuckled, and his smile creased his rugged

face. "Well, that's understandable. We just came through what you might call a hair-raising experience." He reached for her seat belt buckle. "Would you like me to help you?"

"Yes, thank you," Yukari answered.

Still pressing the handkerchief to his wound with one hand, Jimmy used his other hand to unfasten Yukari's restraint and help her out of her seat. They stepped over the bulkhead of the small door just behind the cockpit and walked through the passenger compartment of the plane. Yukari was short enough to walk standing up, but Jimmy, who was six-feet-two, had to bend to avoid hitting his head as he passed through the cabin. Normally any of Jimmy's passengers would have ridden back here for the one-hour flight from Port St. Jacques to Saigon. However, Jimmy, the sole owner of the small unscheduled air service, had to make money any way he could, so on this flight the passenger seats were filled with revenue-producing sacks and boxes of freight. Even so, he could have made room in the cabin for Yukari, but, as he had informed her when he picked her up, it would be more comfortable for her up front with him. Smiling shyly, she had accepted his offer.

In the course of the flight Jimmy had learned that Yukari, who had been enjoying a three-day vacation at the seashore in the French resort town of Port St. Jacques, was the twenty-one-year-old daughter of Commander Hiroshi Amano, an aviator in the Japanese Imperial Navy. Commander Amano was in French Indochina as a military attaché to the Japanese consulate; because his duty was considered diplomatic rather than military, he had been granted the very rare privilege of being allowed to have his family accompany him. The Japanese consulate had made quarters available for the Amano family on rue de Pasteur, an avenue of well-kept lawns and stately villas. Hiroshi's wife, Yuko, had gasped in delighted surprise when she saw where they were to live: a large, Western-style, high-ceilinged house, cooled by spinning overhead fans and set in the midst of a shaded garden behind twelve-foot-high walls.

That was all coming to a close, though, for Commander Hiroshi Amano and his family would be returning to Japan the next day. It was because they were about to leave that Hiroshi had allowed Yukari to make an unaccompanied visit to the seashore. Hiroshi's wife and sixteen-year-old son were at home making preparations to leave, while Hiroshi would be meeting Yukari on her return from Port St. Jacques.

Jimmy opened the aircraft's door and spotted a Japanese man dressed in crisp naval whites complete with diplomatic braid waiting on the docks. Hiroshi Amano, to be sure, Jimmy thought. Though certainly, like everyone else, Hiroshi had seen the sudden engine fire, he displayed no outward emotion. He stood with his legs slightly spread, holding a small riding quirt behind his back, as he waited stoically for his daughter. Jimmy helped Yukari from the plane, then walked with her as she went to greet Hiroshi.

"Hello, Father," Yukari said in Japanese, bowing politely.

"Was your visit to the seashore pleasant?" Hiroshi asked.

"Yes, Father."

"I am glad. Wait in the car, please."

"Yes, Father." Yukari turned to Jimmy and bowed slightly. Jimmy bowed back, and then Yukari walked over to her father's staff car. The driver opened the back door for her, bowing deeply as she slipped inside.

Hiroshi watched until his daughter was safely inside the car, then turned back to Jimmy. "You are injured?" he asked, switching to English. It was excellent.

Jimmy took the handkerchief down and looked at it. It was blood-soaked. "It looks worse than it is," he replied, putting the handkerchief back. "A cut, that's all."

"You should have it seen to," Hiroshi said. He called over his shoulder to his driver, and the driver, bowing sharply, barked a one-word reply, then hurried off. "I have sent for a doctor," the commander said.

"Thank you."

"It is I who should be grateful, Mr. Blake," Hiroshi insisted. "Your skill as an aviator saved my daughter's life."

"I appreciate your expression of gratitude, Commander Amano," Jimmy answered dryly, "but the truth is, I was trying to save my *own* life. Your daughter just happened to be with me."

"Yes, to be sure. Nevertheless, that was a display of skillful flying on your part. And to show my appreciation, I would like to invite you to be the dinner guest of my family tonight. I apologize for giving you so little notice, but we will be leaving the country tomorrow."

"You're going back to Japan?"

"Yes. We will be flying back. I do hope the incident today hasn't so frightened my daughter that she will be unable to fly."

Jimmy smiled, and his face was filled with admiration. "Your daughter is a very brave young lady, Commander Amano. She didn't show the slightest bit of fear."

"That pleases me," Hiroshi replied. "You will accept my invitation?"

"I am honored by it."

Hiroshi's driver returned then, leading a man in a white suit carrying a small black satchel.

"This man is a doctor," Hiroshi said. "Please allow him to look at your wound."

"Yes, I will. Thank you again," Jimmy said.

The Japanese naval officer bowed, and Jimmy bowed back, then watched as Commander Amano returned to his car. Not until the car was driving away did Jimmy turn his attention back to the airplane. Already it was being unloaded by a couple of Annamese, and it bobbed up and down each time one of them entered or left the cabin. The native workers were wearing only khaki shorts and rope-and-leather sandals, and in their half-naked state it was easy to see how thin they were. But looks were deceiving, because they moved the heavy sacks and boxes with little apparent effort.

The man in the white suit stepped in front of Jimmy and held up his medical bag. "*Bac si*," he said, and Jimmy recognized the local term for doctor.

Jimmy nodded. "All right, fix me up, Doc. I don't have time for this."

The doctor looked at the wound; then, by gestures, he indicated that Jimmy needed stitches.

"Yeah, well, can you do it here? I've got to look after my plane." Jimmy pointed to the dock. "Here," he said. "Do it here."

The doctor said something, but Jimmy didn't understand him.

"What?"

"He says if he does it here, it will leave a bad scar," a bystander translated for him.

Jimmy laughed. "A scar, huh? Hell, what difference does that make? I wasn't pretty to begin with. Tell him to sew me up."

The bystander relayed the message, and, finding an empty crate, Jimmy sat down while the doctor cleaned his wound, then began sewing it shut. The operation drew a crowd of curious onlookers, and, through the translator, the doctor apologized for them.

"Oh, hell, let 'em watch," Jimmy said. "I disappointed 'em when I didn't crash. They ought to have *some* kind of a show."

The doctor sewed for another moment or two; then he cut the thread and tied it off. After that he put a clean bandage over the wound.

"Thanks," Jimmy said, pulling several bills from his wallet and offering them to the doctor.

The doctor looked at the money, then waved his hands in protest. He spoke to the translator.

"He says the Japanese man has already paid," the translator said.

"Then tell him this is a tip," Jimmy said. "I don't have enough to fix my airplane anyway, so I may as well be generous."

The doctor accepted the money, smiling broadly at his good fortune.

When the doctor left, Jimmy walked back over to his plane, stepped onto the bow, then scrambled up top and crawled between the two engines. The right power plant was undamaged, but the left engine hung in its mountings, grotesquely twisted and blackened.

"What happened, Monsieur Blake?" a man called.

Jimmy recognized André LeGrand's voice and groaned. LeGrand was the chief loan officer for the Banque de Saigon—and the last person Jimmy wanted to see. Jimmy owed the bank twenty-five hundred dollars on his plane. Now he wouldn't be able to make the money to pay the bank until his plane was repaired. And he wouldn't be able to repair his plane until he made some money.

"I had an engine fire," Jimmy grumbled. He managed to disconnect one of the cowling latches, even though it was warped by the fire. With the latch disconnected he was able to open the cowling and look down on the blackened engine. The smell of burned rubber and oil wafted into his nose. When he saw the fuel line, he let out a sniff of disgust. "And here's the culprit," he added, holding the rubber hose in his hand. "A broken fuel line."

"Such a shame," the banker said, making *tsk-tsk* sounds. "How difficult is it to fix a broken fuel line?"

"The fuel line's no problem," Jimmy said. He pointed to the engine. "But the crankshaft, propeller, cylinder walls, and pistons are shot. It's going to take a major rebuild, if not a new engine."

"I see," LeGrand said. "And that means what?"

"That means time and money," Jimmy replied. He smiled thinly. "Neither of which I have at this moment."

LeGrand cleared his throat. "What do you plan to do?" he asked.

Jimmy shut the cowling and pushed the fastener shut. It was an automatic move, though in truth the engine was so badly damaged that it made no difference whether the cowling was shut or not.

"I guess the only thing I can do is try and raise enough money to replace the engine," Jimmy said.

"Yes, to be sure," LeGrand agreed. "And while you are about it, perhaps you will be so kind as to raise enough money to pay the note at the bank as well. It is due by noon tomorrow."

"I thought maybe you could give me a ninety-day extension," Jimmy said. "And loan me enough money to make the repairs," he added halfheartedly.

"Yes, I thought as much," LeGrand said. He shook his head slowly and clucked his tongue. "I wish I could, Monsieur Blake. I rather like you, you know. But, unfortunately, one cannot let business decisions be clouded by friendship. You mustn't forget that I have a board of directors to satisfy, and they are not disposed to wait any longer. You do understand."

Jimmy sighed. "Yeah, I understand. And you understand, I hope, that without that extension and the additional loan, there's no way I can pay you. You'll have to take the airplane. And in its present condition, I'm afraid that it's not even worth what I owe you."

"Such are the risks of business," LeGrand said.

Jimmy climbed down from the airplane, then turned around and took one long, wistful look back at it. He sighed. "Okay, there it is. It's all yours."

"There is no hurry. Noon tomorrow will be soon enough," LeGrand replied with a shrug. "I have no fear that you will fly it away. It is too bad that your idea of a Southeast Asia airline didn't work out. But with only one airplane and one pilot the odds were against you."

"Yeah," Jimmy said. "I guess they were."

"What will you do now? Will you fly for Pan Am?"

"Pan Am? Hell, no. I hate those bastards. I guess I'll go back on with World Air Transport."

"Will they rehire you?"

"I'm sure they will. The president of the company, Willie Canfield, is a good friend of mine. And he told me when I left that if this didn't work out, he'd take me back. Although I probably won't get on as captain," Jimmy admitted. "But it doesn't matter. I'm not too proud to fly in the right-hand seat, and Willie knows that."

"I wish you good luck, Monsieur Blake," LeGrand said.

"Thanks."

Jimmy turned and walked away from the seaplane without looking back.

"Monsieur Blake, wait! Don't you want to remove your things from the plane?" LeGrand called.

"I'm wearing my leather jacket," Jimmy answered over his shoulder. "There's nothing else I want."

Hiroshi Amano was taller than the average Japanese man, and he accentuated his height even more by the ramrod erectness of his carriage. He was forty-two, a commander in the Imperial Navy, and though the caste system had been officially abolished in the previous century, he was by entitlement—and still considered himself to be—a samurai, a practitioner of the feudal Bushido code of chivalry, whose motto was: "Always live a life prepared to die."

Though the job of military attaché might seem a very tame assignment for a warrior, Hiroshi's job in Indochina was actually more than it seemed. Japan, which was being boycotted by the Western nations for its "adventures" in China, would soon face a serious shortage in oil, steel, and many other of the critical raw materials it needed to keep its economy going. One possible solution to that problem lay in the mineral-rich regions of Southeast Asia. However, as Southeast Asia was entirely controlled by Great Britain, France, and Holland, it was becoming more and more evident that Japan's only route to the raw materials it needed would be by military action. Hiroshi's objective, then, performed under cover of military attaché, was to gauge the strength of French Indochina's defenses. It was to make his actual duty less obvious that he had been allowed—in fact, encouraged—to take his wife, daughter, and son with him for the six-month assignment.

Hiroshi's family was present to greet Jimmy Blake that evening when the Annamese servant took the pilot's shoes and showed him into the parlor. Because of the French influence in Indochina, the architecture of the house was European. The clothes Hiroshi and his family were wearing were also Western-style, but the furnishings of the house and the conventions of the Amano family were strictly Japanese. They had been sitting on pillows on the floor around a low table, and when Jimmy arrived, they stood and bowed formally. Jimmy somewhat self-consciously returned their bow, then presented the box he was carrying to Hiroshi.

"How is your wound?" Hiroshi asked, accepting the present.

"Fine, fine," Jimmy said, putting his hand to the bandage. "Nothing to it."

"I am glad it was of no consequence."

"I brought you a fifth of Kentucky bourbon. I hope you like it."

"Thank you," Hiroshi said. "I must confess that I have developed a taste for American whiskey. Your gift pleases me very much. And now, if you would, allow me to introduce the rest of my family."

Hiroshi's wife, Yuko, like his daughter, Yukari—who smiled shyly at Jimmy—was an exquisitely beautiful woman, and to look at the two of them, Jimmy thought, he'd be more inclined to say they were sisters rather than mother and daughter. Saburo, the teenage son, was making an obvious effort to maintain as erect a bearing as his father. He shook hands firmly with Jimmy when he was introduced. Yukari withdrew with her mother to see to the preparation and serving of dinner; Saburo, on the other hand, asserted his right as a male by standing alongside his father. But Saburo's prerogative extended only so far as to be present, Jimmy saw, because conversation was carried on exclusively by Jimmy and Hiroshi.

Dinner was ready, and everyone sat on cushions arrayed around the low table. There was perfect symmetry to the way the dinner of rice, fish, fruit, and vegetables was displayed, as if the meal was a work of art. Then, as Jimmy looked at it, he realized that it *was* a work of art. He could imagine that Yukari and her mother had gone to great lengths to arrange the colors, shapes, and sizes in such a way as to make the most pleasing presentation.

Jimmy was offered a fork but he declined, choosing instead to use chopsticks. He could see that his adroitness with the implements pleased his hosts, and he was glad. He decided, though, that it was probably best not to tell them that he had learned the skill from a bar girl down on Cong Ly Street.

Throughout the dinner Jimmy could feel Yukari's eyes on him. Each time he'd feel her gaze, he looked over toward her, but he never managed to catch her in the act so that he was unable to exchange the slightest communication with her, even through glances. When he did glance toward her, he saw that she and her mother were looking down at their plates as if they were totally remote from the proceedings. Jimmy would have thought that they were paying no attention whatever had they not been so quick to respond to the slightest signal from Hiroshi, or even from Saburo, when a cup was to be filled or a plate removed.

At the meal's conclusion Yukari and her mother

cleared the table quickly; then Hiroshi dismissed the two women and his son with a slight wave of his hand. Bowing deeply, they withdrew, leaving Jimmy and Hiroshi alone.

"I know it is difficult for Westerners to sit for so long on the floor," Hiroshi offered. "There are some chairs in the living room, if you prefer."

"Whatever you wish, Commander," Jimmy said. "I'm quite comfortable here."

"Good. Then here we shall stay. You eat with chopsticks, you sit on the floor, you pay the proper respect to our customs. . . . You are a diplomat, Mr. Blake, as well as a fine aviator," Hiroshi said with admiration. He opened the whiskey and poured two glasses, handing one of them to Jimmy. "To our two countries," he suggested.

"To our two countries," Jimmy replied, touching his glass to Hiroshi's.

"My wife's brother lives in America," Hiroshi said after they took a sip. "His name is Yutake Saito. He is a gardener in Los Angeles."

"Is that so? Well, there are many Japanese living in Los Angeles, from what I understand," Jimmy said.

"Yes, that is true. I visited Los Angeles in 1932, when I represented my country in the Olympic games. While there, I met not only my wife's brother, but many Japanese-Americans."

"You were in the '32 Olympics?"

Hiroshi smiled. "My event was pistol shooting, in case you are wondering what event an old man could enter."

"No, I . . ." Jimmy started to protest, but then he smiled. "You're right. I was a little surprised," he admitted. "I always think of Olympics as running and jumping . . . sports for the very young. So tell me, how did you like America?"

"I liked it very much." Hiroshi took another swallow of his drink and studied Jimmy over the rim of his glass. "That is why I hope our diplomats will be able to avoid a great Pacific war between our countries."

Jimmy's eyes narrowed. "Why do you say that? Do you think there *will* be a war between America and Japan?"

"I am a professional military man, and I think a war with America would be a very bad thing for Japan," Hiroshi replied. "I am afraid, however, that there *will* be a war. Do you think not?"

"I don't know. I have to confess that I had no idea things had gotten to that state. I guess I've just been minding my own business, trying to make my airline work. I should have been paying more attention."

"Let us speak of something other than war," Hiroshi said and smiled. "Tell me about your airplane. Will you be able to repair it?" He lifted the bottle to fill Jimmy's empty glass.

"Thank you," Jimmy said, holding his glass out. He sighed. "No, I won't be able to repair it," he said. "But it doesn't matter because it isn't even my plane anymore. I had to give it back to the bank. Today was my last flight."

"I am so sorry."

"Don't be," Jimmy replied. "It was very foolish of me to think I could make a go of it with my own unscheduled air service. At least if I start flying for World Air Transport again, I'll get paid. That's more than I can say about the last eighteen months, when every penny I've made has gone back into that plane."

"You will be flying the Clipper, then?" Hiroshi asked.

"No, Pan American flies the Clipper. World Air Transport flies the Windjammer."

"Ah, yes, the Windjammer. I know of it. It is a four-engine flying boat, built by Rockwell-McPheeters Aviation," Hiroshi said. "The engines develop fifteen hundred horsepower each, the craft will carry seventy-five people at a cruising speed of one hundred seventy-five miles per hour, and it has a range of four thousand miles."

Jimmy laughed with surprise. "You seem to know a great deal about the Windjammer."

Hiroshi smiled easily. "When it was first introduced there was a great deal published about it. As I, too, am an aviator, I found the information most interesting. You have flown this airplane?"

"Oh, yes. Before I tried to start my own airline, I was a captain for World Air Transport."

"And how does such a huge ship handle?"

Jimmy grinned. "Like a dream. I mean, when you see it alongside a dock, it looks as ungainly as a battleship. But when it's flying, it handles like a speedboat." He tossed his drink down.

"When you were flying for World Air Transport, did you fly the Pacific route?" Hiroshi asked, pouring more whiskey into Jimmy's empty glass.

"Yes, I did," Jimmy replied. "Well, I wound up here, but I actually started out flying the Atlantic on the New York-to-Lisbon run. I switched to the Pacific last October. Then I found out that World Air Transport was selling the Grumman they'd been using for route development, so I decided to borrow some money to buy it and start my own airline. The rest, as they say, is history. Only, in my case, it's a very *short* history. As you can see, I didn't last very long." Jimmy tossed this drink down, too, then put his hand to his forehead and smiled crookedly. "These things get to you pretty fast, don't they?"

"I am interested in your experience with World Air Transport," Hiroshi said, ignoring Jimmy's remark. "Four thousand miles isn't enough range to allow you to cross the Pacific without landing somewhere. Where do you have bases?" He held up the whiskey bottle, offering Jimmy another drink.

Jimmy smiled. "Commander, are you trying to get me drunk so you can get information out of me?"

"That would be a waste of good whiskey, wouldn't it?" Hiroshi replied smoothly. "Have I asked you anything that isn't public knowledge?"

"No," Jimmy admitted. "No, I guess you haven't."

"Then in that case I am not asking for military secrets. I am merely an aviator like you, talking about something for which we both share a passion. You do have a passion for flying, do you not?"

"Oh, yeah," Jimmy said. He got a faraway look in his eyes. "There's nothing quite like watching the sun come up over the rim of the earth when you're flying at ten thousand feet above a solid-blue ocean. One minute it's so dark, you feel that you're flying inside an inverted bowl; then, in the very next second, there's an explosion of light that touches the ends of the earth. It is, at the same time, the loneliest and the most wonderful feeling in the world." Jimmy smiled, a bit self-conscious over the fact that he had allowed someone else to look into a secret part of his being. "I'm sorry. I guess I got a little carried away there."

"I am very pleased by your observation. Do you realize that you have spoken of our national symbol, the Rising Sun?" Hiroshi asked.

Jimmy smiled. "Yeah, I guess I have, at that."

"Do you understand haiku?"

"Yeah, it's a sort of poem, isn't it?"

Hiroshi nodded. "Perhaps it would be more properly described as an exercise in discipline than as poetry. You see, you must express a thought that will send ripples of association through the reader's mind the way a pebble sends ripples through a still pool. And you must do this in three lines that comprise exactly seventeen syllables. I have composed a haiku about flying. Would you care to hear it?"

"Yes, very much."

> "High above the crystal sun
> I await the destiny
> of my soul."

"Yeah," Jimmy said. "Yeah, that's the way it is. You got it just right." He held out his glass. "If you don't mind, I guess I *will* have another. After all, I'm the one that brought the whiskey over here, so if I get drunk, it's my own fault, isn't it?"

Hiroshi laughed. "After your harrowing experience today, you deserve to get drunk if you wish."

"Damn right," Jimmy slurred, then tossed the drink down as if it were water. He looked around the room. "Your wife and daughter have retired for the night?"

"Yes. It is not our way for women to participate in conversation that is best left for men."

"I see your point. And it's just as well. I seem to be getting a little light-headed, and I wouldn't want the women to see me like this. I don't want to embarrass myself in front of your daughter."

"My daughter thinks you are a hero," Hiroshi said. "Your flying skill impressed her greatly."

Jimmy grinned. "Is that a fact? Well, I'm very honored that she thinks so highly of me. You know, it's a shame that you're leaving so soon. I'd like to . . ." He let the sentence hang uncompleted. "On second thought you probably wouldn't let me call on her, anyway."

"No," Hiroshi agreed, "I wouldn't. Yukari's mother and I have already chosen her husband, and it would be unseemly to allow any other man to call on her for any reason."

"I didn't mean anything by it. I hope you don't take offense."

"No offense taken," Hiroshi replied.

"Honolulu, Midway, Wake Island, Guam, the Philippines, and Hong Kong," Jimmy said, ticking off the names on his fingers.

Hiroshi smiled. "Those are the bases I asked about?"

"Yep. And of all of 'em, Wake Island is the most important."

"Why is that? Wake Island is very tiny . . . so small that it doesn't even have its own water supply."

"Yeah, it's small, I agree. But it's damned important. You see, if we're going to carry anything besides gasoline in our planes, then we must land at Wake to refuel. That means whoever controls Wake Island controls the entire Pacific. And right now that's Pan American Airways. We have to pay them for the right to land and for every drop of water and gasoline we take on."

"Yes, I can see now how important Wake Island must be," Hiroshi said. He reached for the whiskey bottle. "Another?"

"No, thanks. I should be getting home. It's been a busy day," Jimmy said. With some difficulty he stood up. "I thank you very much for your invitation—and despite what you said, I can't help but feel that I may have disgraced myself somehow."

"No, you were merely relaxing after a trying experience," Hiroshi said lightly.

"I didn't insult you by speaking of your daughter?"

"There are some Japanese among my acquaintances who would have been greatly insulted," Hiroshi conceded. He smiled. "But I have visited America, and I have relatives who are now American, so I am aware of your ways. I am not insulted."

"I'm glad," Jimmy said. He looked down at his stockinged feet and wiggled his toes. "I wonder what that fella did with my shoes?"

"I'm sure he left them by the door," Hiroshi said. "Come. I will help you find them."

"You're a good man, Commander Amano-san," Jimmy said, speaking the words slowly and distinctly so as not to slur them.

"I thank you for your kind thoughts," Hiroshi replied.

"Ah, there're my shoes," Jimmy said when they reached the front door. He slipped his feet into them, then bent down to tie the laces. While he did so he looked up at Hiroshi and smiled. "Tomorrow you and your family are going one way and I'm going another," he remarked.

"Yes," Hiroshi replied.

"Who knows? Someday our paths may cross again."

"They may indeed."

CHAPTER TWO

JUNE 4, 1940, DUNKIRK, FRANCE

Sir John Paul Chetwynd-Dunleigh, Earl of Dunleigh and Colonel of His Majesty's Royal Essex Fusiliers, now in active service with the British Expeditionary Force, looked at the glowing dial of his wristwatch. It was 3:15 A.M., and he was at the final defensive position, approximately one-half mile from the beach at Dunkirk. Over the last week almost 340,000 soldiers had embarked from Dunkirk for England. The vaunted Maginot Line, living up to its promise, had not been breached. But it *had* been flanked, and France, which had based its entire defense on those static fortifications, had fallen. With the fall of France the British Army suddenly found itself outnumbered and outflanked. It had no choice but to retreat, though the English Channel had seemingly cut off even that route.

The British High Command had sent out urgent requests to its citizens, asking that they go to France in anything that would float. All England had responded with ships of war, ships of commerce, yachts, fishing boats, barges, and scows. The channel was packed with thousands of overloaded vessels as the troops were withdrawn. Newspapers in England and in the United States were already hailing it as the greatest strategic withdrawal in the history of warfare.

The end result was that France had been abandoned, and now practically the whole of Europe belonged to the Germans. John Paul had volunteered to stay behind and command the rear guard, thus buying enough time for the troops to withdraw. During the rear-guard action his men fought bravely and well, turning back three separate German thrusts. The fighting had been ferocious, and of the 323 men John Paul had started with, only 141 had lived long enough to get onto the evacuation ship, boarding it just after midnight that morning.

John Paul would be staying behind only long enough to coordinate the final defense with the French officer who was taking over. The major general who was John Paul's immediate superior had informed him that he was being recommended for the Distinguished Service Order with Bar for his heroism. But that didn't mollify John Paul's dissatisfaction. General Halfacre and the British press could paint it any way they wanted, he thought. In his mind the "strategic withdrawal" was still a defeat.

The commander of the French rear guard reached John Paul's position and introduced himself. "Please excuse me for saying so," Major Pierre Aubron said, shouting to be heard over the constant roar of shells from German tanks and field artillery that continued to rain deadly barrages down on the beach, "but you seem awfully young to be a colonel."

John Paul laughed. "If you think I'm young now, you should have seen me when I was five."

"*Pardon?*"

"That's how old I was when I inherited the commission," John Paul explained.

"I thought people who inherited commissions never used them except for ceremonial dinner parties," Aubron said dryly. "What are you doing over here?"

"When the war started, I asked to go into active service," John Paul replied. "I'm afraid I must plead temporary insanity."

Aubron laughed. "Temporary, you say? We will see about that. The last ship is about to sail. If you don't get down there, your insanity could become permanent."

"Some host you are," John Paul joked. "Rushing me off as if I had overstayed my welcome."

They glanced to the east, where the sky bloomed red with the false dawn of repeated cannon flashes.

"I'll come see you off," Pierre suggested.

"What about your men?"

"They have instructions to hold here for thirty more minutes; then they are on their own."

"Feel like a little run?" John Paul asked.

"But of course," Aubron replied, grinning. "After all, exercise is supposed to be good for you."

As the two men started running toward the beach they heard an incoming howitzer round whooshing down out of the blackness. It hit about one hundred yards ahead to the right of their path, and the shell's brilliant flash was followed a second later by the sound of its explosion. They were so used to such things by now that they didn't even alter their run. By the time they topped the last hillock, they were gasping for breath. Despite that, they were stopped short by what they saw.

"*Mon dieu!*" Aubron breathed. "Look at that!"

The beach was well lighted from nearly a hundred fires as trucks, tanks, and motorcars burned fiercely. For every vehicle burning there were at least ten more that weren't, and they stood abandoned on the beach. Most were in perfect condition, with keys still in the ignition, gas in the tanks, and doors open, as if inviting the Germans to drive them home.

John Paul shook his head sadly. "It shames me to see us abandon all this," he said.

"You have no cause for shame," Aubron replied, bitterness in his voice. "Your army has abandoned some equipment . . . my army has abandoned an entire country."

Another shell rushed over them, sounding like a runaway freight train. It plunged into the channel about a half mile offshore and exploded with a roar and a geyser of water.

John Paul spotted a British noncom and called, "Sergeant! Who is the senior officer remaining on the beach?"

The sergeant saw John Paul's rank and came to attention. "Blimey, Colonel," he said. "I imagine you must be."

"I just got here. Who else?"

"That would be our Major Heath down at the edge of the water, sir," he said, pointing toward the surf where a handful of men were getting into a boat. "He's been in charge of loading."

Thanking the sergeant, John Paul and Pierre Aubron hurried down across the beach to the British officer.

"Step lively, lads, do step lively now," Major Heath was saying to the soldiers who were climbing into the boat. "We wouldn't want to be late, now, would we?"

"Major Heath?"

The major turned toward John Paul, and John Paul saw the same look in his face that he had seen in the faces of all the officers he had spoken to during the last three weeks: exhaustion, shock, and anger. But he didn't see defeat, and somehow the major's look of defiance compensated for all the military equipment lying around on the beach.

"Ah, you must be Colonel Sir Chetwynd-Dunleigh," Major Heath said. "I was told you were still here."

"Yes."

"I'm damned glad you made it, sir. You're the last one, you know. And you, Major?" Heath asked Aubron. "Will you be going with us as well? A lot of your countrymen have."

"No, I will be staying in France," Aubron answered. He took off his heavy steel helmet and rubbed his hand across the crease in his forehead caused by the weight of the helmet.

"Major Aubron's men relieved our chaps at the barrier," John Paul explained.

"Good for you, Major," Heath said.

"Yes, well, I should warn you, I told my men they could disperse in thirty minutes," Aubron said. "After that there will be nothing between the Germans and the beach."

"No matter. We'll be gone by then," Heath said. He pointed to a black silhouette lying a half mile offshore. "Do you see that ship? That's the destroyer *Shikari*, and it's the last military vessel of the entire evacuation armada. Once we're aboard her, we'll head for England, and the Boche can jolly well have this bloody beach. No offense, Major," he quickly added.

"Where will you go now, Pierre?" John Paul asked.

"I'm not exactly sure," the Frenchman replied. "My military orders go only as far as the evacuation. After you are gone, I suppose I will try to make it back to Paris. My brother has a café there."

"Really? What's the name of it?" John Paul asked. "When this damn war is over and the Germans have been kicked back to their own border, I plan on returning to France on holiday. I'll come to the café and look you up."

"It is called Marcel's."

"Marcel's? That sounds familiar. Would I have heard of it?"

Pierre smiled. "You may have. Many famous writers have been there. Hemingway, Dos Passos, Twainbough, Gertrude Stein."

"Oh, yes, of course," John Paul said.

"Colonel," the sergeant said, coming down to the waterline. "I've had a final look around. Everyone has come in now."

"Very good," John Paul said. "Get your men into the boat, Sergeant. Major Heath, after you." He turned back to the Frenchman. "Oh, and Pierre, when you get to your brother's restaurant, do put away a bottle of his finest wine for me, won't you? I wouldn't want to be disappointed when I show up."

"I'll pick it out myself, John Paul," Aubron said, shaking John Paul's hand.

John Paul stepped into the shallows and climbed onto the boat. He was the last one to board, and even before he sat down the operator started the boat toward the destroyer. The small outboard motor popped loudly as the boat climbed up one side, then slid down the other of the heavy, rolling swell of an incoming breaker.

Turning, John Paul gave a quick look over his shoulder back at the beach littered with mutilated bodies, strewn with twisted debris, pocked with mortar craters, shells still raining down. . . . If anyone had asked him what hell looked like, he would have replied, "Dunkirk."

John Paul was quite surprised by the turnout to meet the *Shikari* when it returned to England. Several hundred people lined the docks, mostly civilians who had come down out of curiosity or out of a sense of patriotism. Someone had erected a huge banner that proclaimed: WELCOME HOME, LADS. ENGLAND IS PROUD OF YOU.

As John Paul walked down the boarding ramp from the deck of the destroyer and read the sign, he snorted. What was there to be proud of? They had run for their very lives, hadn't they? He knew that the evacuation of Dunkirk was being passed off by the War Office as a "strategic withdrawal," but the truth was, it was a retreat.

In addition to the civilian well-wishers, there were also military debriefers.

"How many German divisions would you estimate there are in the Dunkirk theater of operations?"

"What type of weapons did you encounter?"

"Do you have a personal theory on why they didn't move onto the beach and prevent our withdrawal?"

"Upon what do you base your theory?"

They seemed to have endless questions.

There were also personnel officers and posting clerks on hand, authorizing brief leaves and issuing next-assignment duty orders. And there were the ubiquitous "Comfort Ladies," volunteers who served tea and biscuits to the returning troops.

When John Paul finished the debriefing, he was informed that he was being placed on inactive status until later notice. The British military gave him an immediate, indefinite leave and told him to go home—home in John Paul's case being Dunleigh Estate.

"How soon before I can return to active service?" John Paul asked.

"I'm afraid we can't tell you that precisely. As I'm sure you know, Colonel, we left so much equipment and kit on the beaches of France that we can scarcely outfit an army right now."

"What about the Home Defense?" John Paul asked. "Surely I can be of some use to you there."

"We have as many officers and men on active service now as we can equip. You will, of course, still be carried on our active rosters, though I must in all candor tell you that it may be as much as a year before we'll be able to outfit another regiment for you. In the meantime, do stay in touch, and enjoy your leave, sir."

When John Paul left the temporary military headquarters, he walked past the Comfort Ladies' tables and smiled courteously at them while declining what they had to offer. Instead, he headed straight for the nearest pub.

"A pint, Colonel?" the barman asked as John Paul stepped up to the bar.

"Yes, thank you," John Paul replied. While his ale was being drawn, he looked around the pub and saw a couple of old men engaged in a game of darts. The men were wearing Home Guard uniforms, both bedecked with World War I ribbons. The dart board they were using was embellished with a drawing of Hitler's face. One of them threw a dart into Hitler's eye.

"Yes, good show," the other said.

The barman's voice brought John Paul's head back around. "Here you go, guv'nor," the barman said, sliding the mug across the bar to John Paul.

John Paul slapped a coin down, blew some of the foam off the top of his drink, then took it to a nearby table and pulled out a chair. For a long moment he just sat there, listening to the soft whish and thump of the darts as he stared into his mug, watching the tiny bubbles rise up from the bottom of the glass.

"May I join you?" a woman asked, her soft, well-modulated voice interrupting his reverie.

John Paul looked up at the woman. She had red hair, green eyes, and a light spray of freckles across her nose, and though one wouldn't describe her as beautiful, she was, John Paul thought, damned attractive.

"You're American, aren't you?"

"Yes," the woman replied. She smiled. "Why do you ask? Do you have something against Americans?"

"If I did, I'd have to answer to my mother," John Paul replied, grinning. "She's American. Please, do join me." He stood up and pulled out a chair for her. "May I buy you an ale?"

"Yes, thank you," the woman replied, and John Paul waved toward the barman, who nodded back at him.

"My name is Shaylin McKay," the woman offered.

John Paul chuckled. "Not just American, *Irish*-American."

"Sure 'n with me red hair and green eyes, what else would you be thinkin' I'd be?" she replied, rolling a perfect Irish brogue off her tongue.

"You do that very well," John Paul said, smiling.

"Thank you. And thanks for the ale," she added as the barman put a mug down in front of her. The barman also brought, without being asked, a salt shaker. Shaylin picked it up and began sprinkling salt into her drink.

"I see he knows you," John Paul said, indicating the salt shaker.

"I've been here a few times," Shaylin admitted. When she saw him looking at the salt, she smiled. "Oh, I'm sorry about this. I don't mean to be unflattering, but I find English ale so tasteless that this is the only way I can drink it."

"Gads, madam. You dare to mock our ale? What's next? English weather?"

"Why, no, I just love cold, rainy mornings and clammy, foggy evenings," Shaylin quipped.

John Paul studied her over the rim of his mug, but he said nothing.

"You must be wondering why I pushed myself on you like this," Shaylin said.

John Paul smiled. "I'm not wondering at all. I'm sure it's my striking good looks."

Shaylin laughed loudly. "Well, you *are* a fine figure of a man, and that's for sure," she said, mimicking an Irish brogue again. "But in truth," she continued, reverting back to American-accented English, "I saw you get off the ship a short while ago, and I know you've just returned from France. I wanted to get to you before anyone else. You see, I'm a working girl, attempting to ply my vocation."

"Are you now?" John Paul said, raising his eyebrows questioningly. "Tell me, Miss McKay, do I look so deprived that I'm in need of the services of a 'working girl,' as you put it?"

Now it was Shaylin's turn to raise her eyebrows, and she looked at John Paul in momentary confusion. Then, suddenly understanding what he was implying, she almost gasped.

"Good heavens, Colonel, you don't think I'm a *prostitute*, do you?"

"The thought did cross my mind, yes," John Paul admitted.

"Well," Shaylin said, laughing again, "I guess my profession is sometimes compared with prostitution. And when such comparisons are made, my profession doesn't always come out favorably. Actually, Colonel, I'm a journalist."

"Who do you write for?"

"Most of what I do is syndicated by the National Press Alliance, though my principal employment and my press accreditation is with *The St. Louis Chronicle*."

"I see. And what do you want with me?"

Shaylin opened her purse and pulled out a small notebook and a pencil. "I'd like to interview you."

"Why? I mean, there've been hundreds of thousands of chaps who came back before me. Surely by now you've had an opportunity to get the story."

Shayin smiled. "Ah, but you were the *last* one to leave the beach," she said. "And that makes your story quite unique."

"I see."

"How about it, Colonel?"

John Paul looked at her for a long moment, then smiled again. "You know, Miss McKay, I can't help but find myself wishing that you really were engaged in that other profession," he remarked. He sighed. "But if you think anything I might say would be of interest to your readers, then you just go ahead and conduct your interview."

As Shaylin began asking her questions, John Paul realized that she was quite good at her job. Whenever she asked questions of a military nature, they were clear and concise, so that it was obvious that she had more than a rudimentary understanding of military science. She also knew enough not to attempt to get into areas that might be militarily sensitive. As a matter of fact, as the interview continued, John Paul found that talking to her was actually a catharsis for him. He was able to get rid of some of the pain, frustration, and bitterness he felt over his part in what he still perceived as a great defeat.

"But it *isn't* a defeat," Shaylin insisted. "In fact, military strategists all over the world are heralding it as a great strategic maneuver."

John Paul threw up his hands in surrender. "Well, who am I to question the world's military strategists?"

"Tell me more about that French officer you left behind."

John Paul told Shaylin about Pierre Aubron. His last view of the Frenchman was as he walked almost nonchalantly across the beach, using his fingers to scoop out goose paté from a tin he had found in one of the abandoned staff cars.

"He was going to try to get back to Paris," John Paul said. "His brother owns a café there called Marcel's."

"Marcel's?" Shaylin said. "My goodness, I've *been* there. I *know* the place!"

"Yes, it has earned quite a degree of fame from all the writers who used to frequent it."

"Eric Twainbough," Shaylin said.

"Twainbough? Yes, he was one of them. And Hemingway and several others as well."

"No, I mean I know the place through Twainbough," Shaylin explained. "We were correspondents together in Spain, during the Revolution."

"You don't say!" John Paul exclaimed. "Twainbough is quite a gifted writer, isn't he? I read *Stillness in the Line* and thought it a wonderful book."

"Just a minute," Shaylin said, holding up her hand. "I read something the other day that I think you might appreciate." She walked over to the wall of the pub where there was a magazine rack, and after looking through a few of the periodicals, she smiled and brought one back to the table. "Yes," she said, "here it is. Eric wrote a piece for *Colliers* about Paris, and in it he described Marcel's." She opened the magazine to the appropriate page and handed it over. "Here's what he had to say about your friend's brother's restaurant."

John Paul began to read:

> In those days when I was writing *A Time For All Things* and Hemingway had not yet published *The Sun Also Rises*, he and I spent a lot of time at a café called Marcel's, owned by Marcel Aubron. Many people now come to Marcel's to see where Hemingway sat when he worked on his great book and where Gertrude Stein held court while Alice B. Toklas sat quietly at her side and where people like Ford Madox Ford or Sherwood Anderson conducted their intellectual arguments. But Marcel's wasn't a tourist attraction when we first found it. It was a quiet place, with good food and drink and pleasant company.

> Hemingway and I would sit at our tables outside and watch the big, green tour buses go by, filled with people looking for the true cuisine of Paris—and we had it all along. And we would drink cold beer and eat *pommes de terre à l'huile*, potatoes covered with ground black pepper and marinated in olive oil, and a *cervelas*, a wide frankfurter split and covered with a special mustard sauce. It sometimes made me sad to know that I was dining so grandly while those poor lost souls on the big green tour buses searched in vain for the true cuisine of Paris.

John Paul smiled and put down the magazine. "I hope Pierre Aubron gets a chance to read this article," he said, tapping the page. "I think he'd very much enjoy it."

Shaylin closed her small notebook and put it back in her purse. "So, what do you do next?" she asked.

"I'm going home for a while. Whatever I do after that is up to the British War Office."

Shaylin stood up and stuck out her hand. "Well, whatever it is, I wish you good luck."

"Thank you. Maybe we'll run into each other again sometime."

"Maybe."

John Paul smiled broadly. "If we do and you've decided to switch to that other profession, you will let me know, won't you?"

Shaylin laughed a low, throaty laugh. "Colonel, you'll be the *first* to know, I guarantee."

John Paul Chetwynd-Dunleigh, wearing his uniform with the newly awarded Distinguished Service Order pinned to his chest, stood at the window of the library in the grand Jacobean palace that was his family home, looking out across the gently rolling and beautifully manicured lawn of Dunleigh Estate. On the walls behind him were towering bookcases containing well over a thousand tomes, including dozens of first-edition, autographed books, some of which dated back to the beginning of the printing press in England. Beyond the library was the great hall, lined on both sides by suits of armor and shields, some of which had actually been worn in ancient battles. Keeping watch over the armaments were the stern portraits of all his forebears. The most recent portrait was of Sir Alexander Percivel Chetwynd-Dunleigh, John Paul's father and the sixth earl of Dunleigh. John Paul was actually the eighth earl. His older brother, dead now, had been the seventh.

Outside the house, on the other side of the garden, was the family cemetery, where under markers of various shapes and sizes rested the bones of those same forebears whose portraits graced the great hall. John Paul's father's plot was empty, however, for Sir Alex had gone down with the *Titanic*. The small grave next to his father's was not empty. This was the final resting place of James Croyden Chetwynd-Dunleigh, the seventh earl of Dunleigh. Jimmy had died of the Spanish influenza in the sixth year of his earldom and the twelfth year of his life.

A burst of laughter came from the salon, and though it was muffled by distance, it was loud enough to cause John

Paul to look over his shoulder toward the sound. His great-uncle Leicester happened to be coming into the library at that moment. Leicester Chetwynd-Dunleigh, who was in his late sixties or early seventies, was a large man with a walrus-type mustache. He was wearing the dress uniform of a major general, but the red tunic was fastened by only one button to accommodate his girth.

"Here you are, then," his uncle said in his inimitable gruff voice. "What are you doing in here, lad? You should be in there with the others. After all, you are the honored guest."

"They seem to be doing quite well without me," John Paul replied. As if to underscore his point, there was another burst of laughter.

Leicester chuckled. "Yes, well, your mother does seem to have the ability to make everyone have a good time."

"It's the American in her," John Paul said, adding cynically, "Americans are such fun-loving people." He took a sip of his drink. "In fact, they are so busy having fun that they can't come over here and give us a hand."

"Here, now, we don't want them anyway, do we lad? I mean, they arrived on the scene in the last war at the very last minute and have gone around patting themselves on the back ever since. I suspect we'll be able to take care of the Boche all by ourselves."

"Will we?" John Paul asked. "How?"

"How? You ask me how? Why, with brave lads like you, that's how." He pointed to the cross that dangled from the blue-bordered red ribbon pinned on John Paul's chest. "They don't just give the Distinguished Service Order away, you know. And I expect there are a few other brave chaps in your number as well."

"No matter how brave our chaps are, they can't fight without weapons," John Paul muttered.

"Without weapons? Why would you even say such a thing? Our army has the finest equipment of any army in the world."

"Wrong. We *had* the finest equipment of any army in the world. Now the Germans have it. Uncle, do you have any idea how much matériel we left on the beach at Dunkirk?"

"Not exactly," Leicester admitted. "I'm a little out of things, you understand. My commission, like yours, came with the title. But unlike you I've performed no active service for several years."

"Well, let me fill you in. Sitting on the beach right now are more than two thousand large-caliber guns, sixty thousand trucks, seventy-six thousand tons of ammunition, and six hundred thousand tons of fuel and supplies. The only weapons we brought back to England were our small arms."

"But . . . what about in the armories and supply depots here?" Leicester asked. "Can't our lads just be issued new equipment?"

John Paul finished his drink, then set it down on a nearby table. "In all of England we have only five hundred heavy guns remaining," he said.

"Only five hundred?" Leicester asked in a shocked voice.

"And that includes obsolete and museum pieces," John Paul added.

"I had no idea. There has been nothing in the papers."

"Well, we would hardly want to announce to the Germans that we're totally defenseless, now, would we?"

"No, no, of course not," Leicester agreed.

"Uncle Leicester, you will keep this quiet, won't you?" John Paul said. "I was talking out of turn . . . it wouldn't do even for our own people to know the extent of our predicament."

Leicester put his finger across his lips. "Oh, mum's the word, my boy, mum's the word," he promised. There was more laughter. "I suppose I had better go back in there. You're sure you don't want to come along?"

"Maybe later," John Paul said.

"You really should, you know. You're a genuine hero, and we need heroes now."

Leicester left, and John Paul returned to the window. He saw a couple of groundskeepers out in the cemetery, on their hands and knees pulling weeds. They were paying particular attention to the very first Chetwynd-Dunleigh, a man who had been dead for several hundred years and yet, even from the grave, managed to hold sway over his subjects. He was the first; John Paul was the latest. The funny thing was, John Paul knew that the two of them weren't even related. . . .

When Lucinda Chetwynd-Dunleigh saw Leicester return without John Paul, she excused herself to the man she was talking with and went over to talk to her uncle by marriage.

"Did you find him?" she asked, her green eyes narrowing in concern.

"He's in the library," Leicester replied. "I asked him to come join the rest of us, but he said he wanted to stay in there for a while longer."

"I'll go see him," Lucinda said. She put down her drink and walked toward the doorway.

"Lucinda," Leicester called.

She stopped in the doorway and looked back at him.

"He lost a lot of good men during that fracas over in France. During the Boer War I saw a few lads going through the same thing. He needs a little time."

"I'm not going to demand anything of him, Leicester," Lucinda said. "I just want to go to him, that's all."

She started down the long, shadowed hallway toward Alex's library. *Alex's library*. The words played over in her head, and she smiled. It was funny. She still thought of it as Alex's library, just as she thought of the house as Alex's house. Alex seemed to have a presence here, even though he had been dead and gone for twenty-eight years.

At fifty-six, Lady Lucinda Chetwynd-Dunleigh still retained much of the beauty that had made Lucinda Delacroix one of the most sought-after debutantes in New York at the dawn of the century. Lucinda's father had been a very wealthy man with a sense of grandeur—a sense of grandeur that had prompted him to arrange Lucinda's marriage to Sir Alex Chetwynd-Dunleigh. Alex had had land and a title and a forebear whose name was in the Domesday Book. What he didn't have was money. But that situation was neatly corrected when Lucinda's father settled a one-million-dollar wedding gift on the groom.

Lucinda stepped into the library, and when she saw her son standing at the window, she couldn't help but think of how much he reminded her of J.P. Winthrop, the man whose heart she had broken when she obeyed her father's wishes to marry Alex. Almost seven years after Lucinda had married her English lord, J.P. had come to Europe on business and visited the Dunleigh estate in England to pay a friendly call on Lucinda and her family. When he had learned that Sir Alex had booked passage to the United States on the maiden voyage of the *Titanic*, J.P. decided to extend his visit by returning on the same ship. The last time Lucinda ever saw J.P., he was standing on the boat deck of the *Titanic* in much the same pose John Paul was assuming now. J.P. and Lucinda's husband, Alex, were among the many who died that night. And that was the night that John Paul had been conceived.

"Hi," Lucinda said to her son.

John Paul turned toward her. "Hi yourself."

"Are you okay?"

"I'm fine," John Paul replied. "But I don't want to go in there." He gestured toward the parlor.

Lucinda laughed. "I don't blame you. It's really quite patriotic in there right now. God save the king, hurrah for the Union Jack, and all that."

"Well, these are times that call for patriotism," John Paul countered.

"Don't get me wrong, I'm all for patriotism," Lucinda said. "I just don't think it needs to be defended with an olive fork."

"At least they're taking up the olive fork," John Paul muttered. "That's more than we can say for your Americans, isn't it? They've done nothing in this war."

"Why should they? This isn't their war."

"It will be," John Paul said with certainty. "They'll stay out as long as they can, and then, after we've been bled quite dry, they'll come in at the final hour to save the day, just as they did in the last war. Only this *isn't* the last war, and I'm afraid if they wait too long, there won't be any day left to save."

"You mustn't be so critical of the Americans. After all, you're half American."

John Paul looked at Lucinda for what seemed an endless moment. "Only half, Mother?"

Lucinda gasped sharply, then was silent. Finally, very quietly, she asked, "How long have you known?"

"Since I was twenty-one," John Paul answered. "When I came into . . . *Father's* papers. Did you know he kept a diary, Mother?"

"No," Lucinda said. "I didn't know."

"I may be the only one who *does* know," John Paul said. "It was unmarked, and I found no record of it anywhere else. I didn't read it for the first month or so because I wanted to respect his privacy. But then I thought that since he had died nine months before I was born, his diary might be the only way I would ever have to know him. In the diary he confessed a secret that he said he had shared with no one. Except with you, of course. It would have been pretty difficult not to share the secret with you. He was impotent and had been for years."

Lucinda bowed her head. "It happened shortly after Jimmy was born," she said. "I don't know why. He wouldn't go to a doctor. He was, as I'm sure you gathered from the diary, very self-conscious about it."

"Was J.P. Winthrop my father?"

Lucinda unconsciously began wringing her hands. "John Paul, why are you doing this?" she asked in a pleading voice. "Why are you bringing all this up now?"

"Don't misunderstand me, Mother," John Paul said. "I'm not feeling sorry for my father. As you know, I never knew him. But I *am* feeling somewhat aggrieved for myself. If I don't have a father, then I would at least like to know who the father is that I don't have."

Suddenly and unexpectedly Lucinda laughed. John Paul, realizing then what he had said, also saw the humor in it, and he laughed as well.

"I'll try and explain it to you, my darling," Lucinda said. "But I don't know if you'll be able to understand. I don't know, really, if *I* understand it. But you see, I loved them both . . . Alex and J.P. I loved them in different ways, of course, and, to be honest, I can't honestly say that I loved one more than the other. J.P. was bold, passionate, and American. Alex was proper, intellectually stimulating, and very, very British. I thought that by keeping the identity of your father secret, I would always be able to see both of them in you. And I have. You have J.P.'s boldness and passion, and you certainly have his looks. But because you have been brought up with Alex's name and in his house, you have a sense of propriety and an exasperatingly stubborn British pride that I think Alex would greatly appreciate." She paused, adding softly, "I never told you because I wanted you to be Alex's son."

John Paul turned toward the window and drummed his fingers on the sill. "I *am* his son," he finally said. "Ever since I've known the truth, I've tried to picture myself as J.P. Winthrop's son, but I can't do it. No matter how hard I try, I can't do it. When I stand here and look over at that cemetery, I know that *those* are my forebears. And when I am buried there, I know I will be accepted by them as one of them. Whatever biological accident may have happened to get me here, I *am* the Earl of Dunleigh."

He turned back toward his mother and held his arms open for her. With a small cry of relief Lucinda went into his arms, and he held her to him.

"You don't know how wonderful it is to hear you say that," she said. "I have carried that burden with me ever since you were born."

There was another burst of laughter from the parlor, and John Paul looked toward the door. "It does sound as if they're having a good time in there," he remarked.

Lucinda chuckled. "They do seem to be. Oh, by the way, another guest arrived, one you haven't seen yet, though she says she knows you."

"She?"

"Yes, quite a lovely young woman. Red hair, green eyes. American."

"Shaylin!"

"My, my," Lucinda said, smiling and shaking her head. "She said she only met you for a few moments, but it would seem that she made quite an impression on you."

"I wonder if she's come to tell me about a career change," John Paul murmured.

"I beg your pardon?" Lucinda asked.

Her son laughed. "Never mind, Mother. It's a private joke."

CHAPTER THREE

When the destroyer *Washita* put into Pearl Harbor at about 1600 hours, the first thing that came aboard was its mail. The ship had been on sea patrol for ninety days, so quite a bit had accumulated; there would have been even more if not for the fact that three times while they were at sea a PBY had managed to rendezvous with them, each time making a low pass overhead to drop a canvas mailbag.

Even with those few intermittent drops some of the men actually had as many as forty or fifty letters waiting for them. Petty Officer Second Class Kevin McKay, on the other hand, had only one, and he wouldn't have gotten it if his friend Bill Raymond hadn't brought it to him. Kevin got mail so infrequently that he never bothered to check, and sometimes an exasperated mail clerk would have to hunt him down almost two weeks after a letter had arrived.

It didn't bother Kevin that he seldom got mail. Truth was, he wrote even fewer letters than he received. He had only his sister to correspond with, and she didn't write very often.

"If you want to know what I'm thinking about, read my articles," she once said.

That was easy enough to do. Her newspaper articles were syndicated, so Kevin saw her byline frequently. He supposed she was even famous because it certainly seemed to impress people when he told them that his sister was Shaylin McKay. In fact, Kevin was sure she was famous when he encountered people who didn't *believe* she was his sister.

Kevin, who was getting ready for shore leave, checked the postmark on this latest letter and saw that it had been mailed almost three months before, from England.

My dear Kevin,

I am very proud of your new rating. Keep up the good work. Who knows? At this rate you may one day make admiral. I'm not surprised by your rapid promotion, though. From the time you were fifteen I had to fight tooth and nail to keep you from enlisting. Is the Navy all you hoped it would be? You seem to be enjoying it, so evidently it is.

I still wonder if I did as well by you as I should have, but I hope you realize that it wasn't easy for a twenty-two-year-old woman to suddenly have the responsibility of raising her thirteen-year-old brother. Of course, to say that I raised you is stretching the truth quite a bit. You actually raised yourself; I did nothing more than provide you with a roof over your head and an occasional meal.

But that's all in the past, and I don't know why I even bother to bring it up now. Besides, you certainly seem to have turned out well. Look at you! A Petty Officer Second Class at the tender age of twenty-two!

You asked me in your last letter (how long ago was that? A year? Eighteen months?) if I was still seeing Eric Twainbough. The answer, dear brother, is no. Eric is a dear, sweet man, but he's a writer and I'm a writer, and I think it may be impossible for two writers to have any kind of a life together. After all, we do both have our fragile egos to contend with. And Eric is also quite a famous fellow, easily recognized due to his "bulk and beard." He claims to be bothered by it, but secretly he thrives on it. So, to be very honest, perhaps what made it impossible for me wasn't so much that he thrived on his fame as it was that I felt like a fifth wheel, basking in his reflected glory. I didn't particularly enjoy that.

Anyway, though he won't admit it, I think Eric still loves Tanner, his first wife. Or, and here's one for the psychiatrists, Eric may even be still in love with Katya. Yes, the same Katya who's a character in his book *Stillness in the Line.* There really WAS a Katya, and she really was a Russian princess who disappeared during the Russian Revolution of 1917.

At the moment I have a new man in my life. Though he doesn't have as exalted a title as Eric's Princess Katya, he is a member of what the English call the "peerage." He is Colonel Sir John Paul Chetwynd-Dunleigh, the Earl of Dunleigh. If you read my article about the British evacuation of Dunkirk last year, you'd have read about him. He was awarded the DSO for his bravery in manning a defensive perimeter that allowed the British Army to escape.

John Paul is actually half American, so he isn't nearly as stuffy as so many Brits, especially the "landed gentry," are. He's very handsome and very nice, and I very much enjoy his company. But I must say that our situation reminds me a little of the radio soap opera drama, *Our Gal Sunday,* when the announcer begins the program with the question, "Can this girl from a mining town in the West find happiness as the wife of a wealthy and titled Englishman?"

Actually, our relationship hasn't advanced to the point that such a question would really be posed. For one thing John Paul hasn't asked, and I don't know that he ever would—or, if he did, if I'd accept. There is a war on, after all, and I know all about wartime romances, having been involved in one during the Spanish Revolution. Who knows, dear brother? Perhaps it's my fate to go through life finding one war after another to cover—and at the same time some man who can help get me *through* the war.

By the way, guess who just showed up in London? Floyd Stoner. You remember him, don't you? The "Mouth of St. Louis"? It seems that he has convinced Kendra Petzold that shortwave radio broadcasts from London would be as effective as newspaper articles are. Anyway, he showed up in the bar of the Savoy the other night, as full of himself as he always was. Lord save the world of journalism from the instant madness of on-the-spot radio reporting. It may be information, it might even be news, but it can never, NEVER be journalism, even in the midst of war.

Speaking of wars, I'm sure glad you're safe out there in the middle of the Pacific. The German U-boats are menacing all shipping in the Atlantic right now, and they don't always stop to see if the ship they send a torpedo into is flying a British or an American flag.

Keep up the good work, little brother, and stay out of trouble. You're the only family I've got, and I'd like to hang on to you for a while.

With much love,
Shaylin

Kevin folded the letter up and put it away in his locker; then he took his middy blouse off the hanger and slipped into it. His weekend pass had started the moment the anchor dropped, and he didn't intend to waste any more time here.

Kevin's friend Bill was on watch, and he came up on deck with Kevin. "Sure wish I could go into town with you," he said. "It's going to be a long weekend, sittin' here on this tub with everyone else ashore."

"Yeah, but think of it this way," Kevin replied. "You can go ashore Monday when everyone else is on duty.

You'll have the bars and the whores pretty much to yourself."

"Yeah," Bill said, a grin spreading over his plain face. "Yeah, son of a bitch, I hadn't thought about that."

"Permission to go ashore, sir," Kevin said, saluting the officer of the day when he and Bill reached the gangplank.

"Permission granted," the OOD replied, returning the salute.

Kevin saluted the flag on the fantail, then started down the wobbling gangplank.

"Kevin! Kevin, you big redheaded Irishman, save somethin' for me!" Bill shouted over the rail as Kevin stepped onto the dock. Kevin looked back up at his friend, who was dressed in glistening whites and leaning over the railing of the equally glistening destroyer. Behind him was the forward eight-inch gun mount with its gun barrels tamponed, and above that the twin-fifty mount, with the machine guns pointing straight up and covered with canvas. It was a picture that could have come straight off a Navy recruitment poster. Kevin felt a momentary exhilaration—though it wasn't something he could share with anyone else. Anyone he told would think the whole idea was pretty much cornball.

"I'll make sure there's something left," Kevin called back, laughing and waving good-bye as he started up the pier toward the liberty bus.

Thirty minutes later he was walking down the street and listening to music from various jukeboxes spill through the doors of Honolulu's bars. For a moment "Blues in the Night" was strong, then "I'll Be Seeing You," followed by "There, I've Said It Again." The music, the neon lights, and the paid barkers competed for the attention of hundreds of soldiers and sailors who had come into town to squander their precious money and their even more precious hours of liberty.

Kevin McKay homed in on the wailing clarinet of Benny Goodman—not so much because he was a Benny Goodman fan, though he was, but because the music was coming from the New Plantation Club, and that was where Kevin was headed. The New Plantation Club was always the first place Kevin headed toward when he got back, and

it was the last place he had been before he left. It was a
regular hangout for sailors when the fleet was in because
the bartender there was a retired bosun who'd rather handle a disturbance himself than call the shore patrol. If his
handling was sometimes a little rough, it was excused; almost everyone would rather have a small bump on the head
than spend two weeks in the brig.

Lé Wong was another reason Kevin went to the New
Plantation. Lé was a Chinese girl with golden skin, huge
brown eyes, and eyelashes as long as palm fronds. She was
a bar girl who hustled drinks—and herself if the price was
right and if she was in the mood. Kevin had spent his last
night ashore with her, and often during the long night
watches while he was on patrol, he'd stare out across the
sea, looking in the direction of Honolulu, where he could
almost see her face floating just over the horizon.

It was during those long, lonely hours that Kevin came
up with "the plan": He was going to buy some time from
Lé, no matter how much it cost. He'd take her out of the
club on Friday afternoon and go somewhere, maybe even to
the other side of the island. And there, in some quiet little
hotel, without the intruding sound of sailors' laughter, jukebox music, clinking bottles, and breaking glasses, they'd
spend the entire weekend together.

Kevin had actually conceived of the plan on the third
night he was at sea. At first it was just a fantasy, elaborately
spun to while away the long, quiet hours of midnight
watch. But he kept returning to the same fantasy each time
he drew the duty, and the more he thought about it, the
more reasonable the idea seemed. He turned the plan over
and over in his mind, disassembling it, putting it back together again, honing it, and refining it, until not the slightest detail was left to chance—where they'd stay, what
they'd eat, the type of room they'd have. And there'd be
chilled wine already in their room, waiting for them. Lé
would comment about that, and Kevin would answer her as
if it were a perfectly normal thing for him to check into a
room with a bottle of wine already chilling.

"It's nothing out of the ordinary, just an ice bucket with
a bottle of wine. May I pour for you?" he would say with
great savoir faire.

And the best part of the plan, the most absolutely beautiful, foolproof part of the plan, was that Kevin didn't have to *ask* Lé to give up a weekend for him; he intended to *buy* the weekend from her. That way she couldn't turn him down.

And now, he thought as he reached the New Plantation Club and opened the door, after all the dreaming and the planning and the anticipation, it was about to happen. The *Washita* was in port, and Kevin had three days of leave and three months of pay. All he had to do was find Lé and they'd be on their way.

He stepped inside the club, then stopped short and looked around in surprise. As usual the place was packed from wall to wall with solid humanity. And as usual it was cloudy with cigarette smoke and noisy with jukebox music, men's voices, and women's laughter. But there was not one article of Navy white to be seen. Everywhere Kevin looked there was nothing but Army khaki.

"Hello, Kevin. Long time no see," Lé Wong said, smiling as she sidled up to him.

"What is all this?" Kevin asked, taking in the bar with a wide sweep of his hands. "Where are all the guys?"

"This is Army bar now," Lé said. "Sailors no come here no more."

"What do you mean, they don't come here anymore? Where's Boats?"

The smile left Lé's face, and her eyes clouded over with sadness. "You don't know?"

"Know? Know what?"

"Very terrible thing. Very sad. Boats die," Lé said, shaking her head.

"Die? You mean he's dead?"

"Yes. He give bump to head of big sailor man. Everyone else get bump to head, they go down. This big sailor man not like everyone else. He take out knife, he stab and kill Boats."

"Damn," Kevin said. "That's too bad. I really liked the bosun." He sighed. "But that doesn't explain all this. Where'd all these soldiers come from?"

"After Boats die, shore patrol come and make the New Plantation off limits for all sailors. Sailors no can come, but soldiers can come. Now we not off limits for sailors any-more, but New Plantation is already Army place, and sailors don't come no more."

"Yeah? Well, by God, *I'm* here," Kevin said. He smiled and patted his shirt just over his waistband. "And I've got money, too."

Lé smiled broadly. "You got money? It's not payday. How come you got money?"

"I've been at sea three months," Kevin explained. "I didn't have anyone like you to spend it on."

Lé laughed and put her arms around his neck. "Oh, Kevin, I love you too much, I think."

"I've got something I want to talk to you about," Kevin said, preparing to introduce the plan.

"Hey! Hey, Lé, get back over here! You're supposed to be with me, goddammit! Let the sailor get his own girl!" a raspy voice, belonging to a big corporal, called.

"Sailor man have money," Lé called back to the man. "You no have money."

"You're in the wrong place, aren't you, mop jockey?" one of the other soldiers shouted.

"He can't help it," another said. "You know how it is with these sailors. They chip so much paint that it gets in their eyes and they can't see good. They don't know where they are, and they get lost."

"Yeah? Well, I'll help him out," the corporal said. "Look, bud, this ain't where you're supposed to be, so why don't you just get the hell outta here?"

"Anybody want to make me get out of here?" Kevin challenged belligerently, squaring his broad shoulders and tensing his powerful arms. It seemed unlikely that any one person could throw him out, and, as he was the only sailor present, it was equally unlikely that the soldiers would gang up on him. Free-for-alls did frequently develop in Honolulu's bars and alleyways, but even in the biggest knock-down, drag-out fight, the men adhered to a strict code of conduct: It was dangerous for ten sailors to go into a "soldiers' bar," but the safety of one sailor was guaran-teed.

When no one seemed anxious to accept Kevin's challenge, he snorted. "I didn't think so," he said. "Come on, Lé. I want you to leave this place with me."

"Leave with you? Kevin, what you talk? I no can leave with you."

"Sure you can. Look, I'm not asking for a date. I'll pay for your time; I'll pay for the entire weekend." He took out his billfold and held it open toward her, showing her that it was full of money. "We'll go over to the other side of the island and get us a hotel. I'll bring you back Sunday night."

Lé shook her head. "Kevin, I no can do that. Don't you know? I am to be marry tomorrow."

"What?"

"Yes. I am going to marry a soldier boy from Fort De Russey. He love me too much. We get marry tomorrow."

"Are you bullshitting me?"

"I no bullshit you, Kevin," Lé said, pouting prettily. "I tell you true. I meet him one month before, and I love him too much. He get all the papers for marry signed, his CO, everything. We get marry tomorrow."

"Well, if you're getting married tomorrow, what the hell are you doing in here tonight?"

"He say is okay I work one more day until we get marry," Lé explained. "After tomorrow, I no can work no more."

"Shit," Kevin muttered, rubbing his chin. "I've been counting on this. I mean, I have been literally counting the goddamn days."

Lé smiled at him. "You remember last time you here? You like what we do then?"

"Like it? Hell, yes, I liked it. What the hell do you think I've been trying to say?"

"You say you want me go with you for weekend. I say I cannot go," Lé said. She pointed at the ceiling. "But if you want to go upstairs, is okay. Can do."

"Forget it," Kevin said, half turning toward the door. "I'll just . . . "

He stopped and looked back at her. The dress she was wearing had a long slit that ran up the side almost to her hip, exposing her leg all the way to its creamy thigh. She wasn't wearing a bra; that was obvious not only from the way her breasts moved under the thin cloth of the dress, but also by the way her nipples pushed against the material. As Kevin looked at her, he felt the old, familiar churning start up in his groin. And he suddenly found the idea of going to bed with Lé on the night before she was to marry someone else strangely appealing. He smiled at her.

"Ah, what the hell?" he said. "Why not? As horny as I am, I might wear you out so that you won't even be any good for that bastard."

Lé rubbed her hand down her thigh and arched her body toward him.

"You not wear *me* out, Kevin," she purred. "I wear *you* out."

ST. LOUIS, MISSOURI

Hamilton Twainbough came out of the library late in the afternoon and shifted his books under his left arm. The name of the library, engraved in stone above the door, was the William Canfield Memorial Library, though it was called Billy Books by students and faculty alike. Billy Books proudly billed itself as the fourth largest university library in America. Six of the books in that library had been written by Ham's father, Eric Twainbough.

Ham stood there for a long moment, looking out across the Jefferson University campus. Dogwood, redbud, and flowering cherry trees joined with the azaleas, tulips, and irises to create a riot of spring color. Just beyond the library on a branch of a sugar maple a brightly plumaged cardinal, newly matured, sang for a companion. A couple of robins, already mated and parenting, searched the grassy quadrangle for worms.

Checking his watch, Ham saw that it was late enough for the grades to be posted, and he started across toward Spengeman Hall, which formed the eastern boundary of the quad. The quad was bordered on the south by the men's dormitories, on the west by the Science and Industry academic building, and on the north by Constance Canfield Hall and Billy Books.

Ham cut across the grass. Only juniors and seniors were allowed to do that, and Ham was technically still a sophomore. But since this was the last week of the school year, he'd only be a sophomore for a few more days—and even if he was pushing his privilege, there was no one around willing to challenge him.

In the center of the quad was Statue Circle, a garden-like area of flowers and marble chips cordoned off by a thigh-high chain and dominated by the two statues that gave the area its name. It was the exclusive privilege of seniors to walk, sit, or recline inside Statue Circle. No one else could even step across the chain barrier.

One of the statues was the life-sized figure of a man standing with his hands resting lightly on a railing, gazing out across the campus. This was Professor William T. Bateman, a former chancellor of the university and the man credited with having moved Jefferson University from a midwestern "cow college" to the status of one of the most academically respected universities in the nation. A simple bronze plaque by Bateman's statue read: KEEPING WATCH.

The professor's statue was often decorated in accordance with the season. At the beginning of the school year Bateman might be wearing a pledge beanie from one of the fraternities. During football season he'd wear a scarf and carry a pennant. He was also dressed up for Halloween, Thanksgiving, Christmas, and St. Patrick's Day. It was all done in fun and under strict guidelines that made certain that no damage was ever done to the statue.

The other statue was that of Henry R. Spengeman, the founder of Jefferson University. The Spengeman statue was four times life size and had the professor sitting in a chair, reading a book. This statue had been done by Rodin in the style of his "The Thinker" and was listed in the National Register as one of the most important pieces of sculpture in America. There were many who would immediately recognize a picture of the Spengeman statue but had no idea that it was located on a college campus in St. Louis, Missouri.

Due to its national importance and because of its significance to the university, the Spengeman statue was never touched except by a select group of seniors known as the Quad Quad—four young men nominated for the honor by the faculty and elected to the position by their class peers. Competition for membership in the Quad Quad was extremely fierce, for it was the greatest honor that could be bestowed upon a Jefferson University undergraduate. The induction actually took place at the end of the first semester of the junior year, and during the second semester the four served as acolytes to the incumbent Quad Quad, thus learning all the secret rites and rituals that had been passed down through the years. Ham had already been told by the faculty that he was being nominated. Whether or not he was selected would depend on a vote held the following November among Ham's class of '43.

"Ham! Say, Ham, where are you going?" Randy Wilson called.

Randy was also a member of the Class of '43, and the student trainer for the JU football team. He idolized Ham because Ham was the Bears' best running back. Randy was a nice, likable young man, though Ham was sometimes embarrassed by his almost slavish devotion.

"I'm just going into Spengeman Hall to check the grades from my finals," Ham answered.

"Are you kidding? Since when do you worry about grades?"

"Well, let's say I'm wondering about them more than worrying about them. How'd you do?"

"Nothing to write home about," Randy said, "but at least I'm not failing anything. Listen, you coming down to Bear Tracks?"

"I guess so," Ham replied. "How about you?"

"Yeah, sure. Can I hold a table for you?"

"Okay. I'll be there shortly," Ham promised.

"You won't forget?"

"I won't forget."

Randy grinned. "Yeah, we're going to have a good time tonight! School's out! We'll celebrate!"

Ham smiled at Randy's enthusiasm and continued on to Spengeman Hall. He took the concrete steps—steps that had been polished smooth over the years by the foot treads of thousands of students—two at a time as he hurried up to the wide double doors.

The high-ceilinged hallway seemed quite dark after the brightness of the afternoon sun, and Ham had to stand just inside the doors for a moment to allow his eyes to adjust. The floors smelled of a recent application of linseed oil, and as he started down the hallway toward the bulletin board, he saw a janitor at the far end of the hall, methodically pushing his oiled mop.

Grades were posted on the near end of the long bulletin board, while at the far end were listed courses and their locations. A girl stood by the far end of the board, looking first at the clipboard she was carrying, then intently studying the information. From the confused look on her face Ham knew that she must be a freshman—or rather, would probably be a freshman next year—and was trying to fix in her mind the course numbers and locations of all the classes. He saw, too, that she was very pretty, tall and sleek with lines that made Ham think of a greyhound. Ham checked his grades and smiled with satisfaction at what he saw, then looked at the girl again.

"Oh, dear," the girl said, knowing she was being looked at.

Ham walked toward her. "Do you need some help?" he asked with a smile.

"Yes," the girl answered. "According to my schedule, I'm supposed to take a philosophy class. But I don't see it on the course board."

"Here, let me take a look at your schedule," Ham offered, reaching for her clipboard. "Oh, here's the reason. This is a new class, see? That's what the letter *N* stands for. And the course board is still showing last year's curriculum. They probably won't get the new curriculum up until just before school starts in September."

The girl laughed self-consciously. "I guess I'm a little anxious," she admitted. She looked up at him, and Ham found himself looking into perhaps the bluest eyes he had ever seen. She brushed a fall of blond hair away from her face. "You're Hamilton Twainbough, aren't you?"

"Ham," he corrected.

"I thought you were. I've seen you play football."

"You've watched only the good games, I hope."

She laughed. "No, the bad ones, too, I'm afraid. I see all of them. At least, all the home games. My father is a big football fan. You may know him. He's a professor."

"He is? What's his field?"

"Physics," the girl said. "I'm Amy Wilkerson."

"Dub? He's . . . I mean, Professor Wilkerson is your father?"

"Wyman W. Wilkerson. Dub," Amy confirmed. "That's all right; even his family calls him that."

"Maybe so," Ham said, laughing, "but his students don't. Not if they want to get a passing grade."

"But you're not one of his students," Amy said. "He would have mentioned it."

"No, I'm not. I knew better than to tangle with physics."

"I'm not going to take it either. My father's having a hard time with that. I think my ineptitude in math and science has been a big disappointment to him."

"I know what you mean," Ham said. "When I was in high school, I once flunked a literature test. My father was extremely upset."

"Well, your father *is* Eric Twainbough, after all," Amy said. "Maybe he's just a bit overly sensitive."

"Yeah, I guess that's it," Ham said. He grinned. "Especially since the test I flunked was on one of his books."

Amy laughed. "Really? *You* flunked a test on one of your father's books?"

"Yeah," Eric admitted.

Amy laughed again. "I can see where he might be a bit sensitive about that."

"Say, listen, I'm about to head down to Bear Tracks," Ham said. "Would you like to come along?"

"Bear Tracks?" Amy's eyes lit up in excitement. "I'd love to, but I don't know if I should. I mean, Dad's never let me go there."

"Well, that's understandable. You were a high school kid, and high school kids aren't welcome," Ham said. "But you're in college now."

"Not yet. Not until September."

Ham laughed. "And I'm not a junior until September, but I just cut across the quad. Come on, what do you say? I'll look out for you."

Amy smiled broadly. "Okay. I really would like to come. But I have to warn you: I can't drink any beer."

"What do you mean, you can't drink any beer?" Ham

asked in mock horror. "Where would my family be if everyone felt like you? Why, the brewery would go broke."

"Brewery? What are you talking about, your family
would go broke? Your father's a writer. What has that got to
do with a brewery?"

"I'm not talking about my father; I'm talking about my
mother. She and my father are divorced, but before her
name was Twainbough, it was Tannenhower."

"Tannenhower? You mean Tannenhower Brewery?"

"Purveyors of fine beer," Ham confirmed.

"My God! That's one of the biggest breweries in the
world! You must be very rich."

"Yeah, I suppose I am," Ham agreed. "I certainly hope
you don't hold that against me."

"Heavens, no! Why should I hold that against you? I
mean, my grandmother always says it's just as easy to fall in
love with a rich man as it is with a poor man."

Ham threw his head back and laughed heartily. "You
should listen to your grandmother," he said. "She's a very
smart woman. And you are a very direct one."

Bear Tracks was *the* college hangout for JU students. It
was a beer-and-sandwich tavern that occasionally had live
music; most of the time, though, it depended on the enter-
tainment provided by the gaily colored jukebox at one end
of the long, narrow building and on the conversation and
horseplay of its patrons. It was owned by Norman Dement,
who had been an all-star football player for the JU Bears in
the twenties. He had earned the nickname "Bear Tracks"
by supposedly leaving his footprints all over the backs of
opposing players. When he had first opened his establishment, he had tried to call it Dement's Bar, but it was so
universally called Bear Tracks that he had given in and
changed the name officially.

One wall was like a minimuseum for Jefferson University football. It had been given over entirely to action photographs from football games, some of the pictures going all
the way back to the turn of the century. One photo showed
a Jefferson player making a bruising tackle on an opposing
runner, both in the rather funny-looking canvas-and-leather

uniforms worn by players in the first and second decades of the century. To the right of the picture was a headline from *The St. Louis Chronicle:* HITLER'S ARMY UNSTOPPABLE. Underneath the headline was a typewritten message:

HITLER COULDN'T HAVE DONE IT
WITHOUT THE
JEFFERSON UNIVERSITY BEARS!

Karl Tannenhower, Oberreichsleiter of Adolf Hitler's Germany, was an all-star football player for Jefferson University in 1913–14, and the tenacity and aggressiveness he learned here are qualities that no doubt have been of great help to Hitler's well-oiled war machine.

Too bad for the world that Tannenhower didn't flunk out his first semester.

Every fraternity on campus had rented a section of wall from Bear Tracks, and each student bought his own beer mug and hung it from a nail on his fraternity's section of wall. Part of the ordeal of pledging a fraternity was to design a personal coat of arms. Those who belonged to a family with an existing coat of arms couldn't use the family emblem but had to come up with one of their own. The coat of arms was then submitted to a "Board of Validation," consisting of upperclassmen, and when the coat of arms was approved, it would be painstakingly painted on the mug, thus adding to the overall decor of the establishment.

A thick cloud of tobacco smoke hung just beneath the ceiling, though oddly it managed to stay just above the whirling ceiling fans. The fans moved the lower, humid air around but did nothing to cool the place. A Glenn Miller record was on the jukebox, though it could barely be heard above the din of clinking glasses, laughter, and the buzz of conversation.

"Ham! Ham, over here!" someone called as soon as Ham and Amy stepped inside.

Looking over, Ham saw Randy waving, indicating that, as promised, he was holding a place. A half-dozen other students were with him, all seated around a table on the far side of the room. Ham began to steer Amy in that direction.

"Oh, Ham, you didn't tell me I'd be the only girl," Amy said.

"What do you mean?" Ham asked, looking around. "There are other girls here."

"Yes, but not at the table with your friends."

Ham laughed. "Well, can you blame them? Look how ugly those guys are. What girl in her right mind would come near them?" he joked.

"My, oh, my, oh, my," one of the boys at the table said as Ham and Amy reached the table. "Would you look at the dish Ham has brought with him? Our vaunted running back seems to have made quite a conquest."

"Hail, the conquering hero," Randy said, standing and holding his arm out stiffly before him in a salute.

"Hey! That's a Nazi salute," someone scolded.

"My dear sir," Randy said, pulling himself together in inebriated dignity, "for your information, before the stinking Nazis appropriated it, this salute was the one rendered to Caesar's legions." He belched noisily. "And I'll be damned if I'm going to let some Bavarian corporal usurp my prerogative to render honor in the style of Caesar."

"Damn right!" someone else shouted, laughing. "Hail, Caesar!"

Soon everyone else in Bear Tracks was on their feet, saluting Ham and, by extension, Amy. To anyone who just happened to wander in it might have looked like a Nazi salute. To the students it was praise.

To Amy it was extremely embarrassing. Suddenly finding herself in the limelight wasn't something she was accustomed to. But she also had to admit that it was one of the most thrilling moments she had ever experienced.

CHAPTER FOUR

> Lieutenant Rudi Schultz
> 41st Panzer Korps in Russia
> 5 July 1941

Oberreichsleiter Karl Tannenhower
2117 Niederwernstrasse
Hamburg, Germany

Dear Herr Oberreichsleiter Tannenhower:
    Heil Hitler!
    This letter comes to you not from SERGEANT Rudi Schultz, but from LIEUTENANT Rudi Schultz. I am quite aware that such rapid promotion would not likely have occurred due to my military accomplishments and is owed to the fact that I was fortunate enough to have served with your late son, Lieutenant Max Tannenhower. Now at last I have the chance to write you to thank you properly for securing my commission.
    I found much honor in being a sergeant and

considered it a great privilege to have served under your son during our campaign in Poland. But as you yourself stated in your letter to me, Herr Ober-reichsleiter Tannenhower, my acceptance of this commission will provide me with an even greater opportunity to serve the Fatherland. This I intend to do to the best of my ability, and I will dedicate that service to our Führer, to you, and to the memory of your son, whom I so proudly served.

This letter comes to you from Dvinsk, Russia, where I have the honor to be a part of Operation Barbarossa. I am glad to be away from France. I cannot decide which kind of Frenchmen I dislike the most, those who make no pretense about hating the Germans or those who smile silkenly as they betray their own countrymen—like Judas, selling information to the authorities for their thirty pieces of silver.

But enough of France. With your indulgence I wish to tell you about an action in which I recently participated and for which I have been recommended for the Iron Cross First Class. As we approached the river Dvina, which separated our advance from the town of Dvinsk, there was fear that the bridge would be blown, thus stranding our tanks on the west bank. I suggested a ruse that my commanding officer immediately accepted.

In order to accomplish the task, I recruited forty men from my company, and, dressed in Russian uniforms and driving commandeered Russian trucks, we sped to the bridge. On our way we passed three companies of retreating Russian soldiers, and so well were we disguised that they waved to us and shouted to give them cigarettes. One of our number speaks Russian without an accent, and he called back to them and tossed out several packs of Russian cigarettes. As they are very strong and foul smelling, we didn't consider that too great a sacrifice for the success of our mission.

As we approached the bridge, a Russian sentry stepped out to challenge us. My driver slowed to a near stop, then grew frightened and stepped on the accelerator. I had planned to use the Russian-speaking soldier to convince the Russian engineers that we should not blow up the bridge, but now our plan was compromised.

We raced to the far end of the bridge, where my men jumped out of the trucks. Some were deployed as infantrymen, attacking the Russian engineers, while others began at once to dismantle the explosives the Russians had put in place. The battle lasted for about thirty minutes, and seven of my men were killed, but we managed to secure the bridge, and less than one hour later I had the privilege of taking the first tank across.

Currently, the battle goes well, and the Russians we have encountered seem no more formidable than were the Polish, Belgians, or French. I have stopped being amazed by the success of our Army. Truly, no army in history has ever known such triumph.

Heil Hitler! In service to our Führer, I remain your obedient servant.

Respectfully,
Lieutenant Rudi Schultz

Karl Tannenhower folded the letter and tossed it into a basket on his desk marked "Personal Handling." During the Polish campaign in the fall of 1939, Rudi Schultz had been a sergeant in Max Tannenhower's panzer platoon. When Max was killed, Sergeant Schultz had taken the time to write a long letter to Karl, giving him all the details of how his son had served and how he had died. It was a heartfelt letter, and Karl had been so appreciative of it that he secured a commission for the young noncom.

Karl was able to pull such strings with the German military because he was one of Hitler's inner circle. In all of Germany there were no more than a handful of men who could get an audience with Adolf Hitler at a moment's notice. Karl was one of them.

He had been at Hitler's side during the abortive 1923 putsch, tearing strips of cloth from the flag he had carried to use as bandages for the wounded. That flag was now the "Blood Flag," the most sacred icon in all of Nazi Germany, and Karl, because of his association with it, had swiftly risen through the ranks of Nazi officialdom. He had started out as the Gauleiter—the district leader—of Hamburg. Then when Hitler eliminated Ernst Röhm and his brown-shirted Storm Troopers to win support from the Army, Karl was rewarded for his loyalty by being appointed to the rank of Obergrupenführer in the SS in addition to his office as Gauleiter of Hamburg. Those two positions not only gave Karl a great deal of power within the party, they provided him with two very generous salaries.

Karl had reached his current pinnacle shortly after the war began. When Max was killed, Karl had inserted a notice in the *Volkischer-Beobachter*, the official party newspaper, that read:

> FOR THE FÜHRER,
> KILLED IN POLAND,
> MAX TANNENHOWER,
> BELOVED SON OF KARL AND UTA TANNENHOWER

In truth, Karl had intended the notice to be a subtle form of protest to remind Hitler that *he* had started the war, and that Max was dead because of *him*. But to Karl's surprise, Hitler had totally misunderstood the intent and regarded it as a personal tribute to him from Karl. The Führer had been so moved by the announcement that he created a special job for Karl, appointing him to the position of Oberreichsleiter, which made him the head of all Gauleiters in Germany. That had put Karl just one notch below such people as Hess, Göring, Goebbels, Himmler, Bormann, and von Ribbentrop. Then when Hess made his mysterious flight to England, Karl had assumed some of Hess's duties, and he, too, became a member of the inner circle.

There was a discreet knock on the door to Karl's office.

"Come in," Karl called.

"Herr Oberreichsleiter, Herr Maas is here to see you," his secretary said.

"Yes, yes," Karl replied. "Show him in." He stood to

greet Paul, for the two had been friends for a long time. In fact, Paul was the man who had recruited Karl into the party. Like Karl, Paul had risen through the ranks, though his ascent hadn't been quite as high or as meteoric. As an Obergrupenführer in the SS, Paul had been appointed Reich Production Director.

Despite the fact that Karl now outranked his old friend, the relationship between the two men hadn't been threatened—a fact evidenced by the broad smile on Paul's face as he came into the room and shook Karl's hand.

"Paul, my friend, it is good to see you," Karl greeted. "What brings you to Hamburg?"

"Do I need a reason to visit with an old friend?" Paul replied. "Even if that friend is the Oberreichsleiter?"

"Never, Paul, never," Karl insisted. "My door is always open to you; you know that. Either here or at home. And speaking of which, will you take dinner with us?"

"Of course I'll take dinner with you," Paul said. "Only a fool would miss one of Uta's meals."

Karl laughed. "As if she cooked them herself."

Paul wagged his finger. "Never underestimate the influence that the woman of the house exercises over her kitchen."

"That is true," Karl agreed. "That is true. Uta fusses over her kitchen like a true hausfrau." He reached for the phone, saying, "I'll call Uta and tell her to expect you."

The phone call was a brief one. As Karl hung up the receiver he studied his old friend through narrowed eyes and said, "But I'm sure you didn't come to Hamburg just to chat with me—or even to have one of Uta's meals."

Paul cleared his throat. "You're right. Herr Oberreichsleiter . . ."

"*Herr Oberreichsleiter,* Paul?"

Paul nodded. "Yes. My problem is more than a friend can handle. I need the help of the Oberreichsleiter."

"All right, what can I do for you?"

Paul held up his finger, then stepped into the outer office. He returned a moment later carrying a briefcase, which he put on a table and opened, pulling out a folder of papers.

"These are invoices," Paul said. "Requests from a gun

producer for optical lenses, requests from an aircraft manufacturing plant for sheet aluminum, requests from a tank
production facility for ball bearings . . . They are all critical requirements, and all have been submitted on the highest priority as approved by the Minister of Armament and
Industry. You would agree that this is matériel that is cru-
cial to the war effort?"

"Yes, of course," Karl replied.

"These are but a few of the invoices I've been dealing
with," Paul explained. "I brought them because they are
typical of those invoices designated 'highest priority,' requiring delivery within seventy-two hours. But"—he
pulled several of the invoices from the folder—"this request is three weeks old . . . this one is seven weeks old
. . . and *this* one, Karl, this request for ball bearings is
three *months* old."

Karl frowned. "But that can't be. I was in Schweinfurt
just last week. The plant director of FAG Kugelfischer took
great pride in showing me through his plant. They were
turning out millions of bearings. Surely we can't be short of
these critical supplies."

"Oh, we aren't short of supplies. In fact, raw materials,
components, and finished products are piling up in ware-
houses and on shipping docks all over the country. What
we are short of is available trains."

"I wasn't aware there was a shortage of trains," Karl
said, somewhat bewildered.

"I wasn't either. But none of the shipping directors of
any of our factories can get them. They came to me, I tried
and failed, and so now I am coming to you. Where are all
the trains, Karl, and why can't I get them?"

"Did you speak with Dr. Dorpmuller of the Reichs-
bahn about this?"

Paul snorted. "Our esteemed Minister of Railroads
was the first person I tried to speak with, but he refuses to
take my calls. That's why I am here." He smiled. "After all,
what's the use of having a friend in a high place if you don't
make use of it?"

Karl laughed, then buzzed his secretary on the intercom and told her to put him through to the Minister of

Railroads. While he waited for the call to go through, he joked with his friend.

"Still not married, eh, Paul? When are you going to get tired of being with a different woman every night?"

"You know what they say, Karl. Life is a banquet. Why settle for a snack?"

Karl laughed. "Yes, why indeed?"

The intercom on his desk buzzed, and his secretary told him she had his party on the line.

Karl thanked her, then picked up the phone. "Dr. Dorpmuller, Oberreichsleiter Tannenhower here," he said.

"Yes, Herr Oberreichsleiter. How may I be of assistance?" Dorpmuller asked.

"This concerns the transportation of priority shipments," Karl said, picking up one of the invoices.

"These priority shipments, they are by rail?" Dorpmuller queried.

"Yes. Well, they are supposed to be," Karl corrected. "The truth is, none of them have yet gone anywhere. And therein lies the problem."

"And may I ask what the Oberreichsleiter's interest is in this?"

"It was brought to my attention and—"

"You will excuse me, sir," Dorpmuller interrupted. "But *I* am the Minister of Railroads. If there is a problem with the railroad, *I* should be consulted."

"Dr. Dorpmuller, I thought that's what I was doing," Karl said a bit testily. "Consulting with you."

"No, sir, you don't understand," Dorpmuller said. "When the Oberreichsleiter comes to me, that means the problem is coming down to me from above. It should first come up to me from below."

Karl sighed. "Very well, Dr. Dorpmuller, but, as you say, the matter is now over your head. The problem has been given to me, and I would like you to solve it for me. For example, I have an invoice for a shipment that was supposed to have been sent on train number fifteen-five-twenty-seven. That shipment has never arrived."

"That isn't surprising," Dorpmuller said. "Train number fifteen-five-twenty-seven was preempted by government order."

"Preempted? Why? Where did it go?"

"I believe that particular train was diverted to Russia, Herr Oberreichsleiter."

"Oh," Karl said, somewhat mollified. "Oh, well, of course, I understand. If it's being used for strategic purposes, then I suppose I can't really complain." He thought of the letter he had just read from Lieutenant Rudi Schultz. "After all, we *do* have men fighting there."

"I am very glad you understand, Herr Oberreichsleiter. There are so many people who don't," Dorpmuller complained.

"Well, anyone who doesn't understand strategic necessity doesn't have the best interests of his country at heart," Karl said. "However, these are priority shipments, which means that they, too, are critical to the war effort. That being the case, do you suppose we might be able to secure some sort of priority for the next train?"

Dr. Dorpmuller laughed. "You can't be serious, Herr Oberreichsleiter. Why, not even the Army has been able to get a priority number for a train, and they have fifteen divisions still awaiting transport to Russia."

"*What?*" Karl was thoroughly puzzled by the statement. "Wait a minute, what are you talking about? I thought you just said the Army already had priority. You said that's where the train went."

"No, Herr Oberreichsleiter. I told you the train went to Russia, and that is exactly where it did go. But it didn't go there for the Army; it went for the SS, and it went empty."

"Herr Dr. Dorpmuller, let me get this straight. Are you saying the train went to Russia empty?"

"Yes."

"But how can this be? How could the SS enjoy a higher priority than a battle unit? And why would anyone send a train to Russia empty when there are goods and matériel needing to be shipped?"

"The SS enjoys a higher priority because their mission takes precedence over the mission of the Army," Dorpmuller explained patiently. "But why am I explaining this to you? You are an SS Obergruppenführer, are you not?"

"It's a position of honor, not of performance," Karl replied. "I am not involved in the details of SS operations."

"Nevertheless, you must know about the Jews."

"Jews? What about the Jews?"

"The Führer has ordered the resettlement of all Jews in all conquered lands. They are to be removed from the conquered territories and taken to special internment camps in Poland."

"I see," Karl said. "But surely such a program could be delayed until the more pressing business is attended to."

"Herr Oberreichsleiter, there is no more pressing business than the settlement of the Jewish problem once and for all."

Karl was silent for a moment. "Yes," he finally said. "Thank you." He hung up the phone, then walked around behind his desk and sat down. Leaning his head back, he plucked at the bridge of his nose.

"Well, what is it?" Paul asked anxiously. "Why can't I have the trains?"

"Jews," Karl answered, as if that one word explained everything.

"*What?* Are you telling me the goddamn Jews have our trains?"

"In a manner of speaking, yes," Karl replied. "We are running empty trains all over Europe to pick up Jews and transport them to internment camps."

"You might know Jews would be behind it one way or another," Paul muttered. He sighed. "Very well. I'd better see what I can do about getting some trucks lined up. They can't do the job as quickly or as cheaply as the railroad, but we can't afford to wait any longer." He started toward the door, then turned and smiled back at Karl. "I'll see you at dinner tonight," he promised.

"Yes, tonight."

As the door closed behind Paul, Karl returned to his desk and sat down. He had a disquieting feeling about all this. Certainly he had been a member of the party long enough to know of the official view of Jews. He knew about the Nuremberg Laws on Citizenship and Race, passed in September 1935, making it clear to every German—as if such clarification was needed—that the Jews were going to have a hard time in Germany.

Karl hadn't protested the passage of the Nuremberg Laws that revoked Jews' citizenship. Jews could not vote or marry Aryans or employ female domestics of German or kindred blood. They could not attend schools, libraries, theaters, or use public transportation. Passports had to be stamped with the word *Jude,* and all Jewish men had to add the middle name "Israel" while Jewish women had to add the name "Sarah." Karl hadn't protested when all Jews were ordered to wear yellow Stars of David pinned to their clothing to readily identify them—and readily target them.

He had accepted the laws when they were passed because they were merely the extension of centuries of anti-Semitic feeling in Germany and an expression of the general public sentiment with regard to Jews. Karl knew that as long ago as the sixteenth century, such respected men as Martin Luther had preached against the Jews, calling them a plague, a pestilence, and pure misfortune. There had been anti-Semitic uprisings in 1805 and again in 1813. In 1840 when the German constitution proposed to grant rights to Jews, anti-Semites collected eighty thousand signatures on petitions opposing Jewish rights, and the constitution was rejected. Hitler was merely carrying out the historical will of the people.

Personally, Karl had never been as obsessed with Jewhating as the others in the Nazi party—but he did recognize that Jews were a brilliantly contrived scapegoat to be used by Hitler as a means for Germany to raise itself from the ashes. However, Germany was anything but in the throes of defeat now. Germany stood at the head of all the nations of the world, victorious in war and master of Europe. The political purpose of the anti-Semitism had been accomplished; it was no longer necessary to use Jews as a convenient vehicle.

Why, then, if they had already served their purpose, would the government go to all the trouble and expense of relocating them? And what made this relocation so important that it took priority even over the movement of combat units and critical production materials? If anti-Semitism as a government policy went so far as to interfere with the conduct of other operations, then wasn't the medicine worse than the sickness? Besides, it wouldn't be looked on favorably by the rest of the world if Germany systematically uprooted the Jews and forcibly resettled them.

Karl knew that his personal feelings about Jews were not in accord with those of any other member of Hitler's inner circle. Goebbels, Himmler, Bormann, and von Ribbentrop, for example, fell all over themselves trying to prove that their hatred for Jews was greater than the others'. Only Göring seemed unconcerned with having to constantly espouse his hatred of Jews, but Karl didn't know if that was because Göring's anti-Semitism was nominal (after all, his stepfather was a Jew, and while still a student Göring had chosen him as the most influential person in his life), or if his interests in other things—lion cubs, model trains, elaborate uniforms, looted art—left the Reichsmarschall no time for Jew hating. Even so, Karl knew intuitively that regardless of how Göring felt, the Reichsmarschall's sense of self-preservation would keep him from being Karl's ally, should Karl suggest a degree of moderation on the Jewish issue. And Karl had no inclination to try it on his own. Perhaps something Paul Maas had told him on the subject long ago was still valid:

"Perhaps not everyone hates the Jews, but no one really likes them."

Karl mentally threw up his hands. The fate of the Jews was sealed, and there was nothing Oberreichsleiter Karl Tannenhower could do about it.

VIENNA

Blumberg's Department Store was now the State Store of Commerce. David Gelbman, who once owned the store, had been forced to sell it because he was a Jew, and Jews could no longer own commercial property, hold a professional position, work as an educator, draw a government pension, have money in an interest-bearing account, or do anything else that made a reasonable life possible.

Soon after his graduation from Jefferson University in St. Louis, Missouri, thirty-six years earlier, David, a native-born American, had been sent by his father to Vienna to help his aunt run her department store. It was to have been a brief sojourn. But shortly after his arrival in Vienna, David met and fell in love with Anna Rosenstein. They were married, David bought Blumberg's Department Store from his aunt, and he never returned to America.

There had been no need to go back. Vienna had been very good to David, and he had prospered. Remaining in Austria during the First World War even though Austria fought against the country of his birth, David by then had considered himself Austrian enough to help his adopted country through bond drives and relief work.

David's cousin, Simon Blumberg, had been attending college in Germany at the outbreak of the Great War. Swept up in a surge of patriotism and excitement, Simon had joined the German Army and fought through the entire war, only to lose his leg in the final months. Ironically, Simon had served in the same company—and even in the same squad—as Adolf Hitler.

David's wife was Austrian, and his daughter, Miriam, had been born and raised in Austria. By now he had spent most of his life in Austria, so when the Nazis came to power and certain friends suggested that it might be a smart idea for him to take his family and return to America, David had laughed off the suggestion. His family had never lived in America, therefore they couldn't "return." And since David's parents were both dead, he had no family left in America. Even the huge department store his father had once owned in St. Louis had been sold and its name changed. There was nothing in America for David and no reason to go.

Now, though, David couldn't help but wonder if he hadn't made a big mistake by ignoring the suggestions and failing to see the obvious. The Nazification of Austria had caused him to lose his store. In addition, the state had leveled various charges against him—such as conspiring with other Jewish businessmen and financiers to manipulate the state economy—and assessed fines for an amount that just happened to be equal to all the assets he had in the bank, and David's account was seized for "damages." He had the responsibility of providing food, clothing, and a home for his family, and now he had to do this with no money and no business. The only way he could fulfill that responsibility was by gradually selling off the personal possessions that hadn't yet been confiscated.

That was precisely the mission that took him out into the streets of Vienna that day.

It was a hot day, and David was sweating by the time he reached his destination. The little bell over the door of the shop jingled as he entered, and the proprietor looked across the counter to see who had come in. The store was one that dealt in what David, resorting to an Americanism, called knickknacks. It sold candlesticks, porcelain vases, bowls, figurines, crystal decanters, and the like. Such stores had been prospering since the Nazi takeover, for the Jews of the city were being forced to sell off all their belongings piece by piece to survive. Since the stores purchased the pieces at bargain-basement prices, they were able to resell them far below their value, and they were finding a ready market among the gentiles of the city who were discovering for the first time a means of furnishing their homes with "nice" things without having to pay too much for them.

Three such women were in the shop when David went in, looking carefully over all the items on display. One of them, a heavyset, buxom woman, was holding a leaded-glass decanter.

"Helga, what do you think of this?" she asked, holding the decanter up for her friend to see.

"How much?" Helga asked, peering at it appraisingly, her thin face becoming pinched.

"Ten schillings."

"Ten schillings?" Helga waved her hand. "Listen, every Jewish cow in the city has one of those. Wait a while longer; the price will come way down."

David felt both shocked and saddened. He and Anna had a similar crystal decanter that his parents had given them for their wedding. They had bought it at Tiffany's in New York and had paid fifteen dollars for it. Ten schillings was about fifty cents in American money.

"What do you want, Jew?" the clerk asked as David approached the counter. He stared contemptuously at the yellow star pinned to David's suit coat. "I suppose you have some more of your pitiful belongings to sell?"

"Yes," David replied, adopting the look of servility that for the most part curbed assaults—both verbal and physical. He reached around and took out a silver tray that he had stuck in the back of his trousers, covered by the jacket. It was a fairly large tray, and it was beautifully engraved.

"What is this picture supposed to be?" the proprietor asked, studying the tray.

"It's an engraving of the World's Fair held in St. Louis in 1904."

"St. Louis?"

"St. Louis, Missouri. It's in the United States."

"Don't get smart with me, Jew. I know where St. Louis is," the proprietor snapped. He fitted a jeweler's loupe into his eye socket and looked at the tray, holding it this way and that. Catching the light, it gleamed as a result of the polishing Simon had given it that morning.

"This is sterling silver," the proprietor said, as if surprised.

"Yes, of course it is," David answered.

"How did a filthy Jew like you come by something like this?" The proprietor looked up at David, and the loupe made his eye appear monstrously large. "Did you cheat an American visitor?"

"I *am* American, you ignorant son of a bitch," David said in English, his servile look never wavering. "I got this when I attended the World's Fair."

"*Bitte?*"

David repeated his statement in German—omitting the epithet.

"Say, I know who you are," the woman shopper called Helga said, pointing to David. "You used to own Blumberg's Department Store."

"Yes, I did," David said. He forced a smile. "You were one of my customers?"

"Are you kidding? I never shopped in that place. Like all filthy Jews, you charged too much. If you must know, I recognize you from your picture in your advertisements." She walked over to the counter. "Let me see the tray," she demanded.

The proprietor showed it to her.

"I have a cousin who lives in St. Louis. If the cost isn't too dear, I may buy it," the woman said.

"I paid thirty dollars for it almost forty years ago," David said. "Six hundred schillings," he converted.

"I will give you fifty schillings," the proprietor offered.

"Fifty?" David gasped. "But that isn't even one-tenth of its value. Even if you melted it down, the silver would be worth much more than that."

"I probably *will* melt it down," the proprietor said. "What value would there be to my customers of a fair in America? This lovely lady is the exception. How many people do you suppose have any kind of sentimental link to a place in America? If she doesn't want it, it is quite worthless as an object."

David looked long and hard at the silver tray, recalling the afternoon he had bought it. He and his three closest friends—Bob Canfield, Terry Perkins, and J.P. Winthrop— had made a day of visiting the fair, taking part in the great automobile parade and then exploring all the exhibitions on the "Pike." There they ate hot dogs and drank iced tea— the first time the beverage had ever been served—and participated in the invention of the ice-cream cone. They rode the two-hundred-fifty-foot-high observation wheel, and from the top of the wheel looked out over the "wonders of the world." David could almost hear again the trumpeting of the elephants, the squeal of children's laughter, the pitches of scores of barkers urging fairgoers to "come on in," and the sound of a dozen bands playing at once. He could smell popcorn, roasting peanuts, beer, a new thing called barbecue, and the exotic and mysterious tang of wild animals. The fair had billed itself as a window into the future, providing exhibitions of the new century. How magnificent those predictions had been and what a rosy future mankind had envisioned for itself!

How naive they had all been back in 1904.

"I can't stand here all day while you make up your mind, Jew," the proprietor groused, gruffly jerking David back from his reverie. "There are thousands of other hungry Jews in this city and just as many bargains. Keep your lousy tray; I don't have to buy it."

And so it has come down to this, David thought. He wasn't on the Pike of the World's Fair in St. Louis, surrounded by friends and laughing children. He was half a world away, surrounded by enemies—and the proprietor was right. There *were* thousands of other hungry Jews in Vienna and just as many bargains. And the shopkeeper didn't have to buy the tray at any price. Realistically, David knew, the price would only go down and down, until one day the Nazis might decide to just take everything. He sighed and handed over the tray.

"I'll take it," he said to the proprietor.

The woman named Helga laughed mockingly at him. "And I thought you Jews were supposed to be such good businessmen. You fool. I would have given you *sixty* schillings for it."

CHAPTER
FIVE

The car radio squawked out the announcer's voice:

"Good afternoon, ladies and gentlemen, this is Eddie Johnson bringing you a play-by-play description of the football game today between Coach Don Farout's Missouri Tigers, led by All-American 'Passing Paul' Christman, and our own Jefferson University Bears, featuring All-American running back Hamilton Twainbough.

"The stadium is filled to near capacity for this game, and below the press box here is an ocean of red and green, Jefferson's school colors. Across the way are the Missouri fans, thousands of whom are from right here in the city, of course, and they're wearing the University of Missouri colors of gold and black.

"Both teams won their openers last week, Missouri besting Nebraska and Jefferson taking the measure of Ohio State. In that game, as many of you know, Ham Twainbough set a single-game rushing record for the Bears, plunging through Buckeye defenders for three hundred eighty-five

70

yards. But he gave JU fans quite a scare when he was taken off the field on a stretcher on the last play of the game. Well, there's good news, folks. When I spoke to Coach Weber Gillis a short time ago, he said that Twainbough has recovered from his knee injury. He assured me that the Bears are ready and anxious to take on the Tigers. So, wherever you are, turn up your radio, open up a bottle of cold Tannenhower Beer, and sit back to enjoy college football on KSLM, your radio station for St. Louis."

Professor Wyman W. "Dub" Wilkerson inched his white Pontiac slowly along Wydown Boulevard toward the policeman directing traffic into the Jefferson University stadium parking lot. The car in front of him had black and gold banners thrust out each window and yellow and black crepe paper bunting tied to the radio antenna. The people in the car were laughing and cheering for Missouri:

> "Mizou . . . rah!
> Mizou . . . rah! Rah!
> Rah, Mizou!
> Rah, Mizou! Rah,
> Missourah!"

The University of Missouri car passed a group of Jefferson students, both boys and girls, and the JU students made a train and returned a nonsensical cheer of their own:

> "Bo-wo-ski wot-en-not,
> gwot-not and why?
> V-I-C-T-O-R-Y.
> Are we in it? Well I guess.
> Will we win it? Yes, yes, yes.
> JEFFERSON! JEFFERSON! JEFFERSON!"

"Here are the starting lineups for the Jefferson University Bears," the radio announcer was saying, and Dub reached down to change stations.

Amy was sitting in the back seat, watching the students cheer and jeer each other, and when Dub changed the radio dial, she leaned over the seat back.

"Oh, Daddy, leave it on that station! I want to hear the announcer say Ham's name again."

"My word, he's already mentioned it six or seven times. How many times do you want to hear it spoken?" Dub asked.

"But he didn't say his name in the lineup."

"I just want to hear a little news before the game starts."

"Oh, let her hear the lineup," Dub's wife, Janet, said. "Haven't we heard enough news about the war in Europe?"

"All right, all right," Dub agreed and tuned back to the station. "I know better than to argue with both of you."

As they approached the stadium gate, Dub rolled down the window. "Hello, George," he said to the guard. "Are you ready for the game?"

"I sure am, Professor. I'm anxious to see how Twainbough does today. I guess he really put on a show for the folks in Columbus last week."

"Yes, well, I didn't see that game either, but he's already made quite an impression around my house. Or maybe I should say *indentation.* Right in the middle of the living-room couch. You can find him sitting there with Amy just about any night of the week."

"Daddy!" Amy gasped.

The guard laughed. "Well, it sounds like at least one person in your car has a personal interest in how Twainbough does. Just go on over to the faculty parking area, Professor. You know the way."

"Sure do. Thanks, George."

"I hope he has a good game," George called as the Pontiac pulled away.

"Daddy, do you have to say such things to just *every-one?*" Amy complained, slumping back against the seat. "It's so em-*bar*-rassing."

"What was embarrassing about that?" Dub asked. "I was just making a simple statement of fact. Ham Twainbough does seem to spend all of his time at our house. What I wonder is, when does he ever find time to study?"

"We study together," Amy said.

"Oh. Is *that* what you call it."

"Daddy," Amy groaned.

Dub laughed. "Let's call a truce, okay?" He lifted both hands from the steering wheel. "I give up. I won't crack any more jokes."

"Good. Oh, and Daddy, do I have to sit with you and Mom?"

"We have a box seat on the fifty-yard line. Where would you rather sit?"

"Anywhere but with my parents," Amy said. "Really, Daddy, don't you understand how a woman feels about something like this?"

"A *woman,* is it?"

"Yes," Amy replied. "After all, I *am* in college now."

Dub sighed. "And you're anxious to leave the nest, right?" he said, his tone indicating acquiescence.

Recognizing it, Amy continued her efforts to persuade him. "Oh, please, Daddy! A day like today is just too perfect to have to be cooped up in a little box."

"Very well," Dub said as he maneuvered the car into a tight parking space. "Sit wherever you like. But if you aren't back at the car by the time we're ready to leave, you'll have to get your own way home."

"Oh, that's all right. You and Mom can go on without me. Several of us are going to Bear Tracks after the game. I'll have Ham bring me home."

"You'll have Ham bring you home, will you? My, my, what a surprise."

"See you later," Amy called, opening the door and hopping out. She had melted into the crowd before Dub and Janet were even out of the car, hurrying as if afraid that her father might change his mind.

"I'm not sure I like her going to Bear Tracks," Dub said as they entered the tunnel that led from the parking lot to the stadium. "She's still kind of young for that, as far as I'm concerned."

"Bear Tracks is just a part of college life, dear, you know that," Janet said. "We used to go to the Purple Orchid, remember? And that was when it was a speakeasy."

"Yes, I *do* remember," Dub said, laughing. "That's why I'd just as soon she not go."

"Ham is a good boy," Janet said. "She'll be all right."

They neared the end of the tunnel. In the truncated space in front of them was a patch of blue sky, the blurred colors and movement of the fans on the opposite side of the stadium, and the bright green field itself. They could hear the hollow thumping sound of footballs being kicked, and a gold-shirted player ran across the opening for a brief moment.

Exiting the tunnel, the Wilkersons climbed the bleachers toward their box, greeted by friends and acquaintances along the way.

"Hey, Professor, Twainbough's your daughter's boyfriend, right? How's his knee?" one anxious fan called. "Will he be at full strength today?"

"I don't know," Dub answered. "All I can say is it seemed okay last night when he was heading for the refrigerator."

That got a laugh.

"Ladies and gentlemen, please rise for the 'Star Spangled Banner,'" the field announcer said, and the entire stadium grew quiet as thirty-five thousand people stood and faced the flag.

It was nearing the end of the first half, and inside the locker room Randy Wilson had the heat balm and tape laid out on the tables, ready for the half-time break. He knew there would be at least three ankles to tape and twice as many bruises to treat, so it was always necessary for him to leave the field about five minutes before the end of the half to be ready for them. Since becoming student trainer to the football team, he had yet to see an entire game.

He heard the gunshot signaling the end of the first half; a moment later the door to the dressing room banged open, and the players lumbered through like so many elephants—huge, padded young men with dirty faces and grass-stained uniforms. Their cleats clattered on the concrete, and they moved sullenly around the room, then settled on the floor, leaning back against the wall. One of them threw his helmet against the wall of lockers in disgust.

"Randy," Ham said, limping over to the table, "see what you can do about this, will you?" He dropped his pants, then hopped up on the table with his bare legs hanging over the side.

Randy didn't even have to ask what was wrong. He could see it. The right knee was swollen to half again its normal size, and it was already beginning to turn blue.

"Ham, you can't go back out on this knee," he said. "I'd better tell Coach."

"No!" Ham shouted, and he reached out and grabbed Randy by the shoulder, squeezing it so tightly that it hurt. "Don't say a word about this, Randy. I mean it."

"But Ham—"

"Not a word. Wrap it. Just give me some tape to support it. I'll be all right."

Randy sighed, then began wrapping the knee, winding the tape so that the leg could still bend, but bracing it against any lateral movement. "What's the score?" he asked.

"Nineteen to seven."

"*Nineteen?*"

"They scored again just before the half," Ham said.

The coach came over to the table. "How's the boy?" he asked. "Did you hurt your knee again?"

"Just a little bruise, Coach," Ham replied, grimacing as Randy worked. "I'll be all right."

The coach looked at the knee, and it was clear by the expression on his face that he knew Ham was lying. It was also clear that he was going to accept the lie.

"Good, good," he said. "I need you out there, Twainbough. Don't let me down."

"I won't," Ham promised.

"There," Randy said, after he finished the wrap. "If this doesn't do it, nothing will."

Ham hopped down from the table and pulled his pants up, then laced and buckled them into place. He took a few tentative steps, and though he tried to hide the limp and the wince of pain, he was unable to do so. But he smiled, then reached over and patted Randy on the shoulder.

"Randy, my boy, you are a genius," he said. "I feel solid as granite."

"Oh, yeah, I'm sure you do," Randy said dryly. "Ham, if you take a good hit on that leg, go down, do you hear me?

Don't try and break any tackles. You could hurt yourself permanently."

"Believe me, Randy, if Lee Austin Bowman hits me on this leg, I will go down. You can count on it."

"Good," Randy said.

"Okay, guys, listen up," the coach shouted, and the green-and-red-clad young men looked toward the blackboard to see what, if anything, they could do to stop Passing Paul Christman.

"Thirty-two to seven," a fan a couple of rows behind Amy said disgustedly. The crowd was filing out in earnest now that the game was over, though many had begun leaving several minutes earlier, when it was obvious that Jefferson had no chance of getting back into the game.

"What was wrong with Twainbough?" another fan asked. "He ran like an old woman out there. He couldn't do anything right today."

"Yeah, well, I always did think he was overrated. I mean think about it: He's got a famous papa and a rich mama. That's the only reason they're letting him play."

"It has to be something like that. Jesus, he missed a field goal *I* could've made."

Amy couldn't take any more. She stood there with her hands on her hips, glaring up a few rows until she found the two loudmouthed fans.

"Then why didn't *you* go out there and kick the field goal?" she asked hotly, fixing them with her most severe glare. "It's awfully easy to criticize. Don't you know he's *injured*? He can hardly walk, let alone play football!"

"That's all the more reason they should get him out of there, girly," one of the men countered.

Amy bit her tongue and turned away from them, not wanting to get into a long-winded argument. She hoped people weren't being this cruel around Ham.

Well, she told herself, *I guess I'll just have to be especially nice to him.*

* * *

The silver-blue Plymouth convertible rolled to a stop on a bluff overlooking the Mississippi River. Ham shut off the engine but left the radio playing, and its soft dial light was the only illumination inside the car. Outside the bright moon shone on the river, turning it into a stream of molten silver.

"I'm glad you didn't mind not going down to Bear Tracks with the others," Ham said. "I didn't want to listen to a lot of theories on why we lost and what we should have done."

"That's all right. This is much nicer, anyway," Amy said, snuggling closer. "And I'm with you. I'd rather listen to the music than hear the game being replayed over and over."

The music was "Harlem Nocturne," and the saxophone was wailing.

"That's sexy music," Ham said.

"Sexy? Oh, my," Amy said. "We'd better be careful, then." She put her hand lightly on his knee, and she could almost feel the heat coming through his trouser leg. "Does it hurt terribly?" she asked.

"It isn't exactly feeling wonderful," Ham admitted.

Beside him, Amy shivered.

"Are you cold?" he asked. "Would you like me to put the top up?"

"Why put the top up when there are *other* ways to keep me warm?" Amy replied.

Ham chuckled. "Well, indeed there are." He put his arm around her and drew her even closer.

The music ended, and the news started. Amy started to reach for the radio to change to another station, but Ham stopped her.

"No, wait," he said. "At the end of the news they'll give the scores of all the other games."

"*This . . . is . . . Floyd Stoner speaking to you from London,*" the voice on the radio said. Behind Floyd Stoner's voice could be heard the long, mournful wail of air-raid sirens and the crash and thump of explosions. "*What you are hearing are the sounds of death and destruction, raining down upon the heads of the innocent civilians of this beleaguered city, women and children alike.*"

There was one very loud crash, then a moment of silence before Fløyd Stoner resumed talking.

"*That one . . . that one was very close,*" he said, speaking breathlessly. "*I don't mind admitting to you that I ducked when that one went off.*"

There was a staccato burst of gunfire, followed by heavier, more distant explosions.

"*That was antiaircraft cannons, firing from just across the street. I am on the roof of my hotel with a ringside seat to the bombing. High overhead I can hear the drone of Nazi warplanes, but as it isn't yet dawn here in London, I can't actually see anything. Wait a minute! Wait a minute! One of the German airplanes must have just been hit! Yes, yes, I can see it quite clearly now! A small flicker of light high in the dark sky has suddenly flared up, and now it's fluttering down, somewhat like a spark drifting down from a campfire.*

"*But that one German airplane, ladies and gentlemen, seems an awfully insignificant repayment for the damage inflicted upon this beautiful city. From here I can look down on the dock area and see dozens . . . scores . . . possibly hundreds of fires, licking up into the night sky. All over the city of London, from horizon to horizon, a soft, orange glow lights the heavens. And there goes another string of blazing tracer shells, zipping up into the sky, a long finger of death reaching out to bring another Messerschmitt crashing down.*

"*The hopes and wishes of all free men everywhere are with these brave Londoners who tonight and every night face a blitzkrieg that makes war against the innocent.*

"*And now, this . . . is . . . Floyd Stoner, signing off.*"

There was a brief pause, and then another announcer came on:

"*And this is the NBC Blue Network in New York, with scores from today's college football games. . . .*"

Ham reached down to turn off the radio, and Amy looked at him in surprise.

"I thought you wanted to hear the scores."

"Yeah, well, they don't seem quite as important now," Ham replied. "I mean, when you stop to think about it, the young people of America are worrying about football games while the young people of Europe are worrying about their lives."

"I see what you mean. You lived in London, didn't you?" Amy asked.

"No. Before my mother and father were divorced, we lived in Paris . . . but, of course, we visited London. As a matter of fact, I was there with my father just two years ago."

"Is your father going to write a novel about this war?" Amy asked.

Ham chuckled. "Well, I don't know why he wouldn't. He's written one about all the others."

"I really liked *Confession at Linares*," Amy said. "Sure, I know it was an English class project that we *had* to read, but I liked it anyway."

"That isn't my favorite of his," Ham admitted.

"Which is?"

"The first one," Ham said. "*A Time for All Things*."

"Why that one?"

"I don't know. I guess because it's a story about his youth. I find it especially interesting since I have a hard time imagining that my father was ever young." Ham smiled, adding, "In fact, no matter what I've read or what he says, I'm still not convinced that he was."

"It must be very interesting to have a father who's a famous novelist."

Ham laughed. "Most of my friends think it's more interesting to have a mother who owns a brewery. I mean, think of it. To have an inexhaustible supply of beer at your fingertips—isn't that every young man's dream?"

"I guess it depends on how shallow the young man is," Amy countered.

Ham laughed again. "Yeah, I guess it does, at that."

They fell silent for a few moments, then Amy asked, "Ham, do you think America will get into the war in Europe?"

"I don't know. Why?"

"Daddy thinks we will. He says Dr. Rosen told him that Hitler won't stop until someone stops him—or until he controls the entire world."

"Dr. Rosen is a Jew who was forced to leave Germany. You can't expect him to have an objective point of view."

"Still, when you consider—" That was as far as Amy got because Ham put the tip of his finger across her lips.

"Hey, what do you say we don't discuss the war anymore?" he suggested.

"You're right. I don't know why I am, anyway. I mean, Mom and I always get upset with Daddy because he listens to so much of the war news, and here I am talking about it. Okay, what do you want to talk about?"

"I don't want to talk."

"You don't want to talk? So what do you want to do, just sit here?" Amy's voice dropped to a near whisper.

"Well, I wouldn't say I just want to *sit* here." Ham put his hand to Amy's cheek and turned her face so that their lips were but an inch apart. He kissed her, gently at first, then deeper and deeper still, savoring the cherry of her lipstick, the mint of her toothpaste, and, most exciting of all, the unique taste that was just her.

Amy had never gone all the way with Ham, but she had allowed him liberties with his hands, and Ham believed he had never petted with a more exciting woman. His hand went under her blouse and lay against her bare midriff, so smooth and incredibly hot despite the fact that the top was down on the car. When Amy didn't offer any resistance, his hand slipped under her bra and cupped her warm breast that pulsated with a desire as raw-edged and hungry as Ham's own.

"Ham, please," Amy protested weakly, though her voice betrayed her longing as surely as her breathing and the temperature of her skin. "Please, we can't do this."

"I love you, Amy," Ham said. "I want you. I *need* you." Ham's hand came out from under the bra and moved back down the burning skin, dipping under her panties and then through the exciting tangle of pubic hair, finding her hot, moist core. He felt Amy's body jerk once, as if she had felt an electric shock, when his finger came in contact with the slick nub of flesh hidden in the folds of her vagina.

"No," Amy whimpered. "No, Ham, please, we mustn't. We can't. Don't do this." She was almost crying, and she twisted away from him, away from the finger that was making her melt like so much hot wax. She reached down and turned the radio back on. "Let's listen to some music," she said. "Ham? If you love me?"

Ham sighed, then moved his hand away and leaned back in his seat.

"I'm sorry, Ham," Amy said. "Really, I'm sorry. But I just can't. . . . We shouldn't."

"I know, I know," Ham said. He put his arm around her and pulled her to him. "Listen, I'm the one who should apologize. I promised you that nothing like this would happen, and then I . . . But dammit, Amy, I love you, and I want you. I've never wanted anything in my life like I want you."

"But it wouldn't be right," Amy said. "Don't you see that? It just wouldn't be right."

A Glenn Miller song began playing, and when Ham recognized it, he laughed. "Boy, is that ever my song," he said. The song was "In the Mood."

Amy laughed, too. "It's almost like they knew what we were doing," she said.

"You mean *almost* doing," Ham corrected.

"Almost doing," Amy agreed. She kissed Ham lightly on the lips. "Thanks for not doing it. You are a dear."

"Yeah," Ham growled. "I'm a goddamn saint."

Both of them laughed.

LONDON

Colonel Sir John Paul Chetwynd-Dunleigh and Shaylin McKay had just come from seeing a Noel Coward play and were laughing and retelling some of the funniest parts of it when they were interrupted by a long, slow-building wail. It was the mournful warning of an air raid, and the sound came from hundreds of hand-cranked sirens mounted on rooftops all over the city.

John Paul was sure there had never been anything else quite like that sound. It was a heart-stopping moan that was at the same time both an anguished cry and a challenge. Somehow those discordant notes seemed to find a harmonic response in the nerves and heartstrings of all who heard it, and one could never hear it without feeling some immediate and physical effect.

"Oh, John Paul," Shaylin said with a slight shudder, "damn them, they're coming again."

In the distance the thumping sounds of antiaircraft guns started, overriding the drone of hundreds of airplanes. Search beacons sprang on and began probing the dark heavens for the German raiders.

"I think there's an underground station in the next block," John Paul said. "We'll have to run for it. They're pretty close already."

They started to run for the shelter, but halfway there Shaylin broke the heel of one of her shoes and then twisted her ankle badly. She let out a sharp cry of pain as she pitched forward onto the cobblestone street.

"Shaylin, what is it?"

"My ankle!" Shaylin said. "Damn! I don't think I can go on."

John Paul reached down to scoop her up into his arms as the sound of the approaching aircraft engines grew louder and some antiaircraft batteries that were very close by began firing. When the big guns fired, their muzzle flashes lit up the entire area as bright as midday. If that gun was already firing, John Paul realized, then the Germans must be nearly overhead. He knew that the bombs released from the German bombers fell one mile beyond the release point. That meant that the bombs being dropped right now would fall right here.

"We aren't going to make it to the underground in time," John Paul said anxiously. "We must go somewhere else."

"Look! Over there!" Shaylin shouted over the cacophony, pointing across the street. "There's a basement delivery entrance to that store."

Carrying her, John Paul ran in shuffling, heavy steps until he reached the stairs. He hefted Shaylin down the steps, then tried the door. It was locked.

"I'll break the glass," John Paul said. "Hopefully it'll be the kind of door you can unlock without an inside key."

He found a brick and smashed through the glass, then reached through the broken window. Fingering a crossbar, he lifted it up and the door swung open.

"Good for you!" Shaylin said. "You got it!" But her words were nearly drowned out by the roar of an exploding bomb that hit out on the street almost at the spot where Shaylin had fallen. They had moved just in time.

John Paul picked Shaylin up again and carried her inside. It was so dark, though, that he couldn't see anything. Then the muzzle flash of the antiaircraft gun lit up the cellar, and he could see that it was a storage room for mattresses.

"This is wonderful!" he said. "We'll pull several of these over us and we should be as safe in here as we would be in the underground."

John Paul laid Shaylin on one of the mattresses, then went to work making an igloolike structure around them, padding them with mattresses until he felt they could survive even if the building above them took a direct hit. He crawled onto the mattress beside Shaylin.

"There, now, isn't this cozy?" he asked.

"Oh, those *bastards!*" Shaylin said in a frightened voice. There was another hit close by, and Shaylin let out a little scream.

"Here, now," John Paul said in a quiet, soothing voice. "You mustn't be afraid. Is this the war correspondent I hear? You've been through things like this before, haven't you?"

"Yes, I have," Shaylin said. "That's why I'm terrified."

"We'll be safe in here," John Paul assured her.

"Hold me, John Paul. Please, hold me," Shaylin begged in a voice not unlike that of a little girl frightened by a thunderstorm.

John Paul reached out in the pitch dark and put his arm around her, pulling her close. He could feel her heart pounding. Wanting to comfort her, he kissed her. At first it was just a gentle touch of his lips, a reassurance that everything would be all right, that he was here with her and he would protect her. The kiss was a familiar one for they had been intimate for nearly a year now, and as they kissed, desire began to grow.

"John Paul," Shaylin gasped, "make love to me!"

"*What?* Are you serious? This is hardly the proper—"

"Damn you, John Paul, forget for once your damned proper British reserve, won't you? I'm *very* serious. I want you to make love to me right here, right now!"

John Paul felt the blood pounding at his temples and a swirling fire raging in his gut. He needed no further urging; he didn't know when he had ever wanted her more than he wanted her now, this minute, in the midst of a German air attack. The whole idea was the craziest thing he had ever heard of . . . and the most arousing.

They thrust against each other, opening buttons, releasing snaps, throwing aside anything that got in the way so that within a moment clothes were askew and there was only skin-to-skin contact. Her smooth, firm breasts pressed against his flat, hairy chest, while his strong erection thrust against her soft, wet cleft.

Tongues tangled, and words of need and moans of passion were lost in the throat as Shaylin positioned herself on the mattress to receive him comfortably, familiarly. She spread her legs as he entered her. They had made love many times before, but never quite like this.

Bombs continued to fall in the streets around them, and a particularly close explosion was followed by the tumbling crash of brick walls and the bursting tinkle of glass. The terrifying, paralyzing fear Shaylin had experienced was now gone, because despite the intensity of the air raid, nothing from the outside could get through to them. They had managed to construct a cocoon of sensual pleasure that bought them a temporary respite from all that was going on around them.

Afterward they lay together until, finally, the all clear sounded, followed by the clanging bells of the fire engines and the whistles of the air-raid wardens.

"I don't think we want to be found like this, do we?" Shaylin asked with a contented little giggle.

"Oh? Who is the proper one now?" John Paul teased. "You didn't seem too concerned a short while ago. Good heavens, woman, what if a bomb had fallen on us? What if they had come in and discovered us this way? What would people say?"

Shaylin's laugh was throaty. "They would say, 'What a way to go!' "

CHAPTER SIX

Of all the cities in Japan, Hiroshi Amano thought, none was more representative of the spirit of the nation than his own native city of Hiroshima. Even its shape was symbolic, for it resembled an *uchiwa*, a fan, formed by the six islands of the seven estuarial streams that branched out from the Ota River. It was early November, and dawn was breaking, and though it was crisply cool, it wasn't cold. The fishermen from nearby villages and the working people of the city were already at their morning duties so that Hiroshima and its waterways were a mélange of sights, sounds, and smells.

The city was a kaleidoscope of color and pattern, from the butterfly-bright kimonos worn by the young women to the geometric alignment of the *tori* gates that led to the grounds of the Gokoku shrine. On the waterways the flat boats glided effortlessly across the surface, the painted eyes of the boats staring back from their reflections as if admiring the beauty of the scene.

The odor of fish carried up from the river, the timeless

pungency somehow conveying Japan's timelessness as well. Mingling with the fish odor were the smells of burning charcoal, steaming soup, and strong soap that wafted from the narrow streets and twisting alleys along with the calls of peddlers hawking their wares. Above the peddlers' shouts, the rattle of iron-rimmed cart wheels rolling on cobblestones, the chatter of women shoppers, and the laughter of children, was the constant, rhythmic clacking of the wooden blocks unique to the fishermen in Hiroshima's waters that they used to attract the Ota River carp, a fat, red fish found only here and prized throughout Japan for its delicate flavor. Taken in concert, all those sounds created a virtual folk symphony, and with a little imagination one could almost hear plucked *koto* strings played in accompaniment.

In a house sitting on stilts at the edge of one of the estuaries, Hiroshi Amano got up with the morning sun. He put on his uniform and walked through the quiet rooms, picking his way carefully around the sleepers whose mats were placed about the floor. His was a house of wealth and status, and it was not necessary that everyone rise as early as the poor people who needed every daylight moment of every single day just to make a living.

Hiroshi slid open the door that led to the porch, then walked outside to stand and look at the river. Much of the predawn mist had been burned away by the red disk of the rising sun, but enough remained to clothe the scene in a diaphanous haze, making it appear as if the city were a painting on silk rendered in pastel blues, purples, and golds.

As soon as Hiroshi had returned from Saigon, he began planning the campaign that led to Japan's invasion and subsequent occupation of all French Indochina. The French, who had surrendered to Germany and were attempting to hang on to their African colonies, paid so little attention to Indochina that, as Hiroshi had predicted, resistance had been minimal, and occupation had been easy. Now Japan not only had a source of raw materials, it also held strategic positions in Southeast Asia.

But there was to be more. After nearly a year of talks with the United States, the government of Japan was now ready to concede that the talks were going nowhere. As a result, Admiral Isoroku Yamamoto had been given instructions to design a plan of action in the event Japan and the United States went to war. Hiroshi, who had been assigned to Admiral Yamamoto's staff upon his return from French Indochina, made several major contributions to the plan, which was called "Operation Z" in honor of the Z signal given by Admiral Togo in Japan's most famous naval battle at Tsushima.

The first and boldest stroke of Operation Z was to be an aerial attack on the giant U.S. Navy base at Pearl Harbor in the Hawaiian Islands. That would be followed by air, sea, and land attacks to secure for Japan the Philippine Islands. Hiroshi's task was to formulate the strategy for occupying the other Pacific islands as well. On his own initiative Hiroshi had added Wake Island to the original plan.

Looking out over his beloved city, Hiroshi recalled Admiral Yamamoto's reaction when he had first told him several weeks ago of the addition.

"Why worry about Wake Island?" Yamamoto asked as they lay naked and side by side on towels in a bathhouse, receiving massages from the young women attendants.

The two senior officers were as unconcerned over their nudity in front of the women as they were about speaking openly of such classified subjects. The young women lived by a strict code of secrecy that would never allow them to divulge anything about any of their clients, and it was that code that safeguarded the officers' seeming breach of security.

Hiroshi explained, "While I was in Saigon, I met a young American aviator, a pilot of one of the American flying boats that cross the Pacific. According to him, Wake Island is very critical to any air operations across the ocean, for it is desperately needed as a refueling point."

"Is he a person who knows what he is speaking about?" Yamamoto asked. "Or is he a cowboy?"

"A cowboy?" Hiroshi asked, puzzled by the question.

Yamamoto chuckled. "We have our samurai; the Americans have their cowboys. It is that attitude that gives them a feeling of independence and individual strength. Here, the samurai is imbued with the knowledge that he is superior in all the martial arts, but we also have those who are born to business, the arts, religion, or just to serve others. There is a place for every Japanese, and every Japanese is in his place. In America that is not true. All Americans have a personal motto, and that motto is: 'There is no son of a bitch around any better than me.' " Yamamoto said the phrase in English, with his own approximation of an American accent, and it sounded amusing in the middle of the conversation in Japanese.

Hiroshi laughed at the mimicry. "I see what you mean, Admiral. *All* Americans have the self-confidence of our samurai."

"Yes," Yamamoto said. "But as it is their strength, it may also be their weakness. They believe that there is no one with the audacity to attack them—and that smug belief will assure our success in achieving surprise."

"That is very true," Hiroshi agreed. "Indeed, when I mentioned the possibility that our two countries might someday go to war, the American pilot, Mr. Blake, seemed very surprised that the possibility even existed. I thought at the time that he was too involved in his own life to be aware of the greater affairs going on around him. But now that you speak of it, I believe you may be correct. He had no concept that war would ever break out between our two countries because he had an arrogant belief in the invincibility of America."

"That being said, do you have confidence in his appraisal of the importance of Wake Island?"

"Yes, Admiral, I do."

"All right, you have my approval," Yamamoto said. "When you draw up the strategy for taking all the Pacific Islands, include Wake Island. Incidentally, do you believe Wake will be heavily defended?"

"There is only a small garrison there, Admiral."

"We cannot get bogged down," Yamamoto said. "It must fall quickly and cleanly."

"The plan I have drawn up calls for six ships and a regiment of marines. We will have sufficient forces to get the job done," Hiroshi said with certainty.

"I want you to monitor the situation from your post on

board the flagship. If you see that last-minute changes are needed, take the appropriate steps."

"Admiral, I beg of you," Hiroshi interjected. "I am a naval aviator. Please, do not let the greatest operation in our history proceed without me being a part of it. I wish to take part in the attack on Pearl Harbor."

"But you would be of more value to me on the flagship," Yamamoto protested. "Besides, all the elements are formed. Would you deprive one of the attack commanders of their rightful position?"

"Sir, I will go as an executive officer . . . as a pilot . . . as a gunner, even. I just beg to be allowed to participate."

Yamamoto sighed, then smiled. "Had I someone who could grant me permission to go, I would be right alongside you, Hiroshi. Very well, you may go . . . as my official observer."

"Thank you, Admiral. Thank you very much."

Since that discussion had taken place, a vigorous training progam had been instigated to guarantee a successful first blow against Pearl Harbor. The training had taken place at Kagoshima City, a beautiful city sometimes known as the "Venice of the Orient." Kagoshima City was located on Kyushu, the southernmost of Japan's four major islands. The training had been exciting because it involved the technique of "buzzing" the city, flying so low that the planes actually had to dodge telephone poles, then race across the bay at an altitude of twenty-five feet until the torpedo launcher pulled a toggle switch that would have sent a torpedo skimming across the water had a torpedo actually been used.

Though no one in the squadron knew why they were training, they were eager and willing students, and the training went so well that soon even those initially skeptical of using torpedo planes in the attack were silenced. They had been concerned that because the water in Pearl Harbor was so shallow, the torpedoes would hit bottom and explode prematurely. Specially designed, shallow-running torpedoes and the tactic of low-level release had circumvented that problem.

Now all the planning and training was behind them. The Japanese fleet was anchored off the coast of Kyushu with orders to sail the very next morning. The operation was so secret that there were very few who had any idea of where the ships were going or what they would do when they got there. In fact, even Hiroshi's presence at home was part of the plan to preserve that secrecy, for it would seem unlikely that someone on the admiral's staff would be granted a leave of fifteen days, as Hiroshi had, if an operation were imminent. However, Hiroshi also had secret supplemental orders requiring him to fly back to the fleet today, ten days early, to be aboard ship when the fleet sailed the next morning.

As the morning shadows lightened, Hiroshi became aware that he was not alone on the porch. Onri Saito, his father-in-law, was sitting quietly at the other end of the porch, watching Hiroshi with deep, dark eyes.

Hiroshi looked away from the old man's scrutiny. To cover his awkwardness at being discovered in this quiet moment, he pointed to the bloodred disk and said, "The sunrise. It reminds me of the Imperial flag."

The old man didn't respond.

"I was unable to sleep," Hiroshi said.

Still there was no response.

"The brazier made the room close, so I came outside for a breath of fresh air."

"You have decided on war," Onri finally said.

"What?" Hiroshi replied, surprised by Onri's comment. "What are you talking about?"

"You and the others like you have decided to make war. You will attack the United States."

"How—where did you hear that?" Hiroshi sputtered, surprised by Onri's knowledge of what was supposed to be a top secret.

"I have heard it here," Onri said, putting his hand over his heart. "And I have heard it here," he added, bringing his hand to his head. "There are no secrets when one can hear in this way."

"All right," Hiroshi said, "suppose I tell you that what you say is true."

"Then I will tell you that Japan as we know it will cease to exist," Onri responded.

"Is that not a natural thought for a Zen follower who fears the thought of war?" Hiroshi challenged.

"Better to fear the thought of war than to fear the thought of peace," Onri countered.

"I do not fear peace," Hiroshi said. "But as a samurai it is my belief that one should always be prepared to make war, if that is what is necessary to preserve the peace."

"You speak in riddles," Onri accused. "You cannot make war to preserve peace any more than you can scoop a cup of cool water from the heart of a burning fire."

"It is obvious that we differ in our philosophies," Hiroshi said, "though the love for our country is equal in each of us. I have chosen to serve my country as a warrior, you chose to serve as a member of government. I am sorry that you are no longer in the cabinet. If you were, perhaps our views would be more similar now."

"As you are aware, I left my post when Prime Minister Inukai was assassinated," Onri said. "I could not serve a government that let the murderers go free."

"The government was only responding to the will of the people," Hiroshi reminded him. "Do not forget that over one hundred thousand people signed a petition in blood, asking for clemency for the assassins. And nine men who asked to take the place of the assassins on trial demonstrated their resolve by sending to the trial officials their own little fingers pickled in alcohol."

"And now such firebrand young men control the destiny of our country. They are leading us down the path of destruction," Onri warned.

"Or along the path to glory," Hiroshi rejoined.

" 'A split-hair's difference, and heaven and earth are set apart,' " Onri said, quoting a Buddhist saying.

The sound of the other family members awakening reached the porch, and the private conversation between Hiroshi and Onri ended. The old man became once again the father-in-law, the responsibility of Hiroshi because Hiroshi had married his daughter. Onri's son, Yutake Saito, would normally have had the responsibility, but he had been living in America for over twenty years. Hiroshi didn't mind the responsibility of Yuko's family. As a commander in the Imperial Navy his social and economic position was such that he could easily maintain a large household.

Hiroshi's own mother and father were both dead, killed in the great earthquake of 1923, but if they had still been alive, he would have had the responsibility for them as well as for his wife's family, and all would have lived under the same roof. Six people lived in Hiroshi's house, and he had unquestioned authority over all of them: His wife, Yuko, his daughter Yukari, his son, Saburo, and Yuko's mother and father, Yoshiko and Onri. Where Onri had once been a member of the prime minister's cabinet and a man with tremendous power and prestige, now he was relegated to the role of a dependent father-in-law.

Onri had served a well-known pacifist prime minister whose policies not only had led to his assassination, but had kept his name in disfavor even to this day. Still, despite the discrediting of the former prime minister, there was status attached to having held such an important position in Inukai's government, and therefore even though his father-in-law's political philosophies were so different from his own, Hiroshi felt that Onri's presence brought honor to his house.

The door from the house slid open, and Yuko stepped outside onto the porch to join her husband and her father. She turned to Onri and bowed in respect, then she bowed to Hiroshi. Pulling her kimono more tightly about her, she shivered slightly as she looked for a moment out across the estuary.

Hiroshi gazed at his wife as if trying to memorize every detail. Yuko was a beautiful woman with skin as smooth and unblemished as the petals of a rose and hair so deep a shade of black that it was almost blue. Her long eyelashes looked like delicate lace fans, and her eyes were as deep as the deepest pools. In a land that placed great store in the beauty of all things, Yuko's exquisite beauty caused all who saw her to feel warmed by her presence.

"Are you not cold?" she asked in a voice that to Hiroshi sounded like the tinkling of wind bells.

As Hiroshi looked at her and realized that he would be leaving her today, he felt such sadness that he could have almost forgotten honor, code, and everything else to violate the orders that would separate them.

"I am not cold," Hiroshi said.

"Oh, how lovely it is," Yuko remarked, studying the vista before her. "It is no wonder that you were out here now. What a magnificent view!"

"I must report to the ship today," Hiroshi said quietly.

There was the slightest gasp, no more than a quickened intake of breath, before Yuko spoke. "You will not be coming back today, will you?"

"No."

"Saburo finishes his second form in school this month. Will you be there to see him?"

"I am sorry," Hiroshi said. "I cannot say."

"I will explain," Yuko said. A weariness seemed to descend over her. "Saburo is the son of a samurai. He will understand. I will see that he understands."

Seventeen-year-old Saburo woke to the aroma of steaming breakfast soup. He sat up and rubbed his eyes, then looked around his alcove. He didn't actually have a room of his own, sleeping as he did in the corner of the great room that served as living room, dining room, family room, and kitchen, but *shoji* screens partitioned off a portion of the room for him, giving the illusion of a separate room.

The sides of the screens that faced Saburo's bed were decorated with pictures. The pictures weren't of Mount Fuji or blossoming cherry trees, as one might expect to find. Instead they were pictures of airplanes. Saburo was very proud of the fact that his father was a pilot, and he wanted to be a pilot, too. His every waking moment was dedicated to the eventual achievement of that end.

Saburo slipped on his kimono, then rolled his sleeping mat into a neat roll, tied it, and placed it where it was stored during the day. Then he moved the dividers so that his alcove disappeared and the great room was enlarged.

Across the room his grandmother and sister were on

their knees by the small charcoal cooking stove. His grandmother was stirring the pot that filled the room with the rich aroma that had awakened Saburo.

Saburo bowed to his grandmother. "What a wonderful smell," he said. "My stomach is ready."

"Your stomach is always ready," his sister, Yukari, teased, and Yoshiko Saito laughed, for Saburo was known for his appetite.

Saburo left the women and stepped out onto the porch. He bowed to his grandfather, then looked around, puzzled that his parents weren't there.

"Grandfather, where are my parents?"

"They went to the market."

Saburo laughed. "My father went to the market? But he would never do that. Shopping is not a manly job for a samurai."

Onri smiled. "A true samurai has no need of convention to establish his manhood. He is what he is because he is."

"Grandfather, do you ever wish you were a samurai?"

"No," Onri answered firmly. "Samurai are not the only nobles of Japan. I have spent my life studying truth, and it is as noble to study truth as it is to study war."

"What is truth?"

"Those who know it do not speak it. Those who speak it do not know it," Onri replied.

Saburo laughed. "I don't understand."

"When you understand, you will understand."

"Oh, there!" Saburo suddenly said excitedly. "There they are now. I see them. Father!" he called. He ran quickly down the steps so he could meet his mother and father as they returned from the market. His mother was wearing her kimono with the family carnation emblem, and his father was wearing the uniform of a Navy commander. Saburo thought they made a very handsome pair, and he stopped to observe them so that he could fix this memory in his mind. That way he could recall this scene anytime he wished.

"So, the lazy young man is awake at last," Hiroshi teased his son when he had reached him.

"I didn't hear anyone leave," Saburo said. "I would have come too, if you had asked me."

"Why, Saburo," Yuko said, smiling sweetly, "often I have asked you to come with me to the market, and always you have said it is not a man's place."

"I was wrong," Saburo said. "A true samurai has no need of convention to establish his manhood. He is what he is because he is."

"Such wise and mature words from your lips?" Hiroshi said in surprise.

"They are the words of Grandfather," Saburo admitted sheepishly.

Hiroshi laughed. "Then they are indeed wise."

"Father, I finish second form this month," Saburo said.

"Yes, I know. Your mother told me. I am very proud of you."

"As soon as I finish, I can enter aviation cadet training, with your permission. I can become a midshipman in the Navy and a Navy pilot, just like you!" he added proudly.

"No," Hiroshi said.

The smile on Saburo's face faded instantly. He hadn't expected such an answer. "Father, I am samurai. It is time for me to begin training."

"You will go on with your education," Hiroshi said sternly. "You will not go into the Navy."

"But, Father . . ."

"Do you dare to question me?" Hiroshi asked, raising his voice slightly.

"No, sir," Saburo replied quietly, and he turned and ran back to the house so that his father wouldn't see the tears that had welled up in his eyes.

"He doesn't understand," Yuko said, watching her son hurry off. "He doesn't know that your desire to protect him causes you to speak so."

Hiroshi was silent for a long moment; then he sighed. "I won't be able to protect him long. When the war comes, the draft will reach all the way down to boys his age, and there will be nothing I can do to prevent him from going."

"Must there be a war?"

"Yes. I am convinced that we have no other choice

now. The Americans are destroying our economy, disgracing our national pride, and taking away our dignity."

"Father says that war is a failure of the national spirit."

"Your father is a rare and great man of peace. He is a prophet without a following. After the war we will need many men like your father. If we win, we will need them to help us establish a new world order of justice and harmony. If we lose, we will need them to help us salvage dignity from defeat and hope from despair."

"Will we win, or will we lose?"

Hiroshi slowly shook his head. "You ask a question without an answer."

CHAPTER SEVEN

Captain Jimmy Blake stood in the bow of the launch as it approached the great World Air Transport flying boat anchored in the bay. The Windjammer *Golden Gate* was being serviced by seven maintenance men in blue jumpsuits, five of them busy on the stubby low wing known as the step-plane wing and two up on the high wing, sitting on the nacelle of the number-four engine. Such was the size of the plane that those men working on the engine were fully twenty feet above the water.

Jimmy squinted up at the mechanics through bluegray eyes that seemed older than his years. The highly visible scar on his forehead, a permanent reminder of his close call a year and a half earlier, in no way detracted from his rugged good looks. In fact it sometimes drew women to him in the way that a dueling scar draws women who are attracted to danger and excitement.

"What did you find?" Jimmy called to the maintenance crew, cupping his hand around his mouth.

"A dead bird was in the oil cooler," one of the mechanics replied. "We've got it all cleaned out now. There won't be any more problems."

"Good, good. I appreciate that."

The mechanics, like everyone else on the island, worked for Pan American Airways. World Air Transport had to pay Pan Am a landing fee and also had to depend on the rival airline for all the services received there. Even the tiny hotel that served crews and passengers of trans-Pacific flights was owned and run by Pan American Airways System.

"Tell me, Captain, how'd you know this here engine was runnin' hot?" one of the mechanics called down. "The thermocouple wasn't workin', so you couldn't've had an indication on the gauge."

"I could feel it coming in last night," Jimmy replied.

The mechanic chuckled. "You could feel it, huh?" He looked at the other mechanic up on the engine nacelle with him. "He could *feel* it, he says. With guys like him flyin', who needs instruments?"

Jimmy climbed from the launch onto the small lower wing of the Windjammer. It was this wing that helped the airplane break free of the water when it began its takeoff run. It also held much of the aircraft's fuel, and the smell of gasoline was strong while the tank was being filled.

The door by the wing led through the dining salon, and the purser greeted Jimmy as he stepped into the shadowed interior of the plane.

"Hello, Elliot," Jimmy greeted back. "Did you get the food loaded on?"

Elliot Smythe, an Englishman who had trained for his profession on the great luxury ships of the White Star Line, was highly regarded by Jimmy for his thoroughness and concern. "Yes, sir," he replied. "Captain, do you have any idea of the weather? I plan to serve a nice redfish for dinner, and I wouldn't want any of the passengers to skip a meal because of a queasy stomach."

"I don't know, but I'll check with Arnold," Jimmy promised. "He probably has the report by now."

"Thank you, sir."

Jimmy climbed the spiral staircase to the upper deck, then took off his jacket and hung it in the small closet. This was a violation of company rules, which required that all crew members be in complete uniform at all times when on board the airplane.

Burt Wyler, the heavyset, balding navigator, looked up from his navigator's table and chuckled when Jimmy undid his tie and loosened his collar.

"Captain, one of these days a company rep is going to climb these stairs and find you in your shirtsleeves," Burt said. "Then what are you going to do?"

"Come on, Burt. A WAT company rep on Wake? What makes you think Pan Am would even let one of 'em on the island? Anyway, I could always let Meeker greet them. Arnold looks nice, don't you think?"

Arnold Meeker was the first officer, and he was sitting in his seat on the bridge. He turned toward Jimmy when he heard his name mentioned. As always, Arnold, a short man with blond hair and watery blue eyes, was impeccably dressed.

"Thanks a lot," he said. "It's always nice to know that I look good for my friends." He ran his hand over his smoothly combed hair, though no checking was necessary.

"Say, Arnold, did you get met?"

"Yes, sir," the first officer answered. "I gave the information to Burt already. It's on his table."

Jimmy saw the meteorologist's report on the navigator's table, and he picked it up, looked at it for a moment, then buzzed the purser's phone.

"Purser, sir," a voice answered.

"Serve your fish, Elliot. It looks like smooth air."

"Very good, sir. Thank you."

Arnold chuckled. "Elliot worrying about passengers with queasy stomachs again?"

"Can you blame him?" Burt asked. "How would *you* like to clean up after an airsick passenger?"

"No, thanks," Arnold replied. He looked out the window and saw two men standing on the protrusion, using long-poled brushes to wash the bottom of the high wing. Arnold pulled the window open and called down to them.

"Hey, you guys make sure you don't get beyond that 'no step' line. Someone did in Hong Kong, and now we've got dinted sheet metal."

"We'll be careful, Cap'n," one of the men called back.

"I'm not the captain," Meeker corrected. "But be careful anyway." He pulled his window shut again.

Jimmy watched his first officer, knowing that Arnold Meeker figured he *should* be a captain by now, and he knew, too, that Arnold felt it was because of Jimmy that he hadn't been promoted. It wasn't anything Jimmy had done; it was just because he had come back to work for World Air after his failure to establish his own airline. When he came back, he was readmitted with his old seniority rating, bumping out the next man in line: Arnold Meeker. But Jimmy knew something else about Arnold. He had learned that once, during a complaint session with several other copilots on the line, someone had remonstrated that Arnold had been held back because of Jimmy's close friendship with the president of the airline, William Canfield. But Arnold himself had countered that Jimmy Blake was the best pilot he had ever flown with, friend of Canfield's or not, and it would have been extremely foolish of World Air Transport not to reestablish him in a captain's position. Jimmy felt that loyalty like that was valuable beyond words.

"Say, Captain," Arnold asked, turning around in his seat. "Is it true that Eric Twainbough will be going on to Hawaii with us?"

"It's true, all right," Jimmy answered. "I understand he was coming back from Manila on a Pan Am Clipper when he got a toothache. It was so bad that he had to get off here and let the Pan Am dentist take care of it for him. Now, to make his mainland connection, he's going to finish the flight with us."

"How about that?" Arnold observed. "Eric Twainbough is riding with us."

"I've met him before," Jimmy replied.

"You *know* him? I'm very impressed."

"I said I've *met* him before. I didn't say I know him."

"Have you ever read any of his books?" Arnold asked.

"Well, I'm not much on these highfalutin authors, but I did read the one about prospecting for gold in Alaska."

"That was *Fire on the Northern Ice.*"

"Yeah. I liked that one pretty much. It had some good

action scenes. And it had some pretty hot scenes between the hero and the whore with the heart of gold."

"Yeah, it was quite a good book, I suppose. But the one I like best is *The Corruptible Dead*. That was a lot better than his last one, *Confession at Linares*."

"*The Corruptible Dead?* They made a movie of that, didn't they? Starring Demaris Hunter? I think I saw it. Of course, I'll see any movie she's in. Demaris Hunter is one beautiful woman."

"She's also a very good actress. She won the Academy Award for her role as Leah in that film, and they don't give Oscars away just because a woman is beautiful."

"No, I guess not."

"Eric Twainbough," Arnold said again. "I can't believe I'm actually going to meet him."

"I had no idea you were such a Twainbough fan," Jimmy remarked.

"Well, I guess you could call me a fan, though I find the man more intriguing than his books. He's lived quite a life. I did a paper on him in college. My contention was that while his books are often thought-provoking and always entertaining, they sometimes lack depth."

Jimmy chuckled. "If I introduce you to him, you won't embarrass me by telling him his books lack depth, will you?"

Arnold grinned. "I'll do my best."

Even as he was being discussed, Eric Twainbough was sitting on the front porch of the small Wake Island Hotel, reading a *Time* magazine. He was wearing khaki pants and a flowered sport shirt that hung loose. His hair was more white than gray, and his bushy beard seemed to add to his overall bulk. He was a big, barrel-chested man with massive shoulders, muscular arms, and a formidable belly. He was scratching that belly as one of the Pan Am stewards approached him, carrying a bottle of Tannenhower beer.

"Oh, thank you," Eric said, taking the bottle and leaving the glass and money for the drink on the tray. "Did you check on the Windjammer for me?"

"Yes, sir," the steward replied. "It is due to take off this evening, as scheduled."

"Good, good. That means I'll be in Honolulu tomorrow, the eighth, San Francisco on the ninth, and St. Louis on the tenth." He sighed. "Damn! I'm going to miss it by one day."

"What is that, sir?" the steward asked.

"My son is being inducted into the Quad Quad," he replied. Noting the steward's look of confusion, he explained, "It's a position of honor at the university he attends. I wanted to be there for it, but there's no way now."

"Actually, Mr. Twainbough, there is. You see, when you arrive in Honolulu tomorrow morning, it will be the seventh again, not the eighth."

Eric barked out a "Ha!" and grinned broadly. "By God, you're right!" he said. "I forgot about the international date line. That saves me one entire day. Which means that if I'm lucky enough to get the right connections, I could make it after all. You're sure the airplane is all right? I saw some men working on it earlier."

"It was just routine maintenance," the steward assured him. "When I checked a few moments ago I was told that the airplane would leave on schedule."

"They'll be serving dinner on board?"

"Yes, sir."

Eric rubbed his hands together. "We live in some age, don't we? In an hour or so I'll get on that airplane, eat a fine dinner, then crawl into a sleeping berth. When I wake up tomorrow morning I'll be in Honolulu, and three days from now I'll be halfway around the world from here in St. Louis, Missouri."

"Yes, sir," the steward agreed. "It's quite amazing."

At 4:30 P.M. a Pan Am launch stood ready to take Eric out to the Windjammer *Golden Gate*. Several Pan Am employees, many of whom had brought rather dog-eared copies of books to be signed, came down to the dock to tell Eric good-bye, and he autographed the books and cracked jokes while the other six passengers got into the launch. These were through passengers who had arrived on the inbound flight from Hong Kong at eight-thirty the night before. Now, after having spent the previous night and most of that day in the small hotel on Wake Island, they were reboarding the plane for the continuation of the flight to Honolulu.

The launch reached the plane minutes later, and Elliot Smythe was waiting there to help the passengers out of the boat. Captain Jimmy Blake was there also, standing just inside the door, and behind him was First Officer Arnold Meeker.

"Welcome back aboard. I hope you had a pleasant rest," Jimmy greeted each passenger coming aboard. When Eric appeared, he smiled and said, "Ah, Mr. Twainbough, it's good to fly with you again."

Eric squinted at him. "We've flown together before?"

Jimmy laughed. "Yes, sir—though it's been quite a few years. I flew you to Portugal when you went over to cover the Spanish Civil War."

Eric grinned broadly at the memory. "Oh, yes, I remember now. You were flying with Willie Canfield then."

"Yes, sir."

"So how is Willie getting along?"

"Just fine, as far as I know." Jimmy chuckled, and added, "Of course, we don't exactly move in the same circles anymore. He's a high-powered executive, sitting behind a desk in his office, and I'm a working stiff, boring holes in the sky with his planes."

"Knowing Willie, I'd bet anything he'd change places with you in a minute, if he could," Eric suggested.

Jimmy laughed. "Yes, sir, I do believe he would. But I wouldn't change with him."

"I don't blame you a bit," Eric said. "The greatest thing that can happen to a man is that he finds a way to make a living doing what he loves to do. Those few of us who do are very lucky."

"You've got that right," Jimmy agreed. "Oh, by the way, I would like you to meet my first officer—and a fan of yours—Arnold Meeker."

"I'm always happy to meet a fan," Eric said, smiling at the copilot.

"I've read *all* of your books, Mr. Twainbough," Arnold said, visibly excited.

"Please, call me Eric. And I hope you found one or two you enjoyed."

"I . . . uh, liked all of them," Arnold said diplomatically. "What are you working on now?"

Eric smiled and shook his head. "Well, I suppose I could tell you, as so many writers do, that I never discuss a work in progress—but the truth is, I'm not working on anything. I just flew to Manila on a pleasure trip. It may be another year or so before I get started on something else."

"Don't wait too long," Arnold said. "I'm anxious to read a new one by you."

"You sound like Sam Hamilton."

"Who, sir?"

"Sam's my editor at Pendarrow House. He's always after me to get started on another book." Eric looked around the plane. By now all the other passengers had boarded and were in their seats. "Any special place I should sit?"

"Anywhere you want," Jimmy answered. "Elliot, will you dog the door shut? Mr. Meeker and I have to go up to the flight deck to get the preflight started."

"Yes, sir, Captain," the purser replied.

Jimmy and Arnold climbed the spiral stairs up to the cockpit and strapped themselves in their seats. Then a boat towed the airplane away from the dock and pointed it out toward the middle of the bay. The towline parted as the boat moved out of the way, leaving the airplane bobbing free on the gentle waves of the sheltered bay.

"Turn on the seat belt and no smoking signs," Jimmy ordered.

"Seat belt and no smoking signs on, Captain," Arnold replied, complying with Jimmy's request.

"Starting sequence for engine number one," Jimmy said.

They went through the starting sequence with each engine until one by one the engines coughed, sputtered, belched smoke, and took hold. Finally, with all four propellers spinning, Jimmy taxied the big flying boat out to the far end of the bay, then turned to head into the wind. He ordered the navigator to contact Wake control.

A moment later Burt Wyler spoke. "I've got Wake on the radio for you, Skipper."

"Thanks," Jimmy replied and raised the microphone. "Wake Island control, this is World Air Transport Windjammer *Golden Gate* requesting permission for takeoff."

"*Windjammer* Golden Gate, *altimeter is two-niner-niner-five. You are cleared for immediate takeoff and departure on a course of zero-niner-zero degrees,*" the voice in Jimmy's headset said.

"Thank you, Wake Island," Jimmy responded. He hung the microphone on the hook and put both hands on the wheel. "Flaps at thirty," he told his copilot.

"Flaps at thirty, Captain," Arnold answered.

"Mixture full rich."

"Full rich."

"Props at increase RPM."

"Increase RPM."

"Okay," Jimmy said, "let's have full power."

Arnold shoved the four throttle levers against the forward stop, and the Windjammer's engines roared at maximum power as the plane started across the bay, leaving a long streak of white foam behind it on the water. The step-plane wing lifted the craft to the surface of the water, and for forty seconds it skimmed along, splashing so much seawater on the windows that it looked like a tropical downpour. Then some of the noise and all the vibration ceased as the plane lifted free and began climbing slowly away from the tiny island, breaking clean from the streak of white foam.

"Wake Island Control, this is Windjammer *Golden Gate* off at four thirty-seven local. Please advise Honolulu."

"*Will do, Windjammer* Golden Gate."

Jimmy hung the microphone on its hook and leaned back, then looked around the flight deck, smiling broadly, and said, "And once again skill, daring, and experience triumph over fear, ignorance, and superstition as we get this big-assed son of a bitch into the air."

* * *

Three hours later Jimmy and Arnold were sitting with their hands idly folded across their laps. The autopilot was engaged, and the control wheels were making tiny movements as if invisible hands were executing the minute corrections needed for air currents.

"How long have we been under way?" Jimmy asked, stretching.

"Two plus zero-five," Arnold answered.

Jimmy twisted around in his seat. "Got a fix on our ground speed, Burt?"

"One forty-five, Skipper."

"Well, looks like everything's going fine here. Arnold, I think I'm going to leave it in your capable hands while I pay a visit to our passengers and spread the old charm."

"Spread it on thick, Captain," the first officer chuckled.

Jimmy started for the spiral staircase, then stopped and returned to the locker for his jacket. With a smile and a wink at Burt, he slipped it on, then went below.

To save weight, only the lower deck of the Windjammer was soundproofed. Whereas the engines were a reassuring but loud roar on the flight deck, here the level was reduced to a subdued drone, no louder than the interior of a high-speed train. Here, too, were all the amenities of a first-class hotel, with plush carpets, wall upholstery, and elegant curtains.

Jimmy stepped into the dining room where Elliot Smythe and his assistant Mark Greer were laying out hors d'oeuvres of cold shrimp, caviar, and sliced fruit.

"Looks good," Jimmy said.

Elliot speared a cold, peeled shrimp with a toothpick and wordlessly handed it to him.

"Um, tastes good, too," Jimmy noted.

"Captain, will you be visiting with the passengers now?" Elliot asked.

"I thought I might."

"If you'd like, I can start the cocktail hour, and you can all visit in here."

"Yes, that would be nice."

Jimmy stepped over to the window and looked down at the sea while he waited for the others. In the gathering darkness below he saw a ship, and from its long narrow shape he knew it was a warship. It rather surprised him, and he wondered what it was doing out here alone . . . and who it belonged to.

His attention was diverted by the arrival of the passengers, and he turned away from the window to mingle with them.

"Captain, what time do we reach Honolulu?" one of the passengers, a slim man of around forty, asked, taking a drink but forgoing the carefully prepared food.

"We should probably touch down around ten in the morning," Jimmy answered.

"And then how long before we go on to San Francisco?"

"We'll leave at about two in the afternoon."

"Isn't that going to be hard on you, flying all that distance?"

Jimmy chuckled. "Oh, I won't be going on to San Francisco," he said. "You'll pick up a new flight crew tomorrow in Hawaii. So while you're flying along at ten thousand feet, I'll be lying on Waikiki Beach, drinking mai tais and looking at the beautiful girls in their skimpy bathing suits."

"You almost make me wish I wasn't going on," the passenger said, and the others laughed.

Elliot came over to Jimmy and asked, "Captain, would you like to eat with the passengers?"

"Yes, Captain, please join us," Eric Twainbough invited.

"I'd be glad to," Jimmy said. He turned and led everyone into the dining salon.

In the middle of the dessert course the phone buzzed, and Elliot answered it. A moment later he motioned to Jimmy.

"Excuse me," Jimmy said to his dinner companions and walked over to the phone.

"Skipper, maybe you'd better get up here," Burt said. His navigator's voice was quiet and calm, but Jimmy recognized a sense of urgency in the tone.

"I'll be right there," Jimmy replied. He walked back over to the dining tables and held up his hand. "Ladies and gentlemen, thank you for allowing me to share your meal with you."

"Anything wrong, Captain?" one of the women passengers asked anxiously.

Jimmy gave her a reassuring smile. "No, it's just time for me to go back to work, that's all."

He took the stairs up to the flight deck two at a time. It had grown dark while he was below, and he had to stand there for a few seconds to let his eyes adjust from the bright lights of the dining salon to the subdued red lamps of the flight deck. He took his seat, and as his eyes grew accustomed to the darkness outside, he blinked a couple of times to be sure that he wasn't merely seeing a reflection in the windshield.

"What the hell?" he muttered, realizing that he *wasn't* seeing things and leaning forward to try to get a better look.

"There are three of them," Arnold Meeker said. "That one in front of us and two more at eleven o'clock."

Now Jimmy's eyes were fully adjusted, and he could see the dark outline of a single-engine fighter plane, flying about fifty yards in front and slightly to the left. The wink of exhaust fire was very bright, but there were no other lights on the plane. The other two planes could be picked out only by the blue exhaust flames from the stacks that protruded from underneath the engine cowling. They were too far away to be seen in silhouette.

"What the hell are those crazy bastards doing up here without lights?" Jimmy asked. "Burt, can you get through to them?"

"I've been trying, Skipper, but they either don't have radios or I can't find their push."

"Have they made any threatening moves or anything?" Jimmy then asked his copilot.

"No, sir," Arnold replied. "They moved up here just a few minutes ago. Two of them drifted up higher, and this one stayed right where you see him. I went off autopilot and had Burt call you."

"Whatever it is they're doing, they're doing it purposely," Jimmy said. "They can do over three hundred easily, but they're throttled back to match our speed. Who are they? Did you get a good look at them?"

"No, sir," Arnold answered.

Jimmy put his hand on the wheel. "I've got the controls," he said. Arnold dropped his hands. Jimmy pressed the left rudder and turned slightly, toward the shadow.

"Captain, what are you doing?" Arnold asked, a bit alarmed.

"I thought I'd line up with him to see if we can catch him in our landing-light beam. Okay, now! Turn it on!"

Arnold reached down and flipped on the lights that were recessed in the leading edge of the wings. Brilliant beams of brightness stabbed ahead of them, catching the fighter plane in their glare. It was painted yellow-green, with orange-red balls on its fuselage and on the tip of each wing.

"He's Japanese!" Jimmy exclaimed. "But what the hell are they doing out this far?"

As soon as the fighter pilot realized he had been caught in the beam of light, he rolled over onto his back and let his plane drop out of sight.

"Keep an eye on him, Burt," Jimmy ordered.

Burt stood up and looked out his window. "He pulled out of his dive and now he's headed east," he reported.

"East? That's odd."

"The others are going east, too," Arnold said, pointing, and Jimmy could see the fiery flashes of exhaust move across the black sky. "What do you think that was all about, Captain? There can't be too many single-engine airplanes operating this far out over the Pacific."

"They're probably coming from a carrier somewhere around here," Jimmy suggested.

"Well, then, that brings up another question. What's a Japanese carrier doing this far east?"

"I don't know," Jimmy answered. "But when we get to Honolulu, I'm going to tell the authorities about it. I'm sure they'll be very interested."

"You're working the 'howgozit' chart, Burt," Arnold said. "What time will we reach Honolulu?"

"At the present speed and wind conditions, we should arrive at nine forty-five, local."

Jimmy stroked his chin, pondering the incident for a moment. "You know, on second thought, maybe we shouldn't wait until tomorrow. Reel out the long-range antenna, Burt. See if you can raise Honolulu."

"Should be able to raise 'em with no problem," Burt said. "We're getting a real good skip effect tonight." He turned the crank that let a long wire trail out from the tail of the airplane, then started calling Honolulu. A moment later he got through. "I've got 'em, Skipper," he said.

"Thanks." Jimmy took the microphone down and held it to his mouth. "Honolulu, this is Windjammer *Golden Gate.*"

"*Go ahead, Windjammer* Golden Gate."

"Honolulu, I want to report the presence of three Japanese single-engine fighter planes at our location."

"*Understand three Japanese single-engine fighter planes?*"

"Yes."

"*One moment, Windjammer* Golden Gate," the radio voice said. For a moment only the sound of the carrier-wave signal crackled in Jimmy's earphones, but then the voice returned. "*The head office wants to know if the fighter planes acted in a hostile manner?*"

"Negative," Jimmy said. "But don't you think it's a little unusual for single-engine planes to be this far out?"

"*Where are they now?*"

"They withdrew to the east. Do you copy that? To the *east* of our present location."

"*Roger, I understand. They withdrew to the east.*"

"Well, that probably means they have a carrier out here, probably between us and Hawaii," Jimmy said. "I think that should be reported to the proper authorities."

There was another pause; then the voice returned.

"*Thank you, Windjammer* Golden Gate. *Your message has been received, and the Hawaiian Defense Department has been notified.*"

"Thank you," Jimmy said. "Windjammer *Golden Gate* out." He hung his microphone back up on the hook.

"Did they get the message?" Arnold Meeker asked.

"Yeah," Jimmy said, grimacing. "For all the good it did."

ABOARD THE JAPANESE CARRIER *KAGA*

When the three Scout planes returned to the carrier with the news that they had been spotted by an American flying boat, there was a great deal of consternation and worry. Had their planned surprise attack been compromised? Had the flying boat radioed ahead to the American naval base at Pearl Harbor? And if they had, would Pearl Harbor understand the significance of Japanese carrier planes being this far out in the Pacific and this far north of normal trade routes?

Many wanted to call off the attack, but cooler heads prevailed, and when Hiroshi went to bed that night, it was with a sense of almost hyperreality that tomorrow he would be part of the attack force on Pearl Harbor.

Hiroshi lay on his bunk in the corner of the pilots' sleeping compartment. As a full commander he was authorized private quarters, even though he didn't have a command and was flying only as an "observer" for Admiral Yamamoto. But he preferred to sleep with his men. The pilots thought he slept with them to show that he was one of them, and they appreciated that, so Hiroshi said nothing to contradict their belief. The real reason he slept with them, though, was so that he would be more attuned to their mood and in harmony with their ability to perform. In this way his report to Admiral Yamamoto would carry much more weight.

Hiroshi listened to the whisper of the ship's blowers and the conversation of the men. He felt more than heard the throb of the ship's engines as it beat its way through the water at twenty-four knots. He turned on his side and watched some of the pilots play a game of cards under the cat's-eye lamp that lighted the troop hold in an eerie yellow glow.

Nearby, someone lit a cigarette, and the cloying smell of its thick, oppressive smoke joined the other odors: the stench of bodies gone four weeks without a proper bath, the lingering sourness of vomit, and the smell of one of the pilot's private cache of food—which was welcomed enough when they all had shared the snacks but was quite irritating right now.

The message that would launch the attack against Pearl Harbor had finally been received. "Climb Mount Nitaka," the transmission read. When it had been given to Admiral Nagumo, the fleet commander, he had read it aloud, then folded it and put it in his pocket. The others in the ready room gave a *"Banzai!"* cheer for the emperor, and only Hiroshi had noticed that Admiral Nagumo had turned to the windows to look out over the sea without participating in the cheer or saying a word. The entire fleet was then told of their secret mission.

That message had been received on December 2, with the instruction that the attack be launched on the morning of December 8, Tokyo time, or December 7, local time. Because they had crossed the international date line, it was now the evening of December 6. Hiroshi looked at his watch. The official time on board the ship was Tokyo time, but Hiroshi had adjusted his watch as well as his calendar to Honolulu time. It was 11:30, one half hour until the day of the attack. The pilots would be called at 3:30 . . . just four more hours. The men should be sleeping now, Hiroshi thought, not playing cards. Perhaps he should order them into bed. And yet even as he thought about it, he knew that he wouldn't. They weren't actually under his command— and besides, *he* couldn't sleep, so how could he expect the men to do what he couldn't?

Hiroshi sat up and left the troop hold, making his way through the ship to the hangar deck. In contrast to the dim troop compartments, the hangar deck was well lighted, and there was a buzz of activity. The maintenance men were all swarming around the airplanes, checking, double-checking, and triple-checking things they had checked, double-checked, and triple-checked the night before. They weren't going to be a part of the mission personally, but the spirit of each maintenance man would be with his plane, and they stayed with them on this last night to be as close to the attack as they possibly could.

On the floor of the hangar deck was a beautiful plaster-of-Paris relief map of Pearl Harbor, and though Hiroshi had studied it many, many times, he walked over to study it one more time. He walked around so that he would approach the model from the north, the same way the approach would be made for real tomorrow; then he stood there and scrutinized every detail.

"Excuse me, Commander Amano. I have no right to interrupt your contemplation," a soft voice said from behind.

Hiroshi turned and saw Sergeant Ota, the mechanic of his airplane. For a moment Hiroshi felt a sense of alarm. Was something wrong with his plane? Was he to miss the attack? Then he put that fear aside because as Admiral Yamamoto's personal observer, even if something was wrong with his airplane, he would merely preempt one of the other pilots. It would be a hard thing to do, but it would have to be done.

"Yes, Ota, what is it?"

Ota handed Hiroshi a small package wrapped in red-and-white tissue paper. "This is for you, Commander."

It was *noshi*, a small strip of dried abalone. In ancient times samurai ate abalone before going into battle. It was supposed to give them strength and wisdom. Hiroshi was very touched by Ota's gift, and he bowed to his sergeant.

"Ota, please give me a fingernail paring and a lock of your hair tomorrow. I will carry them in the plane with me."

Ota smiled his delight. "I will, Commander! Thank you! Thank you very much!"

Hiroshi turned back toward the relief map and perused it again as Ota returned to his work.

After examining the map for several more minutes, Hiroshi left the hangar deck and climbed the ladder to the flight deck. A guard was standing just outside the hatch, and he came to attention at Hiroshi's approach. The fleet was running without lights because they were close enough to Hawaii now to be seen by long-range patrols, so it was extremely dark. Hiroshi stood there for a moment to allow his eyes to adjust to the darkness; then he walked across the deck, past the hulking shadows of the fighter planes already in position, until he reached the bow.

Hiroshi stood at the bow with his legs spread and his hands on his hips, riding the pitching deck as the ship plowed through the rough seas, savoring the splash of water on his face as some of the waves broke high enough to spray onto the deck. He licked his lips and tasted the salt water, and he squinted into the blackness ahead of him. There was his future and the future of his country. If he could take off now and fly far enough, swiftly enough, perhaps he might glimpse that future; then he could return and govern his life by what he had seen. With a slight shake of his head he turned around and started back across the flight deck to the hatch leading down to the pilots' compartment. He didn't believe that anyone could see into the future, though many went to fortune tellers to try to learn what was yet to be. Even if it were possible to do so, Hiroshi didn't think he'd want to know what was going to happen to him.

"Commander, Commander, it is time to go," an insistent voice said, and Hiroshi became aware of a hand on his shoulder. So, he had been able to sleep a bit after all. That was good. Any sleep, no matter how little, had to be better than no sleep at all.

The compartment was a beehive of activity. The soiled clothes that had been contributing to the foul smell were now all piled in the center of the room, and the pilots pulled on fresh, clean clothes—from their underwear out to their flight suit and from fresh socks up to the *hachimaki* headbands, traditional white bands with the red sun of the Empire. A new smell permeated the compartment as joss sticks and candles were lighted at the several Shinto shrines, where many were drinking small jiggers of sake and praying for their success.

Breakfast consisted of *sekihan*, rice and red beans, supplemented in Hiroshi's case by the abalone he had received from his maintenance sergeant the night before. After breakfast all the pilots went to the briefing room, and there the leader of the attack, Commander Fuchida, held a seat for Hiroshi.

The briefing contained up-to-the-minute data on wind direction and velocity and a detailed analysis of where their ships would be after the attack so that all the airplanes could be successfully recovered. They were cautioned against using their radios lest the attack be discovered by an errant radio transmission.

"Before you go I wish to read you a poem, composed by Admiral Yamamoto," Hiroshi offered. The pilots remained in respectful silence as Hiroshi cleared his throat and began to read the *waka*, a haikulike poem:

> " 'It is my sole wish
> to serve the Emperor as his shield.
> I will not spare
> my honor or my life.' "

"Banzai!" someone shouted at the conclusion of the reading; then the others joined in, and, laughing and shouting, the pilots swarmed to the flight deck, where their planes and the deck crews stood in readiness.

As Hiroshi approached his plane, he found Sergeant Ota standing by the wing. His navigator-bombardier and machine gunner were already aboard, and as Ota held the boarding step for Hiroshi, he handed him a tiny wrapped package. Hiroshi knew it contained the fingernail and hair he had asked for, so he smiled and put it inside his tunic, then climbed into the cockpit of his plane.

The engine was already running, having been started by Ota, so Hiroshi merely watched the flag at the top of the mast. When it dropped, that would be the signal to take off. It dropped.

"Pull chocks!" Hiroshi shouted and opened the plane to full throttle. The plane roared down the deck and dropped off the end; then the wings caught hold, and the craft began to climb. As the others took off behind him, Hiroshi climbed to the specified approach altitude of thirty-five hundred meters and sped toward his destiny.

CHAPTER EIGHT

Petty Officer Second Class Kevin McKay rested his elbows on the railing of the destroyer *Washita* and leaned forward to look out over the ships nestled in the harbor. The fleet was in, and the ships, secure in their moorings in the morning mist, ranged from cruisers and tenders to submarines, minesweepers, and destroyers. Additionally, alongside Ford Island in the middle of the harbor stood two lines of battleships, exercising a haughty dominance over all the other craft present. Only the absence of aircraft carriers prevented a muster roll call of the entire Pacific Fleet.

The water of the bay was as smooth as glass and Sunday-morning quiet. A couple of church party boats were moving across the bay, leaving small V-shaped wakes on the blue-green water as they carried white-clad sailors ashore. The sailors had rejected church call on board their vessels in favor of going into Honolulu and attending civilian church services. Kevin could understand that; he had often joined the church parties to attend mass—not so

117

much for the Christian enrichment of a civilian church as for the frequent invitations the soldiers and sailors received from the parishioners to take Sunday dinner in their homes. Generally those invites were no-lose propositions for the servicemen, for at best there would be single, young daughters in the homes, and at the least there would be a good home-cooked meal.

Today Kevin planned on staying aboard his ship, though daydreaming about young women made him think about Lé. She really did get married to a soldier from Fort De Russey, just as she said she would. Kevin had sneaked down to the courthouse the next day and waited around until she and her soldier showed up. He was a tall, thin, goofy-looking sort with thick glasses and a very prominent Adam's apple. Kevin had told his good friend Bill Wheeler that he couldn't figure out whether the soldier had married Lé because he fell in love with the first piece of ass he ever had, or whether he just figured he was so ugly that he'd never get another chance.

Kevin had yet to come up with another bar he liked as much as the New Plantation, which, since it was now strictly an Army bar, he never went to anymore. But the night before Kevin and Bill had gone to the Bloch Recreation Center to see the Navy-sponsored "Battle of the Bands," being held to determine the best band in the fleet. The three bands who made the finals were from the *Pennsylvania, Tennessee,* and *Detroit.* The band from the *Pennsylvania* had won, but their victory wasn't without some controversy, and after a night of drinking, several sailors had continued to press for their own favorites until, inevitably, a fight had ensued. The shore patrol had been called, and this morning scores of sailors who should've been on board their ships were sleeping off their hangovers in the base brig. Kevin had managed to avoid that unpleasantness by slipping out through the back door of the bar, pulling Bill along with him, the moment he had heard the whistles blowing. A much drunker Bill, who'd been negotiating to go upstairs with a bar girl, hadn't wanted to leave, protesting so vehemently that Kevin had to drag him out by force. Later, as they were riding the barge back to the *Washita,* they heard an accounting of how many sailors were spending the night ashore in brigs, and Bill sheepishly expressed his thanks.

It wasn't that a night in the brig was all that bad, Kevin thought, but such incidents meant there was a possibility of losing a rating. In peacetime, Navy ratings were too hard to come by to squander foolishly. For the time being, thanks to Kevin's quick action, the ratings of both men were safe.

As Kevin was thinking about the events of the night before, he heard the hatch behind him open and shut.

"How's your head this morning?" Bill Wheeler asked.

"Fine," Kevin answered.

Bill stepped out onto the deck to join Kevin at the railing and look out over the harbor. He was carrying two bunches of grapes.

"Where'd you get those?" Kevin asked, nodding at the grapes.

"They put 'em out in the serving line this morning," Bill responded.

"Really? I didn't see them."

"That's because you're such a goddamn early bird. They didn't even put 'em out until half the people had already been through," Bill explained. "That's why I got one for you," he added, offering one of the bunches to Kevin.

"Hey, thanks," Kevin said and popped a grape into his mouth.

"Well, seein' as how you might've saved my rating, I figure I owe it to you." Bill screwed up his face, asking, "So, you really don't have a headache, huh? I mean, after all we drank last night? How come?"

"There's a difference between getting drunk and getting stinko," Kevin said wryly, "and I've learned that difference."

"Yeah? Well, one of these days maybe *I'll* learn that trick, too. So, tell me, are you going into town today?"

"I don't know. They're showing a movie down in the petty officers' mess this afternoon," Kevin said. "I thought I might catch it. It's one with Gary Cooper and Demaris Hunter. Want to see it?"

"Depends. Does Cooper kiss the horse or Demaris Hunter?"

"What do you think?"

"For me, it wouldn't be a contest. But you never know about the guys in the movies. Sometimes they can be incredibly dumb."

Kevin laughed. "Well, I think he kisses the horse. Anyway, what do you care? Demaris Hunter is kinda old for you, isn't she?"

"So what? I bet she'd love to teach a young fella like me the facts of life," Bill countered.

"Yeah, well, now that's an idea," Kevin suggested. "We could write her a letter. 'Dear Miss Hunter,' we would say. 'We're a couple of young sailors who don't yet know the facts of life. If we come to Hollywood, would you teach them to us?' "

Bill laughed. "If we're really going to write it, we ought to get your sister to write it for us. She'd be really good."

"Ha!" Kevin said. "I can see my sister helping me set up a piece of ass with a movie star."

"I read her column in the Honolulu newspaper this mornin'. It's a real good piece."

"Of course it's a good piece," Kevin agreed, his pride showing. "Shaylin's a good writer."

"She's pretty brave, too," Bill added. "I mean, living over there in London with bombs dropping on her head every night. I sure wouldn't want to do that. Don't you worry about her?"

Kevin smiled. "Naw. Shaylin and I have a deal: I don't worry about her, and she doesn't worry about me."

The sound of aircraft engines reached them, and as Bill popped another grape into his mouth, he raised his hand to shield his eyes against the sun.

"Look at all those planes," he said, pointing toward a large flight coming in from the north.

"Damn! That's a lot of them, isn't it?" Kevin said. "Looks something like a flight of geese heading south."

"Man, wouldn't I like to be up in one of them, though?"

"You like airplanes so much, you should have gone into naval aviation," Kevin remarked.

"Why? You can't fly unless you got at least two years of

college, and that, I ain't got." He continued to look at the approaching formation. "What are they, Army planes?"

"Yeah, I guess so," Kevin agreed. "I mean, they'd have to be, wouldn't they? The carriers are all at sea."

"That's funny," Bill mused.

"What?"

"Well, I can't figure out what the hell kind they are. I mean, they aren't P-36's, and they aren't P-40's. Hell, some of them don't even have their gear up."

Kevin chuckled. "They 'don't even have their gear up.' That's something only an airplane nut like you would notice."

"Well, whatever they are, they're making a mock attack on battleship row. Look at them peeling off," Bill said.

Suddenly a column of water shot up; then a big red ball of fire *whooshed* into life, enveloped almost immediately by rolling black smoke. A second later there was a loud boom, followed by an oil-scented pressure wave of hot air hitting them in the face.

"*Holy shit!*" Kevin shouted. "Have those bastards gone crazy? That was a real bomb!"

Three of the fighter planes turned then and started toward the *Washita*. For a moment Kevin stood there, watching them approach, fascinated by the little winking lights on the leading edges of the wings. Then he saw that the lights were detaching themselves from the wings and racing toward the ship. They were live tracer rounds—and they were coming right toward him.

Bill had the same realization. "Kevin, those are Japs!" he shouted. "Those are Jap planes, and they're shooting at us! Why the hell are they—"

"Get down!" Kevin screamed, diving for the deck just as a hail of bullets whizzed and popped over the top of the rail, clanging into the deck and superstructure behind him.

But even as Kevin was shouting for Bill to get down, he was shouting at a dead man, for Bill's sentence had been cut off by a round of slugs slamming into his chest.

The three planes pulled up out of their strafing run just over the top of the destroyer's masthead—so close to it that Kevin thought they might snag the antenna wire in their wheels.

With the planes gone, Kevin got up and hurried to check on Bill. His friend was sprawled on his back with his white blouse red with blood, his eyes open, and his face still set in an expression of surprise. His arms were thrown out to either side of his body, and the bunch of grapes he had been eating were lying alongside his open hand.

Another plane came over, also shooting, though not quite as accurately as the first ones had. Kevin looked up and saw the orange-red ball on the fuselage and the sunburst on the wingtips. He furiously shook his fist at the plane as it roared by.

"Bastards! You yellow bastards!" he shrieked.

There was a mounted twin-fifty pod just above where he was standing. Under normal battle stations each of the fifty-caliber machine guns would be manned, but Kevin knew that both gunners had gone ashore with the church party. The guns were unattended.

Climbing up to the guns, Kevin jerked off the canvas cover, then opened the ammunition chest and threaded the belts. He closed the bolts and cleared the head space; then, with the guns ready to fire, he leaned his shoulders into the crescent-shaped pads and swung them toward battleship row. There, one after another, he saw ships exploding in great, roaring balls of fire.

The OOD on board the *Washita* was only then beginning to sound general quarters, and the bell clanging incessantly over the ship's loudspeaker added to the deafening din. Those sailors who had still been at breakfast and the ones who were sleeping late were now tumbling out onto the deck in various stages of dress and undress, confused by the noise and the bedlam. It took but one look at the burning ships and at the sky full of snarling airplanes and explosive antiaircraft shells for them to realize what was going on. This was no drill! They were actually under attack! Galvanized by fear and excitement, they hurried quickly to their battle stations.

Kevin's usual battle station was at the eight-inch guns on number-one turret. But eight-inch guns were useful only when firing at another ship or at a target ashore. They were useless when it came to engaging aircraft, and aircraft were what was attacking them. Because of that, Kevin didn't bother to report to his battle station, but chose instead to stay right where he was.

"McKay!" Phil Hall, the gunner's mate, shouted. "McKay, get your ass over here!"

"Can't do it! I'm busy!" Kevin shouted back. He saw a plane just coming out of a torpedo release, and he started firing at it, giving it a lead as if he were back in Missouri, shooting at a dove on the wing. The double line of tracer shells spit out from the twin barrels of his guns, and Kevin moved the lines up, hosing them toward the Japanese torpedo plane. The plane flew right through the tracer shells; then a little finger of flame licked up from the wing root. No more than a second later the plane exploded in a ball of fire, then tumbled out of the sky.

Even as those of his shipmates who had been watching gave a frenzied cheer, Kevin was already swinging his guns toward another target.

"McKay! You get over here to your battle station! *Now!*"

"You sure you want me to do that?" Kevin asked as he brought down a second Japanese airplane.

"Leave him alone, goddammit!" somebody yelled. "Can't you see he's shootin' the hell out of 'em!"

The second airplane Kevin shot down crashed into the water about two hundred yards away from the *Washita*, and its death brought on another cheer.

The gunner's mate now realized what Kevin already had—the number-one gun wasn't going to make the slightest contribution to this particular battle—so he stopped yelling at Kevin and ordered instead that more belts of fifty-caliber ammunition be brought up from the powder locker so that Kevin wouldn't run out.

"Thanks, Phil!" Kevin shouted back.

Suddenly, over on the *Arizona*, an enormous ball of fire and smoke *whooshed* more than five hundred feet into the air. There was a low, stomach-shaking boom, followed immediately by a concussion wave so powerful that it knocked Kevin away from his gun. He was hurled halfway across the deck, but he managed to get up onto his hands and knees and crawl back toward the gun.

"Look out!" someone shouted, and Kevin looked up to

see a bomb falling from one of the high-level bombers, heading straight for the *Washita*. It came down in a perfect arc, and Kevin could almost imagine that he was playing outfield in a baseball game and watching a long, lazy fly ball drift toward his position. It was as if he could reach up and catch it as it came in, and he followed the bomb down, almost mesmerized by it. It plunged right through the top of turret one, then exploded in a loud, fiery blast. In that instant Phil Hall and everyone else in gun turret number one, Kevin's gun crew, disappeared. A cold chill swept over Kevin. If he had gone to his assigned battle station, he'd be dead now.

There was another, secondary explosion way down in the bowels of the ship as the bomb struck the powder magazine. The second explosion lifted the front half of the ship out of the water, raising it to about a thirty-degree angle before slamming it back down again.

The ship began an immediate roll to port, and Kevin started climbing up the slanting deck. Below him he could hear the ship breaking up as the furnishings and heavy equipment tumbled to port. As the roll deepened, it became increasingly difficult to stay on the deck so that by the time Kevin reached the starboard railing, he had to throw one leg over to stay up. He looked around and saw the other sailors who were topside. Some of them had also made it to the starboard rail, but most were still trying. A few of the less fortunate were dumped into the sea. The uniforms of two sailors were on fire.

The ship continued to roll, and as it turned over, Kevin and the others who had made it all the way to the starboard railing merely stood up and walked with the roll, finally ending up standing on the bottom of a ship that had turned turtle. Now, completely out of the fight, the men of the late *Washita* could do nothing but sit on the bottom of their capsized ship and watch what was going on around them, having a front-row seat to a drama of immense proportions.

Everywhere Kevin looked he could see ships burning, listing, or sinking. Several oil smears were spreading out across the bay as well as flotsam and jetsam . . . here a hatch cover, there a life preserver, pieces of wood from smashed launches, bits of clothing, some bottles and water-tight canisters, and, incongruously, even a flower lei.

Kevin could also see sailors . . . dozens of them . . . scores of them . . . hundreds of them . . . oil-covered and burned, swimming through the water or being pulled out of the bay by the many lifeboats and gigs braving enemy fire and bombs for just such a purpose. Several sailors floated by, facedown and perfectly still. They were being recovered, too, but with grappling hooks rather than hands.

A second wave of enemy planes came roaring low over the harbor, firing machine guns and dropping more bombs at already-burning ships before pulling up and away through the black puffs of antiaircraft fire that chased them —for the most part unsuccessfully—across the sky. Finally the last of the Japanese planes flew away, and the sounds of explosions and gunfire stopped, replaced by the rush and roar of the many fires, the shouts of fire fighters and rescue workers, and the low, wailing moans of the wounded.

"McKay, are you all right?"

Kevin looked over to see who had asked the question and could barely recognize Tom Kirby, the ensign who had been the officer of the day, because he was so covered with oil.

"I'm okay, sir," Kevin replied. "What about you?"

"I'm all right," Kirby said. He looked at the others sitting on top of the ship. There weren't more than twenty men, their faces reflecting pain, shock, and disbelief. "My God," the OOD said. "Don't tell me we're the only ones who got out."

"I think several made it into the water," Kevin said quietly.

"Jesus, I hope so," the ensign groaned, burying his head in his arms. "I wish I knew just what the hell happened."

Kevin shook his head slowly. "Well, sir, it's only a wild guess, you understand, but I'd say we just got ourselves into a war."

The Japanese attack planes observed strict radio silence as they returned to the carriers, so Hiroshi Amano was unable to share his elation with anyone else. Nevertheless, the attack had been an overwhelming success, and he felt a tremendous sense of pride, not only in having participated in the raid, but for having been one of the architects of the plan. It was a magnificent victory.

It took about an hour to return to the carriers, which meant that it was four hours since Hiroshi had taken off before he saw his ship, the *Kaga*, again. The weather had worsened during those four hours, and the carriers' decks were now pitching very badly. As Hiroshi turned his plane into the landing approach and started down toward the *Kaga*, he caught a flash of light out of the side of his eye. Glancing over, he saw that a returning plane landing on one of the other carriers had just crashed and exploded. Hiroshi felt a sinking sensation in the pit of his stomach. What if that happened to him? What if he had survived everything else, only to waste his life and the lives of his crew by crashing onto the deck of the pitching carrier?

No! He put such thoughts out of his mind. It would *not* happen to him.

Hiroshi jockeyed the throttle and control stick and kicked the rudder bar left and right, watching the landing flag officer until his eyes hurt from the strain; then finally he found himself over the end of the pitching deck. He chopped the throttle and slammed the plane down. His tail hook caught the landing wire, and the roll of the plane was arrested almost immediately. He was safely landed.

Hiroshi sat in the cockpit and laughed.

"Are you all right, sir?" his navigator-bombardier asked.

"Yes, yes, I am fine," Hiroshi replied. "I am fine."

He couldn't explain to the young man exactly why he was laughing. It was a sense of relief over still being alive, yes, but there was something else. Hiroshi had suddenly realized that in all his planning, he hadn't extended his plans beyond this moment. He had thought only of attacking the target and doing the job well, but he had not considered the fact that he might *survive* the attack, and therefore he had no idea of what to do next. He knew only that he was alive and life was sweet. Oh, life was so sweet!

Greeted by the deck crew when he climbed out of the plane, Hiroshi waved and shook hands. A beaming Sergeant Ota was waiting for him, and he returned Ota's fingernail and hair lock so that the maintenance man might keep them as personal relics. It was then that he realized what must be done.

"Get the planes fueled and reloaded," Hiroshi ordered. "We must go back again!"

"Yes, sir!" Ota answered with a broad grin. He in turn began issuing orders to the others, and they rushed to rearm and refuel the aircraft.

When Commander Fuchida, the attack commander, returned a moment later, Hiroshi greeted him, then walked with him toward the bridge where they would report to admirals Nagumo and Kusaka.

"It was a fantastic success," Hiroshi said as they started to the bridge. "But I am worried about one thing."

"The American carriers," Fuchida said. It was a statement, not a question.

"Yes, that is what troubles me."

"We must go back," Fuchida said. "We must go back and finish what we started. Do you agree?"

"Of course I agree," Hiroshi said. "I have already begun the rearming of my airplane. Do you think the carriers will be there when we go back?"

"I don't know," Fuchida admitted. "I don't know why they weren't there or where they were. They were supposed to be there. But it makes no difference whether they are there or not; we must go back. We have the opportunity now to knock America completely out of the Pacific for years to come. If we finish the rest of the ships and the planes at the airfields, America will be fatally crippled, and victory shall be ours."

Hiroshi and Fuchida were welcomed to the bridge by the two admirals, whose smiles were as broad and happy as those of the crewmen on the flight deck below. Both pilots found celebration sake thrust into their hands.

"We have already sent a signal to Tokyo, detailing the magnitude of our victory," Admiral Kusaka said. "What a great day for the emperor this is!"

"Admiral, we are having the planes refueled and rearmed," Fuchida said without preliminaries. "I request your permission to return and strike the Americans' fuel tanks and other targets of opportunity as well as seek out the carriers."

"I think a second attack would not be wise," Admiral Nagumo said.

"But, Admiral, we have them on the run! Now *is* the time!"

"This was a precisely planned operation," Admiral Nagumo said. "Our mission was to deliver one swift thrust and then return like the wind. To do otherwise would be to place the entire fleet in jeopardy."

"But Admiral Nagumo, their planes have all been wiped out," Fuchida protested. "The Americans have nothing left but a few antiaircraft guns. If we go back now, those ships that we only damaged can be destroyed."

"But you didn't destroy the carriers, is that right?"

"The carriers? No, sir, we didn't even see them."

"Do you know where they are?" Kusaka asked.

"No, sir."

"Commander, surely the element of surprise is no longer with us. By now the American carriers know of the attack, and they would be ready for us. In fact, even now they may be looking for our fleet. I have no intention of placing this fleet in jeopardy. Add to that the fact that the weather is getting worse every minute, and you can see why I insist upon retiring. We will not attempt to perfect perfection. There will be no further attacks of any kind. We will withdraw now."

Hiroshi and Fuchida looked at each other for a long moment but said nothing. Hiroshi's mood had changed sharply from elation to despair. It seemed to him that he had just witnessed the loss of the best opportunity Japan would ever have to win the war decisively.

The rising sun slipped in through the slit in the window curtain, filling Eric Twainbough's sleeping berth with light and waking him up. He lay there in his bunk for a moment, listening to the steady, reassuring throb of the Windjammer's engines; then he raised up on one elbow and pulled the curtain aside to look out. The bottom of the wing and the engine nacelles were glowing pink from the sun, which was a bright-red orb just a disk's width above the lip of the pearl-blue sea. He slipped into his robe, picked up his clothes, then parted the curtains and stepped out of his berth onto the slightly vibrating carpeted floor and headed for the lavatory. There he brushed his teeth, washed his face, combed his hair, and dressed, and then he walked up to the front of the airplane to the dining salon. Elliot Smythe was laying a fresh gleaming-white cloth on the table.

"Good morning, Mr. Twainbough," Elliot said. "Would you like breakfast? Or just coffee?"

"What have you got for breakfast?"

"Corned beef hash, eggs, English muffins, and marmalade," Elliot replied.

"Can you poach the eggs?"

"Of course, sir."

"Sounds good. I'll eat."

"Very well, sir," Elliot said and headed forward to the galley, which was located in the nose, just under the flight deck.

Some twenty minutes later Eric was spreading marmalade on the last of his English muffin when Jimmy Blake descended the spiral steps from the flight deck. He signaled for a cup of coffee, then sat down across the table from Eric.

"Anyone else up yet?" Jimmy asked.

"I haven't seen anyone," Eric answered.

Jimmy rubbed his chin. "I guess I'm going to have to get them up."

"Why's that? Is something wrong?"

"Yeah," Jimmy said. "We just got a radio message from Honolulu. They're under air attack."

"*Air attack?* Are you serious? By *whom?*"

"The Japanese," Jimmy replied.

"My God, how did they get there?"

Jimmy sighed. "I have a good idea. Last night we were visited by three Jap fighter planes. They were single-engine planes, and they were so far out to sea that they could have only come from carriers. After they buzzed us, they left, heading east. Actually, sort of northeast."

"Northeast? Well, we're already a bit north of the normal shipping lanes, aren't we?" Eric asked.

"Yes."

"Then that's how they pulled it off. They sneaked in by taking a route that they knew no one would see them in."

"Yeah," Jimmy said glumly. "Only someone *did* see them. *We* saw them." He took a long swallow of coffee. "We saw them, and I reported it. *Dammit!*" he exclaimed, angrily hitting the table with his fist. "I reported it and they didn't do a goddamn thing about it. For all I know, the message is still sitting there on the desk of the radio operator I talked to."

"Maybe you can follow up on it now," Eric suggested.

"Oh, I've already followed up on it. I thought they might at least be able to send some planes out after them. Whether they listened to me any more this time than they did last night, I don't know. Even if they did listen, there's a question as to whether or not they'll be able to get the message through to the Army and Navy. From what they said, Pearl Harbor is pretty much a mess right now. In fact, it's so much a mess, they've advised me to land at Midway."

"Are you going to?"

"No," Jimmy said. "In the first place, I don't have enough fuel to make it to Midway. And in the second place, I don't think the Japs'll come back to Pearl Harbor, whereas they might hit Midway. I'm going to go on in. That's what I wanted to tell the other passengers about. I need to convince them that I think going on to Pearl Harbor is the best bet."

"Were you ordered to Midway or just advised to go there?" Eric asked.

"I was advised," Jimmy replied. "I was told I could use my own judgment."

"Then you do what you think you should without regard to what the passengers think," Eric urged. "Tell them Pearl Harbor was attacked, but don't tell them you were advised to go to Midway."

"Yeah," Jimmy said, finishing his coffee. "Yeah, that's probably the best way to handle it."

*   *   *

An hour or so later, when the Windjammer started its descent into Pearl Harbor, Eric and the other passengers looked out the windows at the remnants of the once-proud Pacific Fleet. The harbor was filled with wrecked ships, some of them upside down so that only the red-brown hull bottoms showed, others so low in the water that their decks were awash, and still others completely sunk so that only their superstructures were sticking up. Many were down by the bow or by the stern, and many others were listing by various degrees, some completely over on their sides. Several were still burning, and the entire end of the island was covered by a billowing cloud of oily black smoke.

It was obvious also that the Navy wasn't the only one hit by the attack. Over on Hickam Field were the remnants of a dozen or more blackened hangars and shop buildings, while out on the flight line wrecked and burned-out airplanes were scattered about.

"Son of a bitch!" one of the passengers said, speaking for all of them. "Those little Jap bastards did one hell of a job of it."

CHAPTER NINE

William Canfield stood at the mirror in the bathroom of his suite of rooms at the National Hotel. Willie, as he was called by everyone close to him, was five-feet-nine, with powerful shoulders and a flat stomach. He didn't have to work to have a muscular conformation, it was just a part of him—like his hazel eyes and auburn hair that were so much like his mother's. He was thirty-three years old, the younger son of Robert and Connie Canfield and the younger brother of John Canfield.

The Canfield family owned Canfield-Puritex Corporation, a multinational food-processing company (cereals, baking products, canned meats, animal feeds) that was headquartered in St. Louis but had additional production facilities in Buffalo, New York, and in Windsor, Ontario. Besides the food-processing company, the Canfields held controlling interest in World Air Transport and owned several thousand acres of farms, ranches, and timberland, making them one of the wealthiest families in the United States.

Bob, Willie's fifty-eight-year-old father, was president and chairman of the board of Canfield-Puritex and Canfield Enterprises, having built up the conglomerate from a small —and failing—animal feed mill.

Connie, Willie's mother, had been at the forefront of human rights issues since college. A zealous suffragette, she had been jailed numerous times for refusing to halt rallies protesting for a woman's right to vote. During the Depression, Connie took up the cause of the hungry and homeless, and now she worked to achieve equality for minorities.

John, Willie's older brother, had started out in the family business, but his driving interest in politics, coupled with a genuine desire to be of service to his country, moved him to leave the business and go to Washington to work for the government. John had begun his government career as an assistant to his father-in-law, Champ Dawson, the senior senator from Missouri. Now he was on President Roosevelt's White House staff, holding the somewhat ambiguous but very important title of National Mobilization Adviser.

Willie, on the other hand, *did* work in the family business, but he had nothing to do with the food-and-grain-processing company. Willie was president and chairman of the board of World Air Transport. He hadn't inherited the job; he had earned it by being the driving force behind the creation of the airline. The entire operation was his idea in the first place, from its struggling beginnings as a small midwestern enterprise to the position it occupied today as one of the world's major airlines, competitive with Pan American and BOAC in the extensiveness of its routes.

The question in Willie's mind now was how long those world routes would continue. With the war in Europe having spread to the Pacific, civilian commerce was sure to be cut back—if not eliminated altogether. Willie was reasonably certain that that was the reason he had been summoned to Washington to meet with the President. He was going to be told personally that his airline could no longer fly overseas. Of course, that was only his surmise, because when John had called on behalf of the President, he had been very guarded over the phone.

After he finished shaving, Willie slapped an astringent on his face, then walked back into the bedroom. Since the suit he was going to wear for the meeting wasn't yet back from being pressed, he slipped on his robe and sat down to the breakfast that had just been brought up by room service: two boiled eggs, two very crisp strips of bacon, whole-wheat toast, orange juice, and coffee. Reaching over to the radio, he turned down the volume. He had turned it up so he could hear the program of Benny Goodman music from the bathroom. Now there was a commercial, leading into a newscast.

"Lucky Strike Greens have gone to war! Lucky Strike Greens have gone to war! Yes, ladies and gentlemen, the familiar green package that has for so long identified Luckies is no more. Why? Because the American Tobacco Company recognizes that Uncle Sam needs green dye in its war effort.

"However, though the package has changed, the cigarette has not. Luckies are still easy on your throat because the toasting process takes out certain harsh throat irritants.

"Remember, L.S.M.F.T. Lucky Strike means fine tobacco."

There was a second's pause after the commercial, and then the high, breathless sales-pitch voice was replaced by the lower, calmer voice of the news broadcaster.

"A special presidential committee, headed by Associate Justice Owen J. Roberts, submitted a report today that was highly critical of the actions of Admiral Husband E. Kimmel and Lieutenant General Walter C. Short. According to the report, these two high-ranking officers were charged with the defense of Pearl Harbor but failed to take adequate steps to defend their commands against the sneak attack of the Japanese on December seventh.

"According to the findings of the special committee, Admiral Kimmel and General Short had been warned repeatedly by their superiors in Washington that an attack was imminent. In addition, hours before the attack, a World Air Transport Windjammer had reported seeing Japanese fighter planes well within the American defensive zone. And finally, Army radar operators had picked up the incoming attack fleet on their radar screens. Despite all this, Admiral Kimmel and General Short failed to maintain the degree of

readiness that would have prevented the Japanese from carrying out a successful attack.

"What disposition is to be made of this report and what action, if any, will be taken against the officers charged is not known at this time."

There was a knock on the door, and Willie put down his coffee cup and went to answer it. The hotel valet stood there with Willie's pressed suit. Willie quickly dressed, and by nine o'clock he was down in the lobby, where he was met by a White House driver. A few minutes later the car came to a stop under the East Wing portico, where his brother, John, was waiting for him.

"Hi, Willie," John greeted. "Come along. The President is already in his office, waiting for us. I'm glad you could come, by the way."

Willie grinned crookedly. "You're glad I could come?" He snorted. "Are you kidding? When big brother calls, I jump."

"Sure you do," John quipped as they walked toward the Oval Office.

"How're Faith and the kids?" Willie asked.

"Faith's fine, and so is Morgan, but I'm afraid Alicia has the sniffles."

"Alicia just needs a little huggin' from her uncle, that's all," Willie said.

John smiled. "She was very excited this morning when she heard you were coming to Washington. She's convinced that you're coming just to visit her. And, of course, Faith is looking forward to you having dinner with us this evening."

"Will anyone else be there?" Willie asked suspiciously.

"Anyone else? What do you mean?" John replied innocently.

"You know damn well what I mean. Will somebody who just happens to be an available female be there? Faith missed her calling, you know. She would have been a perfect matchmaker."

John laughed. "The truth is, I don't think she had time to set anything like that up. I didn't even tell her you were coming until this morning. Anyway, she's just trying to be helpful."

"What is there about women that they can't stand to see a bachelor?" Willie asked.

"Well, to a woman, an unmarried man is just like a vacuum," John explained, laughing. "And you know how nature abhors a vacuum."

They left the hallway and stepped into a reception area. The appointments secretary looked up from her desk.

"Good morning, Mr. Canfield," she said. "Go right in. The President is expecting you."

"Thanks," John responded. He pointed toward the door on the other side of the room. "Well, here it is, little brother. Behind this door lies the seat of all power."

"Covetous, big brother?" Willie teased.

"Not really," John replied, opening the door for them. "I'm more like a moth, hovering around a flame. I like the light, but I have enough sense to stay out of the fire."

They stepped into the Oval Office, and President Franklin Delano Roosevelt's big-jowled face split with a wide grin. The cigarette in the holder that had become his trademark protruded from one side of his mouth, thrust up at a jaunty angle. He greeted the two brothers jovially as they walked across the deep, wine-colored carpet to his desk. It was cluttered with ship models, and Willie noticed that one of the models was of a World Air Transport Windjammer. He wondered if the President had put the model plane there just for his benefit, then decided that he probably hadn't; Franklin D. Roosevelt had no need to impress Willie Canfield.

The President gestured at two chairs in front of his desk, indicating that the brothers should sit.

"Well, Willie, old sport, it's nice to see you again," Roosevelt said. "Tell me, how is your father and that beautiful mother of yours?"

"They're doing very well, Mr. President," Willie replied as he sank onto the leather-covered chair. "And they both send their regards."

"Salt of the earth, your parents," Roosevelt said. "Absolute salt of the earth." He took the cigarette out of its holder and ground it out, then lay the holder down before he looked up again. It had been a while since Willie had seen FDR in person, and he was struck by how old and tired he looked. The bags under his eyes were heavy and dark, and he wondered if the photographs he saw in the newspapers and magazines might not be touched up a little, for he had never noticed the bags before. On the other hand, he was looking at the President of a country that was at war, and that would have to have some telling effect.

"Willie, how much do you know about the amount of damage the Japs did to us at Pearl?" the President asked.

"I have a pretty good idea, Mr. President. As you may know, one of our planes arrived in Honolulu shortly after the attack. My pilot got a very good perspective of the damage as he was coming in. He told me it was"—Willie paused to select the right word—"I think it would be described as extensive."

"Extensive, yes," Roosevelt agreed. "You might say that. In fact, we have purposely been vague about just how extensive the damage really was. If the Japanese knew how badly they actually hurt us, the panic going on out in California right now might really be justified." The President paused for a moment; then suddenly he smiled broadly. "But that was then, my boy, and this is now. We are ready to hit back!"

"Very good, sir!" Willie enthused. Though he didn't say it aloud, he wondered just how the President planned to make a strike against the Japanese with the Pacific Fleet so badly decimated.

Roosevelt held his smile for a moment longer, and the smile made him look exactly like his pictures. "We are going to bomb Tokyo," Roosevelt said, answering Willie's unasked question.

"Bomb Tokyo?"

"Absolutely," Roosevelt said. "That will make those— to borrow a colorful phrase from Secretary Hull—'pissants' over there have second thoughts about whom they're dealing with. I mean, there they are, ensconced on their little island, content in their smug belief that they are safely shielded by the Pacific Ocean. It would have to be most disconcerting to look up and suddenly see bombs falling from American airplanes on their capital city, don't you agree?"

"Oh, yes, sir, I quite agree," Willie said.

"Good, good, I thought you would," Roosevelt said. "Now, how can we do it?"

Willie blinked in surprise. "I beg your pardon, Mr. President?"

Roosevelt laughed loudly and slapped his hand down on the desk. "I guess I threw you a curve ball there, didn't I, old sport?"

"Yes, sir," Willie admitted. "High and inside."

"High and inside," Roosevelt said, laughing again, until the laughter was interrupted by a coughing fit. When it subsided, he picked up his cigarette holder and began to fit another cigarette into it. "Of course," he went on, "I understand that's just the kind of pitch Joe DiMaggio likes . . . high and inside."

"I guess it is," Willie agreed, not yet sure where the conversation was going.

"I have to be honest with you, Willie. I came up with the idea of bombing Tokyo," the President continued, "knowing full well that it is impossible. But when I mentioned it to your brother, he informed me that it is my job as President to come up with the ideas. Other people will figure out how to make the impossible possible." Roosevelt put the holder in his mouth, and John leaned down to snap a cigarette lighter under the cigarette. Roosevelt puffed until the cigarette caught, then gazed up at Willie. "And he tells me you are a master of such things. That's why I asked you here, Willie. I want to bomb Tokyo, and I believe you can make that happen. Now, tell me, can your long-range Windjammers do the job for us?"

"No, sir, I'm afraid they can't," Willie replied.

It was obvious that this wasn't the answer Roosevelt wanted, and he leaned back in his chair and looked at Willie through the cloud of cigarette smoke. His eyes narrowed, but he said nothing, and Willie felt compelled to explain his position.

"There are a dozen reasons why we couldn't use the Windjammers, Mr. President, or Pan Am's Clippers, for that matter. Number one, with the Pacific bases in Japanese hands, Tokyo is out of range, even for those aircraft."

"But those planes will land on the sea, won't they?" John put in. "What if we had a fueling ship waiting at a forward location for you? Your planes could land, take on fuel, then attack."

Willie shook his head. "People have the wrong idea about flying boats," he said. "They're designed to land and take off in sheltered bay areas only. They can't do it in the open sea because the waves are too high. Oh, they could probably set one down, all right, in an emergency. But they'd never get back up again—especially not with a full load of fuel and bombs. And even if they could make it all the way to Tokyo, how would the bombs be delivered? You couldn't just roll them out the door. In fact, the doors of both Windjammers and Clippers open over the step-plane wing, which is where we carry our fuel. If the step-plane were damaged, we'd at best lose fuel and at worst risk an explosion. Also, there's no way to mount guns for protection, and the airplane only cruises at about one-seventy-five or so. It would be a one-way mission for the pilots and crews. Surely you wouldn't want to send men out on a mission that you *knew* was suicide."

Roosevelt drummed his fingers on the desk for a moment or two; then he sighed. "No, of course not." He sighed again. "I guess bombing Tokyo isn't such a good idea at that."

"The idea of using *seaplanes* isn't very good," Willie said. He smiled. "But the idea of bombing Tokyo is great. It's a very good idea."

"Yes, but how are we going to do it? My generals tell me the Flying Fortress simply doesn't have the range."

"I could give you a suggestion," Willie said. "But it might sound so crazy that no one would take it seriously."

"Would it work?" Roosevelt asked.

"Yes, sir, I think it would."

"Then let me hear it. The crazier it is, the better. That just means that the Japanese would be less likely to consider it."

"I think we should use B-25's."

"B-25's?" John said skeptically. "Come on, Willie, that doesn't make any sense. Those are twin-engine planes with much less range than the B-17's."

Willie smiled. "I agree they don't have as long a range or as heavy a bomb-load capacity as the B-17. But they will carry a good-sized bomb load, and they do have good range. And they can do something the B-17 definitely cannot do."

"What's that?" Roosevelt asked.

"They can take off from an aircraft carrier."

"An aircraft carrier!" John said. "Willie, B-25's are *Army* planes."

"So what?" Willie replied. "The war belongs to the Army and the Navy equally, doesn't it? All you have to do is get them to work together. I know the capabilities of the B-25. It isn't designed for it, but I know it can be coaxed off the deck of a carrier by a good pilot. All you have to do is have the Navy cruise close enough to Tokyo to be within the range of the B-25, but out of range of the Japanese land-based fighter aircraft."

"You say you can take them off—but can you *land* them on a carrier?" John asked.

"I very much doubt it," Willie said, shaking his head.

"Why not?"

"Well, in the first place, landing on an aircraft carrier requires a great deal of skill . . . a skill that Navy pilots practice for months to learn and maintain. In addition, a carrier plane has to be specially designed with arresting hooks and so forth. No, I'm afraid that when the airplanes return, they'll have to either ditch in the water alongside the carriers and the crews be picked up by the Navy, or circle overhead while the crews bail out."

"That would be very dangerous for the crews, wouldn't it?" Roosevelt asked.

"Yes, sir, it would," Willie admitted. "And to keep the aircraft carrier on station would also be dangerous. The entire operation would be risky, but it would be an acceptable risk."

"I understand," Roosevelt said. He drummed his hands on the desktop. "Army bombers flying off Navy carriers." He looked at Willie and smiled broadly. "You know, crazy as it sounds, I *like* that idea," he said. "It would show that our fighting forces are a team. Okay, Willie, thanks for the suggestion. Now I'm going to turn this over to the Army and Navy geniuses to see what they can come up with. I'm sure that their first thought will be that I'm crazy.

Then they'll probably decide I'm a genius. I'm afraid, for security reasons, you'll never get credit for the idea, my boy."

"That's quite all right, Mr. President. I'm only sorry I can't be of more help to the war effort than to make a mere suggestion," Willie replied.

Roosevelt laughed and winked at John. "That's just what we were hoping you would say, eh, John?"

"Yes, sir," John agreed, his eyes twinkling with good humor.

"There *is* more you can do, Willie," the President explained. "If you're willing to accept the job—and the rank that goes with it."

"Job? Rank?" Willie asked, confused by the President's words.

Roosevelt looked over at John and grinned. "Have you really told him nothing, John? Or is he just that good at hiding the truth?"

"I haven't told him a thing, Mr. President," John replied. "Go ahead and make the offer."

Roosevelt leaned forward on his elbows and eyed Willie. "We have been talking about the Japanese, but the truth of the matter is, our *real* enemy is Germany," he said. "Our grand strategy is going to be to keep Japan at bay, so to speak—hold them off with our left hand while with our right we concentrate all our efforts on defeating Hitler. We intend to fight Mr. Hitler in Africa first, because that is where the war happens to be right now. But we won't win a real victory until we can get back onto the European continent and kick that house painter out of France. And to do that, we intend to convert England into the world's largest military armory, storing there guns and tanks and ammunition and everything it will require until we are ready to invade Europe. Are you following me so far?"

"Yes, sir, I think so," Willie said.

"Good, good. Now, in the meantime, the British and the Germans have been carrying on a long-distance war by bombing each other's cities and towns. So far it has been pretty much of a stalemate between the two of them—but if we add our air power to that of the British, we might hasten the day of the invasion. Now, the British have agreed to give us airfields; all we have to do is fill those airfields with our planes and our boys. That's where you come in."

"I'll do anything I can, Mr. President," Willie said, still not knowing what Roosevelt wanted of him.

"I thought you might. Willie, it seems to me that your experience not only in running an airline but in building one would serve us in great stead. With your permission, I would like to submit your name before Congress with the recommendation that you be appointed to the rank of brigadier general and in that capacity assume the task of commanding one of our bomber wings."

"Won't I be stepping on the Air Corps' toes? Surely you have high-ranking men in the Army who deserve the promotion," Willie said.

"None who have had your experience of managing large fleets of big aircraft," Roosevelt replied. "Willie, I didn't come up with this idea; the top brass in the Army Air Corps did. You wouldn't be stepping on anyone's toes. You would be doing us a great and needed service."

"In that case, Mr. President, I would be deeply honored to accept the commission and the assignment."

"Then I suggest you go back to St. Louis and begin putting your affairs in order. And while you're there, visit your nearest tailor and order a set of brigadier general's uniforms, because, my boy, you are going to war."

"How soon will you be leaving?" Faith Canfield asked her brother-in-law that evening.

"I don't have an exact date," Willie replied, "but I imagine it'll be very soon."

"Uncle Willie, what do you think about this airplane?" six-year-old Morgan Canfield asked, holding up a model of the twin-boomed P-38. "Isn't it a beauty?"

"Oh, it's a beauty all right. That's a fine airplane."

"I'll just bet it can shoot down every German and every Jap airplane in the sky," Morgan said, and he went running across the room, holding the airplane up over his head and making appropriate engine sounds.

"Morgan, don't be quite so rambunctious," Faith ordered. "You'll wake your little sister."

"But Mama, airplanes are *loud*," Morgan insisted.

"Airplanes might be loud, but little boys who have little sisters who are trying to sleep off a cold had better not be. Now, you can either fly your plane quietly, or you can go to bed. Which will it be?"

Morgan gave an exaggerated sigh. "I'll be quiet. I've never heard of a quiet airplane," he complained, "but I'll be quiet." He retired to a corner of the room, where he continued to fly his plane quietly.

Willie took an appreciative sniff of the air. "I don't know what's cooking in there," he said, gesturing toward the kitchen, "but it sure smells good."

"Rack of lamb," Faith replied.

Willie grinned. "It's no coincidence, is it, that that's my favorite?"

"Well, you are a soldier, after all, and we must all do our part to keep up the morale of our brave boys."

Willie laughed. "I'm not a soldier yet, and when I do become one, I'm going to be a brigadier general involved with the transfer of aircraft. I hardly think I'd qualify as one of our brave boys. Nevertheless, I really am looking forward to the meal—and I must add, it's refreshing to just spend the evening with the two of you, without being put on the auction block for the latest available female."

"Uh-oh," Faith mumbled.

"Faith, you didn't!" John scolded.

She smiled crookedly. "Well, it just seemed awkward to have only the three of us. And the rack of lamb was certainly large enough for another guest."

"Who did you ask?"

"Candy Keefer. You know her, John."

"I've never heard of her."

"Of course you have. We met her at the Christmas party for the White House staff, don't you remember? She's the sister of one of the secretaries. Very pretty girl—tall, nice shape, blond hair, green eyes." Faith looked at her brother-in-law. "She'll be perfect for you, Willie. She's a knockout."

Willie sighed, then smiled in resignation. "Okay, Faith.

I don't suppose I'd be much of a 'soldier boy' if I didn't appreciate the company of a pretty girl. I'll be on my best behavior for her."

Willie had kept his promise all through dinner.

The meal finished, Candy Keefer accepted a cup of coffee from Faith with a smile of thanks, unconsciously brushing back a fall of tawny hair with one hand. As Faith had said, Candy was an exceptionally beautiful woman, with wide green eyes set above high cheekbones and a mouth that was perhaps just a bit too full to be perfect—as if that was a flaw, Willie thought to himself. She was quite possibly the most beautiful woman he had ever met. Yet despite that, or maybe even because of it, he withdrew more and more into himself, answering questions only when he was directly asked and then responding in as few words as he could.

"I've been wanting to meet you for a long time," Candy said to him.

"Oh?" Willie looked at Faith. "Just how long has my sister-in-law been trying to get us together?"

"I beg your pardon?" Candy asked without guile.

"I'm sure you know what I mean, Miss Keefer," Willie countered. "It seems that every time I come to Washington, Faith brings out someone else for me to meet. You will understand, I'm sure, that when I decide to marry someone, I'll make the choice myself."

"Willie!" Faith chided.

Candy took a sip of her coffee, studying Willie for a long moment over the rim of her cup. Finally she lowered it, her green eyes sparkling with great humor.

"And when you do make this big decision to marry me, Mr. Canfield, will you also be making the decision as to how many children we're to have? And what kind?"

For a moment there was shocked silence; then Willie burst out laughing, and the others, relieved that the tension was eased, laughed with him.

"I'm sorry," Willie said. "I guess I did sound a little like a self-centered boor, didn't I?"

"Why, not at all," Candy said, smiling sweetly. "I would say you sounded more like a conceited ass."

"Touché," Willie said, laughing again. "I guess I really had that coming."

"To clarify why I've long wanted to meet you, it's because I regard you as one of America's true aviation pioneers. I mean, you flew the Atlantic within weeks of Lindbergh's flight, and you did it with an airliner that carried passengers. I feel you did far more to open up commercial aviation than Lindbergh ever did."

"Well, thank you," Willie said. "But I have to confess that the flight wasn't my idea. And I was only the copilot."

"While still in your teens," Candy said. "Perhaps that's why I found the whole thing so appealing."

"Are you an aviation enthusiast, Miss Keefer?"

"Yes."

"Perhaps if the opportunity presents itself the next time we meet, I could take you for a flight," Willie suggested.

"That would be nice," Candy said, taking another sip of coffee and studying him through those cool green eyes of hers.

Willie loosened his tie. He wished Faith hadn't brought this woman around. There was something very disconcerting about her . . . and being disconcerted wasn't what he needed when he was about to embark on a mission that, from the sound of it, would be affecting history.

CHAPTER TEN

MARCH 27, 1942, HOLLYWOOD

Del Murtaugh was on his hands and knees, pruning the rosebushes in Demaris Hunter's backyard. Several yards away, alongside the glistening blue swimming pool, Demaris was sitting in a lawn chair, reading the newspaper. It was a balmy, clear day, not quite warm enough to swim, but warm enough for Demaris to be wearing a "sun suit," as the shorts and halter set was called.

Demaris Hunter was one of the most beautiful and respected stars in Hollywood, and when people discovered that she was one of the clients for the Saito-Murtaugh Gardening Company, they would invariably ask Del, "What's she really like?"

"She's nice," Del would answer.

It was all he would ever say about her. She *had* been nice to him, often having one of her servants bring him coffee or lemonade or sandwiches. But at times she did things that made him feel very uncomfortable. For example, he had often seen her naked—not because she was flirting with him, but because when she wanted to take off her bathing suit and she happened to be outside, she never gave him a second thought and would undress in front of him as if he weren't even there.

It was almost a year before Del could tell his wife about that peculiar habit of Demaris's. He had been nervous and tongue-tied when he told Rubye, worried about how she would take it, frightened that she'd demand that he not work there anymore. And he didn't want that to happen because Demaris Hunter was his and Yutake's single biggest account.

"When she takes off her clothes like that, does it make you get hard?" Rubye had asked.

Del had cleared his throat before mumbling, "Sometimes."

"Well, I don't reckon you can help that," she had said. Then she had laughed. "But whenever it does happen, you just be sure you bring that hard thing home to *me.*"

Rubye's reaction had surprised Del—but then, though they'd been married for six years now, Rubye still had a few surprises left. For example, two years earlier, when Del's then-boss, Yutake Saito, had decided to put off buying a new truck and several new pieces of equipment because he didn't have enough cash on hand and didn't want to take out a loan, Rubye had suggested that Del make an offer to buy in as a partner. Del had laughed off the suggestion, saying that they didn't have enough money. That was when she had presented him with fifteen hundred dollars, money that had been left to her by her parents. She had not only kept it carefully hoarded in a bank back in Missouri, she had kept its very existence secret throughout the long, lean, hard years of the Depression. Now, as a result of that money, Del was a full partner in a business that was doing quite well.

"You have the garden looking lovely, Mr. Murtaugh," Demaris called, breaking into his thoughts.

Del looked up from his work and over at her. "Thank you, ma'am." He started to go to her.

"No, no, you don't have to get up," Demaris said, and she walked over beside him, removing her sunglasses and sticking the earpiece in her mouth.

She *was* a very pretty woman, Del thought, though somehow in person she seemed to bear little resemblance to the larger-than-life figure he saw on the screen.

"What are you doing now?" she asked.

"I was just working on the rosebushes here."

"Oh, they look gorgeous," Demaris said. "You and Mr. Saito are doing a marvelous job."

"Thanks again. And if you don't mind, I'll just pass that along to Yutake. He could prob'ly use a bit of cheerin' up."

"Oh? Why? What's wrong?"

Del rubbed the back of his hand across his cheek, leaving a smear of dirt. "Folks are givin' him a pretty hard time of it," he said. "You know, him bein' Japanese an' all."

Demaris licked her fingers, then reached up to rub the dirt off Del's face. It was a terribly erotic sensation, and he felt himself beginning to stir.

"Well, heavens, *he* didn't have anything to do with starting the war," Demaris said as she rubbed her fingers across his cheek.

"Yes, ma'am, Miss Hunter, you know that, and I know it. Problem is, there's lots of folks who *don't* know it. And they're the ones that's causin' all the trouble."

"Well, I'm sure they'll get over it," Demaris said, drawing her hand back.

"Yes, ma'am," Del replied, putting his hand to his cheek where her fingers had been. "I reckon so."

At that moment the back door opened, and Demaris's maid stepped outside. "Miss Hunter, you wanted me to remind you about that meeting you have down at the studio at four o'clock," she called. "I've got your clothes all laid out for you."

"Oh, thank you, Lois, you're a dear," Demaris replied. Smiling, she turned back to Del. "You will tell Mr. Saito how pleased I am with the work you and he have done in my garden?" she asked. As she spoke, she began to remove her halter.

"Uh, yes, ma'am," Del replied, clearing his throat. He looked down at his feet in embarrassment, but he peeked up, allowing himself a quick glance at the pink nipples of her perfectly formed breasts. The arousal he had felt earlier was now a raging erection, and he hoped Demaris wouldn't notice it.

"Good," she said, giving no clue that she was thinking about anything other than Yutake Saito. "I always like to give praise when praise is due." She started toward her house, carrying the halter in her hand.

Demaris walked hurriedly through the cool interior of the two-story, Spanish-style stucco house to her bedroom. She kicked off her sandals as she entered the room, enjoying the feel of the deep carpeting on her bare feet as she crossed the room to her bathroom. The maid had already drawn the bath so that when Demaris stepped into the bathroom, it was filled with the scent of bath oils and expensive perfume. Standing beside the tub, she pushed the shorts down over her long, shapely legs, then stepped in and slid down into the fragrant water.

She grinned. When she was wiping the dirt off Del's face, she had noticed the front of his pants. He had grown a hard-on. She hadn't expected that, and his reaction to a simple, friendly gesture had surprised her. After that she couldn't help herself and took off her halter in front of him just to add fuel to the fire.

Whatever innocent fun she had hoped to get from the incident had backfired on her. As she bathed in the oil-scented water, tiny flames of sexual arousal licked at her body. It had been several weeks now since she'd had sex, and the prolonged abstinence was beginning to gnaw at her. After the meeting at the studio she'd have to go down to the set and see who was there.

Demaris was still young enough, firm enough, and beautiful enough to be able to select a sexual partner at will from the army of young, virile extras who abounded at the studio lot. But she had to be careful. She had heard shocking stories of established female stars who'd been sexually experimentative only to find themselves being blackmailed by ambitious young men who wanted to parlay an afternoon in the sack into a big break in their careers. So far Demaris had been lucky. Every man she'd had sex with had accepted the act as its own reward and had considered himself fortunate to be granted sexual favors by one of

America's most desired women. She prayed her luck would last.

Finished with his work, Del loaded the tools onto the truck, then drove back to the office to check the schedule for what jobs he had the next day. When he arrived, he found an official-looking notice nailed to the front door. Puzzled, he walked over to read it.

INSTRUCTIONS TO ALL PERSONS OF JAPANESE ANCESTRY:

In accordance with an executive order signed by the President of the United States, you are hereby ordered to report immediately to a designated evacuation point, there to be relocated to an area that represents safety for you and security for the United States.

You are authorized to take only such personal belongings as you can easily carry. There will be no cars, trucks, motorcycles, horses, bicycles, or other private conveyances authorized. All assets not carried with you must be disposed of through immediate sale. No houses, commercial establishments, farmland, or fishing boats may be retained in trust or escrow. No third-party sales are authorized. All sales must be immediate and final, or said property will be confiscated by the United States Government in accordance with the provisions of this act.

You have forty-eight hours to dispose of all assets and holdings and report to Baker Street Station, where you will board the train for relocation. Failure to follow the instructions promptly will result in your removal by force. The military is empowered by the Act to use as much force as is deemed necessary in carrying out the directives, up to and including the right to shoot to kill.

NOTICE

HEADQUARTERS
WESTERN DEFENSE COMMAND
AND FOURTH ARMY
CIVILIAN EXCLUSION ORDER NO. 20

Del raced back to his truck and over to Yutake's house, where he found his business partner standing on the front porch, talking to an Army sergeant. Two other soldiers were there as well, armed and looking grim.

"What's going on here?" Del demanded, hurrying from the truck to stand beside Yutake.

"This ain't none of your business, mac," the sergeant said. "This is between the United States Government and this here Jap."

"Mr. Saito is my business partner," Del said.

The sergeant chuckled. "Not for long he ain't. Accordin' to the law, all Japs got to sell everythin' they own, and that includes businesses."

"The business is yours, Del," Yutake said softly, "if you want it."

"I'll take out a loan, Mr. Saito," Del said. "I'll pay a fair price."

"Long as you do it in forty-eight hours," the sergeant said.

"That's impossible," Del replied angrily. "The loan won't come through that quickly."

"Pay me nothing for it," Yutake said. "It is a gift."

"No!" Del said. "I'll raise the money some way."

"It ain't just the business," the sergeant said. "It's *everythin'.*" He looked around at Yutake's house and let out a low whistle. "Sure wish I had the money to buy this place. Wouldn't the old lady like it, though."

"Never mind," Del said. "We'll find a buyer for his house."

"What do you mean *'we'*?" the sergeant asked. "No third-party sales are authorized. The Jap here has to handle it his own self."

"I'll help him find a buyer," Del said firmly. "He'll do the selling."

The sergeant looked at Yutake's yellow Oldsmobile sitting in the driveway. "Tell you what, you don't have to look no further to sell that car. I'll give you a hundred bucks for it. And I'll let you keep it till it's time for you to leave."

"One hundred? It's worth seven or eight times that!" Del protested.

"Yeah, ain't that the truth?" the sergeant said, grinning slyly. "But try to get it now, when everyone knows it has to be sold by ten A.M., day after tomorrow."

"I'll buy the car," Del said. "Eight hundred and fifty dollars."

"Are you crazy?" the sergeant sputtered. "You can get a *new* one for that."

"I want this one," Del said resolutely.

"It's your money," the sergeant fumed. "But do-gooders like you are goin' to make it hard on the rest of us." He turned to his soldier colleagues. "Let's go. We got some more Japs to run out," he said. "But mind you," he told Yutake, facing him again, "don't try to run out. Remember, the U.S. Army has the right to shoot to kill to bring you into compliance."

When the soldiers had left, Del followed Yutake back into the house where Yutake's wife, Fumiko, and his daughter, Miko, were huddled in fear. On the table in the dining room behind them was the uneaten meal that had been interrupted by the soldiers' appearance.

"Why are they doing this?" Miko asked, tears running down her cheeks. "We are good Americans." Miko, an exceptionally pretty girl of nineteen, was wearing a typical teenage outfit of a light-blue blouse, a blue-and-white plaid skirt, bobby socks, and saddle shoes. "Why does the government question our loyalty?"

"It would seem that our loyalty is directly proportional to the color of our skin," Yutake said.

"Our food is getting cold," Fumiko said. "I will reheat it."

"Don't bother for me," Yutake said quietly. "I have no appetite now."

Demaris Hunter was warm and damp, her breathing was ragged and gasping, and the nerve endings in her thighs twitched and jumped as she opened herself to receive her lover. She felt him slide through the wetness, then heard him groan in satisfaction as he buried himself deep inside her.

She thrashed on the bed beneath him and raked her fingernails across his shoulders and down his back. She raised her hips to him, giving and taking in a way that maximized her pleasure. Then the pressure that had been building inside spilled over in a sudden, torrential spasm of sensation, matching his as he spent himself inside her. As the passion slowly drained away, she shuddered from head to toe.

They lay together for a few moments longer, his hot, sweaty body pressing against her. Their breathing grew more regulated, and the throbbing flesh inside her gradually stilled. Finally she pushed against his shoulder.

"For God's sake, Roger, you're squashing the shit out of me," she grumbled.

He pulled out of her and rolled off, and they lay side by side, looking up at the shadowy patterns cast on the ceiling by the orange trees just outside the small house. The house and the orange grove it sat in had originally been an investment in tranquillity—"*A place where you can come to be alone, relax, and study your lines,*" her agent had told her. "*We'll keep the ownership under a corporate name so no one can trace it to you. Trust me; there'll come a time when you thank me for this.*"

The agent was right; she was thankful for the hideaway. It provided tranquillity and relaxation, true enough, but it also gave her a place to conduct her assignations without fear of being interrupted by unwanted company. Or of being seen.

"I have a big favor to ask," Demaris's latest lover said after several seconds of silence. "I almost hate to ask it."

"Then don't," Demaris countered coldly. She reached over and fished a cigarette from a pack by the bed, flicked open the lighter and lit it, then snapped the lighter shut with a loud click.

"But I don't know where else to turn," Roger said. "Demaris, I am in terrible trouble. I owe some money—a great deal of money—to a very unpleasant person." He paused, adding, "Like, break-my-legs unpleasant. Or acid-in-the face unpleasant."

"Damn, Roger, you don't mean to tell me you've borrowed money from a loan shark!"

"Yes."

"I know you're very young, but you can't be that young, can you? Surely you had better sense than to do something like that!"

"It . . . it was a matter of image," Roger replied. "I needed clothes, a car, a nice place to live if I was going to project success. You have to have that if you're going to make it in this business."

"Is that a fact?"

"Yes. Well, you know, Demaris. I mean, look how successful you are. Beautiful clothes, beautiful car, your house in Beverly Hills, and this place."

"In my case success came first. The other things came afterward."

"It's different now from the way it was in the old days," Roger protested.

"The *old* days?" Demaris asked, raising up on her elbows and glaring at him. As she moved, bars of shadow and light from the half-closed blinds rippled across her naked body, looking like the stripes on a tiger.

"Well, that is, I don't mean the *old* days," Roger stammered. "I mean, not *real* old or anything like that. I just meant . . ." He let the sentence die in a frustrated sigh.

"How much money, Roger?"

"Seven thousand five hundred."

"That's a lot of . . . success," Demaris said.

"Yes, but not to someone like you," Roger insisted. "I mean, I know that you have so much money that seven thousand five hundred dollars doesn't mean anything to you."

"Is that a fact?" she repeated.

"Yes. And I thought that you—I mean, well, seeing as how we have become, uh, *friends*, you might say, I thought you wouldn't mind letting me have it."

Demaris got out of bed and walked naked over to the dresser. She fished the checkbook and a pen out of her purse, then began writing.

"You have very poor timing, Roger," she said. She finished making out the check, then tore it from the book, blew on it to dry the ink, and brought it back to bed.

"Poor timing? I don't understand," Roger said.

"Asking me for money this way makes it seem like I'm having to pay for cock," she said coldly. She laid the check on his spent penis. "It's a nice cock," she said, patting it, "but it isn't worth a thousand dollars an inch."

"Thank you, Demaris," Roger said, reaching for the check. "I'll never do anything like this again, I promise. From now on it'll be just loving and—"

"No," Demaris interrupted him. "There will be no 'from now on.'"

"What . . . what do you mean?"

"We'll never see each other again."

"But why? I thought you liked sex. I don't understand."

"I'm sure you don't," Demaris said with a sigh. "Now, take your check, get dressed, and get out of here."

"Demaris, I—" Roger started, reaching for her.

"*Go!*" Demaris snapped, slapping his hand away.

Quietly, sullenly, he climbed out of bed and got dressed. He left the check lying on the bed until he was fully clothed; then he reached for it. He looked at her one last time.

"Thanks," he mumbled.

Without replying, Demaris waved him away. She remained sitting on the bed unmoving until she heard his car drive away; only then did she get up and go into the bathroom. She felt the need for a bath . . . a very hot bath.

When Yutake Saito and his family reported to the railroad depot on the morning they were to depart, dozens of armed soldiers were standing on the street in front of the station. There were more soldiers inside the depot itself and out on the platform, alongside the train that was waiting for the internees. Signs were posted all over the place, some detailing Exclusion Order Number 20, by which all Japanese-Americans were being relocated, and others that merely gave instructions:

UPON ARRIVAL,
ALL JAPS MUST REPORT IMMEDIATELY TO THE
DESIGNATED ASSEMBLY CENTER ON TRACK 9.

There were over five hundred Japanese-Americans present, all of whom, like Yutake, had been forced to liquidate their life's savings during the previous forty-eight hours. They were carrying an assortment of bundles, bags, boxes, and baggage, and as they stood there with their few remaining belongings, it made a poignant, pitiful scene.

Yutake looked up and down the line to see what each family considered important enough to take. One woman was carrying a sewing machine, another an iron. One man clutched a can of paint and a paintbrush, and Yutake would have laughed had it not been so sad.

A little boy, carrying a light-blue-and-yellow pennant with the letters *UCLA* printed on it, ran by. His mother shouted sharply to him, and he returned to sit on a suitcase beside his older sister, whose expression was a numb bewilderment as she sat silently eating an apple and staring off into space.

An Army captain came over to the group and cleared his throat.

"All right, you Jap people," the officer shouted, "I want you to count off into groups of seventy-five. There will be seventy-five people in each car."

"Seventy-five? Captain, these cars are designed for no more than forty people," one of the men complained.

"Forty *Americans*," the captain said. "You people are smaller. We can easily get seventy-five of you in each car."

"But we have our baggage," the man protested.

"If you brought too much, you'll have to get rid of some of it," the officer stated, shrugging.

"You've left us nothing as it is," one of the other men shouted. "We will not get rid of another thing."

"Then work it out somehow," the captain said. "You are going to get seventy-five to a car. Now, count off and get aboard." He started to walk away, then stopped and looked back. "Oh, I almost forgot. That's seventy-five adults. If you have children, they'll have to double up."

"No, that's impossible!" someone shouted, but the

captain was already walking away with a deaf ear, and they knew they'd have to do just as he said.

By packing and repacking, squeezing, turning, contorting, and bending, seventy-five adults and fifteen children got into car number 1317. It wasn't for nearly another hour that the train—with jerks, squeals, and groans—got under way. The destination was the Heart Mountain Relocation Center in Wyoming.

Two days later, in the predawn darkness, the train reached Heart Mountain, drawing to a stop at a siding in the middle of the Wyoming desert. Despite the crowded conditions of the cars, most of the occupants had finally managed to sleep, though it was more from sheer exhaustion than any ability to find a position of rest.

The door at the front of the car was unlocked, and an Army sergeant stuck his head in the open doorway and yelled, "All right, slants, we're here." He was a large man with a fat neck and a double chin. His hair was cut very short, and what there was of it was very blond. "This is your home away from home—only since you got no other home now, that makes this your *only* home. Everybody out! Everybody out! We have a nice apartment waiting for each and every one of you. Let's go! Everybody out, chop chop!"

"What does 'chop chop' mean?" Fumiko Saito asked her husband.

"Americans think it is a universal Oriental word," Yutake answered. "I think they believe it means 'hurry,' though they use it for just about everything, and the more ignorant Americans use it more often than most."

"Cut the chatter," the sergeant yelled at Yutake. "We don't have time for that. You got to get out here and find your apartment, and then we have to free this train up for another load." He laughed. "Heart Mountain's going to wind up as big as Tokyo. Hell, we could even use it for bomber practice."

"Mama!" one little girl gasped and started to cry. "They're going to drop bombs on us!"

"Pay no attention to him, dear; that is not a man, but a pig," the child's mother answered, speaking in Japanese, and with that statement she gave the sergeant the name that all the inmates would come to know him by: the Pig.

A few minutes later everyone was standing outside, blinking from the harsh spotlights mounted on poles that shone brightly down on the pathetic group. It was very cold, and many who had dressed for their accustomed Los Angeles weather weren't prepared for the brutal temperature of the Wyoming desert. They shivered and clamped their arms together and shuffled around, trying keep warm.

The Pig marched back and forth in front of them, giving them their camp "orientation," as he called it. He was wearing a warm coat and mittens, and as he spoke his breath puffed out in vapor clouds. He had to be aware that some of the less-warmly dressed people were suffering greatly from the cold, but he gave no indication of it.

"It is our aim," the Pig was saying, "that you people turn Heart Mountain into your own community . . . your own city, if you will. Here you will all be given comfortable barracks, cooking facilities, and safety. You will have the right to elect your own council, appoint your own police force and fire department, and live your own lives. But there are rules you must follow. No weapons of any sort will be allowed . . . all letters coming in or going out of camp will be subject to censorship . . . families may stay together, but anyone over the age of seventeen will be placed in a special dormitory whether their parents are here or not. Also, you will notice that the camp is surrounded by barbed wire. Under no circumstances is anyone allowed to approach the fence, and to do so will bring immediate action. There are machine guns in all the guard towers, and our guards have orders to shoot to kill." The Pig smiled brightly. "You would do well to avoid such unpleasantness and to allow us to be the gracious hosts we really wish to be. My name is Sergeant Caviness, and I am the noncommissioned officer in charge of this camp. Colonel Bailey is the officer in charge, but he is a very busy man, so you won't see much of him. If you have any complaints, you must take them up with me. Do *not*, I repeat, do *not* bother the colonel. If you bother the colonel, he will be most displeased with me, and if the colonel is displeased with me, I will be most displeased with you. That's the way it works, you see. Now, are there any questions?"

"Sergeant Caviness," a young man called, "could we go into the barracks now? Some of us aren't dressed for this cold. We had no idea the temperature would be so severe."

"And who are you?" the Pig asked.

"My name is Eddie Yamaguchi." The man was about twenty or twenty-one, and he was wearing a letter jacket from the University of Southern California.

"Well, Eddie Yamaguchi, you seem warm enough. Where'd you get that jacket?"

"I earned it," Eddie replied. "I'm a pitcher for the USC Trojans baseball team."

"Wrong," the Pig answered snidely. "You *were* a pitcher for the USC Trojans baseball team. Now you're a Jap in charge of heating." The Pig looked at the others. "If any of you have any difficulty getting coal or getting your furnace going, see Eddie Yamaguchi, the former baseball pitcher for USC. He'll take care of it for you."

"Excuse me, please," Eddie interrupted. "How can I carry out this task? I know nothing about such things."

"Then learn," the Pig said dryly. "And learn, also, to keep your mouth shut when I'm talking. Now, as I was saying, you people can elect a slant mayor, a slant police chief, and a slant fire chief, but always remember: *I* am the boss. You would do well not to forget that. Now, all unmarried men report to barracks number four-eleven. All unmarried women to barracks four-twelve. Married personnel to barracks four-thirteen through four-sixteen. You'll find that the barracks have been fixed into nice apartments, compliments of Uncle Sam. Yamaguchi, you'll see to it that all coal bins are full and all stoves are working before you report to your barracks. Understand?"

"Yes," Eddie replied. "I understand."

The Pig smiled. "Ah, good, Yamaguchi. Understanding is the basis of all harmony, don't you agree? But of course you do. Slants are big on things like harmony, ain't they?"

Having finished with his announcements, the Pig

turned and walked away, leaving all the Japanese still standing in a group. They looked around at each other in confusion. The sergeant hadn't formally dismissed them, though he had assigned them to their barracks. Did that mean they could go? Someone voiced the question.

"*I'm* going," another said. "I've been told what to do for four days now, and no one is going to have to tell me to get in out of the cold."

"What is a slant?" another asked.

"What?"

"A slant. The Pig used the term 'slant.' I don't know what that means."

"It's a derisive word for Japanese."

"Not just Japanese," another put in. "For any Oriental. It is in reference to our eyes."

"Ah, so the round-eyes are jealous of our eyes, are they?"

Laughter greeted the comment, though it was nervous laughter. Still, it seemed to galvanize everyone into action. Children were gathered, bags collected, and the group trudged off through the cold, early-morning air to find their barracks and apartments.

Though Miko Saito would be billeted in the unmarried women's barracks, she went with her parents first to see where they'd be living.

"Oh, Yutake," her mother said in a wailing tone as they reached their new home. "Surely they don't mean we are to live here?"

Yutake looked around and sighed. "I'm afraid they do, Fumiko. I'm afraid they do."

The "apartment" was a twenty-by-twenty-five-foot single room in an uninsulated, tarpaper-covered wooden barracks. The floor was of rough-hewn wood, the walls were unpainted and unpapered, and the entire room was lighted by one bare bulb hanging from a cord. In one corner were two army bunk beds covered with olive drab blankets, and a wooden vegetable crate standing on end and fitted with crossboards for shelves was the only visible storage.

Fumiko began to cry. "We had to give up our lovely home for this? For this? Oh, Yutake, what is to become of us?"

Yutake put his arm around his wife's shoulders and patted her reassuringly. His eyes were moist, but he didn't allow a tear to form. "We will survive, Fumiko. We will survive," he promised her.

"Excuse me. Do you need help with your fire?" a voice asked from the doorway.

Yutake turned. It was Eddie Yamaguchi, the baseball player. "No, thank you," he replied. "I can build the fire myself. I'm sure there are others who need your help."

"If you need anything, call on me," Eddie said. "My name is . . ."

"Eddie Yamaguchi," Miko Saito spoke up. She smiled. "We saw you pitch against Stanford in the championship game last fall."

"Did you?" Eddie asked, grinning. "Then you also saw that I was knocked out in the fifth inning."

"My friend Del Murtaugh says you pitched brilliantly until then," Yutake said. "He is my business partner—that is, he *was* my business partner—and I respect his opinion because he knows baseball very well. He used to be a catcher for the pitcher Swampwater Puckett."

"Swampwater Puckett? Boy, it was a sad day when he retired. He was the best there ever was," Eddie said. "And your friend was his catcher?"

"Yes. But before Puckett went into the major leagues. They played on a local team in some small town in Missouri."

"I'm very impressed," Eddie said. He grinned again. "If you'll excuse me now, I'll see to the others. Perhaps we can visit and talk about baseball sometime."

He had addressed his suggestion to Yutake—but he was looking at Miko, and she replied quickly, "Yes, that would be a good idea. I . . . that is, my father loves baseball. I'm sure he'd enjoy it very much."

"Until then," Eddie said, touching the bill of his baseball cap and bowing slightly.

"He seems like a nice young man," Yutake said when Eddie was gone.

"And very handsome," Miko added.

"Miko, such boldness is most unbecoming," Yutake scolded.

"Perhaps such things were unbecoming before, Father. But not any longer. Times have changed," Miko said.

"Times may change, but good behavior never will."

CHAPTER ELEVEN

APRIL 1942, BERCHTESGADEN, GERMANY

When Karl and Uta Tannenhower stepped off the train, a middle-aged, rather stiff-looking SS officer approached them from across the station platform. He was bearing a bouquet of long-stemmed yellow roses, and with a click of his heels and a stiff bow he presented them to Uta.

"Frau Tannenhower, allow me, please, to give you these flowers on behalf of the Führer. Herr Oberreichsleiter, welcome to Berchtesgaden. I am Oberführer Max Brandt of the Berghof guards. The Führer has detailed me to attend to your every wish."

"Your name is Max?" Uta asked plaintively. "We named our son Max."

"Oh? And where is your son now, Frau Tannenhower?" the officer asked politely.

"He is . . . he is dead."

"He was killed in the first days of the war, when we invaded Poland," Karl explained.

"You have my sympathies," Brandt replied, bowing his

head slightly. "And my admiration for being the parents of a true hero of the Fatherland."

"Thank you," Karl said.

"Oh, Karl, aren't the roses lovely?" Uta asked in a too sprightly voice, looking at the bouquet Brandt had given her.

"Yes, they are quite nice," Karl agreed.

"I'm very excited to be here," Uta said. "You, of course, have been to the Führer's summer residence before. Where exactly is the Berghof?"

Karl pointed to the mountain that rose just behind the railroad station. Perched near the top, overlooking the valley, was an imposing-looking home. "Up there."

"But it appears so formidable!"

"Well, it is, rather. Now. When the Führer first purchased it back in 1928, it was called Haus Wachenfeld and was a simple country house that needed heavy rocks to hold down the shingles to keep them from being ripped off in a storm. He had it completely reconstructed into a showplace—Bormann oversaw the construction—and renamed it the Berghof. Aside from the main house, the expansive complex takes up a goodly section of the mountainside. And as you can imagine, it is all exceedingly well guarded."

"Herr Oberreichsleiter, there is someone waiting in the coffeehouse who wishes to meet Frau Tannenhower before we go," Brandt said.

"Meet me?" Uta asked.

"Yes. Would you follow me, please?"

"Oh, our luggage," Uta said, handing the claim ticket to Brandt.

"I'll have it taken care of," Brandt said, and when he snapped his fingers, a soldier seemed to appear from nowhere, clicking his heels together sharply. Brandt handed the soldier the claim ticket, and the soldier started off on his errand.

Karl and Uta followed Brandt to the coffeehouse to learn the mystery of who was waiting to meet Uta. A group of tables was on the sidewalk in front of the coffeehouse, each one occupied. At one of the tables sat a very handsome young man in the uniform of a Luftwaffe major general. He was drinking beer and reading a newspaper. AMERICA BOMBS TOKYO, the headline read.

The Luftwaffe officer looked up and, recognizing Karl, jumped up and clicked his heels together sharply.

"Good morning, Herr Oberreichsleiter," he said.

"Good morning, General," Karl replied. He pointed at the paper. "Does that say America bombed Tokyo?"

"*Jawohl*, Herr Oberreichsleiter."

Karl frowned. "How the hell did they do that?"

"That is not known, Herr Oberreichsleiter," the officer answered. "But I am certain the Americans would never be able to bomb us with such impunity."

"Why not? The British have," Karl replied.

"But at a heavy cost to themselves," the young general argued.

"Yes," Karl agreed. "Well, let us hope we can keep them away." He smiled, putting the officer at ease. "And so far the Luftwaffe has done a very good job of defending our cities."

"*Danke*, Herr Oberreichsleiter," the officer said, clicking his heels and bowing again.

"Carry on, General," Karl said, and the officer sat down again and resumed reading.

Brandt led Karl and Uta inside the coffeehouse, where a pretty blond woman was sitting at the corner table normally reserved only for the most important of guests.

"Karl, is that . . . ?" Uta's whispered question trailed off.

"Eva Braun, yes," Karl replied softly. Hitler's girlfriend was one of the best-kept secrets of the Reich; few knew of her, fewer still had ever met her. Karl had met her several times and had told Uta about her, but this would be Uta's first encounter. That she was here to meet them personally was an indication not only of Hitler's confidence in Karl, but of how close he had let Karl come.

"Hello, Oberreichsleiter Tannenhower. And, may I call you Uta?" the young woman asked.

"Yes, yes, of course," Uta said, flustered at being so close to the woman who was so close to Hitler.

"And you must call me Eva," she said. "Do be a good

fellow, Max, and fetch the car for us, will you?" Eva asked the SS guard with a peremptory wave of her hand.

"Yes, of course, at once," Brandt replied, and he clicked his heels—as obedient to the young woman as his aide had been obedient to him a few moments earlier.

Eva laughed a rich, throaty laugh. "Being the Führer's mistress does have its advantages," she said.

Uta gasped slightly at hearing Eva describe herself in such a way.

Again laughter bubbled forth from Eva's throat. "Are you surprised to hear me say openly what others say behind my back?" she asked.

"Well, no, uh, I mean, uh . . . " Uta stammered.

"I am not ashamed to speak the truth," Eva said. "The Führer and I are not married because he feels it would be wrong to marry before the end of the war. But our commitment is as strong as if we were married."

"I'm sure it is," Uta said—because she could think of nothing else to say.

"So tell me, how is your daughter? Liesl, isn't it?"

"Yes, Liesl. She is at home with our maid. She wanted to come, of course, but she is only sixteen—an awkward age, of course, so I feared she would be a bit underfoot."

"That is true, I suppose. Still, the Führer loves children so," Eva said. Then, seeing the car arrive, she smiled broadly. "I see that the good major has brought the car around. Shall we go up to the Berghof, then?"

"Oh, yes," Uta said. "I'm very much looking forward to seeing it."

"I think you'll like it," Eva said. "It's a little like a museum sometimes, filled with paintings and armor and the like, but we do have a marvelous time during our weekend get-togethers."

Brandt held the door open for the two women, and they got into the back seat of the large, open Mercedes. Karl rode in the front with the driver, while Brandt hurried back to ride in a second car.

The road kept curving back on itself as they climbed up the mountain, and when they looked over the side, they were often unable to see the roadbed because it was so narrow that the car actually hung over the shoulder. They could, however, see all the way down to the bottom, where the road began as a narrow ribbon winding up out of the small village that was now no more than a cluster of toy houses far below.

All the way up the side of the mountain Eva kept Uta laughing, regaling her with funny stories and describing in unflattering terms all the men whose names were synonymous with power: Göring, Himmler, Goebbels, von Ribbentrop, and many others. Uta couldn't help but wonder how Eva described *Karl* to people when he wasn't around.

The car finally reached the top of the road, where they were stopped by a closed gate. The driver honked the horn, but no one was there to open the gate for them.

"I wonder where the guard is?" the driver asked.

"Guard, yoo-hoo! Come and open the gate quickly, or you will be sent to Russia to fight in the real war!" Eva shouted, standing in the back and cupping her hands around her mouth as she called.

About twenty meters off the side of the road was a small outhouse, and the door of the outhouse suddenly banged open as a man, still adjusting his pants, hurried to the gate. Eva laughed gleefully, and the others in the car, including Karl, joined in. The guard stood at attention as the car passed through the gate and drove the rest of the way up to the house.

Uta was overwhelmed by Hitler's beautiful chalet. The large and luxurious villa made the most of the ground it stood on to provide the occupants with a spectacular view.

"Do you know the rules of the stay here?" Eva asked.

"Karl explained them to me," Uta said. "But why don't you go over them one more time, just to make certain he didn't leave anything out."

"All right," Eva agreed. She smiled. "Understand, now, that these aren't *my* rules, they are the Führer's rules, and even I have to abide by them. Which reminds me . . . I could have smoked two more cigarettes while I was down there. Now it's too late. Do you smoke?"

"No," Uta replied. "But Karl does."

"Not up here, he doesn't. That is the first rule. The Führer doesn't smoke and does not wish to be around anyone who does."

"That must be awfully hard on a lot of people," Uta observed.

"Yes, it is. By the way, the Führer doesn't know that I smoke, and if you tell him I do, I will deny it. Do you know what he wants to do? He wants to force the cigarette companies to put a slogan on all their packages of cigarettes, warning that smoking causes cancer and can kill!" Eva laughed. "Can you imagine the cigarette companies actually going along with something like that?"

"Hardly," Uta agreed.

"Oh, and whistling," Eva continued. "He hates whistling. He says it hurts his ears. I think he's still shell-shocked from the last war."

"And Karl says no dancing," Uta noted.

"That's right. The Führer says dancing is a waste of time. I love dancing." Eva laughed. "Come to think of it, I'm not sure what I see in him."

She then continued, "No heavy makeup or nail polish."

Uta touched her cheeks. She had applied rouge and eye makeup before leaving the train.

"Don't worry," Eva said, noticing Uta's reaction. She chuckled. "Really, I think the only one who wears more makeup than he can stand is Göring, and somehow the Führer finds the strength to accept even that."

Uta laughed loudly. She had often joked with Karl about the makeup Göring wore.

"No letter writing or diary keeping," Eva went on. "I'm sure that when this is all over the Führer plans to write another book, and he doesn't want anyone else's book to be in competition with his."

"I promise you," Uta said, "he has nothing to worry about from me on that score. I seldom even read a book, let alone plan the writing of one."

"Finally," Eva said, smiling, "and this is most important—this is the one that *I* asked him to put in—no political discussions. I hate politics. To tell the truth, I don't even understand what National Socialism is supposed to be about. So we talk only about fun things while we are here."

"That, too, will not be a problem for me," Uta said. "I have no love for politics, either."

When they reached the chalet a few moments later, SS officers, dressed in white jackets and black trousers, opened the doors for them.

"Where are the others?" Karl asked one of the SS men.

The officer clicked his heels and snapped to attention. "The Reichsmarschall, the Reichsführer, and the others are in the parlor, Herr Oberreichsleiter," he replied.

"Dear, I have a few things to discuss with them," Karl said, excusing himself. "Fräulein Braun?" He bowed toward Eva.

"Go," Eva said lightly with a wave of her hand. "You enjoy yourselves with whatever it is you and the others find to talk about. Uta and I will entertain ourselves."

"Thank you, Fräulein." He turned and left, his footfalls echoing down the long hallway.

"How soon before we see the Führer?" Uta asked, turning her attention back to Eva. "Shouldn't we go pay our respects?"

Eva laughed. "Oh, my, didn't your husband tell you? Nobody but nobody sees the Führer before noon. He'll rise at about twelve, and we'll take our lunch at one. That is when you can pay your respects."

"I'm sorry, I didn't mean to be presumptuous," Uta apologized.

"Nonsense, you weren't at all presumptuous. Now, while the Oberreichsleiter is in there talking to Göring and Himmler and Goebbels and the others, let me show you around the place."

"I would love that," Uta said. Some distance away she saw a woman surrounded by children. "Oh, isn't that Magda? I mean Frau Goebbels?"

"Yes," Eva said. "Poor woman. She devotes herself to her children because Goebbels is such a *schurke* with other women. He pretends that he's faithful only to her, and she pretends that she doesn't know, but everyone talks about it. Even the Führer has spoken to Goebbels and told him to quit his womanizing."

Uta nodded thoughtfully. "I must remember to say something nice to her."

Eva merely smiled knowingly.

Like a hausfrau proudly showing off her home, she escorted Uta through the spacious rooms of the luxurious villa. It was constructed of beautiful woods and liberally embellished with Carrara marble. Expensive Oriental rugs were on the floor of every room, and heavy, richly upholstered furniture displayed both elegance and comfort.

"Here is the terrace," Eva said, opening the French doors and sweeping out onto the stone and cement veranda.

"Oh, Eva, how beautiful!" Uta said, walking over to the low wall that surrounded the terrace and looking out over the magnificent vista displayed before her. Far below she could see Königssee Lake sparkling in the sunshine, and in the distance the Alps in all their grandeur.

"Do you like it here?" Eva asked. She stepped up onto the wall, then struck a ballet pose. "I could do *Swan Lake* here—only Wagner didn't write it, so the Führer probably wouldn't like it."

Uta laughed at the younger woman's antics. Then Eva jumped back down to continue the tour, leading Uta across the large flagstones and into a well-tended garden.

"Often we have tea here, just the Führer and I," Eva explained. "Also, I like to read here. I like romantic novels very much. The Führer sometimes scolds me for reading such books. He says they do little to enrich my mind. But I tell him that I like them, and he hasn't ordered me to stop reading them."

Two Scotties bounded across the garden to greet Eva, and she stooped down to pet them. "Ah, here you are, my lovelies," she cooed as the small black dogs happily jumped and rolled under her stroking.

"These are my babies," Eva explained. "The Führer has a big German shepherd named Blondi, and he thinks Blondi is the only dog that ever lived." She let the dogs lick her face. "Yes," she said, speaking in a mincing voice to the dogs, "you missed me, didn't you?" She resumed her normal tone for Uta. "But for my money, you can't beat Scotties for companionship."

"Fräulein Braun, the Führer is coming," one of the white-uniformed servants said, appearing from inside the house.

"Ah, His Royal Highness has awakened," Eva quipped, standing up again. "Come. As mere peasants we must take our place in line to receive our morning greetings." She looked at her watch. "Well, surprise of surprises, it actually *is* a morning greeting. He has five minutes until noon." Eva cupped her hands to her mouth and blew into them, smelling her breath. "Oh, dear, I hope I don't stink from cigarettes," she muttered.

Adolf Hitler stepped through the French doors onto the patio and looked around. He was uniformed in dark brown trousers and a double-breasted jacket of a lighter shade of brown. A red-banded, visored military hat was perched on his head so that the famous forelock of hair wasn't immediately discernible. Over his breast pocket he wore the Iron Cross First Class. He looked at Eva and Uta, then smiled and walked toward them.

"Ah, Frau Tannenhower, I am so delighted you could come with your husband. These weekends are much gayer when there are beautiful women about."

"You are too kind, my Führer," Uta murmured shyly.

"Well, then," Hitler said, his greeting completed. "I believe the men have all gone to the dining room. Shall we join them for lunch?"

"Lunch so early?" Eva joked. "Whatever makes you think someone might be hungry? Is it just because we've been up for several hours with nothing to eat?"

"We could wait until later, if you prefer," Hitler retorted.

"No, no, now will be fine," Eva said quickly, and Hitler laughed at Eva's easy surrender.

Uta followed the couple back into the house, down the hall, and into the dining room. As Hitler had said, the others were already there, and the dining room was full. Karl was sitting next to Göring, and he had kept a chair empty for Uta. She knew that for some reason Göring was Karl's favorite among Hitler's inner circle, though she didn't know why. Perhaps it was because Göring was the only other member of the group to have been awarded Germany's highest military decoration—the Blue Max—during the First World War. Whatever the reason, it still seemed strange to her, because she regarded Göring as little more than a clown in heavy makeup and fancy uniforms. Even now he was wearing a light-blue uniform with a broad gold stripe down each pant leg, an array of medals was spread across his broad chest, and diamond rings glistened and sparkled from his fat fingers.

Hitler spoke to the others, and they returned his greeting, then waited patiently as Hitler helped Eva into her chair. After that the other ladies present, including Uta, were seated; then, with a scrape of chairs, the men sat down.

The meal, for the guests, was typical Bavarian fare of bratwurst and kraut. Göring filled his plate with a particularly generous serving of the sausages. Hitler, being a vegetarian, had potato soup.

Though this was the first time Uta had ever been to the Berghof, she had taken meals with Hitler before, so when he started the monologue that passed for conversation, she wasn't surprised. Hitler's conversations weren't really conversations—at least, not in the normal sense. There was no exchange of ideas from the others, no input or differing points of view. Hitler postulated a thesis, and then he expounded upon it. His audience was merely a sounding board.

After lunch Hitler invited everyone to stroll through the grounds to a place he called the teahouse. Here they were served apple-peel tea and cake. Hitler had as large an appetite for cake as Göring had for sausages, and here, too, the monologue continued. He spoke about such things as art, travel, astrology, and the importance and sanctity of motherhood, mentioning not only the Goebbels children, but Liesl as well.

Everyone returned to the main house shortly after six, where they watched a movie. It was an American film, starring James Stewart and Carole Lombard. Though the movie had German subtitles, Uta, and of course Karl, could follow the English dialogue. At the end of the movie a brave pilot had to fly through a blizzard and over mountains to deliver a special kind of medicine to save the couple's baby. Though the pilot arrived in the nick of time, it was a heartrending ending. When Uta looked over at Hitler and Eva, Eva was unashamedly wiping the tears away, and, incredibly, even Hitler's eyes were red rimmed.

One of the rules was that no one could go to bed before Hitler, so later that night Uta had to stifle her yawns as Hitler continued his monologue, often repeating the same things he had said earlier in the day. Finally, at two in the morning, Hitler stood abruptly, bowed stiffly, then wished everyone a good night. It was obvious to Uta that the other guests were as tired as she was and as eager to go to bed, for there was absolutely no lingering after Hitler's departure. Everyone left immediately.

"Well," Karl asked as he and Uta prepared for bed in the room they had been given, "what did you think?"

"I thought it was"—Uta wanted to say boring, but she was afraid to—"fascinating."

Karl chuckled, then reached over to kiss her on the cheek. "Spoken like a true diplomat's wife," he said.

"Bring hot tea, *Brötchen*, and marmalade to the terrace," Eva was saying right ouside the door to Uta's room early the next morning.

"At once, *Gnädige Fräulein*," a man's servile voice answered.

There was a light knock on Uta's door, and when Uta turned over, she saw that Karl was already up and gone.

"Uta, Uta, are you awake?" Eva called, her voice muffled by the closed door.

"Yes, just a minute," Uta answered. She sat up, put on her dressing gown, then hurried over to open the door.

Eva came into the room, smiling as brightly as the morning sun streaming in. She was dressed as a Bavarian peasant in a dark print skirt, a puff-sleeved blouse, and a white apron.

"As you may have gathered, the Führer doesn't like anyone to eat until he rises. Then we must all take lunch together as we did yesterday," Eva said. "But sometimes I do manage to sneak in a small snack. Otherwise, I couldn't make it. Would you join me?"

"Of course," Uta said. She started toward the closet to

select her dress. "Tell me, Eva, why do you call him Führer and not Adolf?"

"Because he is my leader, just as he is the leader of everyone else in Germany," Eva replied easily.

"Yes, but you are also his . . . good friend. Surely you call him by a more personal name?"

"He wishes me to call him that," Eva said. "That way there is never any problem of my slipping and saying something I shouldn't before someone who shouldn't hear."

Uta took down a red dress.

"Oh, yes, that will be lovely," Eva said. "The Führer likes red."

Uta quickly dressed and joined Eva out on the terrace for their light breakfast, and as she drank her tea, she also drank in the magnificent scenery of the mountains and lake. Eva asked Uta if she would like to complete the tour of the chalet that had been interrupted by Hitler's appearance the day before.

"Yes, I would like that very much," Uta said. She looked around. "Though I haven't even seen Karl to tell him good morning. I probably should try to find him."

"Oh, you don't want to interrupt their meeting," Eva warned. "The Oberreichsleiter and the Reichsführer are having a heated discussion right now."

"Oh? What about?" Uta asked.

"Jews. What does Himmler ever want to talk about except the Jews? At least the Führer has other interests besides the Jews."

"Are they having an argument?" Uta asked, concerned.

Eva laughed. "Don't worry about it," she said reassuringly. "Your husband has Göring on his side, and Göring makes a formidable ally."

"Yes, I suppose so," Uta said, realizing then why Karl tended to link himself with Göring over all the others.

"Let's start downstairs, shall we?" Eva suggested. "Then we'll come back up here and I'll show you everything except the Führer's room. I can describe that room to you if you wish," she added, with a possessive smile.

Eva led Uta inside and down a spiral staircase to the antechamber, one wall of which was glass opening onto a courtyard. The other side of the antechamber led into a very large drawing room that featured an enormous fireplace of green faience and a tremendously large picture window looking out toward Untersberg Peak.

"Why, I've seen photos of this!" Uta said.

"You should have," Eva said matter-of-factly. "It's on about twenty million postcards. Come, here is the dining room. I know you ate two meals here yesterday, but did you get a chance to really look it over?"

"No," Uta admitted. "I did notice that everyone sat in armchairs rather than straight-backed chairs, though."

"That's the Führer's idea. He likes to make his meals last two hours or more, and he feels that armchairs are better suited for that pace."

Silently, Uta agreed. She remembered the long, drawn-out meals and Hitler's rambling monologues and realized how much more uncomfortable she would have been had she been subjected to all that while seated in a straight-backed chair.

The dining room was paneled with pine, and the furniture was of matching wood. There were several medieval-type lamps of heavy wrought iron, and along one wall was a cupboard filled with exceptionally beautiful china and vases.

Beyond the dining room was the main hall, where the movie had been shown the night before. Uta hadn't noticed then, because they had been pulled up to expose the screen, but one wall was covered with exquisite tapestries.

"Oh, how beautiful!" Uta said, walking over to the tapestries and runing her hand over one of them.

"They are authentic Aubussons and Gobelins," Eva said as proudly as if they were her own. "Oh, and these mosaic tables and the fireplace are a gift from Mussolini." She chuckled. "Mussolini is a comical character. He follows the Führer around like an obedient puppy. But his son-in-law, Count Ciano . . . ahh . . ." Eva folded her arms across her chest and made a move as if she were dancing. "How handsome he is, and how beautifully he dresses! I have some photographs of him that I sometimes look at and dream about. I do believe it makes Woulfe jealous."

"Woulfe?"

"The Führer," Eva explained. "You wanted to know my pet name earlier? When I first met him, he was introduced to me as Herr Woulfe. It is the name he used when he wished to be incognito. But I never really use it anymore, for he doesn't like me to. Now, come upstairs."

Uta started toward the spiral staircase, but Eva called out to her. "No, come this way."

There was another staircase, one Uta had not seen. It was covered with red velvet carpet, and Eva explained that it went up to the main apartment. "My rooms are up there. And so are the Führer's," she added.

Uta hadn't seen this part of the house, and she was struck by the size of the upstairs corridor, which was every bit as imposing as the main hall on the first floor. The walls were covered with huge paintings and lined with tables of marble and expensive woods. Vases, busts, small statues, and expensive bric-a-brac were clustered on the tables.

"Take off your shoes and walk quietly," Eva whispered, taking off her own shoes. "The Führer is still sleeping."

Uta followed Eva's instructions, laying the shoes beside Eva's on the stairs, and tiptoed down the long, thickly carpeted hallway beside Eva. Two SS guards stood totally immobile outside one door, and Uta didn't have to be told that it was the door to Hitler's apartment.

"This is my room," Eva whispered as they reached the next room, and she opened the door and ushered Uta inside. The walls were lined with silk, and the room was heavily furnished. Above the sofa hung a painting of a seminude woman.

Uta gasped when she saw it.

"Yes, it's me," Eva said, smiling proudly. "The Führer claims that it is scandalous to have such a painting of oneself on display, but I think that he secretly likes it. Besides, it's certainly better than the photograph he wishes me to keep of him."

Eva pointed to the photograph of Hitler on her night table. The background of the photo was completely black, the face staring out in an almost spectral image. The eyes,

always intense, were absolutely hypnotic in this picture.
"Frightening, isn't it?" Eva asked.

"Yes," Uta agreed, so compelled by the picture that
she didn't even stop to think that her answer might not be
diplomatic.

Eva opened a door at the far end of the room, and Uta
looked in. It was a large bathroom with a huge marble tub
with gold fixtures. There was another door at the other end
of the room.

"That leads into the Führer's apartment," Eva whispered. She let Uta look around, then pulled the door shut.
"Now you've seen everything," she said. "What do you
think of it?"

"I think it is absolutely beautiful," Uta breathed.
"What a grand place to live."

"Or to be imprisoned," Eva replied. "For that's what I
am."

Uta was surprised by the strange comment. "I don't
understand. You mean you can't leave here?"

Eva smiled sadly. "Of course I can leave here. But
when I do, I must be completely guarded, unable to let the
world know what I feel in my heart. Here, at the Berghof, it
isn't necessary for me to keep everything a secret, for all
who visit this place are people who can be trusted."

At that moment Uta felt an almost overwhelming pity
for the young woman who, on the surface at least, would
seem to have everything she could ever want.

The rest of the day passed much the same as the previous one. Hitler came down at a few minutes after twelve,
greeted all his guests with an almost shy formality, then
treated them to another long afternoon of rambling monologues. Finally, during a pause in the Führer's speech,
Himmler spoke up.

"It seems, *mein Führer*, that there are some among us
who do not entirely share your goal of a Jew-free Europe."

Hitler looked up at Himmler, but he said nothing.

"The Reichsmarschall," Himmler said, pointing to Göring, "and the Oberreichsleiter," he added, pointing to

Karl, "think that we are making a big mistake by relocating all the Jews we encounter in the conquered territories."

Hitler's dog, Blondi, scooted over to him, and Hitler began stroking the dog's head. He continued to stroke in silence for a long moment—so long that Himmler felt compelled to clear his throat and speak again.

"I have told them that there is nothing, absolutely *nothing*, more important to the Third Reich than the total and absolute settlement of the Jewish problem once and for all!"

"My Führer," Göring said, his voice firm, "Himmler's relocation of the Jews from Eastern Europe is using up every available train. That leaves no trains available to ship critical parts from one industry base to another. It also denies the Wehrmacht and Luftwaffe desperately needed trains."

Hitler studied Göring for a long time. "It is not Himmler's relocation of Jews," he finally said. "It is *my* relocation of Jews."

"Yes, of course," Göring replied.

Karl sighed resignedly. He had hoped at some point during the weekend visit to discuss with Hitler the issue of preempting all the trains just so Jews could be hauled from the captured lands to the concentration camps. But Hitler's response to Göring made it clear that whatever objections Karl might bring up about the transfer of the Jews would go unheeded. He therefore said nothing.

For the next few moments everyone sat quietly, just gazing through the window at Untersberg Peak. After several moments Hitler spoke again.

"If I am successful with all that I have set out to do, I will be considered one of the greatest men in the world. But if I fail . . ."

"*Fail*, my Führer?" Göring interrupted, protesting that Hitler might fail.

Hitler impatiently waved Göring's interruption aside, as if it were imperative that he finish his thought. "If I fail," he went on, "I shall be condemned as the most dreaded criminal in the history of mankind, and I will be damned for eternity."

There was such an ominous tone to Hitler's voice as he made the statement that it chilled Uta and caused her to tremble. She thought of the expression she had heard often as a child but had never understood: "Someone just stepped on your grave."

CHAPTER TWELVE

Hamilton Twainbough could feel rivulets of sweat running down the middle of his back as he stood at rigid attention at the foot of his bunk in the hot, dank barracks. Through the open doors of the barracks came the sound of a platoon of lowerclassmen going through the regimen of dismounted drill. The drill sergeant's voice and the sound of the marching platoon's boots drumming against the macadam pavement in perfect syncopation floated in on the stifling midday air.

Ham Twainbough and the nineteen other members of the third platoon of OC Class 42-4 were standing for inspection. Because the residents of the barracks slept head to toe, the foot of Ham's bunk was nestled between the heads of the bunks to either side of him. The olive drab blanket on Ham's bunk was stretched so tightly that a quarter dropped from a distance of one foot would flip over—which Ham knew to be the case because he had had to

180

remake his bunk three times that morning until that feat could be accomplished. Ham's spare blanket, like all the others, formed a "dust cover" over the pillow. Ham's wall locker, like all the others, was open for inspection, the extra uniforms displayed with exactly one inch of the bar showing between the hangers as prescribed. On the floor beneath his bunk was an extra pair of boots and one pair of shoes, the leather of each glistening from the painstakingly applied spit-polish shine. At the foot of the bunk was his foot locker, the lid open and the tray set at an angle and lined with a white towel that showed off, in a precise pattern, the never-used toilet articles—socks, handkerchief, extra belt and belt buckle—that were kept spotless just for the "inspection kit."

This was Saturday afternoon, and it was Ham's final weekend in Officer Candidate School. Actually, the training part was already completed, and the men were going to be given a pass for the weekend, then return Monday, at which time they'd be commissioned as second lieutenants. To get the pass, however, they had to get through this final inspection.

One of the tactical officers—called "tacs" by the candidates—stopped just in front of Ham. He studied Ham for a moment, looking for "gigs"—infractions—and when he seemed unable to find one, Ham breathed a bit easier. But Ham's relief was premature, for just before the tac turned away, his eyes lit up. He had spotted a gig.

"Candidate Twainbough, how dare you insult your fellow officers-to-be and the United States Army by standing your last inspection with your uniform in such a deplorable condition! What is that hanging from your pocket?"

"*Sir!* Candidate Twainbough. Permission to look, sir."

"Permission granted," the tac, Lieutenant Andrew Quinn, replied. Shortly after Ham had arrived at OCS, Lieutenant Quinn had told him that he once flunked an English literature assignment in college because he couldn't successfully posit the values in Eric Twainbough's book *Then Came the Gladiators*. "I can't get even with the author for that humiliation," Quinn informed Ham, "but I can take it out on his son. And, mister, while you're here, I intend to make your life hell on earth."

Lieutenant Quinn had been true to his word—he *had* made Ham's life hell on earth—but he hadn't been any harder on Ham than on anyone else, and he hadn't been any harder on Ham than any other tac had been. Ham realized that Quinn's threat wasn't anything personal, it was just a scare tactic, a part of the game, the hazing that all Officer Candidates were subjected to.

Ham glanced down at his shirt to see what the infraction was and noticed a tiny thread hanging from the button on his left pocket—no doubt the gig that Quinn was talking about.

"*Sir!* Candidate Twainbough. It appears to be a thread, sir."

"Mister, you call that *rope* a *thread*?"

Quinn leaned forward until his face was but a half inch from Ham's face, and Ham had the sudden, rather incongruous thought that he had never been that close to another human being's face without kissing it. He unconsciously smiled.

"Candidate Twainbough, wipe that smile off your face!" Lieutenant Quinn sputtered.

Ham quit smiling.

"No, Candidate Twainbough. Put the smile back!"

Ham forced the smile back onto his face.

"Now, wipe it off. Wipe it off, I say!"

Ham had neglected the prescribed OCS ritual. He kept the smile frozen in place, then raised his right hand and stiffly moved it across his face, "wiping" off the smile.

Invariably, every time one tac found a candidate to pick on, it would draw the attention of all the others, so Ham was quickly surrounded by at least five tactical officers. The other officer candidates remained absolutely silent, their eyes glued straight ahead, thankful that they weren't the one singled out for attention.

"What is it, Lieutenant Quinn?" one of the other tacs asked.

"Candidate Twainbough found something to smile about," Quinn replied. "I don't know what he found so funny, especially as he's standing here with a rope hanging off his pocket."

"A rope, Lieutenant Quinn? That's not a rope," one of

the other tacs said, "that's a *lanyard*. Candidate Twainbough, what is your excuse for having a lanyard hanging off
your pocket?"

"*Sir!* Candidate Twainbough. I have no excuse, sir."

"What school are you in, Candidate?"

"*Sir!* Candidate Twainbough. I am in Officer Candidate School, sir."

"You are wrong, Mr. Dumbjohn. You are in Infantry
Officer Candidate School. And I want you to understand
the problem. You see, here you are, about to graduate from
Infantry OCS, after which you will be given the great and
glorious honor of serving your country as an infantry officer"—he stepped back and held his hand out to take in all
the other candidates—"as indeed are all these gentlemen."
He smiled benevolently, then turned back toward Ham and
roared, "*AND YET YOU HAVE A LANYARD HANGING
FROM YOUR SHIRT. DO YOU WANT TO BE A CAN-
NON SHOOTER, MISTER?*"

"*Sir!* Candidate Twainbough. No, sir."

"Then jerk that lanyard off your shirt!"

"Wait a minute, Candidate," yet another of the tacs
said. He leaned over and looked at the offensive thread.
"You know, that looks to me like the lanyard for an eight-
inch howitzer, wouldn't you gentlemen say?"

The other tac examined it closely. "Yes, I agree."

"Then when the lanyard is jerked, don't you think
there should be an appropriate sound?"

All the tacs grinned. "Oh, absolutely," one of them
said.

"You may proceed, Candidate . . . with the appropriate sound," Lieutenant Quinn ordered.

"*Sir!* Candidate Twainbough. *BOOM*, sir!" Ham
shouted, as he jerked the offending thread from his pocket.

Fortunately for Ham one of the other candidates let
his curiosity get the better of him at that precise moment,
and he looked around. One of the tacs caught him in the
act.

"*KEEP THOSE EYEBALLS GLUED TO THE
FRONT, CANDIDATE!*" the tac bellowed, and, like sharks
at a feeding frenzy, the tacs all gathered around the offending candidate, leaving Ham alone.

The other candidate was chewed out for several minutes, and then the inspection continued. The "lanyard" was considered a minor enough incident that Ham, and indeed all the candidates of the Third Platoon, Company OC-4, were able to get their final passes.

Dressed in his khaki uniform, with his tie properly tucked in between the second and third buttons of his shirt, his brass buckle glistening in the sun, his brown shoes shining nearly as brightly, and with a crease in his trousers so sharp it could just about cut paper, Ham caught a taxi from Fort Benning's front gate into the town of Columbus.

He still owned his Plymouth convertible, but officer candidates weren't allowed to keep a car on post, so he had left his car in St. Louis. The previous week he had called Amy Wilkerson and asked her to bring the car down to Columbus in time for his graduation and commissioning.

Amy was still a student at Jefferson University, but school had just let out for the summer, so he didn't think it would be difficult for her to get away to come see him. Amy was somewhat reluctant at first, questioning the propriety of such a visit, but Ham's argument was persuasive, so she finally agreed to come, and they made arrangements to meet at 1700 hours, ("five o'clock in the afternoon," he explained) in the lobby of the Upatoi Hotel on Victory Boulevard.

When Ham entered the hotel lobby, he spotted Amy sitting in an overstuffed chair, holding her purse primly in her lap and biting nervously on her bottom lip. Ham had almost forgotten how pretty she was—though in truth, given the twelve weeks of intensive training under very difficult conditions he had just gone through, *any* woman would probably look good to him now.

Ham stood just inside the door of the hotel, watching Amy. She didn't yet realize he was there. Enjoying the gentle voyeurism, he took off his hat and stuck it in his belt, staying put to better savor the moment. Finally Amy saw— or felt—that he was there, and she looked toward the door. There was a moment's hesitation, as if she wasn't sure who he was. The last time she had seen him his hair was longer, he was a little heavier, and he'd been wearing civilian clothes, including the green-and-red letter sweater of Jefferson University. Then his identity sank in, and she flashed him a smile and started toward him. He did likewise, and they met halfway across the lobby.

Ham took her in his arms and kissed her deeply. She kissed him back as deeply, her body going limp in his arms. Then suddenly she let out a little whimper of alarm, as if she were just now realizing that they weren't alone . . . that they were, in fact, standing in the middle of a hotel lobby.

"Ham!" she scolded, pulling away. He let her go, and she stepped back from him, a bit unsteadily, and reached up to adjust the pink hat that had become skewed by the embrace.

"What's the matter?" Ham asked with a grin. "Aren't you glad to see me?"

"Yes, of course," she replied. "But this is a public place, for crying out loud."

Ham chuckled. "I know. That's why I was so reserved. Wait until I get you in a *private* place."

"Ham!" she scolded again.

"Come on," Ham said, laughing and leading her toward the door. "I've been cooped up on that base for three months, eating nothing but Army chow. The first thing we're going to do is find us a restaurant where we can get a huge, thick steak."

"There's a nice restaurant here in the hotel," Amy suggested.

Ham shook his head. "We'll order breakfast from here in the morning," he said. "We'll have it sent up to our room," he added.

He pretended not to notice Amy's nervous shiver.

The restaurant Ham chose was just up the block from the hotel. Due partly to hunger and partly to the awkwardness they felt with each other after their lengthy separation, dinner was a quickly eaten affair with little conversation until they got to dessert.

"They're fine," Amy said, spooning up some ice cream as she responded to Ham's question about her parents. "Of course, they don't know I'm down here."

"You didn't tell them? How did you avoid that? I mean, aren't they going to know you're gone?"

Amy shook her head. "They don't live in St. Louis anymore."

Ham was surprised. "Surely your father didn't give up his professorship at JU. I find that very hard to believe. I thought he was about as permanent a fixture there as the statues in the Quad."

"Yes, well, he still is," she explained. "I mean, he isn't gone for good. He just took a sabbatical from the university. He's working on some war project for the government. He and Dr. Rosen."

"Both of them?"

"Yes. I have no idea what it is they're working on. I don't even know *where* they are. In fact, the only way I can write to my parents is by sending my letters to a post office box in Washington, D.C."

"Can you call them?"

"No. I have a number I can call in Washington, and the person there gets in touch with my parents and they call me back. It's all very strange."

"Not when you figure that your dad's a physicist," Ham teased. "Physicists are strange people. I mean, look at Dr. Rosen."

"Surely you don't think my dad is as strange as Dr. Rosen?"

Ham laughed. "Amy, *nobody* is as strange as Dr. Rosen. I mean, anybody who'd wander around the campus with a message pinned to his jacket that reads 'I am Dr. Rosen. If I am lost, please notify the Physics Department, Jefferson University, St. Louis, Missouri' is really strange."

"Well, they had to do that," Amy said with a giggle. "Dr. Rosen once got on a train and rode it to Louisville; then he got off and started wandering around. When the police picked him up, they thought he was drunk or a madman because he didn't have any idea what city he was in or why he was there."

Ham sniggered. "I'm not sure he even knows what *planet* he's on."

"My father says Dr. Rosen is the most brilliant man he's ever known," Amy defended.

Ham smiled gently and reached across the table to take Amy's hand in his. "Sweetheart, no offense against your father or Dr. Rosen, but this is the first weekend I've had off in three months, and if you don't mind, I would rather not spend it talking about physics or absentminded professors. I intend to have a good time."

Amy laughed. "All right. What would you like to do first?"

"Well, they're having a dance out at the country club for the graduating officers of my class. Would you like to go? You could meet some of the other men and their wives."

"Wives?"

"Yeah. Nearly half of the guys I've been training with are married."

"And they live on the base?"

"No. They live in small apartments here in Columbus. And they've not had a fun time of it, I can tell you. This is the first weekend any of us have been able to get off. Those poor ladies have just had themselves for company." Ham squeezed Amy's hand. "So how about it? Feel like celebrating at the country club?"

"I'd love to. But I'd like to change into something more appropriate—and festive—than this suit."

"Fine. I'll help you."

"Ham!"

He grinned. "Okay, okay. I'll just sit and watch."

A number of Ham's fellow officers-to-be were sitting with him and Amy at one of the tables at the country club, laughing and telling stories of things that had happened during the training. Ham's "Sir! Candidate Twainbough, BOOM, sir!" story seemed to be the one everyone enjoyed most.

"Why did you even bother to come here if you couldn't see each other?" Amy asked one of the wives.

The young woman chuckled. "Oh, we found a way around that. We were able to see each other every Sunday morning when we went to church together on the base. And we learned that if one of us happened to be Catholic and the other Protestant, we could double the time we got to be together."

"Believe me, all the Protestant wives had a quick catechism class from the Catholic wives," someone said.

"And vice versa," a dark-haired girl put in. "Though I think the Protestant chaplain was beginning to wonder what a couple named Bertelli was doing in his church."

"Bertelli? You should see the way he looked at the Goldblooms," one of the wives said. "*Oy vay!*" She spread her fingers and held them to her chin in a self-caricature.

The others laughed.

"Where do you think most of us will be going?" Tony Bertelli asked.

"Africa," Neil Goldbloom answered. "I got a buddy who works down in personnel. He said our whole class is going to Africa."

"Shit," one of the others said. "They're *fighting* in Africa. There's folks getting killed there."

His somber pronouncement caused a moment of silence, and a number of couples tightly squeezed each other's hands, as if reassuring one another that nothing so unlucky would happen to them.

The merriment quickly resurfaced, and Ham and Amy spent most of the evening on the dance floor. When the celebration finally wound down, they walked arm in arm out to the parking lot, stopping periodically for kisses. The drive back to the hotel was short—mercifully, Ham thought. The anticipation of how the evening would, hopefully, conclude was almost more than he could take.

"I had a wonderful time tonight, Ham," Amy said as they stepped into their hotel room. She closed the door behind them.

"I'm glad," Ham replied. He brushed her hair aside and kissed her temple, feeling her shudder slightly.

"Ham?"

"Yes?" He kissed her again.

"Is there really fighting going on in Africa?"

"Yes."

"I'm frightened for you. I wish you were going somewhere else."

Ham smiled. "I'm glad you're frightened for me. But where else would I go? There's fighting everywhere."

"I just wish you hadn't gone into the infantry."

Ham thought of the incident in the barracks this morning, when the tacs were accusing him of being disloyal to the infantry, and he smiled.

"No, I'm serious," Amy said, not understanding his smile. "I mean, the infantry gets right in the middle of the fighting."

"Look," Ham said, sighing, "if I'm going to go off to fight in a war, I may as well get right in the middle of it."

"Right in the middle of it," Amy echoed. "Damn. That sounds like something your father would say. You are not your father, Hamilton Twainbough. He's the bigger-than-life adventurer, not you. You're your own man; you don't have to live up to him."

"I'm not trying to live up to him," Ham defended. He paused for a moment, then sighed. "No, that's wrong. I guess maybe I am, in a way. I mean, just about everything I've ever done I did for his approval. When I was young and I'd spend my summers with him, I always wanted to catch the biggest fish, shoot the biggest antelope, ski the highest mountain. . . . Now I guess I'm going off to fight in the biggest war."

"To outdo him?"

"No," Ham said, smirking, "I'm sure he'll find a way to get into this war, just like he has every other war that's come along in his lifetime. There's no way I can outdo him—or even stay even with him."

"Then why are you doing this?"

Ham laughed and chucked Amy on the chin. "What did you do, take an advance course in psychology or something? Why are you playing Dr. Freud with me?"

"I'm just scared, that's all," Amy said softly. "I don't want you to go over there and get yourself killed."

"I don't plan to," Ham said. He lifted up her chin with his finger and raised her lips toward his. "But it makes me feel good to know that I've got someone here who'll worry about me."

"I'll worry about you," Amy murmured.

Ham put his arms around her and pulled her to him,

pressing his lips to hers. Her tongue lightly touched his, setting fire to him, driving him mad with desire for her. Then, gasping for breath, Amy pulled away from him again.

"Oh," she gasped. "That makes me dizzy."

"Then maybe we'd better sit down," Ham suggested.

"Yes, perhaps we should," Amy replied, and when he sat them down on the edge of the bed, she made no protest.

Ham kissed her again, and this time his hands began to roam over her. He started to push his hand inside the top of her low-cut dress.

"No, wait," Amy said, pushing his hand away gently.

"Amy, I—" Ham started, but, smiling, Amy put her finger across her lips to shush him.

"I just want to make certain the door is locked," she said and walked over to set the bolt. When she turned back to him, she began unfastening the catches on her dress. "I may as well take this off. There's no sense in getting it all mussed up."

Ham grinned broadly. "No. There's no sense at all!" He stood up then and began undoing the buttons on his shirt while stepping out of his shoes.

"Let me go into the bathroom for a moment," Amy said. "I'll be right back."

While she was gone, Ham got out of his uniform and laid it carefully across the back of the chair. He took off his undershirt as well, but he left his skivvies on. Turning down the bedcovers, he slipped in under the sheet, then watched the bathroom door expectantly.

A few minutes later Amy came back out, wearing a long, black-silk gown that clung to her curves and was punctuated at the bodice by her nipples. She walked over to the bed, then sat down on the edge and looked at Ham, her eyes wide and vulnerable.

"Ham, I'm afraid," she said in a small voice.

"Of me?"

"Yes. And of me. Of this."

"Don't be afraid," he whispered.

"I knew this was going to happen," Amy went on. "From the moment I bought this nightgown, I knew this was going to happen. In the car on the way down here I figured out a hundred different ways to keep it from happening, a hundred things I could say that would stop you. But I knew, even as I worked out each scenario, that no matter what I said, no matter what I did, it was going to happen. And I knew why." Amy licked her lips. "We're going to make love because I *want* to make love. And that's why I'm afraid. I'm afraid of what you must think of me."

"No, don't be afraid of that," Ham said gently, persuasively. "Don't *ever* be afraid of that."

He pulled the cover aside for her, and Amy slipped in under the sheet, then pressed herself up against him. He could feel the heat of her skin, the hardness of her nipples, the curve of her hip, even the soft bush of her pubic hair, all covered from his view but not denied to his tactile sensations by the thin, black silk of her nightgown.

Her hands moved down through the hair of his chest, then across his flat stomach to the elastic waistband of his shorts. She hesitated there for a moment, then boldly stuck her hand down inside his shorts and wrapped her fingers around his rock-hard penis. Though his fingers had dipped into her own hot wetness on several occasions, this was the first time she had ever felt him.

"Oh, my!" she gasped.

Ham shoved his shorts down across his hips and legs until they reached his ankles, where, using his feet, he worked himself out of them. Then he grabbed the hem of Amy's nightgown and began slowly pulling it above her hips, all the time kissing her, pressing himself against her, and speaking soft, loving words to her. He then pulled the top of the gown down and kissed her breasts, drawing one nipple in between his lips and sucking it gently.

The foreplay went on for several more minutes, each of them becoming more venturesome as they grew more familiar with the territory. Finally, Ham moved over Amy.

She was so lost in the languorous sensations of the moment that when the connection between them was made, she gave a small cry—more from surprise than from the sharpness of it. But the cry was immediately replaced by long sighs and groans.

Ham felt a brief pang of conscience—he was, after all, deflowering a virgin whom he would soon be leaving—but it was quickly vanquished by sheer animal pleasure . . . and all-too-human need.

UNION STATION, LOS ANGELES

"Deanna! Miss Durbin! Would you look this way, please?" one of the photographers called.

The young movie star looked toward the photographer, who raised his camera to take her picture but then lowered it when Mickey Rooney used his fingers to make "rabbit ears" grow from the top of his co-star's head. Deanna turned and swung at him good-naturedly, and, laughing, Mickey Rooney scurried away.

In addition to Deanna Durbin and Mickey Rooney, there were nearly a dozen other Hollywood stars assembled here, including Bing Crosby, Risé Stevens, Jimmy Cagney, Judy Garland, and Bob Hope. They were gathered on the station platform alongside the "All Star Special" train, which would carry them to a number of Army bases on their cross-country tour. The movie stars were surrounded by reporters and newspaper and newsreel photographers as well as by the hundreds of fans who had come down just to see their favorite stars off.

"Bob, this train is carrying a regular 'Who's Who' of stars, isn't it?" one of the reporters asked Bob Hope.

"Who's who?" Hope cracked. "Mister, the soldiers don't care who's who. All they're interested in is 'What's what's what's what?'" He accompanied his wisecrack with leering eyes and a wolfish grin. Everyone laughed uproariously.

"Here you go, fellas," Hope said, grabbing a basket full of rolls. "Are you hungry?" He began tossing the rolls out to the gathered fans, accompanying each toss with a joke or a quip that made everyone laugh. When the last roll was gone, he tossed out the basket.

"What else have you got, Bob?" someone shouted, and Hope took off one of his shoes and tossed it, much to the delight of everyone there. "Oh, that was real smart of me. That's thrown off my gait," he said. "Now for the rest of the trip I'll be walking in circles." He demonstrated by stomping around in a circle. "Of course, now I can just join Bing. He's been walking in circles all his life," he added, pointing at Bing Crosby and making a funny face, which drew another laugh.

Demaris Hunter was also making the tour, and when she arrived, riding in the back seat of a studio convertible, several photographers and newspaper reporters hurried over to greet her. One was a radio announcer, and he thrust his microphone toward her.

"Ladies and gentlemen of our radio listening audience, stepping out of her car now—and, I must say, presenting a vision of loveliness—is Demaris Hunter. Miss Hunter has appeared in nearly two dozen movies but is probably best known for her Academy Award-winning performance as Leah in *The Corruptible Dead*. Miss Hunter, would you say a few words for our listeners?"

"Of course I will," Demaris said, smiling for the photographers. "Hello, everybody. This is Demaris Hunter, greeting you from Hollywood."

"Demaris, tell us why you are making this trip," the announcer queried.

"Why, that's an easy question to answer. I'm making this trip because I want to play some part, however small it may be, in helping the war effort. If by a song or a dance or even by a little joke we can bring some joy into the lives of our brave soldiers, sailors, and marines who'll soon be off to fight in foriegn lands, then we of the motion picture industry will feel gratified."

"Will you be thinking about Carole Lombard during this tour?"

"Yes, of course," Demaris replied solemnly. "Carole Lombard is the inspiration to us all, and our hearts go out to Clark Gable in his time of sorrow. But we do hope that he takes some consolation in the fact that Carole truly gave her life for her country, just as our brave soldiers and sailors now fighting in this war may be called upon to give theirs."

"Thank you, Miss Hunter. And now, ladies and gentlemen, I see Claudette Colbert is arriving, so I'm going to try and get a word or two from her as well."

Demaris started walking toward the entrance to the cavernous station when she heard her name being called.

"Miss Hunter? Miss Hunter?" A harried young man carrying a clipboard came running up to her. He was wearing a button on his jacket that said *Boarding Official*. "If you'll show me what luggage you have, I'll get it taken care of for you."

"Why, thank you. That's very sweet of you," Demaris said.

"Oh, and, uh, you'll be in the third car, roomette four. You'll be rooming with Greta Gaynor."

"Great," Demaris said sarcastically. "We're old friends."

Though not exactly enemies, Demaris and Greta Gaynor could hardly be called old friends. But they were old acquaintances. Demaris's first role had been originally intended for Greta Gaynor. It had been one of Goliath Studios' earliest talkies, and Greta, a silent-movie star, had had a difficult time with the new technology—so difficult, in fact, that Goliath's only recourse had been to pull her from the picture.

Being replaced in the part had been quite a blow to Greta's ego, but being replaced by a complete novice had been almost more than she could handle. After all, Greta Gaynor was a star, known and loved by millions of fans all across the nation; Demaris Hunter was an unheard-of nobody.

That had been the start of Demaris's career. Since then she had become one of Goliath Studios' biggest stars and box-office attractions ever. Greta, on the other hand, never regained the popularity or achieved the star billing she had enjoyed as a silent-screen actress. However, to Greta's credit, she had eventually managed through study to make the transition to talkies. Now she was a very good actress, much better than she had been even at the peak of her stardom, though all her roles now were supporting character parts. She had even been nominated for an Oscar in a supporting role. And, as a bonus to everyone else, moving from star to character actress had not only improved Greta's dramatic performances, it had made her a much nicer person. People who had disliked her intensely now had kind things to say about her.

Greta was sitting on the bench seat in the roomette, looking through a copy of *Life* magazine, when Demaris stepped inside.

"Do you want the top or bottom?" Greta asked, looking up from her magazine.

"You were here first; you choose," Demaris replied.

"No, no, you're the star, I'm in the supporting role. I feel lucky just to be along for the ride."

Demaris grimaced. "Really, Greta, why don't you cut out this poor-little-bit-player shit? Damn if I didn't like you better when you were the bitch of Hollywood."

Unexpectedly, Greta laughed. "My God, I did wield some power then, didn't I?"

Demaris laughed with her. "I'll admit that you sure had *me* scared to death," she said. "That's the trouble with the kids coming up nowadays. They don't scare the way we did."

Greta put down her magazine and, spontaneously, they embraced.

"You really are going to let me choose?" Demaris asked.

"Sure, why not? I mean, if you have a preference. It's no big sacrifice on my part, believe me. It doesn't make any difference to me whether I'm on top or bottom."

"For me I guess top or bottom has always depended upon the man I was with," Demaris quipped. She was rewarded by a hearty laugh. "But, with bunks, I must say that I prefer the lower." She sat down and looked through the window at the activity on the platform outside. "My, my, they are really making a big thing of all this, aren't they?" she remarked. "Newsreel men, photographers, reporters, radio people . . . There isn't this much ballyhoo at a world premiere."

"Well, you know how the studios are," Greta replied. "They're all for doing the right thing—provided they get enough coverage out of it. The way I figure it, we'll probably entertain half-a-million soldiers, sell a million war bonds . . . and one hundred million extra tickets."

Demaris chuckled. "Now, there's the cynical old broad I know and love so well."

Greta laughed with her, then asked, "By the way, have you heard from Guy lately? How is he doing?"

Guy Colby had been an additional complication between the two women when they first met. At the time he had been Greta's husband . . . and became Demaris's lover. The initial relationship between Demaris and Guy didn't last long, however, and Demaris subsequently married the male lead of her first picture, a cowboy star named Ken Allen. That marriage ended in divorce, and Demaris married Ian McCarty, one of the leading box-office stars and the heartthrob of female moviegoers everywhere. That marriage ended before it was even consummated, when Ian —secretly homosexual—committed suicide on their wedding night by jumping off their yacht into Santa Monica Bay, unable to go through with the sham marriage or even confess the truth to Demaris.

Guy Colby, too, had gone on to marry again. He took as his third wife April Love, a starlet whose talent didn't measure up to her looks or to the imaginative name her agent had dreamed up for her. Now they, too, were divorced.

"Guy's doing well," Demaris said, answering Greta's question. "He called when he heard I was coming on this tour, and we had a going-away dinner last night."

"He's a sweet man," Greta said. "Sometimes I think that of all the foolish and bitchy things I did in those early days, mistreating Guy Colby was probably the most foolish and the most bitchy of all."

"Well, I wasn't exactly the answer to his prayers either," Demaris admitted. "But you're right. He is a good man. He deserves better than either one of us."

Suddenly there was a loud *whoosh* of steam from outside the car, then several shouts, a blast from the train's whistle, and an increase in the activity on the platform.

" 'Board!" the conductor shouted.

"Well, I guess we're about to get under way," Demaris

said, looking out the window. "Incidentally, have you seen all the liquor and food they brought on board?"

Greta nodded. "I hear they're going to keep the club car open twenty-four hours a day for the entire trip. It's going to be one long party." She sighed happily. "I just love trains—and this is going to be a train trip to remember!"

CHAPTER THIRTEEN

JUNE 1942, WADDLESFOOT, ENGLAND

"It is preposterous," said Air Group Captain Todd Whitley, the British liaison officer to the U.S. Army Air Corps Base at Waddlesfoot, as he held a dripping teabag over his cup and examined the color of the water. It wasn't quite ready, so he dipped the bag again. "The whole idea of daylight precision bombing is utterly preposterous."

"But you must admit that there are advantages to the concept if we can pull it off," Brigadier General Willie Canfield countered. Having earlier rejected the offer of a cup of tea, he took a swig of his coffee.

"If you ask me, the only advantages are all to the Jerries," Group Captain Whitley replied. "I mean, think about it. There your Forts will be, all strung out in a nice queue, like fat geese ready for the plucking, just waiting for the Messerschmitts and Focke Wulfs to pounce on them."

Lieutenant Colonel Jimmy Blake, who was the 756th Bomber Squadron Commander, chuckled. "Ah, but that's where we have you, Group Captain," he said. "We don't plan to line our planes up in a long row the way you British chaps do. We'll be flying in a very precise formation."

"Oh, yes, I quite forgot about the combat box and the wonders it will do," Whitley said wryly.

"Don't dismiss the combat box out of hand," Jimmy said. "If it's properly flown, there won't be any area of the sky that a German fighter can use for an unopposed approach. And don't forget, there are many more guns on a Fortress than there are on a Halifax or a Lancaster."

"Oh, I know the concept, Colonel. The question is, do you really believe it will work?"

Jimmy refilled his coffee cup. Then he grinned. "Hell, if I didn't believe it'd work, I'd still be flying Windjammers across the Pacific."

Willie laughed. "Yes, I know how anxious you were to continue doing that," he said. "As soon as you found out I had a new job, you started bombarding me with requests to get into the fight. You're like an old fire horse, Jimmy, jumping into harness at the sound of the bell."

"Well, I don't want you to get the wrong idea. It's not because I'm brave or anything," Jimmy said. "It's just that I got to thinking about it, and I realized that if the Japs decided to attack me while I was flying a Windjammer, there wouldn't be anything I could do about it. But a B-17, now —well, that's a different story. It has guns all over the place."

"And the combat box," Whitley added sarcastically.

"The combat box will work," Willie said. "I'll admit, it hasn't actually been tried in battle yet, but it's been quite well thought out."

"So has attacking under the cover of darkness been well thought out," Whitley said. "I'm sure the concept wasn't new with Caesar's legions."

"We have to make our attacks in the daylight," Willie explained. "That's the only way we can utilize the effectiveness of the Norton bombsight. With it we can drop a bomb into a pickle barrel from thirty thousand feet. Precision bombing means we can take out aircraft factories, oil refineries, whatever we're going after, with far fewer bombs and far more devastating effect than can be achieved with carpet bombing attacks."

"Yes, well, don't forget, in order to hit a pickle barrel from thirty thousand feet, you first have to *see* the bloody thing," Todd said. "And with cloud cover, smoke, and flak, not to mention a few German fighter aircraft who might try to get in the way, you're going to find that you'll have a hard time putting this pet theory of yours into operation."

"*My* theory?" Willie replied. He laughed. "It's not my theory. I'm just over here to help gather enough airplanes to give the theory a chance to work, that's all."

"You're going to have to gather quite a lot of them, I'm afraid," Whitley said.

"We will," Willie insisted. "We have hundreds here already, and more are arriving every day." He got up from his desk, then walked over to the window to look out. Within his field of vision he could see a dozen or more B-17 bombers recently arrived from the States. He would've been able to see even more if it hadn't been so foggy.

"Is it still socked in out there?" Jimmy asked.

"Yeah. The clock says it's nearly sunset, though I haven't seen the sun all day long. Will this damned fog ever lift?" Willie complained.

Whitley chuckled. "Good heavens, my dear fellow, you haven't even *seen* a fog yet," he said. "Why, when I was a lad, we used to call this a bright and sunny day."

"Don't pull that 'you haven't seen a fog' stuff on me," Willie rejoined. "I'm from St. Louis, and we don't just have fog, we have something the newspapers call 'smog.'"

"Whatever is smog?"

"It's a combination of smoke and fog."

"You don't say." Whitley made a disapproving clucking noise. "Well, leave it to you Americans to take a perfectly good language like English and screw it up with your quaint colonialisms."

Willie laughed; then hearing the buzzer on his intercom, he nodded at Jimmy. "Get that, would you?"

Jimmy pushed down on the lever. "Go ahead," he called into the box.

"*General, the tower just called,*" a voice said over the intercom speaker. "*The B-17 that was overdue? It's just reporting in. The pilot is asking for permission to land.*"

"In this fog? That's impossible," Willie replied. "The

pilot must be out of his mind. Tell the tower to send him somewhere else."

"*There isn't anywhere else he can go, General,*" the voice on the box said. "*It's like this for a hundred miles in every direction. And the pilot has declared a fuel emergency. He has to set it down here.*"

"Damn," Willie said. He sighed. "All right, tell the tower to clear him to land. I guess we have no choice."

"Sergeant, this is Colonel Blake," Jimmy said into the box."

"*Yes, sir?*"

"Tell the tower to get all the runway lights turned on. Then call out the fire truck and ambulance, and have them standing by."

"*Will do, sir.*"

Jimmy snapped the intercom switch off and looked around toward Willie and the British officer. "I don't know about you two, but I'm going outside to sweat this one down."

"We should all go," Whitley replied, grabbing his hat from the top of the file cabinet. "It'll be good practice for sweating in the stragglers when you chaps start your daylight bombing."

The field lights were coming on just as the three officers left the small, white-block building that served as Willie's office. Once outside they could see the glowing yellow halos the lights made in the heavy, white vapor that blanketed the entire airfield. Over in the emergency vehicle station a couple of truck engines started, and the ambulance and fire truck moved out to the edge of the airfield, ready to dash through the fog to provide whatever assistance they could for the plane, should it crash-land.

"Do you see anything, Jimmy?" Willie asked.

"No, not a damned thing," Jimmy replied. After a moment he said, "Wait a minute, do you hear that? There it is."

"Yeah," Willie said, "I hear it."

The noise of the approaching plane's overstrained engines was becoming increasingly loud.

"Damn, listen to that howl," Willie said. "Those props are badly out of synch. It's not enough he's nearly out of gas and trying to put down through the fog, he must be having engine trouble besides."

"He's not going to make it, chaps. I hope you're ready for that," Whitley said grimly.

By now most of the men on the base had heard about the approaching B-17, and they spilled out of the hangars, barracks, BOQs, and mess halls to see what was going on. In groups of threes and fours, cooks, clerks, mechanics, and pilots gathered on the perforated steel planking that the engineers had laid down to form the runway, apron, and environs of Waddlesfoot Airfield.

"Who is that up there?" someone asked. "One of our regulars?"

"No, it's a new delivery, just comin' in from the States. It's a ferry job, probably no more than three on board—pilot, copilot, and navigator."

"Why don't they just bail out?"

"They can't do that. There's no tellin' where the plane might come down. It could crash right in the middle of town."

"Hell, it could do that anyway."

"Here he comes," another said. "Looks like he's getting it lined up with the runway, all right."

"Good," Jimmy said, breathing a sigh of relief. "That means he can at least see the glow of the lights well enough to be *able* to line up."

"There's a lot more to landing a plane than just getting it lined up properly, as you well know, Colonel," Whitley cautioned.

"Yes, well, first things first, Todd," Jimmy said.

Still unable to see anything of the airplane, everyone stood around in anxious silence, listening to the B-17's engines, trying to gauge by the sound how high it was and how it was doing.

"Man, we can't see shit," one of the mechanics complained. "How're we goin' to know whether or not he makes it?"

"Oh, don't you worry any about that," one of the others said. "If he don't make it, we'll know, all right."

"Oh, yeah," the mechanic agreed sheepishly. "Yeah, I see what you mean."

Suddenly a loud roar rolled across the field as the pilot opened all four engines to full power. A moment later someone shouted, "Look!" and pointed toward a large brown shape coming right toward them, charging through the haze, its four engines bellowing loudly but discordantly, its propellers leaving four long vapor trails of feathery cork-screws. The airplane was skimming along at no more than thirty feet above the runway as it thundered over their heads, rattling the windows and shaking the very ground before the nose pitched up, and it clawed its way back up into the enveloping mist.

"Jesus!"

"What's that crazy idiot doing?"

"He nearly crashed into us!"

"General, you better get out of here! It ain't safe!" one of the sergeants said.

"No, it's okay," Willie answered. "I don't think the pilot even intended to land that time. He was just taking a look around at whatever obstacles he might have to contend with. Listen, he's making a go-around. He'll set it down this time, and I'm betting he makes it."

"Really? Well, I hope you're right. I'd sure as hell hate to be on board that thing right now. I mean, I'd be scared to death."

"I imagine it would be frightening if you didn't have anything to do," Willie said. "But I suspect the pilot has enough to keep himself occupied."

"Enough to keep himself occupied?" Todd snickered. "You, my dear Willie, are a master of understatement."

"Listen, here he comes again!" someone shouted, and everyone stopped talking to hear the sound of the engines as the B-17 lined up with the runway for a second approach.

The pilot throttled back, and there was a series of loud popping sounds followed by a slight change in the pitch of the engines.

"Son of a bitch! He just lost an engine!" Jimmy said.

"I'm afraid so," Willie replied.

"Be lively, lads," Whitley said. "That means he's just committed himself to this go."

The men stood waiting in anxious silence as they listened intently to the engine sounds of the approaching plane. The sounds grew quieter and quieter, until they all but disappeared.

"What happened to it?" someone asked.

"Shhh!" another ordered.

All was silent for a moment longer. Then someone shouted excitedly, "Look! There he is, on the ground!"

The large, lumbering airplane abruptly emerged, rolling out of a billowing cloud of fog with its nose high and its tail dragging behind it. Three of its four engines were turning over quietly, while the fourth was still and feathered. The brakes squealed in protest as the pilot brought the plane to a halt. A moment later the remaining three engines fell silent, and after a few more revolutions the giant propeller blades slowed to a stop. For a moment there was an absolute hush among the onlookers; then, spontaneously, the men began to cheer.

"Sergeant!" a grinning Willie shouted to one of the men standing nearby.

"Yes, sir?"

"Have the pilot report to me in my quarters. I want to buy that man a drink. If he balks, tell him I've got the only ice on base."

"Yes, sir!" the sergeant replied.

Still grinning, Willie turned to his squadron commander and to the British Liaison Officer. "Will you two join me?"

"Hell, yes, I will," Jimmy said. "If that fella is a civilian ferry pilot, I'm going to try and recruit him for my squadron. That's the kind of pilot we're going to need over here."

"I'd like to have a look at this chap myself," Whitley admitted.

The three officers hurried back to Willie's quarters, where he took a tray of ice from the freezer compartment of his refrigerator and put it in a large beaker to begin assembling martinis. He was peering into the refrigerator, searching for the bottle of olives, when his sergeant knocked gently and opened the door.

"General, you wanted the pilot to report to you here?"

"Yes," Willie replied, still bent at the waist, his head

practically inside the refrigerator while he looked for the olives. "Send him in, send him in." He paused, then called, "Jimmy, where the hell are the olives?"

"Bottom shelf, behind the beer," Jimmy replied in an odd-sounding voice. "Uh, General, I think maybe there's something you should know about this pilot."

"What about him?" Willie replied.

"That's just it."

"What's it? Oh, there they are."

"It's not a him," Jimmy said quietly.

"What did you say?" Willie asked, pulling his head out so quickly that he bumped it on the refrigerator door. "Ouch!"

"Oh, dear, I do hope you aren't hurt," a soft, well-modulated woman's voice said.

Willie turned around in surprise. Standing there just inside the room was a beautiful, tall, blond-haired, green-eyed woman. She was smiling broadly.

"Hello, Willie. We meet again," she said. "Or should I call you General now?"

"Candy?" Willie said to the young woman he had met at his brother and sister-in-law's house back in Washington. "My God! Candy Keefer, what in the world are you doing here?"

Candy's cheery little laugh bubbled forth. "Well, you asked me here. You *did* offer to buy me a drink, didn't you?"

"*You?* You're the one who flew that B-17?"

"General, you know this woman?" Jimmy asked, appraising Candy appreciatively.

"Yes. Yes, I do."

Jimmy smiled. "Well, in that case, perhaps Whitley and I should leave and let you two catch up on old times."

"Uh, yeah, thanks," Willie said.

Taking their drinks with them, Jimmy and Whitley slipped quietly out of the room, leaving Willie and Candy alone.

"You were flying that Fortress?" Willie asked again.

"Yes. Why do you find that so hard to accept?" Candy asked. "I'm not the only woman ferrying airplanes."

"True, but none of the others asked me to take them

for a flight just a few months ago," Willie said, and there was an edge to his voice. "Dammit, you were mocking me, weren't you?"

"No, I wasn't," Candy answered easily. "Just because I know how to fly doesn't mean I wouldn't enjoy flying with you. After all, I know how to drive a car, too, but I've ridden with men."

"It's not the same thing," Willie protested.

"Isn't it?" Candy asked sweetly. "What's the harm, other than perhaps a slightly bruised ego?"

Willie looked at her for a moment longer, then broke into a grin. "Nothing, I guess." He opened the olives and dropped one into each glass. Then he filled the glasses with the clear liquid from the beaker and handed one to Candy. "Here's to a hell of a good job of flying," he said, holding his glass toward her.

"Thanks," Candy replied. "And thanks for turning on the lights. They provided just enough difference in the intensity of the fog that I was able to use them for my guide."

"Oh, that was Colonel Blake's idea," Willie said. "I didn't introduce you, did I? I want you to meet Colonel Blake and Group Captain Whitley—" Willie stopped and looked around the room. "What the hell happened to them?"

Candy laughed. "They left just a moment ago, remember? Something about giving us an opportunity to 'catch up on old times'?"

Willie smiled. "Oh, right. That was damned decent of them. So, how are my brother and sister-in-law getting along?" he asked. "Or do you ever see them anymore?"

"I saw Faith a couple of weeks ago," Candy replied. "She and John are doing fine, and so are the children. I guess you know you're Morgan's hero. To hear him tell it, you're going to win this war practically single-handedly."

"Yes, well, Morgan is pretty easy to impress. It's Alicia you have to look out for. She's always been the skeptical one."

Candy laughed. "A healthy dose of skepticism is a very good trait for a girl to develop," she said. "Otherwise, any man who wanted to could talk a girl into anything."

"What about you?" Willie asked. "Do you have a

healthy dose of skepticism, or could a man talk you into something?"

Candy took a sip of her drink before she answered, and she smiled at Willie, looking at him with smoldering green eyes over the edge of her glass.

"Depends on the man," she said in a low, husky voice. "And it depends on what he's trying to talk me into."

"I'm the man," Willie replied. He looked at her intently, his gaze practically stripping her naked. Then he smiled. "And for now, I'm just trying to talk you into going into London with me tomorrow, for dinner. What do you say?"

"I've got a return flight to the States tomorrow night," Candy said. "If you can get me out to the airport in time to catch that flight, you've got yourself a date."

In the Bucket of Blood pub on Fleet Street, Shaylin McKay brought six bottles of ale back to the table and passed them around to the other journalists, all of whom were men. All of them, including Shaylin, were wearing olive-brown U.S. military uniforms but with a shoulder-flash that identified them as correspondents.

"Hey, you do that really well," one of the others said. "If you ever run out of stories, you can always turn a buck by waiting tables."

"There are a lot of other ways to earn money besides waiting tables," Shaylin said with an exaggerated smile. "More profitable—and a hell of a lot more fun."

"*Whoowee!*" one of the others hollered, which was followed by a few catcalls and whistles.

"Yeah, but the question is, are you any good at it?" someone asked.

Shaylin took a drink of ale, then wiped her mouth with the back of her hand. She smiled sweetly at the man who had asked the question.

"Well, now, Charley, that's something you'll never find out unless it becomes necessary for me to go into the business. And then it'd cost you a bundle. You maybe more than anyone else."

"Boys, what do you bet old Charley starts putting

some money back for the occasion?" someone asked, and the others laughed.

Over in the corner of the pub someone started playing the piano, and a bunch of American voices began a boisterous rendition of "Deep in the Heart of Texas."

"What the hell is it with that song?" someone asked. "Everywhere I go, I hear it. There can't possibly be that many men over here from Texas."

"There aren't," someone else explained. "But there's a certain élan to being from Texas. It has a much more glamorous sound than, say, telling someone you're from some place like Ohio or Arkansas or Missouri."

"Sir, I protest!" Floyd Stoner said, holding up his forefinger. "It just so happens that I am from the Show Me state and damned proud of it."

"The Show Me state?"

"Missouri," Shaylin explained. "And watch what you say about it, because I'm from there too."

"You won't find *me* saying anything bad about Missouri," one of the other correspondents said, seizing the opportunity to get on Shaylin's good side. "I'm not from there, but I went to school there. I studied journalism at the University of Missouri."

Shaylin smiled. "Well, I'm a Jefferson U girl myself, but I won't hold it against you that you went to Mizzou."

"I should hope not. Especially after we humiliated you in the football game last year. Everyone was touting Hamilton Twainbough as the greatest football player since Red Grange, but when he came up against us he couldn't do shit. He didn't know whether to wind his watch or scratch his ass."

"You played in that game, did you, Dirkson?" Floyd asked.

"What? Why, no. No, of course not," Dirkson sputtered.

"I just wanted to be sure," Floyd said.

The others laughed.

"Hey, I've got an idea," someone proposed. "Let's start a countermovement against all those would-be Texans. We'll all be Missourians or honorary Missourians. Now, does Missouri have a song?"

"The Missouri Waltz," Shaylin replied.

"How does it go?"

Shaylin began to sing, but she couldn't remember all the words, and the tune failed to make an impression on the group.

"Shit, that's it? I mean, that's the best we can come up with?"

"That's it," Shaylin said.

"Well, so much for that idea. Come on, guys, what do you say we become Texans? Let's go join them."

With whoops and shouts of "*Ah hah!*" most of the group got up from the table and walked over to the piano, where they were welcomed by the growing throng of "Texans" and joined in the singing.

"Look at them over there," Floyd scoffed. "Damned if you wouldn't think every one of them had been born on the banks of the Brazos."

"All they need are ten-gallon hats," Shaylin answered with a laugh.

After a pause while they sipped their ale, Floyd asked, "What do you hear from your English colonel?"

"He's now serving in His Majesty's forces in the Burma-China theater of operations."

"Well, for someone who's lived his entire life in a castle, I'm sure the whole experience is quite a change."

"Dunleigh Estate isn't a castle," Shaylin said. "And don't sell John Paul short. He's not some drawing-room colonel."

"I know, I know. Distinguished Service Order and all that," Floyd said. "I suppose there must be something to him, or you wouldn't be interested. By the way, what does he think about Eric Twainbough coming to England?"

"I don't know. I haven't mentioned it in any of my letters."

"Do you think you'll be seeing Twainbough?"

"Yes, I suspect I will."

"I don't blame you for not mentioning it. I can't imagine that Colonel Chetwynd-Dunleigh would be too happy about it."

"Floyd, all this isn't really any of your business, is it?"

"I guess not," Floyd replied. He sighed. "Though I

like to think that if I'd played my cards right, it would have been."

Shaylin thought back several years, to when she was a reporter for *The St. Louis Chronicle* and Floyd was a broadcaster for KSLM Radio. They had seen quite a bit of each other, but despite being compatible in many ways, including sexually, the relationship hadn't gone anywhere because they had been too busy pursuing their own careers, Shaylin in newspapers, Floyd in radio. Her career eventually took her to Spain, where she covered the Spanish Civil War—and where she met and had an affair with Eric Twainbough.

"Let's talk about something else, shall we?" Shaylin asked.

"Okay, I'll go along with that," Floyd agreed. "Tell me about Kevin. What do you hear from your kid brother?"

"Well, Kevin isn't much of a writer, as you know," Shaylin said, smiling. "Though he did write and tell me all about his experiences the morning Pearl Harbor was attacked. His ship was sunk, you know, so he's got a new ship now. He's on a DMS."

"DMS?"

"Destroyer/minesweeper. The *U.S.S Sharpe*. But I have no idea where it is. All I know is that he's somewhere in the Pacific. I just hope he's all right. From what I've heard, the Japs have us outnumbered out there about ten to one."

Floyd shook his head. "I hardly think it's that bad. And anyway, even if it is, you don't have to worry about Kevin. He's a survivor."

Shaylin smiled proudly. "He is, isn't he?"

A British airman walked up to their table then, the crown and wings over his jacket pocket looking outsized when compared to the wings worn by the American aviators. "Mr. Stoner?"

"Yes."

"I am Flight Lieutenant Pyre, sir. I am here to inform you that your request to go on a bombing mission has been approved."

"It has? Great!"

"Floyd, I didn't know you had put in to go on a bombing mission," Shaylin said.

Floyd smiled. "Well, I wanted to go Edward R. Murrow one better," he said. "It's one thing to get the drama of broadcasting from a rooftop during an air raid, but what's it like from the other side? I mean, how does it feel to actually be in the plane during a raid?"

"Are you going to try to broadcast it?"

"No, I've got a wire recorder. I'm going to transcribe it, then play it back."

"Oh, what a wonderful idea!" Shaylin enthused. "I wish I could do something like that."

"Well, it's taken me quite a while to get it approved," Floyd said. He turned to the British officer. "When will I be going?"

"Why, tonight, sir," the flight lieutenant said, as if surprised by the question. "We sortie one hour from now."

"Tonight?" Floyd asked, his voice suddenly much weaker. It had been one thing to think in the abstract of going along on a bombing mission with the RAF. It was quite another to actually do it.

"Yes, sir. I was told to collect you and take you out to the field, straight away."

"Wait a minute, not so fast," Floyd stammered. "Must it be tonight? I mean, I need a little time to get ready."

"Floyd, if you don't go, I will," Shaylin said quickly.

"I'm sorry, madam, I have no authority to take a lady," the flight lieutenant said. "It will have to be Mr. Stoner or no one. If you would like, Mr. Stoner, I'll tell the group captain that you were unavoidably detained. Perhaps you can get another mission approved."

Floyd waved a hand in protest. "No, no, don't be silly. I'll go. But if you would, please, take me by my hotel so I can get the wire recorder."

"Yes, certainly, sir. But you must hurry. The group captain gets quite irate if his sorties don't get off on time."

"Good luck, Floyd," Shaylin called as Floyd followed the RAF officer out. "I'll be listening."

*   *   *

"Would you like more wine?" Willie Canfield asked, reaching for the bottle.

"Sure, why not?" Candy Keefer replied, holding up her glass. "After all, I don't have to fly back."

"I can't tell you how shocked I was to see you at the controls of that B-17 yesterday."

"And I can't tell you how glad I was to see anybody, yesterday. When that fog moved in on us like that, I didn't know if I was going to be able to put us down or not."

"What about the man flying with you?"

Candy laughed, her green eyes sparkling. "He's one of my students," she said.

"Your *student*?"

"I'm a flight instructor . . . or I was, until I took the job for Ferry Command."

"There is no end to your mystery," Willie said, grinning crookedly.

"Well, don't you think a woman should have a little mystery about her?"

"Oh, absolutely," Willie agreed. "It makes her so . . . mysterious," he said, and they both laughed.

"Speaking of surprises," Candy said, "when you invited me to dinner tonight, I had no idea you meant room service in a hotel room."

"Yes, well, the dining rooms are much too noisy, and if my friends saw me sitting at a table with a beautiful woman, they'd be buzzing around, angling for an introduction."

"But aren't your friends all high-ranking officers? I thought only common soldiers horned in on their friends."

"That's where you're wrong. Generals get as horny as privates."

Candy laughed heartily at the double entendre. "Oh, that was a good one."

"You liked it?"

"Yes."

"Good. That means you've passed the first test."

"And what was that test to determine?" Candy asked. "The sharpness of my wit?"

"Hell, no." Willie smiled at her. "It was to determine

whether or not I could move the conversation into a sexual area without being slapped."

"I see. And have we moved the conversation into a sexual area?" Candy asked with a surprising amount of throatiness to her voice.

Willie got up and walked around the table, then leaned down and kissed her. He could smell and taste the wine, clean and antiseptic, as he kissed her. Her mouth opened and her tongue met his. After a moment of dizzying sensation, Willie pulled away. "I rather think we have," he said, finally giving her an answer.

"Willie," Candy said in a small, plaintive voice, "please don't do this unless you're prepared for it to get serious. I won't be a one-night stand."

"I don't want a one-night stand," Willie answered. "There are enough of those around."

Candy stood up and leaned into him, kissing him again. The kiss was long and demanding, and Willie could feel her trembling in his arms.

"Then in that case," she said, "let's do it before I lose my nerve."

"I'll put the table out in the hall for the waiter, so we won't be disturbed," Willie said. He quickly shoved the table through the door, then locked the door and set the chain latch. When he turned back around, he saw that Candy had gone to the other side of the bed to begin undressing in the shadows. Willie turned the lights off, then moved to the opposite side of the bed, where he quickly stripped his muscular, compact body of clothes.

A moment later they met under the sheet, naked body to naked body, open mouth to open mouth. Willie's hands caressed her curves, and when his tongue touched the nipple of her breast, her body arched and quivered in delight, and a soft moan came from her throat.

Candy's quick, shallow breathing filled the room as Willie's hands roamed her body and his tongue went from nipple to nipple. Finally, one hand slipped down her body, lingering briefly in her pubic hair. Then his finger slid inside to her moist, hot core. Hungrily, she reached for him; finding him amply ready, she shifted her body under his and joined with him.

"Yes," she whispered, and began to gyrate her pelvis, pushing up against him, meeting his thrusts, taking all of him into her. She soon climaxed, crying out from the ecstasy and the joy of it.

Willie sat in the back of the staff car with his arm around Candy as his driver drove them out to the airport for her to catch the flight back to the States, not giving a damn about protocol. The general's star plate on the car afforded them passage through the restricted areas so that they were able to drive right out on the runway and up to where the airplane, a four-engine C-54 transport, sat gleaming under the lights. The plane was a tricycle-gear craft, making the entry door quite high off the ground. Boarding stairs had been pushed up to the door, on which was painted MILITARY AIRLIFT COMMAND. A few people were in the process of boarding, being checked on by a man holding a clipboard.

"Willie, that's what you're going to have to get for your airline when this war is over," Candy said, pointing to the plane. "A Douglas DC-4. The time of the flying boats is over. They're just too slow."

"I know," Willie answered. "But I won't go to Douglas. Rockwell-McPheeters is working on something that's even better. They'll have it developed by the end of the war, I'm sure."

Candy smiled. "Well, for now this will do me just fine. Just thirteen hours from now we'll be setting down in New York."

"How long before you'll be back?"

"You tell me. You know how many bombers we're flying over."

"A lot," Willie replied without being too specific.

"Then I'll be back soon."

"And I'll be waiting for you."

"*Attention please,*" a voice said over a loudspeaker, "*anyone holding a boarding pass for MAC flight forty-one for New York, please board now.*"

"Well, that's me," Candy said.

"I'll walk out to the plane with you."

The driver opened the door for Willie. Candy slid across the seat and got out on his side; then they walked toward the brightly lighted airplane, which was humming loudly, the power provided by a heavy electrical cable plugged into the aircraft. The inside of the airplane was lighted as well, and Willie could see the pilots going over their prestart checklist.

"Boarding passes, please," the man with the clipboard said as they reached the boarding stairs.

Candy produced hers.

"You aren't going, General?"

"No, I've just brought the lady to the plane."

"Then I'm sorry, sir. This is as far as you can come."

"That's all right," Willie said with a smile. "I can kiss her good-bye here."

Willie pulled her to him and kissed her, holding the kiss long enough that some of the men waiting to board whistled and gave a few catcalls. Finally Willie released Candy.

"That should hold you until you get back," he said.

"Only if I get back soon enough," she retorted with a laugh. She climbed up the stairs then, and Willie stood on the ground and watched her ascent. At the top, just before she stepped in through the door, she turned to wave down at him, and he waved back. Then he walked back to his car and got in, ordering his driver to stay right there until the plane took off.

The door was closed and the stairs pulled away; then the engines started one by one. The plane taxied out into the darkness, and Willie lost sight of it. A few moments later he heard the engines roar and got a glimpse of the plane as it started to climb out, the wheels sucking up into the wheel wells and the four propeller disks shining silver in the ambient light. After that it slipped away into the darkness, its winking red, green, and white lights eventually lost among the stars.

Willie settled into his seat and nodded to his driver, who was watching him in the rearview mirror. "Take me back to Waddlesfoot."

*   *   *

"Willie? Willie? Wake up."

Willie opened his eyes and saw Jimmy Blake standing by his bunk. It was still dark, and Willie reached over to snap on his lamp. The clock said 3:45. He groaned.

"Jimmy, it's oh-three-forty-five. What the hell do you want?"

"I'm sorry, Willie," Jimmy said, his voice quiet and solemn, "but I thought you might want to know, seeing as you had a friend on board the flight."

"Know? Know what?"

"MAC flight forty-one. It crashed into the sea on the way back to the States. There was a Brit ship nearby, and it got to the scene."

Willie sat up abruptly. "Candy?" he asked anxiously. "Is she all right?"

Jimmy slowly shook his head. "I'm sorry, Willie. There were no survivors."

DMS STARKE, NEAR MIDWAY ISLAND

DONG! DONG! DONG! DONG! DONG! DONG! DONG!

The alarm bell sounded through every part of the ship. It was breakfast for the second watch, and the sailors jumped from the tables and headed on the run toward their assigned stations. Kevin McKay, who was eating in the petty officers' mess, managed to grab a handful of bacon and a couple of pieces of bread on his way out, which he fashioned into a sandwich as he ran.

"Now hear this! Now hear this! Enemy airplanes approaching. All hands, man your battle stations. All hands, man your battle stations. Don flak jackets, helmets, and antiflash cream," the loudspeakers blared.

Kevin was in charge of number-two and number-four tubs, which were quad-mounted, forty-millimeter antiaircraft guns.

"Let's go! Let's go! Let's go!" he shouted to the six men under him, two gunners, two loaders, and two ammunition runners.

Kevin had drilled his two crews until they were the

fastest on the ship. He did it partly out of pride and partly out of a determination to wreak as much revenge on the Japanese as he could. He intended to make the yellow bastards pay for attacking Pearl Harbor, for killing his friend, and for sinking his ship. The *Starke*, though ostensibly a minesweeper, was being used as a screening destroyer for the aircraft carrier *Yorktown*.

"No matter what's out there," Kevin had told his men when they were drilling, "it'll have to come through us. Submarines, airplanes, destroyers, battleships . . . if they're going after the *Yorktown*, they're going to have to take us on first."

"They'll wish they never tangled with the *Starke*," one of the younger men boasted proudly. The others laughed at him, but Kevin didn't discourage him. That was the kind of spirit he wanted in his men.

"All loaded, all ready," the tub-two gunner said.

"All loaded, all ready," the tub-four gunner said immediately after.

"Good men," Kevin replied. "Tubs two and four ready, sir!" he reported into the headset he was wearing.

"*Acknowledged, two and four. Aircraft will be approaching from the port side. Be ready.*"

"Okay, you guys, they're comin' from our side!" Kevin shouted down to his men. "So look alive!"

"There go our planes!" someone shouted, and Kevin looked over toward the *Yorktown* as it began launching planes. The other carriers in the task force were also launching planes, and within a few moments a large flight of dark-blue American planes were racing through the pale, rose-streaked dawn, heading west.

"Maybe they'll run into the Jap planes, and we won't even see them," Smitty, the loader, said. "Maybe—"

"Oh, shit! Oh, shit!" the gunner of tub two swore.

"What is it?" Kevin asked.

"Petty Officer McKay, I just now noticed, there ain't no tracer rounds in any of these packs!"

"Dammit, that's *your* job, Smitty!" Kevin shouted to the loader. "How come you didn't check that out?"

"I did!" Smitty insisted. "At least, I thought I did!" he added more dubiously.

"Bailey, go with him," Kevin said to the ammo bearer. "You two get down to the magazine and get some tracer packs. Then get back up here fast!"

"Okay," Bailey answered.

"*Petty Officer McKay,*" a voice came over his headset.

"Aye, sir?"

"*Where are your loader and ammo bearer?*"

"We had a slight problem with our ammo, sir," Kevin replied. "They went to correct it. They'll be right back."

"There's the Jap planes!" someone shouted, pointing to the western horizon. Kevin picked up his field glasses and looked in the direction the sailor had indicated, then saw the planes approaching. He had seen this type of plane before, yellow-green in color with longer wings and a somewhat sleeker appearance than the American planes that had taken off a few moments earlier. There were three levels of approaching Japanese aircraft. The low level was armed with torpedoes—Kevin knew that because he could see them strapped under the belly of the planes—and he assumed that the other two levels were armed with bombs, though they were still too far away from him to be sure. It was funny, Kevin thought: The American planes were out bombing the Japanese fleet while at the same time the Japanese planes were here, bombing the American fleet.

"Here come Smitty and Bailey," the gunner said. Kevin looked around in relief and saw the two men returning, one pulling and the other pushing a cart loaded with antiaircraft packs, which were the clips that the loader fed into the loading chute while the guns were actually firing.

"Get the new packs in there now!" Kevin ordered.

The Japanese airplanes came closer and closer; finally, they began peeling off for their attack. It was clear that they were only going to pay perfunctory attention to the *Starke*. Their real target was the *Yorktown*, and they went after the carrier with a vengeance.

"Commence firing!" Kevin shouted, and not only his gun mounts but every gun mount on the *Starke* as well as all the antiaircraft guns on the *Yorktown* and all the other American ships in the fleet began firing. The sound of hundreds of guns going off at once was deafening, but even above the roar of gunfire Kevin could hear the high-pitched scream of aircraft engines at full power.

The early-morning sky was alive with hundreds of flashes of light, followed immediately by puffs of black smoke. It looked as though the air were filled with countless dirty cotton balls. Kevin could also follow the long, fiery streaks of the tracer shells as they arced up toward the attacking planes. Each tracer round, Kevin knew, was separated by five more explosive shells that didn't have the marking powder that caused them to glow in flight.

Suddenly a huge ball of fire erupted on the wing of one of the attacking planes, and it spun down into the sea, sending up a shower of water. So fierce was the battle that no one even took time to cheer. They just switched their attention to another attacking plane.

One of the Japanese planes heading for the *Yorktown* passed right over the top of the *Starke*, so low that Kevin imagined that he could have thrown a rock and hit the pilot. The canopy on the Jap plane was pulled back and Kevin could see the pilot sitting there, hunched forward slightly, concentrating on the task before him. For a fleeting moment Kevin felt a strange but very strong sense of admiration for that Japanese pilot, respecting a man who could fly his craft through such devastating antiaircraft fire and keep his concentration on his mission. The Japanese plane was gone in a moment, and then Kevin saw the torpedo fall toward the water, hit with a splash, and start toward the *Yorktown*, leaving a long, white streak on the water, pointing toward its target like an arrow painted on the surface of the sea.

When the torpedo hit on the *Yorktown*'s port side, the explosion was heavy enough for Kevin to hear, even above all the other noise.

"Shit!" he shouted. "The carrier's been hit!"

He turned back to watch the ongoing action with the swarming Japanese planes. Another attacking plane was hit, then another, and another still. At one instant he counted four Japanese planes falling at the same time, yet the others continued to press on with their attack. The *Yorktown* took another torpedo hit, and then a bomb plunged down through the flight deck and exploded somewhere deep inside. The Japanese planes started back, but by now the *Yorktown* was burning fiercely and listing severely. The *Enterprise* had also been hit, as had several smaller ships. And though Kevin hadn't realized it during the heat of battle, the *Starke* was one of those damaged, having taken a couple of hits near the fantail. Kevin heard the PA system calling for all fire fighters to lay aft. But a quick glance back at the damage convinced him that the *Starke* was in no danger of going down.

Kevin took off his helmet and ran his hand through his sweaty red hair, then leaned his head back to get a breath of fresh air. He felt his knee shaking, and he knew that he couldn't stop it, so he hoped nobody noticed. After a moment or two he looked down at his crew.

"Son of a bitch," he said, grinning. "This is what it's all about. You know what I mean?"

WITH THE JAPANESE SQUADRON

It was a torpedo from Hiroshi Amano's plane, followed by a torpedo from the plane just behind him, that did the most serious damage to the *Yorktown*. As Hiroshi pulled out of his torpedo run, he saw violent explosions on board the carrier, and he watched in fascination as the shock waves made ripples on the surface of the sea. Oil and fuel poured out of the ship and ignited on the water, and the ship began an immediate list.

Hiroshi radioed back to the *Hiryu*, "Enemy carrier burning."

After the successful strike on the *Yorktown*, Hiroshi led the remaining planes, less than ten of the thirty-four that had started out, back to the *Hiryu*.

Hiroshi had no sooner landed on the carrier when he ordered the planes refueled so that they could return and destroy the American carrier *Enterprise*, which was also badly damaged, though not as severely as the *Yorktown*. One by one the planes landed, and the pilots hopped out to join Hiroshi, waiting for their planes to be refitted.

He and his fellow pilots were waiting on the deck of the *Hiryu*, well out of the way of the bustling mechanics, when suddenly twenty-four American dive-bombers attacked the Japanese fleet. With gasoline, torpedoes, and bombs stacked on deck for the refueling and rearming operations, Hiroshi's carrier was a prime target.

Four bombs hit the *Hiryu*, and they set off the planes parked on the flight deck. The forward third of the flight deck became a solid wall of flame, and as the American bombers returned to the *Enterprise*, Hiroshi and the other pilots could only stand impotently on the deck of the burning ship and watch. There were no flyable Japanese planes left, and no way to launch them if there had been. Their grand scheme to capture Midway had been foiled.

For the rest of the day and far into the night, the *Hiryu* burned fiercely despite the best efforts of the crew to save it. Finally, just before midnight, an explosion ripped out her insides, killing hundreds more in the blast. Captain Tomeo Kaku instructed his officers that the ship would be abandoned.

For the attack on Midway, Admiral Yamaguchi had made the *Hiryu* his flagship. Now he addressed the crew just before the order to abandon ship was given.

"I have given orders for the fleet to turn back. I alone am to blame for our grievous losses," he said. "I alone am to blame for our defeat here. I shall stay aboard. I am ordering the rest of you to abandon this ship and find another so that you may fight again for the emperor."

"Admiral, I shall stay with you," Captain Kaku said quickly.

"Of course," Yamaguchi said. He saw Hiroshi and motioned him over. "You led your men bravely," he said, "and you struck a blow for the Empire by attacking the American carriers. Go now to Admiral Yamamoto. Serve him as you have served me. Take him this hat as a token from me."

Admiral Yamaguchi handed his black cap to Hiroshi, who bowed and received it solemnly. "I will do as you ask, Admiral," Hiroshi said.

"Good, good," Yamaguchi replied. He turned toward Captain Kaku. "Isn't the moon beautiful tonight? Come, let us enjoy it together."

The general alarm to abandon ship was sounded, and the remaining crewmen jumped into the cold sea. Admiral

Yamaguchi and Captain Kaku died with the ship, but Hiroshi and eight hundred others survived. Hiroshi, who was fished out of the water by one of the screening destroyers, got some compensation the next morning, when he received the report that the badly damaged *Yorktown* had indeed gone down. An American carrier was lost—but, oh, at what a cost.

CHAPTER FOURTEEN

JULY 1942, VIENNA, AUSTRIA

Several dozen flags, bloodred with white-encircled black swastikas, floated from cables suspended over the station platform, lifted by heat waves shimmering up from the ground. Beneath the Nazi banners more than three thousand people milled about in increasing agony. It was now three o'clock in the afternoon, and they had been standing in the same place for twelve hours, having arrived, as ordered, at three o'clock that morning.

They were there, according to the notices they had received, to be deported. The first thing everyone had had to do upon arrival at the depot was report to one of the several reception tables the Nazis had set up. There, after filling out a number of official forms, they had been given stamped boarding passes for a train that would deliver them to their new places of residence.

Loudspeakers had been erected at all four corners of the platform so that the Germans could announce each train as it was formed. Between these announcements the

Germans played a prerecorded message over and over again:

"*Attention, do not lose your boarding pass. You will not be allowed on the train without a boarding pass.*

"*Attention, do not lose your boarding pass. You will not be allowed on the train without a boarding pass.*"

The deportees had been told to bring only what they could carry, and suitcases, backpacks, even cardboard boxes sat beside them on the hot pavement. In a pathetic effort to bring more than their luggage would hold, many were wearing extra layers of clothes, including sweaters and overcoats, despite the fact that it was a sweltering ninety degrees.

Only one water faucet was working, and a long line of people waited to use it. An armed guard stood by the faucet, keeping a stern-faced lookout for anyone who might try to fill a bucket or a bottle or even a cup to take with them. The orders were that anyone who wanted a drink had to stand in line for it, no exceptions, no matter how young or old or sick they might be.

David Gelbman had at least anticipated the water problem, and before he and his family had left their house that morning (though officially it was no longer their house, having been confiscated by the government to pay the "special assessment taxes" levied against all Jews), he had filled a tea kettle. Nevertheless, even that had to be rationed, so they drank from it very sparingly.

The deportation order hadn't come as much of a surprise to David, since the situation had continued to deteriorate for all Jews not only in Vienna, but everywhere they were under German control. In the early days of National Socialist Party control David had managed to convince himself that their anti-Semitism was merely a passing stage —the Nazis were antagonistic toward the Jews for political reasons, he had told himself, and once the Nazis had consolidated their power, the persecution would ease up. When that didn't happen, he then had convinced himself that his status as an American citizen would, in the final analysis, be his and his family's saving grace. But now Germany was at war with America, so even that questionable bit of logic was invalid. After those various stages of denial,

David had finally come to grips with the fact that no matter what kind of face he tried to put on it, he was a Jew in a Nazi state—with all that that implied.

At first singly, then a few at a time, the Jews in Vienna began disappearing. Everyone knew, or thought they knew, what was going on, but no one was in a position to do anything about it. Instead, everyone moved about on cat's feet, struggling to stay alive, cringing with fear at the sight of a Mercedes loaded with black-uniformed SS men. The Jews of Vienna held their collective breath as they awaited whatever cataclysmic event might be in their future.

When orders came down that all remaining Jews were to report to the depot for "resettlement," it was almost a relief. "What could be better?" everyone asked. "If they don't want us here, then it's only reasonable that we resettle somewhere else, where we're surrounded by our own kind."

That sense of relief was still felt by all those now waiting for their train to be called, even though they were by now drenched in sweat and dizzy from heat and thirst on this long and sweltering departure day.

Simon Blumberg, who had come to the depot with the Gelbmans, had gone off somewhere at about ten o'clock that morning, and Anna and Miriam were increasingly anxious about him.

"Don't worry about Simon," David said. "He's very resourceful."

"He also has only one leg," Anna reminded him. "If the Nazis see him somewhere where he shouldn't be, he can't run; he won't be able to get away from them. I don't care what you say, I'm worried about him."

David sighed. "Do you want me to go look for him?"

"Attention, do not lose your boarding pass. You will not be allowed on the train without a boarding pass."

"No!" Anna said quickly. "No, you mustn't do that."

David looked at his wife, and for a moment he didn't see the sallow, hollow-cheeked, sunken-eyed woman who had grown old before her time. Instead, he saw the exotic, olive-skinned, sloe-eyed beauty he had fallen in love with when first he had met her, nearly forty years before. He put his hand gently to her cheek.

"Anna, I'm sorry," he said. "I should have taken you back to America long ago."

"No," Anna said, shaking her head. "It isn't your fault. I didn't want to go, remember?"

"I should have made you go."

Anna smiled. "David, have you ever been able to make me do anything?"

David chuckled. "Only what you wanted to do anyway."

"You see, Miriam," Anna said to her daughter. "If you have the right husband, you don't have to give anything up, even when you get married. So be like me. Choose the right husband."

"Yes, Mama," Miriam said, smiling at her parents. She was now thirty, and she had been a librarian before the Nazis made such employment unlawful for Jews. Until the lack of food and other deprivations began working their effects, she had been a very pretty woman, and though over the years she had caught the eye of many men, she had discouraged them all.

At one time Anna had been so worried about the fact that Miriam wasn't married that she wanted to hire a marriage broker. But Miriam had absolutely refused. She didn't want to get married, she always said, because she wasn't prepared to bring a baby into this world. And what was the point of getting married if not to have children?

"Oh, look," Miriam said now, relief in her voice. "There's Simon."

Turning, David saw Simon coming toward them, maneuvering deftly and swiftly through the crowd, even though he walked with the awkward gait imposed by an artificial leg. Simon's mother had been David's aunt, and his father had been Anna's uncle, making him a first cousin to each of them.

"Attention, do not lose your boarding pass. You will not be allowed on the train without a boarding pass."

"Simon, where were you?" Anna asked anxiously when he came up to them.

"I'm sorry if I worried you," he replied. "That wasn't my intention." Reaching into his pocket, he took out three hard rolls and gave one to each of them.

"My God! Where did you get these?" David asked.

"Don't ask, just eat."

"Maybe we should save them until later," Anna suggested. "We might need them more later."

"You *will* need them more later," Simon agreed, "but eat them now. If you try to save them, the Nazis will take them away from you."

"He's right, Anna," David said, taking a ravenous bite. "Besides, I'm starving. I can't wait."

"Oh, it is so good," Anna said, eating her own roll as voraciously as David was eating his.

Miriam began eating her roll, too, though she was cognizant of the hungry-eyed, envious glances of those around her.

"I was afraid they would call our boarding numbers before you got back," Anna said, speaking with her mouth full. A large crumb fell onto her chin and she stopped it with her finger and poked it back into her mouth. "If you missed the train and we got separated, there's no telling when we might see each other again."

"Let us speak English," Simon said in a low voice. "It will lessen the chance of being overheard."

"All right," David said, switching to his native language. "But what is it you don't want overheard?"

"I'm not getting on the train," Simon informed them.

"Attention, do not lose your boarding pass. You will not be allowed on the train without a boarding pass."

"What? What are you talking about?" Anna asked. "Of course you are getting on the train."

"No, I'm not," Simon replied. "It is not work camps we are being sent to. It is death camps. The Nazis are killing all the Jews."

"Killing all the Jews?" David echoed. "Oh, that's not possible. Why would they kill all the Jews?"

"Why would they kill us? Why would the Nazis do *anything?*" Simon asked bitterly.

"Papa," Miriam said, touching her father's shoulder, "Papa, can it be true? I'm very frightened."

"Don't be frightened," David said. "Simon, conditions are bad enough without you spreading even more fear," he chided.

"I am not spreading fear, David, I am spreading truth. I am telling you, I was down there a short time ago, watching the Jews who have already been shipped out. There are two trains, and as the stream of people walked toward the trains, they were divided into two branches. Some went to the left, some went to the right. Some went to labor, some went to die."

"But which is which?" Anna asked.

"I don't know which is which," Simon admitted. "That's why I'm not going to get on either one of them." He thumped on his wooden leg. "Besides, can you see the Nazis keeping me alive with only one leg?"

"But you lost that leg fighting for them," Anna said.

"No," Simon corrected, "I lost this leg fighting for Germany, not for the Nazis."

"But that's the same thing."

"It wasn't then," Simon insisted.

"Simon, are the Nazis telling the people which train to board?" David asked.

"No. They're letting people decide for themselves."

"Well, there you go. If they're letting people make their own choice, then you must be wrong."

"No, I'm not wrong," Simon said. He laughed bitterly. "Do you want to know what I think? I think they are enjoying the fact that those who go to die are choosing their own destiny."

"*Attention, do not lose your boarding pass. You will not be allowed on the train without a boarding pass.*"

They were all silent for a long moment; then finally David spoke. "Maybe you're right. God knows you were right about Hitler all along."

"David, what should we do?" Anna asked, clutching at her husband's arm.

"If we were younger—" David stopped and shook his head. Inexplicably, he smiled. "And if a frog had wings, he wouldn't bump his ass every time he hops."

"What?" Anna asked.

"Never mind. It's an old Americanism," David said. "Simon, are you seriously going to try and get away?"

"Yes."

"How are you going to do that with only one leg?"

"I have a spare," Simon said resolutely.

"I want you to take Miriam with you," David said.

"Papa, no! I want to go with you and Mama."

"Don't be foolish, girl," David said. "Don't you realize that once we leave here . . . well, even if we survive, we'll be separated. You'll go one way, Anna will go another, and I'll go another."

"Oh, David, no!" Anna gasped, and her eyes suddenly filled with tears.

"I'm sorry, Anna," David said, putting his arm around her, "but we need to face this now and draw whatever comfort there is to be drawn from these last few minutes together."

"Your father is right, Miriam," Simon said quietly. "By nightfall you'd be separated from them anyway. Do you want to come with me?"

"It will be dangerous for her, won't it?" Anna asked.

"My dear Cousin Anna," Simon said solicitously, "don't you understand? There is very little chance *any* of us will survive this." He looked at Miriam. "If you want to go with me, Miriam, I will take you. If you want to stay, I will understand."

"Go with him, child," David urged.

Miriam, her eyes glistening, started to embrace her mother, but Simon stopped her.

"No!" he hissed. "Don't make any outward sign that you are parting."

"You mean I can't even kiss them good-bye?"

"No."

"He is right, Miriam," David said.

"But, Papa . . . "

"Don't cry," David said through clenched teeth. "Do you hear me, girl? You must not cry!"

Attention, do not lose your boarding pass. You will not be allowed on the train without a boarding pass.

Miriam bit her lip and blinked several times. "I won't cry," she said in a small voice.

"Simon," Anna said, forcing a smile, "Simon, I look at you, and do you know what I see? I see the boy who, as my oldest male relative, spoke for me at my wedding so long ago. And I see the fine man you have become. And I thank

God that, in His goodness, He let you be a part of our family."

David felt Anna's hand reaching for his and he let her take it, then squeeze it. She squeezed it very hard, and he knew that it was a physical indication of the emotional effort it took to hold back her tears. She squeezed his hand so hard that it actually hurt him, and yet that squeeze was as necessary for him as it was for her and was as meaningful as the tenderest embrace.

"Mama . . . ?" Miriam's voice was like that of a very young child.

"I'm thirsty," Simon interjected loudly, once again speaking in German. "Come, Miriam, let us go stand in line for some water."

"I don't—"

"Go with him, girl," David hissed.

Miriam understood then what Simon was actually saying. It was time for them to go.

"Yes, Papa," she replied.

"Attention, do not lose your boarding pass. You will not be allowed on the train without a boarding pass."

David and Anna stood close together, watching their cousin and their daughter move through the crowd toward the water faucet. David felt as if a vise had clamped down on his heart and as if two needles were stabbing his eyes. He prayed hard that he could hold back the tears, for he feared that if one of the guards saw Simon and Miriam walking away and saw him crying, they might somehow figure out what was going on—as improbable as that was in such a sea of doleful humanity.

"Attention, all persons with boarding passes beginning with the number six, report to the end of the platform."

"Oh, David," Anna said, flinching. "Number six! That's us!"

David reached down to pick up their bundle. "Come," he said.

They moved through the hundreds of people still waiting for their own number to be called until they reached another group whose boarding passes, like theirs, started with the number six. Here, as everywhere, there were dozens of armed guards. As the people queued up, they shuffled by one of the guards, who was examining their boarding passes. The guard turned several people back, and they began protesting immediately that a mistake had been made, that the receptionist had given two people in the same family different boarding pass numbers.

"Surely this is just a simple mistake that can quite easily be cleared up," they complained.

"Get back!" the guards ordered, enforcing their orders by shoving them none too gently with their rifles held high.

"Thank God," Anna breathed quietly. "At least our numbers are the same."

As the Gelbmans approached the end of the platform they saw that there were, indeed, two trains waiting, one on a track to the left, the other on a track to the right. The crowd became silent at that point. Here was a decision to make. What did it mean? Which was the right way for them to go?

At the spot where the decision was to be made, a handful of German guards stood watching impassively, their bodies motionless, their faces expressionless. They were like the point of a plowshare, breaking the flow into two streams, one to the left, one to the right.

"At least for this while longer," David said, "we will be together. The guards are not interfering in the choice the people make."

"But which choice?" Anna asked urgently.

"To the left," David said.

They began drifting toward the left, but just before they got there, Anna suddenly pulled David to the right. "No!" she said. "This way!"

David didn't question her decision. Instead he went with her, changing direction so swiftly and so smoothly that no one even noticed.

A moment later they were already beyond the wedge, the decision, an irrevocable one, having been made.

"Why did you want us to change?" David asked quietly.

"Did you not see the face of the German standing on the left side?" Anna asked.

"No."

"He was looking with pity at the people who were

getting on that train. He knew where they were going, and when I saw his face, I knew, too."

Ahead of them were more guards, this time forming a double line toward the open doors of a cattle car. Many of them had dogs that they held on a tight leash. The dogs were snarling and snapping at the line of Jews.

"Into the car!" one of the guards bellowed. "*Schnell, schnell!* Into the car!"

"Surely you don't mean for all of us to get in that one car?" a man objected.

The guard nearest the man hit him with a policeman's billy club, and he went down with blood streaming from his forehead. Once the man was down, the guards began kicking him—until he was absolutely motionless.

"Into the car!" one of the guards shouted again. "Quickly, quickly! Into the car!"

This time everyone rushed toward the car, running up the cattle ramp that led into it. An old woman slipped and fell and someone stooped over to pick her up. That caused a temporary blockage in the flow of people, so a couple of the guards nearest the old woman and her would-be rescuer dragged them both off the ramp and onto the rocky ground beside the track. That drew several more guards, and they began kicking and stomping the hapless pair until they, like the man who had earlier complained, were bloody . . . and still.

As David and Anna started up the ramp, Anna slipped, and David reached out and grabbed her, managing to save her from falling at the last minute. Even that slightest hesitation caused them to be shoved from behind by others who were themselves being prodded into the car by guards with long poles. Finally they were inside the car, and David almost gagged at the smell. It reeked of vomit, feces, urine, body odor, and other smells that were as bad or worse, though unidentifiable. They were shoved by the crowd into one corner, then pushed hard against the slats. A man standing right next to them stuck his hand through the space between the slats in order to hold himself up. There was a loud, thumping noise against the side of the car, and the man let out a yelp of pain and drew back mangled fingers. Through the space between the slats David could see that one of the soldiers had hit the man's hand with the butt of his rifle.

"Hands inside!" the guard shouted. "Keep your hands inside!"

David could see the far side of the depot through the slats of the cattle car, and he watched a truck just pulling away. The back of the truck was covered with a canvas, but a corner of the flap was pulled to one side. Protruding from that corner was a strong pair of arms, and those arms were pulling onto the truck a lithe, beautiful, dark-haired woman.

"Anna," David said.

"What?" Anna's voice was strained as she fought hard to be brave.

"Anna, she made it," David said quietly.

"What?"

"She made it," David said again.

"She made it?"

"Yes. I saw them."

"Oh, thank God!" Anna leaned into her husband, and he managed to wrap his arms around her. When she looked up at him her eyes were filled with tears, but this time they were tears of happiness. "I don't care now," she said. "I don't care what happens to me."

CHAPTER FIFTEEN

Private First Class—soon to be Aviation Cadet—Travis Jackson settled into a chair in Professor Loomis Booker's living room. As soon as he sat down, young Deon Booker climbed up onto his lap.

"Grandpa, Deon is sitting in Travis's lap," seven-year-old Artemus said.

"He said I could!" his nearly six-year-old brother argued.

"He was just being nice," Artemus said.

"No he wasn't!"

"Are you saying he isn't nice? Grandpa! Deon said Travis isn't nice."

Loomis Booker, who was on the other side of the room tuning the radio, turned back toward his grandchildren. The boys had been his responsibility since their parents had been killed in a car wreck five years earlier. Dr. Andrew Booker, the boys' father and Loomis's son, had been on his way to Washington to receive an award for his role in developing blood plasma when the accident occurred. Ironically, Andrew's life might have been saved had the very plasma he helped develop been made available to him. But the allocation of blood plasma was strictly by race, and the available plasma had been reserved for whites. Dr. Andrew Booker had been black.

"I thought you boys wanted to listen to Fibber McGee and Molly," Loomis said.

"We do," they answered in unison.

"Well, then sit there quietly and listen."

"But Deon—"

"If Deon starts bothering Travis, I'm sure Travis is big enough to take care of it."

"I don't mind Deon sitting here," Travis said. "He isn't bothering me."

"See!" Deon said, sticking his tongue out at Artemus.

"You're just a baby," Artemus grumbled.

"Shhh! Be quiet and listen," Loomis said as the tubes warmed up enough for the radio to come on. "Here it is." Loomis walked over to sit on the couch beside his wife, Della. He reached over and took Della's hand as they listened to McGee's voice over the radio.

"So, the boys down at the lodge don't think I can bowl, huh? Well, I'll show them. It just so happens that I've got a bowling trophy."

"You have a bowling trophy?"

"Of course I do."

"What trophy?"

"Why, you know what trophy, Molly. It's the trophy I won over in Carterville three years ago. Surely you remember. They had a ceremony and everything."

"McGee, you won that trophy in a pie-eating contest."

"Yes, but the pie-eating contest was for bowlers only. It was held in a bowling alley."

"That was only because it was raining, and the bowling alley was the closest building they could hold the contest in."

"I don't care. It was a trophy, and I won it in a bowling alley. Wait a minute, I'll get it out and show you. It's right here in the front closet."

"McGee, no! Not the front closet!"

"Not the front closet!" Artemus echoed, and he and Deon put their hands to their ears and squealed with laughter in anticipation.

Through the radio came the sound of a door opening, then a muffled shout of alarm, followed by a rolling, crashing, tumbling, clanking cacophony of noise as McGee's closet spilled everything onto the floor.

The radio audience howled with laughter, joined by the laughter of the five people sitting in the Booker living room.

When the radio show finally ended, a golden-voiced announcer came on with a commercial message:

"Ladies, what kind of breakfast did you feed your family this morning? With the wartime demand for high-energy nourishment, smart wives and mothers everywhere are serving a delicious bowl of Corn Toasties.

"Packed with energy and vitamins, this tasty cereal is helping to win the war by providing the energy needed by the men and women who work in our nation's factories and by the boys and girls who are studying in school today so that they may be the leaders of tomorrow. Yes, and Corn Toasties are enjoyed by our boys in uniform as well. Testimonial letters arrive in the Canfield-Puritex offices daily, telling us how much our soldiers, sailors, and marines love Corn Toasties."

"What about the Air Corps?" Artemus added. "He didn't say anything about the Air Corps. Travis, do you like Corn Toasties?"

Travis laughed. "I'd rather have grits with a couple of eggs," he said.

"When do you start your actual flight training?" Loomis asked.

"I report to Tuskegee next week. I expect we'll start our flight training soon after. Professor Booker, is it true you're against a colored flying squadron?"

"Yes," Loomis replied. "It's true."

"But why, Professor? Don't you think colored men can fly as well as white men?"

"Of course I do," Loomis said. "That has nothing at all to do with it."

"Well, why, then?"

"If Negroes are going to fight for America, let them fight right alongside the white men. If Negroes are going to be aviators, let them fly right alongside white men. Why must there be two armies and two air corps? There is only one America."

"That's the way it's always been," Travis said, shrugging.

"That doesn't mean it's the way it always *has* to be. Or the way it *should* be."

"I can't be bothered with thinking about things like that," Travis said. "I've got enough to worry about living my own life without trying to change the world."

"That's why God, in His wisdom, put people on earth who *would* change the world."

"I'm going to change the world," Deon said.

Loomis chuckled. "Maybe you will."

"My daddy changed the world," Deon said proudly.

"Yes, he did," Loomis agreed. "Over the years there will be hundreds of thousands, possibly millions of lives saved as a result of your daddy's work."

"I sure do wish Brother Doctor—as we folks down in Delta called Dr. Booker—were still alive," Travis said.

Loomis shook his head sadly. "There isn't a day that goes by that I don't wish he and LaTonya both were still alive. I miss my son." He squeezed Della's hand. "My wife misses her daughter. And these little ones need their parents. I'm too old to give them the kind of attention they deserve."

"You're not old, Professor. You're just now coming ripe," Travis retorted.

Loomis laughed. "Maybe. But you know what happens to fruit once it gets *over*ripe. Anyway, I'm glad that my son made such a favorable impression during his time in Delta."

"Yes, sir. And not just on the colored folks. The white people of Delta thought he was a fine man, too. Everyone down there misses him, but when you get right down to it, Pop misses him the most."

Travis's father was Professor Henry Jackson, principal of Delta's colored school and the man primarily responsible for recruiting Andrew Booker away from Boston and a promising career in medical research to a small Mississippi town to act as general practitioner to the Negro community.

"I wonder if Brother Doctor would be proud of me, or would he be like you and think I was doing the wrong thing?" Travis asked.

Loomis reached over to put his hand on the young soldier's shoulder. "Hold on there, son, don't think I'm not proud of you," he insisted. "My condemnation is of the idea of establishing a separate colored flying corps. It in no way lessens my respect and admiration for you and the other brave young men of color who are going to join its ranks. No, indeed, I'm very proud of you, son."

Travis looked down at his lap. "Thank you. That means more to me than you'll ever know. If there's one person in this whole world my pop respects more than he respected Brother Doctor, it's you, Professor Booker."

Della chuckled and patted her husband's hand. "Travis, you're going to give this man even more of a swelled head than he already has."

Loomis laughed. "That isn't possible as long as I've got you around to deflate me, woman." He glanced over at his grandchildren, who were intently following the conversation. "And you two boys, don't you think it's about time you went off to bed?"

"Grandpa, we want to stay up and listen to Travis tell stories about flying."

Travis smiled. "I hate to disappoint you boys," he said, "but I don't have any stories to tell. The truth is, I've never even been in an airplane yet."

"Come along, you two," Della said, getting up from the couch and holding her hand out toward the boys. "Grandma will get you all tucked in."

As the two youngsters scurried off after their grandmother, Travis said, "They're quite a pair."

"Yes," Loomis agreed. He sighed. "Well, they're Andy's only legacy, so I'm doing my best to bring them up the way I think he would have wanted." He looked at the clock. "It's about time for the news," he noted, getting up and going over to fiddle with the radio dial.

"Professor Booker, Pop says you worked with General Eisenhower during the First World War. Is that true?"

"In a manner of speaking," Loomis replied over his shoulder. "We both worked in the same office, though we didn't have the same job."

"Do you think if you'd stayed in the Army, you'd be a general today?"

Loomis shrugged. "I don't know. I strongly doubt it."

"But there is a colored general, you know. Benjamin Davis," Travis pointed out. "His son is in the Army, too. He's a captain, and he's the chief of our flying school," he added.

"Yes, I've met General Davis, and I know of his son. They're fine men. Ah, here's the news," he said. He sat back down to listen.

"The Germans are said to have pierced the Russian defenses in northwestern Stalingrad. Meanwhile, heavy fighting is also reported in the Caucasus. German troops are advancing along the coastal highway from Novorossijsk.

"From London comes word that the British Royal Air Force has conducted a massive and very successful raid against the German city of Munich. Radio correspondent Floyd Stoner went along on that raid and recorded the sounds and his own thoughts by means of a wire recorder. Here is that transcription—"

For just a moment Loomis thought something was wrong with the radio because of the noise. Then he realized that what he was hearing was the sound of airplane engines. After a few seconds of such sound, Floyd Stoner's voice, breathless, excited, and noticeably tinged with fear, came over the airwaves.

"I don't know if you can hear that or not . . . that sort of low, thumping sound. That's antiaircraft shells exploding nearby. Actually, we can see them more than we can hear them, for when they go off, they light up the sky in a brilliant flash of light. Sitting here in my vantage point I can look out through the glass blister of the gun turret and see the antiaircraft shells winking all around me, like hundreds of fireflies on a summer's night."

There was one particularly loud, heavy-sounding thump, followed by a rattling sound, then the whistle of air.

"Whew! Did you hear that? That was a really close one, and the sound that seemed like hail was bits and pieces of shrapnel striking the skin of our airship. No one was hurt —at least, I don't think anyone was—but you can well see how they could be, for it's just like spraying the plane with machine-gun bullets.

"And now in the sky before us I can see searchlight beams, hundreds of them, stretching their long, bright fingers upward, sweeping back and forth as they attempt to trap a hapless victim in their beams. It's my fervent prayer that they don't find this plane, for when the spotlights have you in their grip, you're an easy target for the gunners below.

"Wait a minute; the pilot is talking to the crew now. I'm going to put the earphone next to the microphone here, in the hopes you can hear what's going on."

The next voice was completely different, not only because of its British accent, but because it was almost maddeningly calm in the midst of all the danger and fright described and recorded by Floyd Stoner.

"Pilot to crew, pilot to crew, look lively, lads. We're beginning our bomb run now."

"Bombardier to pilot. Hold her steady. Steady. Bomb bay doors open."

"Pilot to bombardier. Bomb bay doors open."

"Bombardier to pilot. Nearly ready now, beginning the countdown. Five, four, three, two, one. Bombs away."

"Pilot to crew. Right, there you go. Our bombs are gone now. Good job, lads. Now we can all run away bravely."

Floyd Stoner's exhilarated voice came back on. "This is Floyd Stoner, speaking to you from on board an RAF Lancaster bomber, somewhere over Germany."

Loomis walked back over to the radio and turned it off.

"Whew, that was quite a report, wasn't it? I mean, it put us right in the airplane with them."

"Yes, sir, it was," Travis agreed. "It was very exciting."

"Such things as radio, wire recorders, and movies certainly bring war home to the average person," Loomis said. He thought about it for a moment and shook his head.

"Maybe the more people get a good, close look at it, they'll realize how horrible war really is. Who knows? Someday they might even get around to outlawing it."

Travis laughed.

"What's so funny?"

"What you said," Travis replied. "I mean about outlawing war, like it's a crime or something."

"It *is* a crime. It's the worst crime of all."

"It's also very exciting," Travis insisted. He pointed to the radio. "You have to admit, Professor, you were listening to that as intently as I was."

"Yes, I was," Loomis agreed. "It's that selfsame attractivness that makes war such a hideous crime. And here you are, going off to do the very thing we were just listening to."

"Not exactly," Travis said. "Those people were on a bomber. I don't want to be on a bomber . . . that would be like driving a truck." He smirked and pointed to himself with his thumb. "I'm going to fly *fighter* planes. I'm going to shoot down a hundred Nazis."

HOLLYWOOD

Dumplin's was a very nice restaurant, with good food, excellent wine, and courteous service. That alone would have made it attractive to the "Who's Who" of Hollywood, despite its pricey menu. But one other thing made Dumplin's a favorite of many of the stars.

Kathy York, the attractive brunette who owned the place, had discovered something that eluded all the other preferred spots in Hollywood. Other restaurants and clubs thrived on the publicity they received by being visited by the stars, making sure their establishments were mentioned in all the gossip columns, on the order of: "The Coconut Grove was jumping last night, as witness the attendance of Gary Cooper, Bette Davis, and Joan Crawford. . . . " The idea, of course, was to entice the average person into the restaurant by suggesting that they might actually see a movie star.

Dumplin's didn't do that. Most of the time the stars

could come in, have a nice meal, and leave with few other customers even being aware of their presence, because Kathy, recognizing an occasional need for privacy, *protected* the stars who visited her establishment. There was a second, unmarked entrance to her café, and she kept several tables reserved in the darker, out-of-the-way corners of the dining room. Often two parties of movie stars would be dining at Dumplin's on the same evening, unaware of the other party's presence.

Dumplin's was a particular favorite of Demaris Hunter's, and that evening she was there with Guy Colby. They were sitting across from each other at one of the small, secluded tables, a single candle lighting the space between them.

"When will you be leaving for Russia?" Demaris asked, spearing her spinach salad. "Um, are you going to eat that roll?"

"I've got a couple more weeks left," Guy said, handing his roll to Demaris. "There's still a lot of red tape to be cleared up in Washington."

"What's the holdup?" Demaris asked, spreading a generous supply of butter on the roll. "You already have the funding, don't you?"

"Oh, yes, the Russian government—or I guess I should say the Soviet government—is taking care of that. They've promised me all the money, equipment, transportation, and time I need to make the movie. But, of course, why wouldn't they? It's pure propaganda."

"What's the name of it again? *Flags over the Fatherland?*"

Guy laughed. "Watch your language, woman. Don't you know that 'fatherland' is strictly German? We have to think Russian for this picture . . . Mother Russia. And don't forget that the Communists have to get in a plug as well. So, it's *Red Banners over Mother Russia.*"

"Is it fiction or a documentary?" Demaris asked. The waiter appeared with their main course, and no sooner had the man set down the plate than Demaris tackled it, cutting a large chunk of the meat.

"Heavens, child, haven't you eaten today? I've never seen you attack your food with such gusto."

Demaris sniggered. "I know, isn't it awful? Oh, you've got sour cream on your baked potato, so can I have your extra butter?"

Guy passed the butter to her. "Yes, and to answer your nonfood question, it's sort of a cross between fiction and documentary. The idea is to follow two fictional characters, Comrades Ivan and Olga, in their heroic struggle against the invaders."

"Any hot scenes between Ivan and Olga?" Demaris quipped.

Guy chuckled. "About as hot as you can get with both of them wearing fur parkas." He sighed. "Of course, that all has to do with getting our government's approval for me to make the film."

"Why all the red tape?"

"I think the U.S. government still doesn't trust the Communists," Guy replied. "I don't know why. I mean, we *are* allies now, and the real enemies are the Nazis."

"Maybe they're afraid you'll turn Communist," Demaris suggested.

"Well, they don't have much worry there. Oh, I flirted with it for a while, but I gave it up."

Demaris looked up from her plate in surprise. "You were a Communist?"

"In a manner of speaking, I suppose I was," Guy said. "I joined a group in the early twenties, before I left New York. I was young and idealistic, and the basic premise of Communism—'from each according to his ability, to each according to his need'—made sense to me. But it didn't take long before I realized that it was as impossible a dream as the utopian society. I paid the first year's dues, but I never renewed."

"I never knew that," Demaris said.

"There's no reason you should. I never told anybody. Besides, who wants to go around bragging about some foolish folly of youth? Although if I thought it would speed up the process of getting approval for this film project I'm going to do for the Russians, I'd write a letter to the State Department, telling them all about it."

"No," Demaris said, "I wouldn't do that if I were you."

Guy chuckled again. "Don't worry. I've got better sense than that."

Demaris suddenly put down her fork and looked intently at Guy. "Before you leave for Russia, I have a proposal for you."

"What sort of proposal?"

"A *proposal* proposal."

Guy just stared at Demaris, his face registering complete confusion.

She laughed. "You don't know what I'm talking about, do you?"

"I'm afraid not."

"I'm asking you to marry me."

Guy gasped and dropped his fork. It clanked loudly against the plate, causing some of the diners at the closer tables to look over curiously. One of the diners briefly eyed Demaris and then whispered across the table to her companion, but the people who patronized Dumplin's were well schooled in appropriate behavior, so they refrained from staring at the star.

"Demaris, are you joking with me?" Guy asked in a choked voice. "Because if you are, please don't. You know how I feel about you . . . how I've felt about you virtually from the very first day I meet you, when you so audaciously parachuted down onto my set—the would-be starlet looking for publicity."

"Yes, I know," Demaris replied in a small voice. "That's why I've come to you to help me out of my . . . dilemma. Believe me, Guy, this is no joke. I want you to marry me. I *need* you to marry me."

"Oh," Guy said. For a long moment he just stared at her across the table in silence.

Unable to stand up to his stare, Demaris put her fork down and her elbow on the table, then rested her forehead against her hand. A choking sob escaped her throat, and a couple of tears began sliding down her face. One of them caught a glow from the candle flame, and it flashed gold against her cheek.

"That explains the strange eating behavior," Guy said. "You're pregnant, aren't you?"

"Yes," Demaris answered in a pained voice.

"Who's the father?"

"I'm not sure."

"You're not *sure*?"

"Well, it isn't some stranger off the street, if that's what you're thinking," Demaris retorted. "I know approximately who it might be—I just don't know for certain."

"Are they married?"

"One of them is."

"Why don't you go to the other one? Or should I say *one* of the other ones?"

"I can't do that. I *won't* do that," Demaris said. "I couldn't marry anyone unless I genuinely felt something for him. Right now you're the only one in my life who fits that description."

"I see," Guy said without further comment.

"I can't let the baby be born out of wedlock," Demaris went on. "The scandal would ruin my career."

"There is an alternative," Guy suggested.

"Abortion?" Demaris asked weakly. "Guy, are you saying I should get an abortion?"

"It's been done before."

"Yes, of course it has. We've all heard about those abortion mills—crooked doctors who charge outrageous prices to operate on you in sleazy hotel rooms. Infections, diseases, uncontrolled bleeding. No, thank you. Never mind, Guy. If you don't want to marry me—"

"Wait a minute. Hold on there," he said quickly. "I didn't say I didn't want to marry you, did I?"

"No, but you didn't say you did."

Guy reached across the table and took Demaris's hands in his. "Dearest girl, this has been a dream of mine forever. I love you as I have never loved another woman. And I would marry you under any conditions you care to name. Only I want you to be *sure* that it's what you want. I couldn't bear to think that by marrying you, I would make you unhappy."

"Guy Colby, will you quit babbling on like a nincompoop and tell me whether the answer is yes or no?"

Guy smiled. "Well, I don't know. I mean, when a man gets proposed to, he sort of expects the girl to get down on one knee."

"I'll give you a knee," Demaris hissed. "Right in your cods!"

"Ouch," Guy said, laughing. "Okay, okay, marrying you is better than a knee in the balls any day. The answer is yes."

"Yes? You'll marry me?"

"Yes."

"When? I want to be married before you leave for Russia."

"We'll get started on it first thing in the morning," Guy promised.

"Good," Demaris said, sitting back with a relieved sigh. She pointed to his plate. "So now that that's all settled, how about letting me have your peas? You never eat them anyway."

DEMARIS HUNTER WEDS GUY COLBY

Hollywood, Sept. 17—Yesterday, in a secret ceremony that caught everyone in Hollywood off guard, Demaris Hunter and Guy Colby were married.

"The only surprise is that they waited this long to do it," an insider said. "It's no secret that Demaris and Guy have been in love from the very first film she ever made."

Demaris has been married twice before, once to former cowboy movie star Ken Allen and once to romantic lead and box-office smash Ian McCarty, who tragically drowned on their wedding night. It is a testimony to the affection that all Hollywood has for the couple that Ken Allen was in attendance to wish the newlyweds well, as was Greta Gaynor, one of Guy Colby's former wives.

The couple will have only a brief time together before Guy leaves for Russia, where he is scheduled to begin shooting *Red Banners over Mother Russia,* a project he has undertaken for the Soviet government in cooperation with the United States government.

Demaris told this reporter, "In this I feel I'm no different from so many of my wonderful fans out there who are having to tell their own husbands good-bye. Of course, Guy isn't going to war in the same sense that they are, but he will be filming some actual combat scenes, and so I am concerned for his safety—and proud of his service in defense of democracy."

CHAPTER

SIXTEEN

Aviation Cadet Travis Jackson was three-quarters of the way through his training flight when the Stearman he was flying coughed once; then the engine stopped turning. With the engine out, the biplane had all the glide angle of a brick, and Travis was barely lined up with a cotton field when he found himself slipping down into it.

His wheels snapped off the top strand of a barbed wire fence, and the loud twang could be heard easily above the sound of the slipstream and the windmilling prop. The wheels began to slap against the cotton plants, and the leaves and twigs thumped into the wing and the fuselage. Finally the tires dug into the soft plowed earth, and the aircraft tipped up onto its nose, then rolled on over onto its back as gently as if being placed down by a giant hand.

Travis unsnapped his seat belt and fell to the ground. Concerned over a possible fire, he started running.

When he reached the other end of the field he saw a girl standing there. Suddenly realizing that he had run more than he'd needed to, to be safe, and feeling sheepish for having run so far, he stopped in front of her, panting from the exertion.

"Why you're . . . you're a *colored* boy," the girl said, smiling broadly.

The girl, who was pulling a long sack half full of cotton, looked to be about eighteen or nineteen, with big black eyes and skin a little darker than Travis's. Her thin cotton dress plainly revealed that she wore nothing underneath, and as she stood there talking to Travis, she threw one hip out slightly, exaggerating her curves. Travis didn't know if that was just a natural movement or a calculated one. If the latter, it certainly had its effect, because he found himself reacting.

"I never knew colored boys could fly airplanes," she said.

"Yeah, well, this colored boy doesn't seem to be doing all that well," Travis replied, looking back ruefully at the wrecked aircraft.

"Are you hurt?"

"No, I'm not hurt. Listen, is there a telephone nearby?"

"There ain't no phone here, honey. Mistah Culpepper —he's the one that owns the place?—he don't believe in havin' telephones."

"I have to get to a phone," Travis said. "I have to let the base know what happened."

"There's a phone down at the South-Y store. That's about seven miles from here. Don't know if they'd let a colored man use it or not."

Travis looked around the field. He and the girl were the only ones there. She brushed a strand of hair back from her face and smiled again. She was very pretty.

"You picking this field all by yourself?" Travis asked.

The girl nodded. "Ever'body else is already gone over to the north fields." She grinned. "Mistah Culpepper says I'm the best there is at cleanin' out the culls, so he keeps me back after ever'one else is gone. It's okay; he pays me by the day, not by the pound, so I make out all right."

"What's he pay for a pound?"

"Two cents."

"Boy, it's a good thing he's paying you by the day. You sure couldn't make anything culling at two cents."

She cocked her head and studied him. "You know cotton pickin'?"

"I've picked a pound or two back in Mississippi," Travis replied.

"I thought maybe you had. You want some water?" she asked. "I've got some in a Mason jar over to the fence 'neath that piece o' sack. The ice is probably all melted, but it should still be cool."

"Thanks," Travis answered, and they started toward the fence, the girl dragging the cotton sack along behind her. "What's your name?"

"Ellie. What's yours?"

"Cadet . . . uh . . . " Travis started, then laughed. "I don't suppose I have to go all through the ritual with you," he said. "My name is Travis."

When they reached the fence, Ellie got down on her knees and took her jar of water out from under a small piece of burlap bag, then handed it up to Travis.

"Thanks," he said, unscrewing the top and taking a drink. He discovered that he was thirstier than he'd thought, but he knew that this water would probably have to last Ellie all day, so he only took a couple of swallows before he replaced the lid and handed it back to her.

"Travis, whatcha doin' up in that airplane?" Ellie asked as she put the water jar back under the burlap. "Did you steal it?"

"Steal it?" Travis repeated, surprised by the question.

"I ain't never heard of no colored man flyin' no airplane 'less he stole it."

"It'd be kind of hard to steal a plane, don't you think?" Travis asked. "I mean, you have to learn to fly them first. If you stole it without knowing how to fly it, you'd crash."

"Well," Ellie said, raising her eyebrows as if her point had just been made, "what do you think you just done?"

Travis laughed. "Yeah, I see what you mean. But I didn't steal it, I promise you. I'm in the Army and I'm learning to fly. I'm going to be an Army officer and a pilot."

"Well, if that ain't somethin'," Ellie breathed. She was sitting on her cotton sack, and she patted the ground beside

her, inviting him to sit also. "A Army officer and a pilot.
Imagine that. You sure are a handsome fella."

Her frankness amused Travis, and he chuckled.
"Thanks," he said.

"You think I'm pretty?"

"Well, yes. I think you're very pretty."

"You don't think these are too small?" she asked, and
suddenly she opened the top of her dress, exposing her
breasts to him.

"Uh . . . no. I think they're just right."

"Here, feel them; see what you think," Ellie said, taking his hand in hers, then placing it on one of her breasts.

Travis rubbed his palm over the smooth, soft flesh of
her breast, noting how it contrasted with the hard, rubbery
button of her nipple. He felt himself beginning to breathe
harder, and the churning in the pit of his stomach was
undeniable.

"I'm gettin' you all hot and bothered, aint' I?" Ellie
asked, smiling at Travis's reaction.

"Well, it isn't every day a beautiful young girl invites
me to feel her breast," Travis replied.

"We can use my sack," Ellie suggested. "It makes a
good bed. I've done it on the sack lots of times."

"I beg your pardon?"

"Don't you want to sport with me?" Even as Ellie was
asking the question, she pulled the dress up and over her
head so that she was nude almost before Travis knew what
was going on. She lay down on her sack with her legs
splayed; a pink, moist slit winked at Travis from within the
darkness of her crotch. Ellie smiled and looked up at him
through half-closed eyes, beckoning him to her with her
hands. "Hurry up, honey, I can't hardly wait no more."

Travis took a quick look around the field. Then he
smiled and started slipping out of his one-piece flight suit.
"I'll try not to keep you waiting," he promised.

As soon as he was naked, Ellie reached up to him. She
grabbed his hands, then pulled him gently but firmly down
onto the cotton sack, then wrapped her legs around his
back and guided him into her.

Travis entered her slowly, and Ellie arched her back
and began moaning with the movement. She bit at her lips

and groaned in ecstasy, and the sounds brought forth a small expulsion of spittle. She clawed his back with her fingers and nibbled at his neck. He thrust harder and filled her, and she thrust against him even harder as she accepted him.

Travis found the entire thing unbelievably erotic, not only because he was making love to this beautiful, young, half-wild creature, but because it had come about so unexpectedly and he was doing it out in the open, with the wind rattling the tops of the cotton plants and blowing softly across his bare butt.

The whimperings and noises of the girl began to grow in intensity as she started up the curve of orgasm. Travis, who had approached climax once or twice already, now started again, pulling out all the stops, coasting with it.

It struck the girl first. She whimpered and moaned and whined in carnal delight. Travis joined her in a powerful orgasm that seemed to start in the soles of his feet and work its magic all the way up to his scalp.

He lay there for several moments afterward, enjoying the sensation of maintaining the connection and a partial erection. Then he rolled off Ellie, letting his breathing return to normal.

"Uhmm, that was real good," Ellie murmured.

"Did you like it?" Travis asked.

"I sure did, honey," Ellie replied. "But I 'spect you better be gettin' up now and get yourself dressed. I hear Mistah Culpepper's truck a-comin'."

Startled into activity, Travis suddenly realized that he could hear it, too. He jumped up and began putting his clothes back on, first whipping into his skivvies and then pulling on his flight suit.

As soon as he was dressed, he looked to see how Ellie was doing. His heart almost stopped when he saw how agonizingly slow she was.

"Hurry up, for chrissake," he urged.

"Don't you worry none, honey," Ellie said, smiling sweetly at him. "I ain't never been caught yet."

True to her word, she finished at the last possible moment so that when the truck stopped and Mr. Culpepper got out, Ellie was standing there fully clothed and as innocent looking as a schoolgirl.

Mr. Culpepper looked to be in his late fifties or early sixties, with a red blotchy face and white stringy hair.

"You the fella crashed that airplane in my field?" he asked.

"Yes, sir."

"You must be one of them nigra pilots they're trainin' over at Tuskegee."

"Yes, sir, I am."

"Yeah, well, I told ever'one it wouldn't work," Culpepper said. "You can train nigras to do lots of things, but you can't train 'em to fly." He ran his hand through his hair and looked at Travis. "Still, I reckon I got to give you boys credit for havin' the courage to try," he said. "I reckon you'll be wantin' to call back to the base an' tell 'em what happened?"

"Yes, sir."

"Well, climb into the back of the truck there. I'll take you down to the South-Y and see to it that they let you use the phone. After that, you're on your own."

"Thank you, sir," Travis said.

"And you, girl," Culpepper said over his shoulder as he walked back to the cab of his truck. "You better get back to work."

"I'm goin'," Ellie said. She smiled at Travis. "It was nice knowin' you."

Travis shook his head and laughed. "You're something else, Ellie," he said as he hopped up into the bed of the truck.

Sitting there, his feet dangling over the tailgate, watching Ellie as Culpepper drove away, Travis saw that though she had promised Culpepper she'd get right back to work, she continued to stand there by the fence row waving at him until the truck was completely out of sight.

ON THE AUSTRIAN-YUGOSLAV BORDER

Miriam Gelbman stood by the stove at one end of the one-room mountain cabin, tending to a soup made from turnips, potatoes, and beets. There was no meat stock, and there was only salt for seasoning, but it was something to eat, and over the last several weeks there had been times when she and her cousin, Simon Blumberg, had had nothing at all.

Simon was amazing. Though he had only one leg, he could move on his crutches every bit as fast as Miriam could on two good legs. In addition, the years of depending upon his arms for part of his locomotion had given him an upper-body strength that was remarkable. Whatever doubts Miriam might have had about being led to freedom by a "cripple" were put to rest by Simon's ability to look out for her.

In addition to Simon's strength, he also had an incredible ability to improvise. This skill was coupled with a talent to find something to eat when it seemed as if nothing was there. ("Organizing," Simon called it, borrowing a term he said the soldiers had used in the trenches during World War I.)

And Simon had another skill, one that was perhaps the most valuable of them all. Aside from his native German, he could speak five languages. In two of them, Slavic and Italian, he was so proficient that he could pass himself off as a native speaker.

Since spiriting Miriam away from the roundup of Jews at the railroad depot in Vienna, at which time they had quickly ripped off the obligatory Stars of David sewn to their clothing—praying no one would notice any telltale stitch marks—Simon had used his skills and talents to get them past dozens of military and police checkpoints. They had ridden on hay wagons, in the back of trucks, buses, and once in a policeman's car—Simon having convinced the policeman that he was a German officer, honorably discharged for having lost his leg in battle. Since he *had* lost his leg in battle, albeit during World War I, he had been able to make that part of the story most convincing.

They had reached the Yugoslavian border two days earlier, and because the border was tightly patrolled, even though Germany was occupying Yugoslavia, Simon decided it would be best for them to hole up for a few days while he determined the best way for them to get across.

His plan was to get to Sibenik, a small port city on the Adriatic in Yugoslavia. More importantly, it was a town at least partly controlled by the Yugoslavian partisans, and because of that a clandestine transport service had been established between Sibenik and Palestine. First, however, Simon would have to get across the border into Yugoslavia. Then he'd have to find a band of partisans who would trust him—and whom he could trust. Then he'd have to depend on them to help get him and Miriam across Yugoslavia and onto the ship, provided, of course, there *was* a ship there. . . .

They had been hiding out in the tiny cabin for four days now, and under other circumstances Miriam thought she might really enjoy it. It was quite a beautiful spot at the foot of a region of steep, forested slopes and rugged peaks. Nearby was a lake with water so clear and still that its surface was a mirror of the striking scenery surrounding it. The cabin, which Simon guessed must have been a sheepherder's cabin at one time, was deserted when they came across it and showed signs of having been deserted for years. In a corner of the cabin they found a yellowed newspaper dated 1933.

"Oh, Simon," Miriam had mused when they had first stumbled on the cabin, "wouldn't it be wonderful if we could stay here, safe, out of the way of the Nazis, until the war was over?"

"Miriam, don't even let such thoughts play on your mind," Simon had replied. "If the Nazis win, then for us the war would never be over. Therefore, we must think of nothing but our ultimate destination. We are going to Palestine. Only there will we be safe. *Really* safe."

"I know what you're saying is true," Miriam had said, sighing. "Still, it would be nice."

Since that conversation, Miriam had worked every daylight hour to clean up the cabin, even though she knew they weren't going to stay. When Simon remarked that she was wasting her time, she replied that there was no need for them to live in filth just because they were refugees. What she didn't tell him was that the cleanliness of the cabin had nothing to do with her basic need to clean it. By cleaning the cabin she could manage to fool herself, if only for a short while, into believing that she actually belonged somewhere. Just as devastating to her as being separated from her parents, leaving her job and friends, and losing all the beautiful things she had taken for granted, was the fact that she felt disconnected from reality. Somehow, getting the little cabin clean and turning it into a home, if only for a few days, gave her that necessary sense of reality.

It was nearly dark before Simon returned to the cabin, though Miriam hadn't been too worried about his tardiness because she knew that he could take care of himself. She had kept the soup simmering all day, resisting the urge to eat any of it until Simon returned, though she was very hungry and the smell, even of this ordinarily unappetizing fare, was making her ravenous.

"I've made contact," Simon said, smiling with satisfaction as he stepped through the doorway. "We're leaving tomorrow." He sniffed loudly. "Uhmm, Miriam, that smells delicious," he said, walking over to look into the soup pot. "You've done a good job."

"All I did was boil it," Miriam said, pushing her dark hair off her face with the back of her hand. She dished out the soup in the only two containers they had, an old automobile hubcap and a teakettle. "Simon, are you sure we should go so soon? I mean, shouldn't we wait a while longer, just to make sure everything is okay?"

They had no spoons, and Simon was sipping his soup out of the side of his "bowl." He looked at Miriam across the lip of the hubcap.

"*Liebchen,*" he said quietly, "remember what I said about not getting too comfortable in this place. Sooner or later someone is going to find out we're here."

"I know, I know," Miriam said. "Still . . ." She let the word dangle wistfully.

"Uhmm," Simon said, slurping as he ate his soup, "as a child, I didn't like turnips. But these . . . these are delicious."

"They're not bad, if I do say so myself," Miriam agreed.

They debated whether to finish the soup now or to save a little something for breakfast, finally deciding to eat it all now because, as Simon said, "The way things are, we should deal only with now and let later take care of itself."

It was dark by the time they finished eating, and Miriam cleaned out the cooking pot and the utensils, perhaps for the last time, since they wouldn't be taking those things with them when they left in the morning. Simon took out a nail that he had converted into a screwdriver by scraping and flattening the point, and began using it to work on the arm piece of one of his crutches. A strong wind had come up outside the cabin, and it sadly moaned through the mountains and whistled around the corners of the cabin. But it was offset by the sound of the fire popping and snapping in the small stove that kept the cabin comfortably warm as well as served to cook on. Perhaps it was the soothing warmth and sound of the fire, combined with the pleasant fullness from their meal, that lulled and relaxed them. Whatever it was that diminished their usual alertness, they soon paid the price for it, because suddenly and without warning the front door of the cabin was kicked open and two black-uniformed SS men burst inside.

"Stay where you are!" one of them shouted gruffly.

"*Simon!*" Miriam screamed, dropping the pot she had been cleaning so that it clanged loudly on the floor.

Simon started to stand up, but the SS man nearest him kicked his crutch away, then shoved him backward. Unable to keep his balance, Simon fell back across the bench he had been sitting on. When he again tried to get up, the SS man punched him in the face. Simon sank to the floor, unconscious.

The SS man who had knocked Simon out laughed uproariously. "Look, Hans, it was like knocking over a bowling pin."

"Bowling?" Hans scoffed. "You think about bowling? I'm going to have some fun with this Jewish sow."

"What are you going to do?" Hans's partner asked.

"What do you *think* I'm going to do?" Hans replied.

"You would contaminate yourself by fucking a Jewess?"

Hans sniggered. "For this one I'll risk it." He shoved his revolver into the holster on his Sam Browne belt, then took off the belt and draped it on the overturned bench.

"Keep an eye on the Jew cripple while I take care of a little business. You," he said to Miriam, "take off your clothes." He started unbuttoning his trousers.

"No, please!" Miriam begged, her eyes growing wide with fear. "Don't do this to me!"

Hans laughed a short, evil-sounding bark. "Don't do this *to* you? Why, you filthy piece of pig shit. I'm doing this *for* you. It should be an honor for any Jew bitch to have my Ayrian cock in her cunt." He pulled out his penis and began stroking it. "Look at it, bitch. You'll be begging me for it before we're finished. Now, take off your clothes!"

Miriam just stood there, whether in defiance or paralyzing fear even she couldn't have said. Whatever the reason, it infuriated Hans, and he brought the back of his hand sharply across Miriam's face. Then he grabbed at the neck of her blouse and jerked down, pulling so hard that he ripped apart not only the blouse, but her bra as well. Her full breasts spilled out, and Miriam tried to cover them with her arms only to be hit again.

"Don't cover up those tits, you Jew-fucking slut," Hans ordered. "Don't you dare cover them up!"

Whimpering, her eyes closed, Miriam dropped her arms. They hung limply at her sides, a gesture of complete surrender.

"Now, that's more like it," Hans said. "What do you think, Otto? I ask you, should tits like that be wasted on a Jewish whore? Let's have a look at the rest of her." He reached for the waistband of Miriam's skirt.

Suddenly the tiny cabin was filled with the roar of a pistol shot. Miriam opened her eyes and screamed as blood and brain tissue spewed from the front of Otto's forehead. Then she saw Simon, still lying on the floor where he had fallen, forgotten by Otto, who was supposed to watch over him but instead had become too interested in watching Miriam's humiliation. Hans, his face gone white, made a desperate grab for his pistol, only to realize that he wasn't armed . . . that it was his gun the Jew was using. His eyes grew wide with terror, and he stuck both his hands out in front of him.

"No! No!" he screamed. "Don't do it!"

"Fuck you," Simon growled, and he pulled the trigger,

the P-38 bucking in his hand and kicking out the spent cartridge as it spit flame. Hans grabbed his chest, then looked down to see blood spilling between his fingers. He took one step toward Simon, then fell facedown and lay perfectly still.

After a moment Miriam asked, "Are they both dead?"

"Yes."

"I'm glad he's dead." Still naked from the waist up, Miriam held her arms crossed over her breasts as she stood looking down at the two dead SS men.

"You'd better put your shirt back on," Simon said as he began to struggle to his feet. "You'll catch cold."

"I don't have a shirt to put on," Miriam said. "He tore it up."

Simon looked down at the two bodies. "You can wear this man's shirt," he said, pointing to Otto. "I'm afraid the other one's wouldn't do."

"Would you . . . would you take it off him?" Miriam asked softly. "I don't want to touch him."

Simon chuckled. "Sure," he said. "It doesn't bother me to touch this dead German pig."

Simon stripped the SS man of his tunic, then removed his shirt. He was just handing it to Miriam when four more men burst through the front door. All four were carrying guns, but none were in uniform. Miriam screamed and Simon started toward the pistol he had just set down.

"Hold it! Hold it!" one of the men shouted. "We're on your side!"

Simon stopped. It didn't make any difference whether they were on his side or not, he knew he wouldn't have made it to the pistol anyway.

"Don't you remember me?" the man asked. "I'm the one you met today."

Simon eyed the man. "The partisan," he said.

"Yes," the partisan replied. He was about thirty, tall and dark with flashing black eyes. "I am Captain Moshe Meir at your service." He looked at Miriam, who was staring unabashedly back at him, and he smiled. "My dear, much as I am enjoying the view, I would suggest that you put that shirt on."

"Oh!" Miriam gasped. Quickly, she turned her back and slipped into the shirt.

"I think, under the circumstances, it would be best if we didn't wait until tomorrow before we get started," Moshe said. "We should go right away."

"I agree," Simon said. "I don't know how these two found out we were here, but we had a pretty close call."

"Oh, I told them you were here," Moshe said easily.

Simon, who had just recovered his crutches, looked over at Moshe in anger and surprise. "*You* told them?"

"Yes, of course."

"Why in hell did you tell them?"

"Well, it was a test, actually. You see, if you weren't who you said you were, if you were working undercover for the SS, then my telling them about you wouldn't have made any difference. But if you *were* escaping Jews, they would surely come out here after you, and I could be sure you were legitimate. If you survived the confrontation, I wouldn't ever have to doubt you."

"*If* we survived? That's a hell of a way to find out who you can trust and who you can't, isn't it?"

"Yes," Moshe admitted. "But it is the most accurate way. Anyway, once I saw that you were legitimate, I planned to rescue you. This time things just got a little out of hand."

"Yes," Simon said. "A little out of hand. Not to mention they could have shot us the minute they stormed into the cabin."

Moshe smiled broadly. "True. But all's well that ends well, and it couldn't be for the better. Come, we have a lot of distance to cover."

CHRISTMAS 1942, LONDON, ENGLAND

In the dark of Shaylin McKay's hotel room the radio was playing Bing Crosby's "White Christmas." On her dresser stood a small Christmas tree, its boughs gaily decorated with accoutrements from American, English, and Free French army, navy, and air force uniforms: wings, brightly colored ribbons, badges, and rank devices, topped off by the three stars of an American lieutenant general.

Christmas Eve in London was cold and wet. The rain rattled against the windowpanes and dripped onto the sill and drummed on the chimney pots of the roof next door.

Scowling, Shaylin turned her head on her pillow and looked over at the window. "I'm getting bloody tired of this bloody weather," she grumbled. She reached over to the bedside table for a cigarette but found only an empty and crumpled pack. "And I'm out of bloody cigarettes."

Lying beside her, Eric Twainbough chuckled. "Bloody this, bloody that. Damn if you haven't gone native."

Shaylin got out of bed and padded naked across the floor to the dresser. She opened the top drawer and took out a fresh pack of Camels, extracted one, then came back to sit on the edge of the bed. She lit the cigarette with the Zippo lighter on the table by the empty package.

"I know," she said, exhaling a stream of smoke. "Isn't it bloody awful?"

Realizing what she'd said, she laughed, and Eric laughed with her. He reached over and turned on the bedside lamp.

"Don't turn that on," Shaylin said quickly.

"Why not?"

"Because I'm naked, dear. I haven't any clothes on."

"I know," Eric said. "Why do you think I turned it on? I like to look at you."

Shaylin reached over to turn the light back off. "I like it better this way," she said.

"Why?"

"I don't know. Maybe so I can hide my sin in the darkness."

"This isn't the first time we've shared a bed, Shaylin. You never worried about hiding your sin before."

"I wasn't in love with another man, before."

"And you are now?"

"Yes, I think so."

"You *think* so."

"I know so."

Eric reached out and took Shaylin's hand in his, held it

for a moment, then raised it to his lips to kiss it, brushing against it with his beard as he did.

"Shaylin," he said, quietly. "My dear, sweet Shaylin. I haven't come in the night to steal your soul. But there are certain times, such as being alone in a foreign country at Christmas during a war, when two old friends can do a lot to comfort each other. And if those two old friends happen to be of the opposite sex, then the options available to them to provide this mutual comfort are significantly increased. You and I are two such friends, taking advantage of those options. No more, no less."

Shaylin took a deep drag and stared at Eric for a long moment over the bright red tip of her cigarette. Then she let the smoke out in an explosive laugh.

"Eric Twainbough, you're as full of shit as a Christmas goose. That's the hokeyest damned excuse I've ever heard."

"Well, which will it be?" Eric asked. "Hokey sex or guilty sex?"

"You're sure there's going to be more sex tonight?"

Eric pulled the cover aside, exposing his erection. "What do you think?"

Her laugh was husky. "My, my. When did that happen? For an old man, you seem to have managed an amazingly quick recovery."

"Hokey sex talk will do it for me every time," Eric said, grinning.

Shaylin ground her cigarette out in the ashtray, then lay down beside him, reaching for his penis.

"Okay," she said, "then hokey sex it will be."

CHAPTER
SEVENTEEN

JANUARY 1943, NEAR STALINGRAD

The tank engine rumbled in the background. Lieutenant Rudi Schultz didn't shut it down because it was so cold that he was afraid he wouldn't be able to get it started again. A blade had been fixed to the front of the tank and used to rip a hole in the cold Russian soil, big enough and deep enough to hold twelve of Rudi's men who had died during the night. They had died not from enemy action, but from the bitter, freezing cold and the lack of warm clothing.

Rudi stood on the edge of the mass grave, looking at the pitiful pile of men. They were lying as they had died, frozen in the same twisted, grotesque positions they had assumed in an effort to keep warm. Some, too, had wrapped odd apparel over their uniforms in pathetic attempts to lessen the cold—several wore curtains they had taken from Russian houses, and one bearded soldier was wearing a woman's beaded and sequined formal coat. Rudi would have removed the garments for his other soldiers had it not been for the fact that they were frozen to the bodies.

The German advance against Stalingrad, which had started out so well in the late summer, was now encountering massive Russian counterattacks. The counterattacks were having a devastating effect, and Rudi had been present at a staff briefing where proposals and counterproposals were put forth by the German High Command.

"We must withdraw," someone had said. "We can withdraw to a safer position, then counterattack in the spring."

"Withdraw to where?" another had asked. "We have no fixed withdrawal positions. Remember, if you will, the Grande Armée of Napoleon. The withdrawal of the French became a full-scale flight of panic. Would you have the Wehrmacht undergo that humiliation and suffer that loss?"

In the end, the decision wasn't made by the field commanders; it was made by the Supreme Commander himself, Adolf Hitler. Hitler's order was printed and distributed not only to the senior officers, but to every officer and soldier in the German Army so that the Führer's words might "inspire and lift the spirits of the fighting men."

> *To the German Officers and Men: I, along with the grateful German people, have watched your heroic battle in Russia with utmost trust in your bravery and dedication to duty. In your current situation there can be no consideration except holding fast; of not retreating one step; of hurling into battle every gun, every man, every round of ammunition. You must resolve yourself, for the national weal, to seek victory or death.*
>
> *ADOLF HITLER*

And so the German troops had dug in and struggled to hold. They were holding, Rudi thought, against impossible odds. Strangely enough, as he stood here watching the dirt and snow being pushed over his men who lay frozen in the bottom of the common grave, he felt a great sense of pride. But his pride wasn't in Germany, or even in the German Army per se, but in this particular army, General von Paulis's Sixth Army. His pride transcended even the pride he had felt during the early, victorious days in Poland and France. The Sixth Army was proving to the world that it could fight not only when conditions were perfect, but when conditions were unbelievably bad as well.

Rudi pulled his Russian private's coat about him while he ran through the litany of troubles: The Sixth Army was outnumbered and fighting on the enemy's home soil; German soldiers were freezing to death, and those who weren't dying were suffering from frostbite and other exposure problems; and machinery and weaponry were suffering along with the men. Tank tracks were locked up by ice, and oil had congealed not only in vehicles, but in guns, rendering the telescopic gunsights useless. And even had they worked, many of the guns were frozen so solid that they couldn't be fired.

But still the Sixth Army held.

"Lieutenant," Rudi's sergeant, Helmut Schilling, urgently called from a few feet away, where he was standing on top of a slight ridge. "Russians." Schilling pointed with an arm that protruded from beneath a woolen blanket, and Rudi scrambled up beside him to see for himself. He peered through his binoculars but saw nothing except a field of snow. After a second or two he realized he was watching Russian troops—hundreds of them!—dressed in snow-camouflage white coming across the field straight toward them.

"*Mein Gott!*" Rudi said, lowering the binoculars and motioning his sergeant down off the ridge. "So many! Where did they all come from?"

"How are we going to get out of here, Lieutenant? The Russians are between us and our headquarters."

Rudi sighed. "Sergeant, I'm not even sure we have a headquarters anymore." He glanced at the other men. There were six of them left, including the four men who made up the tank crew.

"We could all crowd into the tank," the sergeant suggested.

"No," Rudi replied. "We'd be sitting ducks. They'd pounce on the tank in a—Wait a minute." He rubbed his chin with his hand as he walked back to the edge of the common grave. "Helmut, we have to dig up some of our men."

"I beg your pardon, sir?"

"Dig them up, Sergeant," Rudi ordered. "I need four men."

One of the other men started to ask what they were doing, but the sergeant cut him off with an impatient "Do as your officer tells you," then led the detail in brushing away the dirt and snow that hadn't had time to freeze again. Within moments four soldiers' bodies, still frozen in their crouched position, were lying beside the grave.

"Now, you," Rudi said, pointing to the tank driver, "get the tank up onto the ridge and depress the gun as far as you can. Open fire on the advancing troops."

"Lieutenant, if we fire from the ridge, we'll be silhouetted against the skyline. We'll be an easy target," the driver protested.

"That's exactly what I want," Rudi said. "Fire no more than two rounds, then put these fellows in the tank." Rudi pointed to the frozen bodies. "If we're lucky, the Russians will hit the tank, and by the time they get here, they'll just see four burning corpses. They may think that was all of us, and it'll give us a chance to get away."

"I hate to do this to our dead comrades," one of the soldiers said.

"It gives them one more opportunity to be of service," another argued.

The driver moved his tank into position on the ridge, and the gunner fired two quick rounds. The sound of the gun was amazingly loud in the stillness of the afternoon, and after the second round was fired, its sound rolled back in a distinct echo from the distant trees. Rudi watched the shells explode in the midst of the approaching soldiers and was gratified to see that one of them, at least, had some effect, when some of the soldiers went down and didn't get back up.

"Put the bodies in quickly, and let's get out of here," Rudi commanded.

The gunner and loader scrambled out of the tank and off to a safe distance while the others dropped the frozen bodies down through the hatch, then scurried away themselves. The first round of Russian artillery burst over them just seconds after the bodies were loaded; two more rounds exploded harmlessly off to the sides; the fourth round scored a direct hit on the tank. It went up with a *whoosh*, and Rudi turned to look back at it as the brilliant red-orange fire and black smoke roiled up against the dazzlingly white snowy background.

Suddenly Rudi felt a searing, burning pain in his thigh, and the next thing he knew, he was lying on the crisp blanket of white, watching almost disinterestedly as the snow began to turn a bright crimson from his blood. Why was he lying down? What was he doing in the snow?

Sound and vision dimmed, and the initial shock of pain gave way as a warming numbness spread through his body. Helmut Schilling came running back toward him.

"What happened?" Rudi asked his sergeant. "Why am I down here?"

"You were hit with a piece of shrapnel, sir," Schilling explained. He bent down and scooped Rudi up in his arms.

"What are you doing?" Rudi asked.

"I've got to get you out of here."

Rudi was a good-sized man, but Schilling picked him up as if he were a child.

"Thank you, Sergeant," Rudi said in a silly sort of formality, as if Schilling had just handed him a dispatch.

Another Russian shell burst nearby, and Rudi could hear the angry buzz of shrapnel as jagged pieces of metal spread out in a lethal fountain. He watched the small smoking fragments as if he were watching a fireworks display. The sergeant started to run, but finally the snow and Rudi's weight became more than he could handle. He tripped and fell, sending both of them sprawling.

"I'm sorry, Lieutenant; I'm sorry," the sergeant said earnestly. He got to his feet.

"Think nothing of it, Helmut," Rudi said easily, calmly. He couldn't understand why his sergeant was so concerned, and he wished he would just stop and relax. Why couldn't they just sit down to rest? He outranked Schilling; he would just order him to stop running.

Rudi could hear voices now, strange-sounding voices. Russian voices.

"They're close," Schilling said, breathing heavily. He looked around. A wrecked truck lay several yards away. "Here," he said, pulling and dragging Rudi. "Get under the truck."

"Get under the truck?" Rudi replied. "No, we must make a stand."

"Dammit, Lieutenant, I've no time to argue. Get under the truck!" Schilling snapped, and he shoved Rudi underneath the vehicle so roughly that Rudi felt a sharp pain return to his thigh. With the return of pain came also the return of awareness, and now Rudi was acutely alert to the situation and to what the sergeant was doing for him.

"Get out of here," Rudi said, and the tone of his voice was such that Schilling knew Rudi was under control again.

"I'll leave in a moment," the sergeant said. "First, I've got to hide you."

From his cramped shelter Rudi wondered what the sergeant was doing, struggling with the snow; then he realized that Schilling was building up a snow pile so that Rudi would be concealed. Rudi helped from inside, and in just a few seconds the snow wall was finished.

"I'll be back," Schilling whispered harshly. "I promise, I'll be back."

Rudi heard the sergeant leave, and then he lay there, feeling a warmth begin to suffuse his body. He didn't know if the warmth came from the numbness of the wound, from the insulating snugness of the snow, or if it was the first sign of dying by freezing. Whatever the cause of the warmth, Rudi welcomed it. Even if he was dying, it would be good to have a momentary respite from the bitter cold.

Rudi lay there for over an hour, clutching the pistol with a round in the chamber, ready to fire if need be. The Russian soldiers were all around . . . he could hear them talking and laughing among themselves. One of the soldiers leaned his rifle against the overturned truck, and when Rudi heard the sound of water spattering on the snow, he realized that the Russian was relieving himself at the truck. A second later another soldier joined the first and then another, by unspoken agreement turning the truck into a urinal.

After a while the stench of the urine drifted in around

the snow and joined with the smell of Rudi's own blood to make him sick. He couldn't keep from throwing up, and he feared that his retching would attract the Russians to him. Blessedly it didn't. Between their own noise and the muffling effects of the snow, they didn't hear him.

Finally the Russian soldiers left, and Rudi lay still for what seemed an eternity. He drifted in and out of consciousness and fought the cold and the pain. Several times he contemplated shooting himself, and once he even went so far as to put the barrel of the pistol into his mouth. He hesitated only because he was afraid that the wound wouldn't be fatal, and he'd be in worse shape than he already was, unable to do anything about it.

It was dark and Rudi dozed off. He was awakened by the sound of digging. His eyes snapped open, and he stared at the wall of snow in fear. Slowly and quietly he raised the pistol and pointed it at the wall. He was terrified, and with every nerve in his body he wanted to pull the trigger, to shoot through the snow, but he managed to hold that impulse in check. Finally the digger broke through the snow, and Rudi saw the dark outline of a man's head peering through.

"Lieutenant, are you all right?" a voice called, and Rudi recognized his sergeant.

"You've come back," was all Rudi could say.

Schilling constructed a travois and placed Rudi on it as gently as a mother would a baby. The night passed in a blur of images, sounds, and pain. Rudi had moments of consciousness when he felt the pain and the cold; then there were long stretches of unconsciousness when he felt nothing and was aware of nothing. There were intervals of hiding; once Rudi came to only to feel the sergeant's hand clamped securely over his mouth to prevent him from crying out, and he was vaguely aware of the passage of several Russian soldiers nearby. Then there was the traveling . . . long, tiring periods of motion with the sergeant plodding along, never complaining, rarely speaking, stopping only periodically to look at Rudi's wound or to adjust the coat around him. And then, after one particularly long period of unconsciousness, Rudi opened his eyes to see a medical officer staring down at him, smiling at him, and he knew that he was back at his own headquarters.

"You are a lucky man," the medical officer said.

"To have surived?"

"No, your survival wasn't due to luck; that was due to the sergeant who brought you in here. The luck comes from the fact that you are going home tomorrow. Back to Germany."

"What? I'm going home? Why? Is my wound that serious?" Rudi asked, surprised by the doctor's announcement.

"Not really," the doctor said. "But there's a JU-52 loaded with wounded flying back to Germany in the morning. My orders are to see that you are on board."

"But I don't understand. Who gave you such orders?" Rudi asked.

"I gave them," a quiet, authoritative voice said, and a man suddenly stepped into Rudi's field of vision. When Rudi recognized him, he gasped.

"General von Paulis!"

"Do you feel up to making the long flight?" von Paulis asked.

"Well, yes, sir, of course. But I don't know why I should go if I'm not that seriously wounded. I believe I should stay here and help my comrades."

"You can help more by going back to Germany," the general said. He stroked his chin. "At least, I hope you can help more. The truth is, the situation may be beyond help even if you can get the orders changed."

"I beg your pardon, sir?"

"I understand, Lieutenant, that you're a friend of Oberreichsleiter Karl Tannenhower."

"I'm not exactly a friend," Rudi replied.

"But you know him, *ja*? You have his ear?"

"Yes, sir, I know him. I served with his son, and he was responsible for my getting a commission."

"Then I will have to prevail upon you to champion our cause," von Paulis said.

"I will, of course, do anything you ask of me," Rudi said.

"When you get home, go to the Oberreichsleiter. Tell him of the conditions here. Tell him that if he does not convince Herr Hitler to rescind his foolish order demanding that we stand until the last, he is going to see the complete destruction of the Sixth Army. The lives of over a quarter of a million men are hanging in the balance."

"I will do what I can, General," Rudi promised.

"And would you also tell my family . . ." Von Paulis's request trailed off. "Never mind," he said. "Please, don't bother my family. They are military. They have been prepared to accept my fate from the day the war began. Have a safe trip, Lieutenant Schultz. God be with you."

"Thank you, General. And with you."

Twenty-two people, including two pilots, rode the three-engine Junkers transport as it winged its way back to Germany. Two doctors walked up and down the aisle of the cabin between the stretchers, which were placed in a double deck along each side. There were eighteen stretchers, and in one of the lower stretchers Rudi Schultz lay. The lower stretcher allowed him to look through the window, breaking up the monotony of the long trip.

"How are you feeling?" one of the doctors asked, stopping by Rudi's stretcher and putting his hand on Rudi's forehead.

"Fine," Rudi said quietly and without expression.

"Good, good, that is good," the doctor said. He moved to the next stretcher, asked the same question, received the same noncommittal answer, and responded in the same way: "Good, good, that is good."

Rudi listened to the doctor's "good, good" float up the aisle until the worthy doctor had moved far enough away so that the drone of the three engines drowned him out. Rudi turned and looked out across the gray-black, corrugated wing, over the black cross on the wingtip, and down to the gently rolling, snow-covered terrain three thousand meters below. Were they still over Russia? Would Russian fighter planes come swooping down on them?

Below, Rudi could see a small house. It was all by itself, miles away from the next nearest structure. Who lived there? Were they ever lonely? Why would anyone want to live in such isolation? Had the war passed them by?

"How are you feeling?" the other doctor asked, stopping at Rudi's stretcher and putting his hand to Rudi's forehead.

"Fine," Rudi answered.

"Good, good," this doctor also replied, already walking on. "That is good."

Rudi turned back to the window.

"We're so glad you could pay us a visit, Lieutenant Schultz," Uta Tannenhower said. She sat on one side of the dining table, having given her usual seat at the foot of the table to Rudi Schultz.

"I am pleased and honored to be a guest in the home of Oberreichsleiter Karl Tannenhower and his lovely wife and beautiful daughter," Rudi replied, bowing his head in respect to Uta and sixteen-year-old Liesl, who sat across from her mother.

Liesl, who preened at the comment, smiled prettily at Rudi, then picked up a bowl and held it out to him. "Would you like some more potato dumplings, Lieutenant?" she asked.

"Thank you, Fraulein Tannenhower," Rudi said. "I should say no, I have made such a pig of myself already. But never have I eaten so well."

"Eat as much as you wish," Karl said from the head of the table. "You have certainly earned it."

"Thank you, Herr Oberreichsleiter," Rudi said, accepting the proffered bowl. "Perhaps I will have a bit more."

"Lieutenant Schultz, would you tell us what it was like in Russia?" Liesl asked. Already Karl's blond daughter was blossoming into a beautiful young woman. Rudi could see much of her mother in her.

"It was cold," Rudi replied. He smiled at her. "And we never had anything this good to eat."

"Is that it? Is that all you can say about Russia?" Uta asked.

"It isn't good dinner conversation," Rudi suggested.

"Lieutenant, I would like to hear the way it really was," Karl insisted.

Rudi looked at Karl, then at his plate. He was silent for a long moment. "I beg your pardon, Herr Oberreichsleiter, but I don't think it would be too pleasant a subject to speak of in front of the ladies."

Karl reached for his wife's and daughter's hands. "I *want* them to hear about it, Lieutenant," he said. "Everyone in Germany should know the sacrifices our brave soldiers really are making for them. And you did say that you were instructed by General von Paulis to tell me of the conditions you soldiers have been enduring."

"But your daughter. She is so young."

"In these troubled times, no one is young," Karl replied.

"Very well," Rudi said quietly. He took a deep breath. "You might be interested to know that on Christmas day, General von Paulis gave the men of the Sixth Army a Christmas present. He allowed us to slaughter four hundred horses for food. The night before, Christmas Eve, men crawled nearly a kilometer on their bellies through the snow to sneak into a wheat field and cut unharvested grain with penknives, bayonets, any tool they could find, and bring the grain back into the dugouts and redoubts. We boiled the wheat and the horse meat to make our Christmas soup. On that same day, nearly fifteen hundred men died from frostbite, typhus, dysentery, and starvation."

Liesl shivered.

"And always, there was the cold," Rudi went on. "You couldn't get away from it, not for one second. The icy wind, which seemed to come straight from the North Pole itself, lashed against our skin like the cut of a million tiny razor blades. Then when someone just gave up and died, the wind and the snow would take them over so that less than one hour after life had left the body, a shroud of snow and ice covered them. There would be only the toe of a boot or a limb frozen to stone to remind someone that this chunk of ice had but a short while before been a living human being. And always behind the ice and snow and cold wind, beyond the last measure of food, there are more Russians, more and more of them, fat and warm and well-armed. We have

been ordered to stand until the last round of ammunition."
Rudi was silent for a moment. "The funny thing is, in many
cases the last round of ammunition has already been expended. I saw men clubbing horses to death, because they
had no bullets for their guns. Then they would smash open
the horse's head and eat the steaming brains raw, as much
for the warmth as for the food."

"Excuse me, please," Liesl said, and, her hand covering her mouth, she hurried from the dinner table.

"I'm sorry," Rudi said quickly. "Please, Frau Tannenhower, Herr Oberreichsleiter, forgive me. I had no
right to paint the picture so graphically."

"Nonsense," Uta said, reaching over to take Rudi's
hand. "Who would have a greater right?"

Karl looked thoughtfully at Rudi. "Lieutenant," he
said, "I don't know what I can do . . . as you may know,
Herr Hitler is a man of rigid thinking. However, I shall try
to persuade him to allow the Sixth Army to withdraw."

Rudi smiled sadly. "I appreciate your efforts, Herr
Oberreichsleiter. But I am afraid that it may already be too
late."

RASTENBURG, GERMANY

The wall of the situation room was covered with a
huge map of Russia, and Adolf Hitler, Field Marshal Alfred
Jodl, General Kurt Zeitzler, and Oberreichsleiter Karl Tannenhower stood looking at it. Behind them more officers
bustled about, while in this room and the next telephones
jangled with the latest reports. Stalingrad was encircled on
the map, and General Zeitzler, his face drawn and haggard,
his eyes puffy from lack of sleep, was trying to convince
Hitler to allow the Sixth Army to break out to the west.

"The red arrows represent the advances of the Russian
Army, my Führer," General Zeitzler pointed out.

Hitler glared at Zeitzler. "Herr General, do you think
me incapable of reading a situation map?"

Zeitzler clicked his heels together sharply. "*Nein,*
mein Führer!"

"And the blue circles?" Karl asked. "What are they?"

Zeitzler cleared his throat, then pointed to them. "They are isolated pockets of resistance, maintained by our forces," he explained.

"You mean to tell me that our lines have been penetrated?" Karl asked. "We no longer have integrity of command?"

"*Nein*, Oberreichsleiter."

Actually, Karl already knew the situation, not only because he could read the map as well as anyone, but also because he had been thoroughly briefed by Rudi Schultz about General von Paulis's plight—and his desperate plea.

"Don't worry, Tannenhower," Hitler said. "The situation is not as desperate as it appears. As usual, General von Paulis is overestimating the strength of the Russians."

"It is hard to overestimate, my Führer, when the Russians are there in such numbers," General Zeitzler said.

"Ah, yes, but what do the numbers mean?" Hitler replied, holding his finger up. "You see, Zeitzler, you are like all the other generals. You only think there"—Hitler tapped the side of his head—"you never think here"—he patted his hand over his heart. "I can think here because I not only have the mind of a brilliant military strategist, I also have the soul of a sensitive artist. That means I have the ability to see the whole picture. And it is with this insight that I can tell you that the Russian soldiers are cowards. Their officers are badly trained. They cannot sustain an offense with such officers. Take my word for it, the Russian counterattack will simply come to a halt. It will run down. All that is necessary for us to achieve final victory is to stay put."

"But without the integrity of a line of battle—"

"Nonsense, nonsense," Hitler said, waving off Zeitzler's protest. "It is better this way."

"Better?"

"Of course. You see, we have pockets of resistance here . . . and here . . . and here, scattered all along the Russian front. Each one of these pockets is tightly defended, impregnable, like steel. Scattering these 'steel' pockets of resistance throughout their front lines is like throwing a handful of ball bearings into the meshing gears of a finely tuned machine. The machine cannot handle the ball bearings, and the Russian Army cannot handle our pockets of steel."

"What a brilliant analogy, my Führer!" Jodl said, slapping his baton against the wide red stripe down the side of his pants.

"Begging the Führer's pardon," Zeitzler continued, "I must inform you that the Army is lacking rations, fuel, ammunition, even a way of keeping warm. We must pull them out of there!"

"Zeitzler, you are a general!" Hitler exploded. "Surely you can see the military importance of our holding Stalingrad. It is, of course, psychologically significant, because it is named after their leader. But beyond that, it sits at a key position on the Volga River. By breaking the flow of river traffic, we can cause the Russians no end of difficulties."

"River traffic? But, my Führer, there *is* no river traffic! It is winter! The river is solid ice."

There was some commotion in the outer room then, and Göring appeared, elegantly attired in a lavender-colored uniform.

"My Führer, I come with good news," he said. "You can keep the Army in place. I personally guarantee that Stalingrad will be supplied—entirely by air."

"By air?" Zeitzler challenged. "With all due respect, Reichsmarschall, that is impossible."

"How do you know?" Göring asked.

"We have over two hundred thousand soldiers there. In food alone it would take over two hundred thousand pounds a day. And there is fuel, ammunition . . . a dozen other necessary items. We couldn't do it with ten times the number of airplanes we now have, even if the weather was perfect and there were no enemy fighters or antiaircraft guns."

"Such calculations are not for you to make," Göring insisted. "The Luftwaffe will decide how many planes it will take. And we alone will worry about the weather and enemy action."

"There!" Hitler said excitedly. "So, do you see, my dear Zeitzler? Our problem is solved. We have Göring's word that we will be able to resupply our brave soldiers. That means that Stalingrad can and will be held. Jodl."

"*Jawohl,* my Führer?"

"See to it that General von Paulis is promoted to field marshal," Hitler said. He smiled at the others. "This is another idea of mine. You see, in the entire history of our country, there has never been an occurrence of a field marshal surrendering to the enemy. This will guarantee that the Sixth Army will stand fast."

"Brilliant, my Führer, brilliant!" Jodl enthused.

"And now, let us take a look at the Afrika Korps," Hitler suggested.

"The map for Africa is in another room," Jodl informed him.

Göring turned to his leader. "If you will excuse me, my Führer, I will issue the necessary orders for the resupply of Stalingrad, and then I will take lunch."

"It is a little early for lunch, isn't it, Hermann?" Hitler posed.

"*Ja,* my Führer," Göring replied. "But I did not eat breakfast."

"Then, go, go. I would not want the Reichsmarschall to be weak with hunger."

Göring saluted, then left.

"I do not believe the Reichsmarschall has ever missed a breakfast," Hitler said after Göring left, and the others laughed. "Well, let's take a look at the Africa situation, shall we?" Hitler and Jodl started out of the room when Hitler noticed that Karl wasn't coming with them. "Are you coming, Tannenhower?"

"Yes. I'll be there shortly, my Führer," Karl answered.

When the others were gone, Karl stood at the map for a long moment, just looking at the hopelessness of the situation.

General Zeitzler sidled up to him and said quietly, "Herr Oberreichsleiter, please, do what you can."

"I have tried, General Zeitzler," Karl said sadly. "Believe me, I have tried."

"He has just sentenced over two hundred fifty thousand men to their doom. If there are that many left," Zeitzler added ominously.

"Yes," Karl agreed. "I'm afraid you are right."

"Now he goes to look at the situation map for North

Africa, but since General Rommel was defeated at El Alamein, the Afrika Korps, too, has fallen into disfavor."

"At least our men in Africa aren't starving or freezing to death."

"Yes," General Zeitzler agreed, "at least Rommel has that to be thankful for."

CHAPTER EIGHTEEN

Second Lieutenant Hamilton Twainbough dipped his handkerchief into a water barrel, then tucked one end of it under his cap and let the rest of it hang, dripping, down the back of his neck. Though it did an adequate job of cooling him as it evaporated, in the desert sun that evaporation process took place all too quickly.

"Hey, Lieutenant, listen," Sergeant Gene Pratt said. "I got Armed Forces Radio Service."

"And now ladies and gentlemen here in America and all you wonderful boys in uniform, fighting for our freedom and listening in on Armed Forces Overseas Radio Service . . . here is 'Hollywood Calling'!"

After the silken-voiced announcer's lead-in, the band began playing "Hooray for Hollywood," while in the background could be heard the applause and cheers of the studio audience.

"Yes, ladies and gentlemen, all of Hollywood is here

279

tonight to do their part to bring a little cheer into the lives of our brave boys overseas. From the icy climes of Alaska to the tropic isles in the Pacific, from England to Australia to the desert sands of North Africa, a hearty hello from all of us here in the good old United States. On the show tonight are Joan Crawford, Barbara Stanwyck, Demaris Hunter, Shirley Temple, Greta Gaynor, Olsen and Johnson, Abbott and Costello, Jack Benny, Mickey Rooney, Robert Taylor, Cary Grant, Frank Sinatra, and me. I'm Wally Wilcox."

"Listen to all those stars they got lined up there," Pratt said.

"And now, here is a letter from the second platoon of Company B, the Seven Hundred Fifty-sixth Tank Destroyer Battalion."

"Hey!" the sergeant whooped. "Hey, I know those fellas! Yeah, they told me they were gonna write a letter. Well, whaddya know? They're really gonna read it. Son of a bitch, how about that?"

"Well, be quiet then, and let me listen," Ham said.

"The boys of the second platoon write: 'We'd like to hear the sound of Demaris Hunter frying a two-inch-thick porterhouse steak, smothered in onions. And let us hear that steak sizzle!' Okay, boys, here she is, Hollywood's own glamour girl, Demaris Hunter!"

The studio crowd applauded, cheered, and whistled.

"Hello, Wally, hello boys," Demaris said.

"Demaris, you heard what the boys are asking for. Can you fry a two-inch-thick porterhouse steak, covered with onions?"

"Well, I don't know."

"You don't know what? You don't know if you can do it?"

"No. I mean, I don't know what a two-inch porterhouse steak looks like, we've had meat rationing for so long."

The crowd roared with laughter.

"You'll learn quick enough when you see this baby. Bring it on out, gents, but you guards better keep your pistols handy. When the crowd sees meat like this, they may attack."

"Oh, I don't know about that, Wally," Demaris cooed.

"The crowd has been seeing ham all night long, and they haven't attacked yet."

More laughter.

"Okay, boys, we've got the burner hot, and here's Demaris, putting in the steak. My-oh-my-oh-my, what a big, gorgeous hunk of red meat that is, just hanging over the skillet. Oops, pardon me, boys; that was my tongue. I'll just stick it back in here."

More laughter.

"Just so you boys won't think this is all going to waste, I'm pleased to tell you that I plan to eat every bit of it, right after the show tonight. Of course, Demaris, you're welcome to join me."

"I'm afraid not, Wally. The stage hands already have dibs on it. I'll be eating this steak tonight, all right, but I'll be with them, not you."

"Just my luck. Okay, that meat is really cookin' now! Get the microphone down here by the skillet, men; you know what the boys of the Seven Hundred Fifty-sixth Tank Destroyer said. They want to hear it sizzle!"

Through the radio could be heard loud sizzling sounds.

"Man oh man, listen to that baby!" Sergeant Pratt said. "Right this moment if I was given my choice between Demaris Hunter and that porterhouse steak, I don't know which one I'd take."

"And now, here's a letter from a group of Army nurses stationed in Hawaii. They want to hear a song by Frankie. Frankie? Frankie who?"

"Oh, that would be me, Mr. Wilcox."

" 'Oh, that would be me, Mr. Wilcox,' " Wilcox repeated, and the crowd laughed at his mimicry. *"Listen to him call me Mr. Wilcox, like I'm so much older than he is. Why, we're just about the same age."*

Laughter.

"Practically."

More laughter.

"Almost."

Louder laughter.

"Nearly."

Uproarious laughter.

"Okay, all you nurses out there, and you fellas too, if you like a mellow sound. Here's Frank Sinatra!"

This time the crowd's applause was intermingled with women's high-pitched screams.

"Don't know what all those dames see in that guy," Pratt said, turning off the radio. "Hey, Lieutenant, how long we gotta keep our guys here?"

"Until Colonel Drake sends word that we can leave," Ham replied. "You've been in the Army longer than I have, Sergeant. You know how it works."

"Yes, sir, I know how it works. That's what's got me worried."

"What do you mean?"

"I don't like bein' this far away from everyone else. I mean, suppose the Germans start a big push through here. Rommel and all his panzers. And suppose somebody high up, like General Fredendall, or Eisenhower maybe, is lookin' at a map and he says, 'I think we ought to make a slight readjustment in our lines.' See, when *we* bug out, it's called running away, but when the *brass* does it, it's called a 'readjustment in our lines.' Now, suppose we have to make one of them readjustments. Why, Second Corps will tell the Third Armored Division, the Division will tell the Nineteenth Regiment, and the Regiment will tell the First Battalion. From there on it's going to be pretty much 'every man look out for himself.' You think word is goin' to get down to us?"

"Don't you?"

"Hell no, sir. What's going to happen is, the whole U.S. Army is gonna be a hundred and fifty, maybe two hundred miles away before some major in some staff meeting somewhere is going to suddenly snap his fingers and say, 'Didn't we leave the Second Platoon of Headquarters and Headquarters Company of the First Battalion out there somewhere?' And one of the other brass hats will take a puff on a cigarette—a stateside cigarette, not one of those things out of the C-ration kits—he'll take a puff, see, and he'll say something like, 'Yeah, too bad about them. But, after all, this is war, and they're expendable.'"

Ham laughed. "Sergeant Pratt, you know what I think?"

"What's that, sir?"

"I think you'd bitch if they hung you with a new rope."

"That's my right, Lieutenant," Pratt replied with a broad smile. "I'm an enlisted man. EMs can do that, you know . . . bitch, moan, and complain. It's only officers who have to stay calm and assured at all times. Are you calm and assured, Lieutenant?"

"I've got it covered," Ham said wryly. "Stay by the radio. I'm going to check the lookout posts."

"Aye, aye, sir."

"What do you mean, aye, aye? Have you suddenly gone Navy on me?"

"I should'a joined the Navy. I got a cousin did that, you know. He's out there in the Pacific somewhere now, floatin' around on a nice big ship, sleepin' on clean sheets every night, eatin' three good squares a day, enjoyin' a cool sea breeze. And here I am in the desert, bakin' in the sun, with scorpions in my boots and sand in my ass."

"It could be worse, Sergeant," Ham said. "It could be the other way around. You could have sand in your boots and scorpions in your ass."

Pratt laughed. "Yes, sir. I guess I could."

Ham left the half-track truck where he'd established his headquarters and climbed up the little hill where he'd set up a series of two-man listening and observation posts. Colonel Drake, the 1st Battalion Commander, had ordered the CO of Headquarters and Headquarters Company to set up an advance lookout point. Captain Poppel then instructed Lieutenant Twainbough to take half of his platoon and do the job by establishing listening and observation posts one mile northeast of the battalion's main position on Djebel Ksaira, the mountain that guarded the north side of Faid Pass. This was the pass through a range of mountains known as the Eastern Dorsal. On the east side of the Eastern Dorsal lay Rommel's Afrika Korps. On the west side was the town of Sidi Bou Zid and the II Corps of the American Army. In between was Colonel Drake's battalion and Ham's outposts.

PFC Richard Edward Parker was at the first lookout post. Ham felt an affinity with Parker because Parker was the only other man in the platoon who was married. Of course, Richard Edward had three sons already, whereas Ham, who had gotten married just after he graduated from OCS, had no children.

"Lieutenant, I'm not one to tell an officer what to do," Richard Edward said as Ham came up to the post. "But with you standin' up on the crest like that, a German sniper with a good scope on his piece could pick you off from a long way off."

"You're right. I wasn't thinking," Ham said, dropping down quickly. "Have you seen anything?"

"A lot of dust plumes," Richard Edward replied. "The Germans are movin' quite a bit of equipment around."

"Maybe they're gettin' ready to go home," Private John Boyd suggested. "Maybe they figure they've had enough now, and they've decided to call the war off and go back home."

"Well, hell, that's all right with me," Richard Edward said. He unscrewed his canteen and took a drink, then wiped his mouth with the back of his hand. "Say, Lieutenant, you think we'll get any more mail while we're out here?"

"I don't see why not," Ham answered. "They got it to us this morning; I guess they could get it to us tomorrow the same way."

Just after daybreak that morning, a Piper Cub, called an L-4 by the Army, had flown over to drop a mail pouch for Ham and his men. Ham got a letter from Amy, one from his mother, another from his father, and one from the Chicago Cardinals, offering him an opportunity to play professional football. He read Amy's letter three times, and then he read his mother's. He then glanced with some amusement at the offer from the Cardinals: "Our scouts tell us that the wide-open running style you exhibited during your playing days at Jefferson University would be much appreciated by the greatest football fans in the world, the Chicago Cardinal fans. If the idea of playing professional football appeals to you, please contact our office so that a contract can be drawn and all necessary arrangements made."

The letter from his father was still in his shirt pocket, unopened.

"I got some pictures this morning. Would you like to see them?" Richard Edward offered.

"Yes, sure, I'd love to," Ham said.

"Wait till you get a look at this beauty," Richard Edward said, taking the envelope out. He removed a small packet of pictures and showed one of them to Ham. "Is she what you'd call pretty, or what?"

Ham's eyebrows rose. He had expected the photo to be of Parker's wife. It was of a tractor-trailer truck. On the side of the trailer was painted BEN-HUR FENCES, on the side of the cab RICHARD EDWARD PARKER.

"I ask you, Lieutenant, what do you think of a man who gets pictures of his wife and kids and his truck, but he shows off his truck?" Boyd teased.

"I'd say he's a man who's proud of his truck," Ham laughed as he handed the picture back.

"I got a paint job out of the Ben-Hur people for lettin' 'em put their sign on the side of my trailer," Richard explained, looking sheepish. "I just thought you might want to see it. Here's Alice and the kids."

Richard Edward's wife, Alice, was sitting in a kitchen chair that had been brought outside of a small, wood-frame house. Two young boys stood beside her, and a baby sat on her lap. One of the boys was about three, the other five. The three-year-old was squinting into the sun and clutching a stuffed bear. The five-year-old was wearing a child's Army uniform and holding a toy rifle on his shoulder.

"The one with the rifle is Bobby," Richard Edward explained. "The one with the bear is Harry, and the baby is Freddie."

"Looks like Bobby has joined the Army already," Boyd said.

"When are you going to get some kids, Lieutenant?" Richard Edward asked, taking the pictures back.

"Hey, give me a break, will you, Parker? I just got married. I haven't had time."

"Well hell, Lieutenant, how long does your part take?" Richard Edward quipped.

Ham scowled good-naturedly. "That, Private Parker, is

none of your damn business," he replied, and with the laughter of the two men ringing in his ears, he moved over to check the other lookout posts. When he got back to the half-track a few minutes later, he found Sergeant Pratt just finishing a radio call.

"What was that about?" Ham asked.

"HQ wants us to be especially watchful tonight," Pratt said. "They think the krauts might try somethin'."

"Did they say why they think that?"

"No, sir, but you know what a bunch of nervous Nellies they are," Pratt replied. He picked up a box of C rations and looked inside. "Beans and franks," he said. "Ah, now there's a meal fit for a king." He started opening a can. "You know, Lieutenant, if you ask me, I wish to hell the krauts *would* attack tonight. I mean, it's pretty borin' sittin' out here, freezin' our asses off at night and burnin' up in the daytime."

"I know what you mean," Ham said. He sat down against a tire and looked through the C ration box for his own supper. When he found a can of mixed fruit, he opened it and began drinking the juice straight from the can, opening his mouth wide enough to take in the tiny pieces of fruit as well. He thought of his father's letter then, so he set the can on the ground beside him and took the letter from his pocket.

> Dear Ham,
>
> Your mail came with the Christmas delivery and thus helped me to have a happy Yule. Hope you spent the holidays pleasantly, though I'm sure you'd have preferred to be somewhere else.
>
> I'm sorry I didn't get a chance to meet Amy before you married her . . . or since, for that matter. But she must be a wonderful girl or you wouldn't be so taken with her.
>
> I'm still in England, though I'm beginning to wonder if I didn't make a big mistake in coming here. I had hoped to find a big story to tell, but the story isn't here, it's in North Africa and in the Pacific. Oh, sure, the Germans were sending their bombers over for a brief while, and we are sending

more and more of ours over there, but that isn't the real war. Most of the reporters here are running around doing stories on each other.

The only good thing about England is that Shaylin McKay is here. We've been spending some time together, though she was quick to tell me that her heart belongs to one Colonel Sir John Paul Chetwynd-Dunleigh, who is serving now with His Majesty's Forces in India. Lord knows I wouldn't want to get between Shaylin and someone with that impressive a name and title. But, as I told her, he's there, I'm here, we're at war, and we owe it to ourselves to take what comfort and pleasure we can, for who knows what the morrow will bring. I know what you're thinking, and you're right, Ham. It *is* a shameless exploitation of the situation, but you don't know Shaylin as I do. I'm not talking her into doing anything she doesn't want to do; I'm just providing her with the excuse she needs to justify doing it.

Give my love to Tanner the next time you write her, will you? Your mother is a beautiful woman in all senses of the word, and if we had been born into a perfect world, I'd still be married to her.

Keep your head down, Ham. The damn Germans took a few potshots at me during WW I, but missed. I wouldn't be surprised if some Nazi bastard didn't have it in mind to make you a special target now because of it.

Much love,
Papa

By the time Ham finished the letter, it was nearly too dark to read. He folded it up, put it in his pocket, drank/ate the rest of his can of mixed fruit, then leaned his head back against the side of the half-track and watched the darkness fall before finally going to sleep.

It was just after sunup the next morning when Ham was awakened by a bansheelike wail. When he sat up, the sound seemed to be all around him, coming from everywhere and nowhere.

"Look! Up there!" Sergeant Pratt shouted, pointing skyward.

Ham looked where Pratt was pointing and saw six airplanes screaming down out of the sky toward them. The planes were German. They were the angular, gull-winged Stukas, and though Ham had seen them in newsreels in theaters, this was the first time he'd ever seen one coming right at him. It was the most terrifying thing he'd ever experienced.

The six airplanes pulled out of their dives at about three hundred feet, but the bombs they released continued to fall.

"Take cover!" Ham shouted, and though he was closer to the half-track, he ran toward a nearby ditch and threw himself into it. As it turned out, that was the wisest thing to do, because three of the six bombs that were dropped scored direct hits on the truck. Within seconds the vehicle was a roaring inferno.

The Stukas, satisfied that the half-track was out of commission, didn't return for a second attack. Instead, they flew toward the middle of the valley some five to six miles distant, where they joined in with another swarm of Stukas that were attacking American positions.

"Look at that!" Sergeant Pratt shouted. "They're poundin' the crap out of our guys!"

"And look back there," Ham added, pointing toward the German lines. "Holy shit! The Germans are launching a major attack through here!"

"Lieutenant, what are we gonna do?" Pratt asked. "We can't warn them; our radio's out."

"Get the men together, Sergeant. Make sure their weapons are loaded. We're going to try and get back to battalion."

But once they got going, it didn't take long for Ham to realize that there was no way they could rejoin Colonel Drake's battalion. The German drive had punched through the middle of the American lines, rolling the main body back and cutting off what had been the American flanks. Colonel Drake's battalion was trapped on the slopes of

Djebel Ksaira. Major Moore and his battalion were trapped on Djebel Lessouda, a hill on the south side of Faid Pass.

It took Ham and his men most of the day to walk out of the area. Sometimes they came so close to the German soldiers that they could hear them talking, and they had to sneak through wadis and creep along behind small ridges to avoid detection. It was late afternoon when they finally rejoined another battalion of American troops, who were now in full retreat.

General Fredendall had completely abandoned the town of Sidi Bou Zid and the Eastern Dorsal. In so doing, he had also abandoned Colonel Drake, Major Moore, and more than twenty-five hundred American soldiers, including Headquarters and Headquarters Company, the company Lieutenant Hamilton Twainbough was assigned to.

"Don't you worry about that, Lieutenant," a colonel named Stark told him. "We're going back to Sidi Bou Zid first thing tomorrow morning and get Colonel Drake, Major Moore, and their men out of there. Meanwhile, I'm going to attach your platoon to Able Company. Report to Captain Quinn."

"Yes, sir," Ham replied, saluting the colonel.

Ham found the men of Able Company spread out alongside a meandering dry streambed. The men had come far today, and they had come quickly. It was a tired and dispirited bunch of soldiers who were gathered around the small guidon stuck in the dirt that marked the location of company headquarters.

"Cap'n Quinn isn't here right now, sir," the first sergeant explained after Ham told him that he and the rest of his men had been assigned to them. "He'll be back in a few minutes, though. You can tell your men to just flop anywhere they want."

"Thanks, Sergeant," Ham replied.

The first sergeant was a short, stout man with a weathered face and closely cropped gray hair. He took in the area with a wave of his hand. "Yes, sir. Well, as you can see, we ain't exactly in what you might call a garrison situation here."

"No, I guess not. Did you lose many men today?"

"Who the hell knows?" the first sergeant answered disgustedly. "They're still comin' in."

"Today was quite hectic."

"Hectic? Is that what you call it, sir?"

"What would you call it?"

"I'd call it a goddamned disgrace, the biggest military blunder since Custer. The only difference is, Custer at least stayed and fought. We ran like whipped pups."

"Would you rather have suffered Custer's fate?"

The first sergeant spat into the dirt. "He at least kept his honor."

A jeep arrived then, and a captain got out of the front seat and started toward Ham and the noncom. Though this was the first time Ham had seen him in several months, he recognized the captain at once. Captain Quinn had been Lieutenant Quinn, one of his tactical officers at OCS. Quinn recognized Ham also, and he smiled broadly.

"Well, if it isn't 'Sir, Candidate Twainbough, BOOM, sir,' " he said, returning Ham's salute, then offering his hand for a shake. 'What are you doing here?"

"My platoon was manning a listening and observation post for Colonel Drake," Ham explained. "After the German attack, we couldn't get back to Colonel Drake."

"Yeah, well, be glad you couldn't. Drake and his men are still trapped back there," Quinn said. He took a drink from his canteen, then continued. "We're going back after them tomorrow, but it's going to be rough."

"I thought we had the Germans pretty well whipped," Ham said.

"They're hardly whipped, Lieutenant. The only thing we've done is push them all together. Think of it as a spring. When it's uncoiled, it's really easy to bend. But when it's all coiled up, it has all that energy sitting there, just waiting to explode. On the east side of the Dorsal, that's what the Germans are—a coiled spring."

"I see."

"I'm not sure you do see," Quinn said, as if he were back at OCS, teaching tactics. "Tomorrow we have to go right into the teeth of that coiled spring, and they know we're coming. It's sort of like a mousetrap when you think of it. Colonel Drake and Major Moore and their men are the cheese, the German Army is the trap, and we're the mouse."

"Perhaps so," Ham said. "But we have to make the assumption that General Fredendall knows what he's doing."

"Assumption, Lieutenant?" Quinn snorted, then looked over at his first sergeant. "Sergeant, you've been in the Army how long now?"

"Twenty-six years, sir," the NCO replied.

"Then, from your twenty-six years of experience, would you please tell this young man the old military axiom concerning assumption?"

"Assumption is the mother of all fuck-ups," the first sergeant said.

"Do you still want to assume, Lieutenant?" Captain Quinn asked.

Ham chuckled. "No, sir, I guess not."

"When you and your guys got out, did you bring any of your equipment with you?"

"Only our weapons. Everything else burned up in the half-track."

"Including rations?"

"I'm afraid so."

"Fortunately, that's one thing we have plenty of," Quinn said. "You can see the supply sergeant and draw three days' worth. Then if you can, you'd better get some rest. We're moving out before first light."

"Yes, sir," Ham said, saluting Quinn and thinking how different he seemed here on the battlefield than he had back at Fort Benning.

True to Captain Quinn's word, Ham and the others were awakened the next morning before dawn. During the night the Army had brought up several two-and-a-half-ton trucks, called by the men 'deuce-and-a-halfs,' and they stood now in several long rows with lowered tailgates, waiting for the troops. Alongside the rows of trucks, large vats of coffee bubbled and steamed over blue-flamed field stoves, and cooks and cooks' helpers ladled out the aromatic brew into canteen cups as the men filed by on their way to the trucks.

"Hey, this is awright," Sergeant Pratt said, holding his nearly full coffee cup carefully as he approached the back of one of the trucks. "In the modern Army, this is the way we're supposed to go to war. I mean, ridin' instead of all this walkin' shit."

"I don't know why they've got me ridin' back here," Richard Edward complained. Like Sergeant Pratt, he was carrying a cup of coffee. "I should be up front, drivin' the damned thing. I'm a truck driver, not a foot slogger."

"You men," the first sergeant called, "check your weapons! Make sure they're not loaded!"

"Sarge, what if we get attacked?" someone asked. "We can't do much with empty rifles."

"If we're attacked, you can load them," the sergeant replied. When he saw Ham sitting on the bench in the back with the troops, he blinked in surprise. "Lieutenant Twainbough, you don't have to ride back here. I can find room in front of one of the trucks for you."

"Thank you, Sergeant," Ham said, "but since we're just attached to your company, I'd rather stay back here with my men, if you don't mind."

The first sergeant smiled. "Good for you, sir. Every now and again I come across a second lieutenant who shows some promise." He closed the tailgate, and one of the men in the truck reached down to snap the safety strap across the back. A moment later the truck's engine started, joining the rumbling sound of the scores of other engines already running. A few moments after that the convoy moved out.

As the trucks sped down the highway that led back to Sidi Bou Zid, the cold, predawn wind whipped against the protective tarpaulins, slapping them against the bowed supports above the men's heads. After a short while the trucks left the road and started out across the plains, approaching Faid Pass. Once off the road the bouncing became so violent that in several cases the soldiers' helmets were jarred off.

From his seat by the tailgate, Ham watched the sky turn from dark to gray to blue. Now it was no longer cold, and the wind, like a breath from hell, filled the back of the truck with a fine, powdery dust that coated the men's sweat-covered faces, clogged their nostrils, and was gnashed between their teeth.

The trucks ground to a halt. The men stayed inside, thinking it was only a momentary halt, but word was urgently passed down that they were to disembark.

"Get away from the trucks! Get away from the trucks and into the ravine! The air corps is coming!"

Ham, doing his best to keep his men together, moved them into the ravine. In front of him he could see the town of Sidi Bou Zid and, nearby, Djebel Ksaira. Colonel Drake's men occupied the high ground, while the Germans controlled the approaches and slopes.

"Here they come!" someone yelled. "Here come our planes!"

"What kind are they?"

"P-40's," the observer replied, shielding his eyes against the sun as he watched the planes approach. There were twelve of them, rumbling overhead at less than five hundred feet, the noise of their engines surging down like thunder. About a mile beyond the ravines they pulled up in a high, arcing climb, then rolled over and came screaming back down straight toward the German positions, firing their machine guns. Then, as they pulled away, they released bombs that plummeted earthward to explode in flame and smoke on the lower slopes of Djebel Ksaira. The lead plane was followed by a second and then a third, until all twelve planes had made a pass. Then each came around a second time.

Rolling off the target, the planes turned back toward the ravine, flying over the American troops at very low altitude, the noise of their engines and propellers so loud that it was almost painful to the troops. The attack planes were so low that Ham could see streams of oil coming from the engines, and he could clearly see the markings on the wings and fuselage.

"They aren't going to leave anything for us," one of the soldiers complained.

"Don't worry," Sergeant Pratt said. "There'll be plenty left."

Suddenly one of the pilots seemed to lose control, just as his plane rolled off target. The P-40 flipped over on its back, then slammed into the side of the mountain, exploding in a large, flaming ball. The men watched the plane burn fiercely, sending thick, oily smoke roiling into the clear sky.

"Damn! What the hell happened?"

"Did he get shot down?"

"No," Pratt said. "He just crashed."

"Jesus! Can you beat that?"

The other airplanes, finished now with their attack, started back toward the American air base, climbing to reassemble in formation.

On the ground the soldiers were stunned by the crash, and they stayed in the ravine for a long time, just staring toward the funeral pyre.

"Look," someone said. "There go our tanks."

Ham looked out to his left and saw an absolutely majestic sight: An entire armor battalion of tanks was moving toward the town—huge, lumbering monsters in perfect parade-ground formation. They raised a storm of dust as they rumbled forward in what seemed to be unstoppable power. At that moment Ham felt genuine pride in being part of an integrated military operation of aircraft, armor, and infantry. He had a feeling that history was being made, and he was enjoying a ringside seat. He wished his father could be here with him, for this was the kind of thing Eric Twainbough could really appreciate.

"We'll get 'em now," someone said.

"Pass the word down to get ready. We'll be going in to mop up, right after the tanks."

"Mop up!" a private complained. "I thought we were in the infantry. I thought we were fighters."

"Are you kiddin'? I'd be just as happy to stay here," his companion joked.

Shortly after the battle commenced, the Americans learned that the Germans, too, had air power, for they launched a Stuka dive-bomb attack against the American tanks.

"Those cowardly bastards!" someone shouted. "Why

didn't they bring their dive-bombers out a while ago, when we had our airplanes here?"

" 'Cause they were afraid we'd shoot 'em down, that's why," another replied.

"They're cowards."

"I'd say they're smart."

Three of the American tanks were hit by the Stuka bombs, and they began burning fiercely, belching up large columns of smoke. There were now four towering plumes of smoke marking the battlefield, three from American tanks and one from the American plane that had crashed.

"Oh, shit! Look at that! Panzers!"

Ham groaned and thought immediately of Captain Quinn's analogy of the mousetrap. The Americans had taken the bait . . . and now the trap was snapping shut. Panzers bore down on both American flanks. The armor battalion commander's tank was taken out of action quickly; then there was a general melee as the American and German tanks swirled around in the dust, exchanging almost point-blank fire. Though much of the action was covered by dust and smoke, Ham could see brilliant flashes of light from the muzzle flashes and tank explosions shining through. He could also hear the thunder of battle, the clank and squeak of tank tracks, and the grinding sound of over-revved engines.

Finally the dust and smoke cleared away, and Ham could see that of the fifty-four American tanks that began the attack, only four had managed to escape the German vise and retreat toward the American lines. In virtually no time an entire armored battalion had been annihilated, while Colonel Drake's and Major Moore's battalions remained trapped behind enemy lines.

"Pull back! Into the trucks, men! Pull back!" The order came quickly down the line. Grumbling, the men who had ridden out in the predawn darkness now climbed back into the trucks for a full-scale retreat. So far not one of them had so much as fired a weapon.

"I don't know about the rest of you guys," one of the soldiers said as the trucks began to pull away, "but I'm gettin' fuckin' tired of runnin' from those sons of bitches!"

Ham thought at first that they'd withdraw no farther

back than to where they'd bivouacked the previous night, but he soon learned that they were going way beyond that. The trucks ground on across the plains of Tunisia for the rest of the day and far into the tracer-illuminated and flare-lighted night. Several times during the day and on into the night the convoy was attacked by German planes, and the ring-mounted machine guns on the trucks would open up, popping loudly overhead and spitting a long string of tracer rounds into the sky. Most of the defensive fire of the Americans was ineffective, but once, while looking out the back of the truck, Ham saw one of the German planes hit. The plane didn't go down, but it did trail a thin stream of smoke as it started back toward its own lines.

It was obvious that the German planes were having a great deal of success because throughout the long day and into the night Ham continued to see burned-out deuce-and-a-half trucks. One of the trucks was particularly gruesome because the charred bodies of a dozen or more GIs were still in the back, sitting on the benches, frozen in that position by death. Even the machine gunner was still at his station, his hands locked in a death squeeze on the grips of the gun.

Finally the American troops reached the range of mountains known as the Western Dorsal. There were five passes through the Western Dorsal, and the column Ham was traveling in went through one of them, Kasserine Pass. The Americans were tired, dispirited, weakened by the loss of three entire battalions, and disorganized to the point that there were several platoons like Ham's, as well as individual soldiers, who were separated from their parent unit. But here at Kasserine Pass, the trucks stopped and the men disembarked to form a defense perimeter. Captain Quinn found Ham setting up fields of fire for his men and told him to come along to an officers' call being held by the battalion commander.

"Are you sure Colonel Kirby wants me at this officers' call?" Ham asked as he followed Captain Quinn past silent trucks and exhausted soldiers. "You know I'm not really assigned to this battalion."

"You are now," Quinn answered.

A few minutes later Ham approached a handful of officers gathered around a small field table. There was a map on the table, and a lieutenant colonel was leaning over the table, looking at the map.

"Sir, this is the lieutenant I was telling you about," Quinn said after the two men had saluted.

"Yes, I remember when you reported," Colonel Kirby said. He smiled at Ham. "Captain Quinn tells me you are Eric Twainbough's son."

"Yes, sir."

"Your father's a damn good writer. *Stillness in the Line* is one of the finest war stories ever written. Better than *All Quiet on the Western Front*, in my opinion, and as good as *Red Badge of Courage*."

"Thank you, sir. I'm sure my father would be pleased to hear that," Ham said.

"Well, you tell him for me, will you?"

"Yes, sir," Ham replied. He thought the conversation rather strange. Here they were, in full retreat from the Germans, and the battalion commander was talking about one of his father's books.

"I didn't send for you to talk about that," Colonel Kirby said, and Ham gasped slightly because it almost seemed as if Kirby had read his mind.

"No, sir," Ham replied. "I didn't think you had."

"I'm giving you Charley Company," Kirby explained.

"Yes, sir, I'll report at once," Ham said. "Who's the company commander?"

Kirby looked up at him. "Didn't you hear what I said? I said I'm giving it to *you*. *You* are the company commander."

"Me? But, Colonel, I'm only a second lieutenant."

"Lieutenant, I have a warrant officer commanding my signal company. Captain Quinn tells me he remembers you from OCS, and he assures me you can handle the job."

"I thank the captain, and you, for your confidence," Ham said. "And I hope I can justify it."

"Yes, well, you may not be thanking me after you find out what I have in mind." He pointed to the map. "Right here in Kasserine Pass we are going to, in the words of General Fredendall, 'pull a Stonewall Jackson.'" He tapped his pencil on the pass. "This far the Germans will get . . .

and no farther. You can see why, I'm sure. Right over here is Tébessa, our most important communications and supply base. If the Germans get through us and take that, they will have effectively eliminated the Americans in the sector. Then they could attack the Brits from the rear. We'd have to abandon Tunisia and maybe all of North Africa. I hope I'm getting the point across, gentlemen," he said to all the officers. "If we don't stop the Germans right here, right now, we're going to have to pull way back."

"Back to where, sir?" one of the officers asked.

"Who the hell can say where we'll wind up?" the colonel replied. "It could be New Jersey, for all I know."

"What do you want us to do, Colonel? Do you have a plan?"

"As a matter of fact, I do. Look how the pass narrows here. What I propose to do is let the Germans come pouring in, like sand through an hourglass. Right here, on the west side of this narrow stricture, we'll be waiting for them. And because of the restriction of the pass, they won't be able to amass any more troops against us than we can have waiting for them. We'll cut them to pieces."

"That's a good plan, Colonel."

Colonel Kirby sighed and stroked his chin. "It's a good plan if you have fresh troops and high morale. Right now I'm afraid we have neither. But we're going to hold this pass, gentlemen. Whatever it takes, we're going to hold this pass. Now, get back to your companies and get them ready."

"Yes, sir!" the officers said in unison as they exchanged salutes with their commander.

Ham got permission to take the remnants of his platoon with him when he took command of Charley Company. It was good that he did because Charley Company was a company in name only. During the long retreat it had lost two truckloads of men to German action, including its only two officers and the first sergeant. Now the company was little more than an augmented platoon, and among the noncoms, only the mess sergeant outranked Sergeant Pratt.

"I'm a cook," the mess sergeant was quick to say. "I'll fight if you want me to, but I've never even been a platoon sergeant. If you're looking for me to be the new first sergeant, you'd better look somewhere else."

"Okay, Sergeant Pratt, I guess you've got the job," Ham said.

"Aye, aye, sir," Pratt said.

Ham chuckled. "Joining the Navy again?"

"Don't I wish," Pratt retorted.

"In the meantime, how about helping me get the men in position? We've got this sector from here to here," Ham said, pointing out the terrain where they'd have to dig in.

Pratt clucked his tongue. "I wish we had three times as many men—or one third the territory to cover," he said.

"If wishes were wings, frogs wouldn't bump their asses every time they jump," Ham replied. "Let's get the men spread out."

Though Ham had told the men of his company to choose a partner so that one could sleep while the other was awake, he himself didn't sleep that night. He tried to, he had teamed up with Sergeant Pratt so that he could, but he was too excited, nervous, frightened, or perhaps all three, to get any sleep. Because of that, when the German panzers began coming through the pass the next morning, he was still awake.

He could feel them coming before he could hear them, a low shaking of the ground as though he were standing beside a railroad track while a train went by. Then he could hear them, a strange combination of low-pitched engine growl and high-pitched squeaking as the tanks' tracks clanked and clattered across all the sprockets and through all the gear wheels. Finally, he could see the huge black shapes materializing in the heavy fog that had rolled in with the break of dawn.

This was it, his first real action. No watching others do battle this time. And no cut and run, either. This time the orders were to stand and fight. The palms of his hands were sweaty, and he felt a hollowness in the pit of his stomach.

"Pratt," he hissed. "Pratt, wake everyone up! Here they come!"

Pratt sat up and wiped his eyes, then looked out through the mist.

"Do you see them?" Ham whispered.

"Yes, sir, I see them," Pratt answered in a normal voice, eyeing Ham sardonically. "What I want to know is, why are you whispering? You really think they can hear us?"

Ham laughed nervously. "No, I guess not."

Pratt passed the word down to the others, and within a few minutes all of Charley Company, and, Ham suspected, everyone else in the battalion, was wide awake.

"Bazookas, antitank guns, mortars, wait for my command!" Ham called.

There was absolute silence along the American lines as the German tanks continued to advance. Then, between the tanks, Ham saw the German infantry. There were tens, scores, hundreds of German infantrymen, faceless, phantomlike figures moving through the fog, holding their weapons at high port in front of them.

"Machine gunners and riflemen, when the antitank weapons open up, you take the infantry," Ham ordered.

He waited a bit, thinking that perhaps one of the other companies would open fire first and he wouldn't have to make the decision. Then he realized that his position was such that *he* would have to engage the enemy first. The decision was his to make whether he wanted to or not. He drew a deep breath and held it for a long moment.

"Fire!" he finally shouted.

Immediately thereafter his company's heavy weapons opened up, the antitank guns making a flat *crack*, the mortars a hollow *thump*, and the bazookas a loud *whoosh*. Seconds later came a ripple of explosions among the approaching tanks, and one went up with a fiery blast.

Now not only Charley Company, but all the companies in line, opened fire, joined a moment later by the much heavier fire of American artillery that was farther back. The Germans returned fire. The exchange was so intense that it was one sustained roar. Joining the heavy fire from the American artillery and German tanks was a steady rattle of small-arms fire. There was the constant flash and gleam of muzzle blasts, puffs of smoke drifting up through the fog, and fire streaks of tracers as they struck the ground, then bounced away, tumbling along their crazed path. The firing continued unabated for a half hour . . . an hour . . . still going long after the fog had lifted. Visibility improved somewhat, though smoke from burning tanks and discharged weapons continued to drift across the field.

Ham's eyes burned from the cordite, and his throat was so dry that he could scarcely breathe, though he wasn't actually aware of being thirsty. A German round exploded nearby, and in the blast effect of the shell he got a quick glimpse of a tumbling arm. With a sickened gasp he realized that the arm wasn't attached to a body, though a watch was still on the wrist, and it flashed gold in the morning sun. The fighting continued for another half hour. Then, finally, the German advance stuttered, halted, and the phantom creatures proved to be human after all as they turned and started running back.

"Cease fire!" someone shouted. "Cease fire! Cease fire!" and Ham realized that word was being passed down from battalion. He, too, took up the call, and a moment later all the guns were stilled.

"They're gone," Ham said. "We held them. Son of a bitch! We held them!"

"That's good," Sergeant Pratt said in a voice that was so quiet that Ham looked toward him in concern.

"Sergeant, are you okay?" he asked.

"No, sir, I'm not."

"Where are you hit?" Ham looked his sergeant over, but he couldn't find any sign of a wound.

"No, it's not that," Pratt said. He raised up and looked around, making sure no one was close enough to hear him. "It's just that . . . well, I think I just pissed in my goddamned pants."

CHAPTER NINETEEN

Yukari Amano and her mother, Yuko, stood on a street corner near Asano Park, stopping strangers on the street to request that they sew a stitch in their *senninbari*. Yuko and Yukari hoped that it wouldn't be long before these sashes containing one thousand stitches from one thousand different people were completed. The idea behind the *senninbari* was that the prayers of all those people would be incorporated into the sash along with their stitches. Yuko was making a senninbari for her husband, Hiroshi, while Yukari was making one for her brother, Saburo, now serving in the Navy.

Saburo had once been forbidden by his father to enter the Navy, but events had moved so quickly as to overtake Hiroshi's objections. He soon found that he had no choice but to allow Saburo to begin naval officer training or Saburo would have been drafted into the Army as a common soldier. Now Saburo, who intended to follow in his father's footsteps, was taking flight training.

"We are lucky to find a place where no one else is

working on the senninbari," Yuko said to her daughter as the two stood on the street corner.

"Yes," Yukari agreed. "There are so many doing the same thing that it makes it very difficult to collect the stitches. Some, I am certain, do not even have a man in the Army or Navy. I think they are just doing it for show."

"No," Yuko answered, "I am certain that no one would do this unless they had a loved one to do it for. It is far too hard. But it will also be most rewarding when they are all finished. And I know that Hiroshi and Saburo will appreciate them very much."

"I hope Saburo will not mind that his was done by a sister, rather than a wife or a sweetheart as they are supposed to be," Yukari said. "Perhaps my doing it will prove to be an embarrassment for him."

"Nonsense. Saburo will appreciate it all the more for it coming from his sister. He loves you so. He has grown much over the past year."

Yukari smiled. "That is true. Do you remember how he used to tease me unmercifully? The last time he was home, he treated me with so much respect that I thought the Navy had made a mistake and sent a different boy home to us."

Yuko smiled with pride. "Oh, but they did not send a boy. They sent a man, and that is the difference."

"Yes, he is a man now, isn't he? Oh, here come three more people. When we get their stitches, we will be nearly half finished."

Yukari was young and pretty and flushed with the confidence of youth and beauty, so she was much more aggressive than her mother. She accosted the approaching strangers, two women and an old man, and offered her sash to them for the stitches. Since many women all over Japan were doing this now, the three obliged willingly and without having to be told what to do. When they had finished, Yukari pointed out Yuko, and, with a friendly smile, the obliging strangers put stitches into Yuko's sash as well.

"Thank you," Yuko said, bowing politely as the three continued on their journey.

"Now we are nearly half done," Yukari said, looking at

her sash. "Mother, do you think . . ." She left the question unasked.

"What is it, dear?"

"Do you think it will make any difference? I mean, even if we get one thousand stitches, will it really protect them?"

"Yes, of course," Yuko said. "And it will do something even more important."

"What is that?"

"It will show your father and Saburo that we love them very much."

"But do they have to be shown? Don't they know that we love them?"

"I am sure they know, but when times are hard, it is good to have some tangible thing to speak of your love. Please, you must not lose heart in what you are doing."

Yukari smiled at her mother. "Don't worry," she said. "I will not lose heart."

KADENA AIR CADET TRAINING BASE

In Saburo's barracks the lights came on while it was still dark outside, and the three NCOs in charge of training came into the room. They and the sudden light burst upon Saburo's restless sleep with the sharpness of a detonating shell, and they screamed and yelled and banged upon the wall and the floors with the grub-hoe handles they carried with them. Within a few seconds Saburo was completely awake, standing at attention at the foot of his sleeping mat wearing only his *fundoshi*—the loincloths they were required to sleep in—and awaiting the sadistic pleasure of the honchos over him. His left eye was swollen nearly shut from a blow he had received the night before, administered by a honcho—as the noncommissioned officers were called —in retaliation for his lack of speed in obeying an order. Every joint and muscle in his body ached from the physical activity of the last few weeks, and his side was still tender from a blow he had received a few days ago. He stifled an involuntary groan, lest it call attention to him, but a cadet four men down from Saburo wasn't able to hold in his moan, and one of the NCOs heard it.

"So you," the NCO shouted. "Mama's little baby, why are you crying?"

"I am not crying, Sergeant," the cadet insisted.

Saburo sensed the inward but silent groans of everyone else as the cadet spoke. It would have been much better for him if he had not spoken at all, for now he had drawn the NCO into conversation with him. Saburo had learned early that you didn't want to engage an NCO in conversation; where one noncom went, the others were sure to follow.

"You were *not* crying?" the sergeant asked, raising his eyebrows. "It sounded so to me." He laughed, and it was a sound of sadistic glee. He looked at the other honchos. "What do you think? Was he crying?"

"I don't know," one of them answered. "I haven't heard him cry, so I don't know what it sounds like. Perhaps he was laughing. Let me see."

The NCO who had just spoken suddenly slammed his hoe handle across the hapless recruit's rear. The recruit let out a gasp, then cut it off quickly. "Now that," the noncom said, turning to the others, "was a cry."

The NCO in charge of all the others had been watching quietly. Now he laughed—a high-pitched sound that was totally without mirth. "But how can you tell with just one sound? Perhaps the baby is right. Perhaps he isn't crying. This may be the sound of one who enjoys having his little butt caressed. They are all mama's baby boys, are they not? The oldest among them is what? Eighteen? Nineteen? They are used to the gentle hand of their mama across their bare butts. Perhaps we should conduct an experiment right now to see. All of you, drop your fundoshi."

The cadets dropped their loincloths, and they stood there naked.

The other NCOs began to point to the genitals of the young recruits and laugh and make derisive comments as to their size. "Look how small they are," one of the honchos said.

"Why do they even bother to wear the fundoshi?" another asked.

Saburo preferred the beating to the humiliating teasing of the honchos, but he couldn't choose the punishment. As it turned out, he and the others had to put up with the merciless teasing *and* a beating, for at the chief honcho's orders, the cadets were ordered to turn to the wall, and all the other NCOs began moving up and down the line of bare buttocks, slamming their hoe handles against them.

Saburo heard them as they approached, and he braced himself. But despite all the mental preparation, he was still shocked by the bolt of white-hot pain that knifed up from his buttocks and through his spine, wrapping around and wrenching his stomach so that he had to fight against throwing up. With an effort beyond anything he would have thought possible, he managed to take the blow in total silence, not even increasing his rate of breathing, for anything—even the slightest acknowledgment—would have brought all the other NCOs to him, each one adding their blow to the first.

Most cadets were able to withstand the blows, but a few, including the young recruit whose groan had brought all the attention down on them, broke, and once they broke they were fair game for the sadistic punches, kicks, and slams of the NCOs. Perversely, the breaking of one generally meant the relief of the others, for all the honchos converged on the hapless victim, leaving the other recruits alone.

After all the NCOs had taken their turn pummeling the ones who had broken, the head honcho called a halt to it.

"So," he said to the cadets. "Did you enjoy our little game this morning? Ah, you did? That is good, that is good, for we will have the chance to play it many more times while you are here. Now, prepare yourselves for today's classes. You must not be late, or we will be very upset." He smiled such an evil smile that he made it clear that far from being upset, the honchos would have liked nothing better than if the cadets were late, giving them an excuse to administer more punishment.

Saburo and the others stood at rigid attention until the door shut on the last of the NCOs. Then, though every fiber in his body urged him to lie down until the throbbing pain had somewhat subsided, Sauburo knew that he must keep moving, so he found the strength to ignore the pleading of his body.

"The bastards," Ikawa, the recruit in the bed next to Saburo's, swore. "There is no need for anyone to behave as those bastards do. Someday I hope someone kills them, and I hope that privilege is mine."

"You could never kill them, Ikawa," one of the others said. "You are like the rest of us. You pee in your pants every time one of them comes near."

"Still, such brutish behavior is unnecessary," Ikawa complained, ignoring the comment. "Why must we be treated like animals in order to learn to fly?"

"There is more to it than learning to fly," another said. "We are learning to be officers in His Majesty's Navy, and defenders of the Empire. They are asking nothing of us that they would not ask of a samurai."

"But I am not samurai," Ikawa complained.

"Neither am I, but Saburo is. Saburo does not complain. The rest of us should learn a lesson from him."

"Are you samurai?" Ikawa asked Saburo.

"Yes."

"And samurai must go through such things?"

"I don't know," Saburo answered. "I suppose my father went through such a thing, but he never spoke of it."

"Of course not. A true samurai would not speak of it, for to speak would be to complain, and a true samurai never complains," the other recruit explained.

Saburo had wanted desperately to agree with Ikawa, to protest against this inhumane treatment of the cadets. But he could not, for he was trapped by the code that governed his life. As a samurai, he had to set the example for the others. He must absorb as much punishment as the honchos wished to give, and he must never utter a sound of protest.

"I will not complain," Saburo said.

"You will be the inspiration for us all."

It wasn't fair, Saburo thought. He didn't want to be the inspiration. He was in pain and he was tired, and he wanted to see his mother and his sister and his grandparents again. He wanted to lie on the sleeping mat and cry

long, bitter tears until all the ache had left his body . . .
until he was no longer tired and his strength had returned.

But he knew that he wouldn't do that because he was
samurai. He had been raised from birth to be cognizant of
the responsibilities of being samurai, and even though such
a caste system had been officially abolished, he could no
more separate himself from its governing code than he
could separate his head from his body.

As Saburo thought about it, the pain began to dull, and
the throbbing in his head went away. Perhaps there was
some secret strength in being samurai after all. Perhaps
pride and duty could act as an effective opiate against suffering and pain. He smiled.

"Look," Ikawa said to the others. "Saburo smiles at
the pain. Let us all be like him. Let us all be loyal to the
Imperial Rescript to Soldiers and Sailors and display the
fighting spirit."

"Banzai!" one of the other recruits yelled, and the others joined in, shouting their war cry and saluting Saburo,
the samurai who was their inspiration.

Saburo had never known such pride.

RABAUL, SOLOMON ISLANDS

The sun rose just after five o'clock, and it spread the
eastern horizon with great smears of yellow and red, touching the surface of the water and setting it afire with color.

Hiroshi Amano watched the sunrise from the beach.
He was sitting on a cut-down oil drum, drinking from a
coconut shell and looking out not only at the sunrise, but at
the Japanese fleet. As the air group commander for the
flagship, Hiroshi would normally be aboard ship right now,
except the oppressive heat in the bowels of the ship had
driven him ashore to sleep on the beach in search of some
relief. But the relief from the heat had been negated by a
swarm of attacking mosquitoes, and today Hiroshi's body
had literally erupted with hundreds of bites, dozens of
which he had scratched into open sores. Many pilots had
tried to sleep ashore but returned to their quarters on the
ship, preferring the stifling heat to the nightly battle with

the mosquitoes. All the pilots had come ashore even before dawn this morning, however, as they were going to hear a speech given by Admiral Yamamoto.

Of all the airfields and bases Hiroshi had visited since the beginning of the war, Rabaul was the most inhospitable. To his thinking, it could have been carved from the regions of hell. The landing strip shimmered with heat under a constant layer of dust, a nearby volcano rumbled and erupted often enough to blanket the area in thick, noxious smoke, and even the trees were naked of foliage. But for all its hostile environment and ugly scenery, Rabaul was the best place to be if one wanted to be in the midst of the war, for it was the headquarters of all Japanese naval and air operations in the southwest Pacific.

Rabaul was even more important now than it had been when first occupied because it was the key to Japan's holding on to everything it had thus far captured. That wasn't just Hiroshi's assessment; Admiral Yamamoto had said the same thing in early March, after a convoy of Japanese transports had been totally destroyed by American and Australian air attacks. The destruction of the convoy, which was carrying nearly seven thousand troops to the Japanese base at Lae, New Guinea, represented one of Japan's most stunning losses of the war, and from that day forth Japanese planners no longer spoke of offense but of defense. Even the emperor was aware of the change in policy now because Hiroshi read the reports of the emperor's briefing concerning the Japanese decision to evacuate Guadalcanal.

"What," Emperor Hirohito had asked calmly, "do you plan to do next?"

"We intend to stop the enemy's westward movement," the warlords had replied. Embodied in that one sentence, Hiroshi knew, was the first official recognition of the turning of the tides of war.

It was a bitter pill for Hiroshi to swallow. From the very beginning he had known that Japan's only hope lay in quick and decisive victory. That opportunity had been lost the previous summer when the American and Japanese fleets clashed in the battle of Midway. Now with the abandonment of Guadalcanal, the distant outposts that protected the Empire were beginning to crumble. When the walls collapsed to the degree that the Americans could begin long-range bomber flights over the main islands of Japan, there would no longer be any hope.

"Ah, Hiroshi, there you are, there you are," Admiral Yamamoto said, smiling broadly as he joined his officer on the beach. "Watching the sunrise, I see."

Hiroshi hopped up quickly from the oil drum and bowed. "Yes, Admiral," he said. "Perhaps it is the symbolism, but I always find sunrises particularly inspiring."

"As do I," Yamamoto replied. "What do you think, Hiroshi? Do I look impressive enough to instill confidence in your pilots?"

Yamamoto, wearing dress whites replete with his numerous awards and decorations, struck a quick pose.

Hiroshi laughed. "Admiral, you would be impressive enough if you spoke in a fundoshi," he said, and Yamamoto laughed a deep, rich laugh.

Hiroshi not only respected Admiral Yamamoto as his commander, he liked him as a person. The admiral was a naval genius, a widely traveled man, and a man who made no bones about his admiration and affection for America. He had spent several years in the United States, and he counted many Americans among his closest personal friends. He spoke English fluently and often imitated various American dialects, entertaining his friends with stories in which he assumed the role of a southerner speaking with an exaggerated drawl, a hillbilly speaking with a flat twang, or a proper Bostonian. Yamamoto was an excellent poker player and had sat across the table from—and beaten, often by bluffing—many of the same senior American admirals he was now facing in war. He was innovative and bold, and he often put thumbtacks on the seats of his staff officers just before a meeting. He did this, he explained with a smile as one by one they encountered them, to "teach vigilance."

Yamamoto smiled. "I would like to see the reaction on your pilots' faces if I spoke to them wearing only a fundoshi. Of course, I would have to wear my admiral's hat and carry my baton, would I not?" He laughed at the ludicrous picture he had painted of himself, then wiped the tears of laughter from his eyes and looked back toward the base. His face became instantly solemn.

"You have built a most formidable line of defense, Admiral," Hiroshi said.

"Yes," Yamamoto replied. He fell silent for a long while. "Defense," he finally answered quietly. "I have built a line of *defense* when we should have a line of offense." He sighed, then slapped his baton against the side of his pants. "But I have a plan, Hiroshi. I have a magnificent plan. With a strengthened line of defense, we will be able to put together another offense, and you would be surprised at what shall be my new target." He chuckled. "Yes, you would be surprised. But the most surprised of all would be the Americans. I promise you, Hiroshi, this will strike as great a blow against the Americans as did our attack on Pearl Harbor."

Hiroshi was more than intrigued. "You have quickened my fighting spirit, Admiral," he said. "Tell me, please, what have you in mind?"

Yamamoto turned toward Hiroshi and raised his finger, wagging it back and forth slowly. "No, no," he said, smiling. "If I tell you now it will spoil the surprise. But keep your fighting spirit, for we will begin planning for it as soon as I return from Bougainville. I'll tell you this, and this only: It will turn the tide of war. In fact, it will *end* the war. It will be the bargaining chip we need to cease all hostilities and to hold on to our gains." Yamamoto chuckled. "Now, what about my flight to Bougainville? Is everything arranged? I want to take off at precisely six A.M."

Hiroshi smiled. Yamamoto's compulsive adherence to a time schedule was legendary throughout the Navy. "We'll leave on time, Admiral. I've made all the necessary arrangements—two bombers and six escorting Zeros. I shall fly the plane you are in."

"Excellent, excellent. I could ask for no finer pilot."

They were suddenly approached by Hiroshi's executive officer. He stopped and bowed to Yamamoto and to Hiroshi.

"Forgive my intrusion, Captain, but the pilots are ready for the admiral's speech."

"Ah, yes, my speech," Yamamoto replied. "Yes, I suppose we must get it over with. I will tell them to go fly bravely . . . something they all do anyway, but for some reason it is expected that I should tell them. You have heard my speech before, Hiroshi; you need not listen," Yamamoto added. "I am sure that you have final preparations to make for the flight to Bougainville."

"Yes, sir," Hiroshi said. "I shall go down to the airfield now."

When Admiral Yamamoto appeared at the airfield a few minutes before six, he had changed out of his dress-white uniform into less conspicuous green fatigues. Just before he boarded the Mitsubishi bomber, he turned to Vice Admiral Jinichi Kusaka and handed him two scrolls.

"You will forgive my simple efforts at calligraphy," he said. "But here are two poems, written by Emperor Meiji, which I have copied. Would you please give them to the commander of the Eighth Fleet with my compliments?"

"Yes, Admiral, it would be my privilege," Kusaka said, bowing.

Hiroshi waited until Admiral Yamamoto was on board and seated before he started his engines. A few moments later, just as the bomber he was piloting broke ground, Hiroshi glanced at the clock on the panel and saw that it was exactly six.

The small air fleet that Hiroshi had put together for the trip consisted of two bombers escorted by six fighters. The bombers flew at just over fifteen hundred meters, while the six fighters hovered protectively overhead. In the clear, early-morning air, the flight was pleasantly smooth, and once, when Hiroshi looked into the back of the plane, he saw that the admiral was napping.

The three-hour flight passed so completely uneventfully that Hiroshi was almost dozing himself when his co-pilot reported, "Captain, I have Kahili airfield in sight."

Hiroshi looked to his left through the spinning propeller blade of his port engine and saw the lush, green island of Bougainville rising from the sea. "Yes, I see it," he replied. He picked up his microphone and keyed it. "Leader to flight, begin descent now."

The change in pitch of the engine noise awakened Hiroshi's sleeping passengers, and they began to prepare for arrival at Kahili. Tunics were buttoned, briefcases were closed, and hats were put on. The descent was long, slow, and gentle; then, finally, they passed over the coastline of Bougainville. Now, instead of water, they were flying over jungle.

"Captain! Captain! Enemy planes to the south!" one of Hiroshi's gunners suddenly called.

"Fighters, drop your fuel tanks! Engage the enemy!" Hiroshi ordered, and the long-range fuel tanks that were suspended beneath the Zeros glistened silver in the sun as they tumbled down toward the green canopy below. The Zeros peeled off and started after the enemy planes, which, Hiroshi noticed, were the twin-boomed, extremely fast P-38 Lightnings.

Hiroshi put the bomber into a steep dive, then pulled out just over the very top of the jungle. The trees were a blur as he skimmed across them at well over two hundred miles per hour, flying so close to them that he could almost stick out a hand and grab a branch. By flying so low Hiroshi had decreased his space for maneuvering, but he had also reduced the attack options of the enemy planes. The P-38's couldn't come at him from below or even from the side; they could only come at him from above. Also, Hiroshi hoped, the color of his bomber would blend in with the jungle, making it more difficult for enemy fighters to see him.

Hiroshi heard his top turret gunner open fire, and he felt rather than saw his copilot turn around to see what was going on. A second later the bomber's cockpit shattered as fifty-caliber machine-gun bullets from the attacking P-38s came crashing through. The instrument panel disintegrated right before Hiroshi's eyes, and he saw blood splattered all over the twisted metal and shattered glass. Though he felt no pain and wasn't even aware that he had been hit, he sensed something wet and sticky on the right side of his face. He put his hand there and discovered that he no longer had an ear.

Machine-gun bullets continued to pound into the top of Hiroshi's plane, and he felt the right wing dip. He turned the wheel to raise the wing, but it had no effect, and when he looked over, he saw that the right wing and right engine were a mass of flames. He was no longer the pilot of a functioning airplane; he was the occupant of a piece of flaming debris, controlled only by gravity.

Hiroshi thought of his beautiful wife, Yuko, and of the magnificent sunrise he had seen that morning. Just before the bomber crashed into the trees and exploded in a ball of fire, he smiled.

Before the two P-38's that had been in on the kill started back to their base, they did a victory barrel roll over the pillar of black smoke that rose from the funeral pyre of the crashed plane. It was the type of maneuver Air Group Commmander Hiroshi Amano would have understood perfectly, had he seen it. But Hiroshi, along with Admiral Yamamoto and everyone else on board his plane, was dead.

LOS ALAMOS, NEW MEXICO

Dr. Wyman W. "Dub" Wilkerson was sitting on a large rock three-quarters of the way up the arid, stony hill, looking down over the cluster of barracks, houses, and Quonset huts that made up the Los Alamos research site. From his vantage point he could see the big sign at the front gate of the high chain-link fence that surrounded the "research" settlement, reading:

> WHAT YOU SEE HERE,
> WHAT YOU HEAR HERE,
> WHEN YOU LEAVE HERE,
> LEAVE HERE.

Dub was one of the scientists working on the "Manhattan Project," the top-secret development of a weapon based on the sudden release of nuclear energy. He had been allowed to bring his wife, Janet, with him, and they were provided with a small, unpainted-plywood house that looked like all the other small, unpainted-plywood houses on the site, even that of Dr. J. Robert Oppenheimer, the project director. The dependents of the scientists who lived in these houses were tightly restricted to the quarters area and had, by necessity, established their own little society.

Janet Wilkerson was taking this spartan life very well

and told Dub often that she didn't even miss the two-story brick home with the sweeping lawn, mature trees, and beautiful azalea garden that had been granted to Dub as head of the Physics Department at Jefferson University. She told him that she didn't miss the campus social life either, or the faculty teas, the receptions, or all the football and basketball games. In fact, she told him so often that she didn't miss these things that Dub knew that she missed them all very much, and he was proud of her for keeping a home for him under very difficult conditions.

As Dub sat there at his vantage point he saw Dr. Sigmund Rosen, Dub's colleague not only on the Manhattan Project, but from Jefferson University as well, coming up the hill toward him. One of the world's preeminent physicists, Sigmund Rosen's credentials were so good that Dub sometimes felt self-conscious about being his superior. But Sigmund, a Jew who had fled Nazi Germany to come to America and join the staff of Jefferson University, felt no resentment at working for Dub. On the contrary, he felt gratitude for his position, and over the past few years the two men had become very close friends. That was partly due to their sharing the same academic field, partly due to Dub's having gone out of his way to make Sigmund feel very welcome when he had arrived in America, and partly because Dub accepted without question all of Sigmund Rosen's idiosyncracies, which were numerous.

The good doctor ran his hand across his forehead as if he were brushing back a shock of hair, but he had such a high forehead that there was nothing to brush back. His eyes were large and brown and slightly drooping, giving him a slightly Oriental appearance. His cheeks were red, as if he had just come in from a cold, brisk wind—though in truth they looked that way all the time—and his hair, what little there was left of it, was an unkempt halo around his head. He was carrying two bottles of beer by the neck in his right hand.

"Hello," he said when he reached Dub. He sat down on the large rock beside his friend and began drinking one of the beers. The other he put on the ground beside him.

"Well, are you going to drink both of them?" Dub asked.

"Bitte?"

"The beer," Dub said. "Did you bring me a beer?"

"Oh, do you want a beer? Here, you can have this one," he said, offering Dub the one he was drinking. "It is okay. I can easily go down and get another."

Dub shrugged and laughed. "Never mind," he said, picking up the second beer. "I can drink this one."

"Gut, gut, you have a beer, too. That means we can drink together."

Dub drank several swallows, then let out an appreciative "Aaah" and wiped the back of his hand across his mouth. Sigmund continued to drink in seemingly deep contemplation.

Finally, Dub broke the silence. "I've spoken with Oppenheimer and all the other team leaders," he said. "We're going with your concept."

Sigmund didn't say anything.

"Did you hear what I said, Sigmund? We've decided that gaseous diffusion is the way to go. We're giving up all the other ideas and putting all of our eggs into your basket. We're going with your theory."

"Ja."

Dub laughed. "Well, I must say, you don't seem very enthusiastic. Everyone has finally admitted that you're right. You should be pleased."

"Ja," Sigmund said again.

Dub sighed. "What is it, my friend? What is wrong?"

"Dub," Sigmund started, his pronunciation making the name sound more like *Dob,* "for many years now I have worked on the principle of atomic energy."

"Yes, I know. You and Fermi and just a handful of the others were light-years ahead of the rest of us."

"Ja. Always I have thought of it as a scientific problem, an intellectual exercise. When I came to America to work, I continued to keep that thought in my mind. But now . . ." He paused in midsentence and shrugged.

"Sigmund, you can't say you didn't understand that we were here to develop a weapon," Dub said.

"Here, I knew," Sigmund said, pointing to his head. "Maybe here"—he pointed to his heart—"I did not know until now."

"I see."

"The weapon, when we make it, if we drop it on a city like Berlin, how many will it kill?"

"I don't know, Sigmund. That's hard to say."

"But I know you have been in on the feasibility discussions, Dub. You must have an estimate."

"Sigmund, it's not for us to consider such things," Dub said quietly. "We are scientists, you and I. Such worries as to whether or not to use the weapon or how many it might kill, those are for someone else."

"*Ja*, and isn't that what is happening now to all of the Jews in Europe? Are not the Nazis rounding them up and killing them because everyone says it is not for them to worry about such things?" Sigmund said heatedly.

"All right, perhaps we scientists *should* think about what we're doing. But, Sigmund, you know yourself that Hitler has scientists, *good* scientists, working on this very same project. Can you imagine what would happen if Hitler got the weapon before we did?"

Sigmund stared into space. "*Ja*, I can imagine," he said somberly.

"It would be disastrous for the entire world," Dub insisted. He sighed. "You asked how many people it would kill if we exploded it over Berlin. Let me fill you in on some other possibilities before I tell you that. There is a very strong possibility, I would say at least three to one, that we won't get the device built at all. And if we do build it, one projection puts the completion date as far away as 1970. There's also the possibility that we might get it built but not be able to transport it anywhere. We'd have to let it sit here like a gigantic rat trap in the desert and lure our victims into it. At any rate, it seems very unlikely that it could be carried in any airplane now flying, though the probability is that the B-29 will be operational soon. So you see, there are many and varied projections about the feasibility of the weapon, and they are all just conjecture, so we won't know until it's tested what the final results will be."

"How many will the weapon kill?" Sigmund asked flatly.

Dub sighed again. "You insist upon knowing this?"

"*Ja*."

"If Hitler beats us to the bomb and drops it on New York or London, it could kill anywhere from one hundred thousand to one million people."

"One *million*?"

"Yes."

Sigmund hung his head. "Dub, what sort of monster have we become?"

"We have not become monsters, Sigmund. But Nazism has exposed us to the darkest side of man. Hitler and his kind are a cancerous growth on the body of mankind, and like a cancerous growth they must be removed or mankind will surely die. Perhaps it will be enough to merely possess the bomb. Perhaps the fact that we have it will convince Hitler to surrender."

"No, I do not think so," Sigmund replied. "Hitler is crazed by the Wagnerian myth of a heroic, Teutonic society. He would rather perish in flames than abandon his perverted sense of purpose."

"Yes, I'm afraid you're right. I just suggested otherwise because I, too, am trying to avoid the truth. It isn't easy to live with the knowledge that what we're doing could result in the instant death of a million human beings. But, Sigmund, my friend, we must be prepared to do whatever has to be done to rid mankind of Hitlerism."

"Will God let us do this thing, Dub? Will God let us build this weapon?"

"I am Christian, Sigmund; you are Jewish. We share the same God. Perhaps your people have had a three-thousand-year longer relationship with Him, but He is the same God that my people pray to. And I tell you now that if the forces of evil that are loose in this world aren't stopped, God will cease to exist. At least, He will cease to exist as far as man is concerned, for Earth will become a literal hell."

"Perhaps you are right," Sigmund admitted with a resigned sigh. "It is just that I have such questions. Please forgive me for asking them."

"There is nothing to forgive," Dub replied, putting a hand on his friend's shoulder. "When the questions stop, you will no longer have a soul."

HOLLYWOOD, CALIFORNIA

Searchlight beams crisscrossed the night sky. These, though, weren't looking for enemy aircraft; they were announcing a special event down below at Grauman's Chinese Theater. Red-velvet ropes looped through brass stanchions blocked off a portion of the sidewalk in front of the theater. The crowd of frenzied movie fans congregated on the other side of the barrier cheered as each celebrity arrived, for the documentary film *Red Banners over Mother Russia* was opening with all the hoopla that only a Hollywood premier could produce.

A number of stars had been invited to the opening, and though quite a few came, a significant number sent their regrets, saying they found it difficult to work into their busy wartime schedule.

The movie had already been critically reviewed, and excerpts from those reviews were prominently displayed on the marquee and on posters and billboards set up in front of the theater.

"RIVETING ACTION." *Los Angeles Tribune*

"NO HOLLYWOOD SPECIAL EFFECTS CAN MATCH THE DRAMA OF REAL WAR. *RED BANNERS OVER MOTHER RUSSIA* BRINGS US THAT DRAMA." *Variety*

"WILL WIN NEW RESPECT FOR THE BRAVE RUSSIAN MEN AND WOMEN WHO ARE FIGHTING THIS WAR." *New York Daily Worker*

In addition to the reviews and blurbs, and just as prominently displayed, were huge posters of blown-up still shots from the film. One of the stills showed a handsome young man, photographed from behind, holding a muscular arm up, his hand wrapped around a rifle. The young man had his head turned back toward the camera, urging those behind to follow him. A beautiful young woman stood beside him, holding aloft a Soviet flag. The image was meant to convey what the Russians were desperate for: getting Allied assistance in their battle against the Germans.

In the lobby of the theater, very close to this poster, a group of volunteer workers were manning tables on which there were several petitions. A sign on one of the tables said: OPEN THE SECOND FRONT NOW!

Another sign urged people to sign one of the petitions:

WHEN YOU WATCH THIS FILM, YOU WILL SEE THE INCREDI-BLE BRAVERY AND SACRIFICE OF THE RUSSIAN PEOPLE. WE FEEL CERTAIN THAT YOU WILL NOT WANT THEM TO FIGHT ON ALONE; THEREFORE, WE URGE YOU TO SIGN THIS PETI-TION NOW!

The petitions would be sent to Washington to show elected officials that the average American was concerned about the fact that while the Allied armies sputtered through North Africa and Italy or lounged in the pubs and private clubs of England, Soviet citizens were being slaughtered as they single-handedly fought the war against the Nazis.

Microphones were set up on the sidewalk to welcome the celebrities to the screening. It was a little different from most premieres because the "stars" of the movie were real people and they were, for the most part, still fighting the battle in Russia, unaware that they were the focus of a major motion picture event.

One celebrity who was present was Guy Colby, the director and producer *of Red Banners over Mother Russia.* His arrival brought a round of applause from those watching the proceedings and enlivened the radio report of the event.

As Guy stepped out of his limousine and onto the red carpet, the announcer rushed to meet him. "And here, ladies and gentlemen of our listening audience," he said into his microphone, "is the inspiration behind this wonderful documentary picture *Red Banners over Mother Russia,* the director and producer, Guy Colby. And with him is his beautiful wife, the fabulous Demaris Hunter, and their infant daughter, Karen. Mr. Colby, would you share a few thoughts with our listeners?" He thrust the mike into Guy's face.

"Yes," Guy replied, "I'd be happy to. Only I would like to correct one thing you said. I am *not* the inspiration behind this picture; the brave Russian men and women who are over there fighting and dying are the inspiration."

"To be sure," the announcer said. "And, folks, I urge all of you to go see this picture when it visits your hometown, because you have to see the genuine bravery to truly understand what Mr. Colby is talking about."

"And, if I may interject," Guy said, "as the picture travels around the country, so will the 'Second Front Now' petitions. I urge each and every American who is concerned about fair play to sign one of these petitions."

"But, Mr. Colby, don't you think we'll open a second front in Europe just as soon as it is possible to do so?" the announcer asked.

"I'm certain that a second front will be opened," Guy answered. "The question is, when? How much longer must we let the Russian people do all the bleeding and dying while we wait for optimum conditions? How much of this delay is due to wartime necessity—and how much of it is due to a philosophical disagreement between the British and the Soviet Union?"

"I see," the announcer said. "And you, Miss Hunter. Do you share your husband's political views?"

"I neither share them nor disagree with them," Demaris replied with a little laugh. "The truth is, I'm afraid, I'm just not at all political. I've got too many other things to worry about, such as my career and my baby, whom, as you can see, I brought with me."

"Yes, I do see," the reporter said. "And I must admit that it's unusual to see someone this young at a premiere. But she is such a beautiful baby that her presence only adds to the luster of the occasion."

Demaris laughed. "What a diplomat you are," she said. "But she is beautiful, isn't she? I'm not just a proud mother talking, am I?"

"Yes, you are a proud mother, Demaris Hunter, but you have every right to be. And now, Guy Colby, Demaris Hunter, and baby Karen, this is your evening and I don't want to hold you up any longer. Thanks for stopping to chat with our listening audience."

"It was our pleasure," Guy said, as he led Demaris into the theater.

As they stepped into the lobby, Demaris said quietly, "Guy, I wish you wouldn't ally yourself so closely with these Second Front Now people."

"Look, some of the people who were very helpful in allowing me to do the picture in the first place came to me and asked for my support," Guy replied. "What could I do?"

"You could have refused."

"But why should I?" Guy asked. "And as I intimated, I'm not sure that I don't believe that the reasons we haven't opened a second front are more political than military."

"Well, what if they are? It's obvious that our government, for whatever reason, feels that a second front isn't possible just now. And if you go on agitating for one, allowing your name to be associated with these petitions, I'm afraid you're going to find yourself in a lot of trouble."

"Trouble for what?"

"Trouble for going against the government," Demaris said.

Guy laughed. "Darling, this is America, not Nazi Germany. The right to petition the government is guaranteed by the Constitution."

"Well, then you go ahead and do whatever you feel you must do. But I don't want to be any part of it. You make sure everyone knows that."

"What if everyone felt that way?"

"Evidently a lot of people do. You *have* noticed the conspicuous absence of big names at this opening, haven't you?"

"Well, this is a documentary; it isn't a real movie," Guy said. "I mean, not in the sense that there are any stars or anything. There's no one for them to come out and support."

"You really believe that that's what it is?"

"Yes. That and the fact that many of them are genuinely busy with wartime commitments."

"My darling, you are naive," Demaris said. "Just

promise me that you won't use my name to solicit signatures for any of those petitions."

"I promise. Your name won't be mentioned. You don't even have to sign the petition if you don't want to."

Demaris snickered. "Oh, I don't intend to sign it."

HEART MOUNTAIN, WYOMING

Private First Class Eddie Yamaguchi was on leave from the U.S. Army, having just completed his training at Camp Shelby, Mississippi as a part of the Nisei 442nd Regimental Combat Team, a unit made up entirely of Japanese-Americans. Many from the 442nd were from areas other than the West Coast, and they were able to go home on leave. But for those soldiers like Eddie Yamaguchi, whose homes and property had been confiscated and whose families had been interned, going on leave meant returning to the detention camp—in Eddie's case, Heart Mountain, Wyoming.

So many young men from Heart Mountain had gone into the Army that the residents' council of Heart Mountain had established a USO for their returning servicemen. Most of the soldiers who lived in the single men's barracks with Eddie were preparing to go to a dance being held at the USO, and they polished shoes and shined brass as they got their uniforms ready for the evening's festivities. Eddie, however, was dressing in a kimono.

"Man," Joe Watanabe said from the bunk next to Eddie's, "what in the hell are you doing in that getup?"

"Miko Saito has invited me to a *chanoyu* ceremony," Eddie replied.

"A what?"

"Don't you even know the term?" Eddie asked. "It's a tea ceremony. Surely you know about the tea ceremony."

Joe laughed. "Yeah, I know about the tea ceremony. I think I even went to one when I was a kid. But if I remember right, it was the most boring damn thing I ever saw in my life. Why would you want to go to such a thing?"

"Because Miko invited me."

"Yeah, well, Miko's a good-looking chick, all right,"

Joe agreed. "But, man, we've been in basic training for three months. Seems to me like you could talk her into some other way to welcome you back, if you know what I mean," he added raffishly.

Eddie looked over at Joe and smiled at him. "Yeah, I know what you mean. But this is a part of our heritage."

"Maybe *your* heritage, not mine. I don't go for any of that old-country stuff."

"A leopard can't change his spots," Eddie insisted. "Someday it'll be important to you."

Joe chuckled. "Yeah? Well, I'll tell you the truth, if I had somebody like Miko asking me to a tea ceremony, hell, I might even go today. In the meantime, I guess I'll just have to impress the girls at the USO with all my medals."

"Medals?" Eddie asked. "What medals? You haven't been anywhere but basic training."

"These medals," Joe said, pulling a handful of ribbons from his pocket. "Found them in a pawnshop."

"Joe, you can't wear those ribbons! You could get court martialed for that!"

"Yeah, I know," Joe said. He grinned. "That's why I'm not going to wear them. I'm just going to carry them in my pocket, see, and when the time is right, I'll pull them out and show them to the girl, explaining that while I won them for acts of bravery, I'm much too modest to actually wear them."

Eddie laughed. "Only a con man like you would come up with an idea like that."

"Yeah, well, I'll tell you what. If the tea ceremony doesn't work out, you can try it. I've got a whole pocketful; you can have some of them."

"No thanks," Eddie said with a laugh, waving good-bye as he left the barracks.

Though the single young women, like the single young men, were required to live in separate barracks, Miko Saito was going to conduct the tea ceremony in her parents' apartment, which was where Eddie headed when he left the barracks.

Miko had written Eddie several letters while he was away in basic training, and he had written back. The letters were very formal because all mail in and out of both the relocation center and the Army camp was censored. Despite the formality of the text, however, Eddie was able to read between the lines, and he and Miko had developed a very close relationship. The tea ceremony was itself an indication of how close they had become because it was a very meaningful ritual to Miko's parents and was therefore a symbol of Eddie's significance to the Saito household.

Under normal circumstances, Eddie would have asked the oldest male member of his family to go to Miko's father and make arrangements for their marriage. But Eddie was the only member of his family at Heart Mountain. His father was dead, and his older brother was in the merchant marines, somewhere at sea. The situation was further complicated by the fact that Eddie had only one week before he had to return to the Army camp, where the rumor was they'd soon be shipped overseas.

When Eddie reached the Saito apartment a few minutes later, he placed his shoes just outside the door and was ushered in by Fumiko Saito. Eddie could see the beauty of the daughter reflected in her mother's face—though Mrs. Saito kept her eyes averted as was proper and said nothing, merely leading Eddie to his place for the ceremony to begin.

To the uninitiated, Eddie knew, the tea ceremony was a practice without purpose. It was developed by Sen Rikyu in the sixteenth century, and in four hundred years not one thing had been changed. The ritual was still performed exactly as he had dictated it should be.

Miko was kneeling by an iron teakettle, and as Eddie took his place, also kneeling, she bowed low to him, so low that her forehead touched the floor. Eddie returned the bow.

Miko's mother acted as the assistant, and she handed Miko the *chabako,* the canister that contained the finely powdered tea.

Miko took a red cloth from the obi tied around her waist and carefully wiped the spoon. Then she spooned some tea into a beautiful blue-and-gold lacquered bowl. Next, she added heated water from the iron kettle, then beat the mixture with a *chasen,* or whisk, until the tea was thick and foaming.

As Miko prepared the tea her mother moved first to Eddie, then to Miko's father, Yutake Saito, and bowing low before each, presented them with the traditional *chagashi,* or sweet cake.

After Miko finished preparing the tea, she poured it into a cup, set the cup on the floor before her, and bowed as her mother picked up the cup. Fumiko then set the cup before Eddie, and she and Eddie bowed to each other, then Eddie picked the cup up with both hands and drank the tea. The same procedure was repeated for Yutake.

When the tea had been drunk and the sweet cakes eaten, very ceremoniously, the bowls and cups were wiped dry and the utensils put away. Only then was the silence broken by Miko, who smiled and said, "Oh, my back is killing me!"

Eddie laughed at Miko's comment. "You did it beautifully," he said. "Sen Rikyu himself would have been pleased."

"You have a fine appreciation for the old ways," Yutake noted. "One doesn't often see that in the young of today."

"I am aware that the ways of centuries can't be improved upon in the few years of a young life, Saito-san," Eddie said.

"Such wisdom for one so young," the older man said, smiling broadly. "A father would be proud to have such a person for a son-in-law."

"Father!" Miko said, blushing furiously. "How can you say such a thing with me in the room?"

"Do not be embarrassed," Yutake told his daughter. "Here is a young man who understands that the exigency of war has made it necessary to speak in such a way. Tell me, young man, is there no one who can speak on your behalf?"

"I have no one to speak for me," Eddie said. "My father is dead, my older brother is at sea. I am alone in this camp."

"Then under such circumstances it is permissible for you to speak for yourself," Yutake said.

"I don't know if I am worthy," Eddie hedged. "I have an uncertain future."

Yutake sighed and looked around the one room that was now his home. "Yes," he said. "Indeed, we all have an uncertain future. I shall not belabor the point, Yamaguchi-san. But if you should wish to speak for yourself, know that I would listen with an approving ear."

"I am flattered and honored that you hold me in such regard, honorable Saito-san," Eddie replied. "And I now make a formal application to you for the hand of your daughter."

"I don't know," Yutake replied with a serious face. "I must give this matter some consideration."

"Father!" Miko gasped.

Yutake laughed. "Do you want to marry him, daughter?"

"Yes, oh, yes!" Miko said. "I very much want to marry him."

"Very well, then; you have my blessing. Both of you. And I will make all the arrangements so that the marriage can take place before you return to the Army."

"Thank you, Yutake Saito-san," Eddie said, bowing his head.

"And now," Yutake said. "I should think that two young people who have just decided to get married would have better things to do than continue a tea ceremony. There is an Errol Flynn movie on at the camp theater."

"Oh, I love Errol Flynn," Miko said.

"Do you now? Well, if that's the case, I don't know if I want to take you or not," Eddie teased.

"Oh, but I love you more," Miko said, taking hold of Eddie's arm possessively.

After the movie Eddie, who had changed from the kimono into his Army uniform, and Miko, who had also changed back into Western dress, went for a long walk, arm in arm, through the night.

"Wasn't it romantic, the way Errol Flynn came back and swept the girl up onto the horse?"

"I suppose," Eddie replied. "But I liked the way he fought off all three of the bad guys with his sword. He had to be pretty good to do that."

"Of course there isn't anyone who is really like Errol Flynn," Miko suggested.

"Yeah, including Errol Flynn," Eddie agreed, laughing at his own quip.

They walked silently for a few minutes. Then Miko said, "Oh, Eddie, look at the moon. Isn't it beautiful?"

"Yeah, I guess so."

"I remember the moon in Los Angeles," Miko said dreamily. "The way it would shine through the palm fronds in our back yard. And the smell of the flowers, and the soft, damp feel of the air, almost like a kiss. I miss that so."

Eddie put his arm around her. "We'll have it all back someday," he said. "When the war is over and we've proven our loyalty."

"But why should we have to prove our loyalty? We're at war with Germany, too, but the Germans aren't in detention camps."

"It's hard to tell the Germans from any other Americans," Eddie said. "Unfortunately, we stand out."

"And you really think when all this is over that we'll have proved our loyalty enough for the rest of the Americans to accept us?"

"I know so," Eddie said. "Listen, do you know what the motto of our unit is? It's 'Go for Broke.' "

"Go for broke? I don't understand."

"It's a gambling term. It means risk everything to win. That's what we're pledged to do, Miko. We're going to risk everything in the Four Hundred Forty-second. There won't be another regiment in the entire United States Army that will fight harder than we will."

"Oh, Eddie, I don't like to hear that," Miko said. "That sounds . . . dangerous."

"War is dangerous," Eddie said. "But if we're very aggressive, it'll be more dangerous for the other side than it'll be for us. And it will prove our loyalty once and for all."

"I shall worry about you every day," Miko said. She smiled up at him. "But I know you'll come back to me."

They walked along in silence, drawing pleasure from their closeness. In an effort to have a little time completely alone, Eddie and Miko had gone quite a distance from the main compound. The lights were fewer here, making the shadows longer. Suddenly ahead of them Eddie saw a movement, a shadow within a shadow, and he stopped.

"What was that?" he asked.

"What was what?"

"There's something up ahead," Eddie said, gently pushing her behind him protectively. "Hello? Hello, who is it?"

Eddie heard a low, ugly laugh, and the shadow within the shadow stepped from the darkness into the moonlight and took form and substance. It was the large, blond bulk of Sergeant Caviness, one of the guards assigned to the camp, the one the internees called "the Pig"—the one who had hated Eddie Yamaguchi at first sight.

"Well, now, if it isn't one of our local heroes. Long time no see. You're the baseball pitcher, aren't you?"

"Yes," Eddie said.

"And now you fancy yourself a soldier."

"I *am* a soldier."

"You're a Jap," Caviness said. He paused for a second, then sighed. "But, you *are* wearing a soldier's uniform. That means you have to salute me, you know."

Eddie shook his head. "No, Sergeant. I will give your rank the respect that it deserves, but I have studied FM twenty-two five. I know all the regulations that relate to drill and ceremony and paying proper military respect to officers and the flag. And I know that I do not have to salute you."

"Oh, yeah, you do," Caviness said. "You see, there's another regulation, one they didn't teach you Japs down there in your camp. It says that Japs, Chinks, niggers, greasers, spiks, wops, and Jews all have to salute white sergeants. Salute me."

"Would you excuse us, please?" Eddie said, starting to walk on.

"I said salute me, you zipper-eyed son of a bitch!" Caviness shouted. "Otherwise, you're going to get hurt—real bad."

Stopping, Eddie shook his head. "I'm sorry, Sergeant, but as the only representative here present of the Japs, Chinks, niggers, greasers, spiks, wops, and Jews, and on behalf of all of them, I'm telling you to go to hell. You aren't getting a salute from me."

"You yellow bastard!" Caviness roared, and suddenly his .45 pistol was in his hand.

"Eddie!" Miko cried. "Do what he says!"

"You'd better listen to your little slanty-eyed slut here, Jap boy," Caviness grunted.

Eddie didn't know if it was his natural competitive spirit, the kind that made him a good baseball player, or his bitterness over seeing so many of his people interned in such an inhospitable place or the training he had gone through for the last twelve weeks, but he suddenly felt very combative, and every nerve in his body was instantly alert. He shifted his weight slightly, coming onto the balls of his feet, ready to spring if need be. He felt the adrenaline flowing, and inexplicably he chuckled.

"Oh, you think it's funny, do you, slant-eyes?" Caviness snarled. He laughed again, low and ugly. "You find the situation entertaining? Well, we'll just see if you're still laughing after I put a bullet in your gut. Do you understand what I'm telling you? I'm going to kill you."

"You mean you're going to try," Eddie said.

"Try?" Caviness sputtered. "Why, you . . . you fucking little . . ." Caviness thrust the pistol out before him.

Just as Caviness started to pull the trigger, Eddie pivoted on the ball of his left foot while shooting his right foot out sharply toward Caviness's gun hand. His foot connected with the gun, and the suddenness of his move so surprised Caviness that the pistol was knocked cleanly from his hand before he could get off a shot.

Caviness let out a yell and came toward Eddie, thinking to overcome him with his size and strength. Eddie leaned slightly aside, showing Caviness a target and then withdrawing it, and Caviness, thrown off balance by his lunge, was unable to correct his thrust. He came up with empty air.

Eddie jammed the fingers of his left hand into Caviness's solar plexus. Then, when he heard the sergeant gasp as the air left his body and the breathing muscles collapsed, Eddie brought the sharp edge of his right hand down squarely on the back of Caviness's neck. He took quite a bit off his blow, for Caviness was now helpless, and if Eddie had wanted to, he could have killed him with the blow.

Instead, he merely stunned a primary nerve, leaving the NCO temporarily paralyzed with pain.

"You fucking bastard!" Caviness spat from his position on his hands and knees. "You'll spend the rest of your life in Leavenworth for this! You attacked a noncommissioned officer!"

"No, he didn't," Miko said, stepping in front of Eddie. "He was just defending me from a rapist. He didn't know who you were until it was too late."

"Rapist? What are you talking about? I never tried to rape you."

"That's what you say," Miko retorted. "But I can get as many witnesses as I need who will swear that you did try."

Eddie reached down and picked up Caviness's pistol. He punched the magazine out of the pistol grip, then jacked out the shell that was in the chamber. "I'll drop this under the flagpole," he said. "You'd better come down and pick it up right away, otherwise someone else may find it, and you'll be paying for a new pistol."

With that, he put his hand protectively on Miko's back and escorted her back to her barracks.

"Bastard!" Caviness called out, still unable to move. "You fucking yellow bastard!"

"Eddie . . . " Miko said when they had covered several dozen yards.

"Yes?"

"You know what I said before about there not being anyone who was really like Errol Flynn?"

"Yes."

"Well, I was wrong. *You* are like Errol Flynn." She reached up and proudly took hold of his arm. "No, I take that back. You are much better than Errol Flynn."

CHAPTER

TWENTY

In the maintenance hangars and out on the revetments, work lights shone through the long night hours as ground crews pored over the B-17's of the 605th Bomb Group. Plexiglas was cleaned, filters were replaced, spark plugs were changed, magnetos were timed, control cables were tightened, holes were patched, machine guns were loaded, bombs were armed, fuel and oil tanks were topped off, and maintenance logbooks were brought up to date. The ground crews' duty started when the sun went down each night, and it ended when the sun came up the next morning.

Over on the other side of the base, in the darkened area, were the bachelor officers' quarters and the aircrewmen's barracks. In theory, they slept while their planes were being serviced so that, come the dawn, they'd be fully rested and ready for the day's mission.

But not all aircrewmen were asleep that particular night. One who was awake was Sergeant Buck Campbell.

332

He had just arrived at Waddlesfoot and was assigned as a replacement waist gunner to B-17 tail number 314389, better known as the *Stand and Deliver*. *Stand and Deliver* was one of the aircraft being prepared for tomorrow's mission, and Buck Campbell would be on it. This would be his first mission, and he was much too excited or nervous or perhaps just plain frightened to sleep.

Buck had gone to bed fully intending to sleep, but he lay awake for hours, just listening to the chorus of snorts, wheezes, and snores from the other men in the barracks. Finally he gave up and got out of bed, quietly moving his footlocker down to the dim firelight emitted by the glass-doored wood stove so he could find the magazine he'd been wanting to read. It was the September 13, 1943 issue of *LIFE*, and the cover was of two young college girls, pretty and sophisticated looking, like girls who came from families with money. They were standing in front of an ivy-covered university building, probably one of those back-East schools, Buck thought. It had a very old, very upper-class look about it.

As Buck leafed through the magazine, he came across one story he would just as soon not have found. It was called "One of Our Bombers Is Missing," and it described what went on back at the air base when a plane went down. It showed lockers being cleaned out, the chaplain writing a letter to an aviator's parents, and a dog waiting patiently for one of the crewmen. It was very sad and a bit frightening, and Buck couldn't help but picture his own locker being gone through in the same way, perhaps as soon as tomorrow night.

The "Speaking of Pictures" section, however, was great! It had an article entitled "Hollywood's Shapeliest 'Shadow Girls'" that showed several actresses' bodies in silhouette. The lighting made them look just as if they were naked, and the pictures gave Buck such an erection that, at about one-thirty in the morning when he was absolutely certain that everyone else in the Quonset hut was asleep, he masturbated while he looked at the pictures.

Afterward, he looked through the rest of the magazine, paying special attention to the ads that featured returning soldiers or sailors being welcomed home by beautiful, smiling women. One day he hoped to be like the men in those ads . . . sparkling in his uniform, with his gunner's wings and a row of ribbons splashed above his breast pocket and with just the right look in his eye to denote reluctant heroism. He would go into a bar somewhere, maybe Memphis, and order a drink and pretend that he didn't notice that all the women were looking at him.

Buck thought he'd like to go to the bar on the roof of the Peabody Hotel. He had looked in once, but at the time he wasn't old enough to go inside and order a drink. Actually, it'd been just as well he couldn't. It had looked a little intimidating. Everyone there seemed so sure of themselves as they laughed and talked and flirted and ordered drinks with strange-sounding names.

It would be different when he went back. Not only would he be old enough to drink, he would also be a genuine war hero. Maybe he'd even play his guitar and sing for some of the women. He wasn't that good a guitar player, he only knew a few chords, but he was a damn good singer. He was so good, in fact, that everyone told him he should try and get on the *Grand Ol' Opry*.

Buck was still looking at the magazine, still fantasizing about the "golden future" all the magazine ads promised, when the front door of the barracks opened, and the CQ came in.

"First mission, huh?" the CQ asked, seeing Buck sitting on the footlocker by the firelight.

"Uh, yeah," Buck answered sheepishly.

"Thought so. There's two times none of you guys can get to sleep. Before your first mission and before your last one. Sometimes, of course, that's the same one," the CQ said, and then he laughed at his own black humor.

"Is it time to start getting ready?"

"It's that time. You takin' Dobbins's place?"

"Who?"

"What ship you got?"

"*Stand and Deliver.*"

"Yeah, you're takin' Dobbins's place. He got killed last week over Bremen. He got killed, and then the copilot got his own ship, so the *Stand and Deliver*'ll be goin' out with two new crew members today. That's bad luck."

"It is?" Buck asked, his anxiety showing in his voice.

"Yeah, anytime a new man comes into a crew, it's bad, and this here crew's got two," the CQ replied. "But you also got Colonel Blake as your pilot, and he's the best there is," he added, easing up a bit. "And the truth is, prob'ly any gunner in the squadron'd change places with you."

"Oh," Buck said, feeling somewhat mollified by the remark.

"So actually, I guess that makes you lucky. The only thing is, he always makes me wake him and his crew first. That's why I had to start in here." He reached over to turn the lights on; then he called out loudly, "Okay, girls, drop your cocks and grab your socks! You've got a mission to-day!"

There were a few groans and moans, and from one bunk a shoe was thrown toward the door. The CQ had pulled the duty before, however, and he was out the door-way before the shoe hit the floor.

It was still dark when the CQ shone his flashlight in Lieutenant Colonel Jimmy Blake's face.

"Briefing at oh-six-hundred, sir," the CQ said.

Jimmy grunted, then sat up and began pulling on his clothes. This would be the thirty-fourth mission since the 605th went operational, and he had flown every one of them, even though he could have stood down after the twenty-fifth.

The Eighth Air Force was still hard-pressed to prove the concept of daylight precision bombing. Despite the vaunted Norton Bombsight and the insistence on target vis-ibility before the bombs were released, the overall results had been only marginally better than those accomplished by the British with their saturation bombing. In addition to the relatively poor performance, American losses had been extremely heavy—much, much heavier than those sus-tained by the British. But the results weren't so bad, or the losses so great, as to give the planners at Eighth Air Force second thoughts about the idea of daylight raids. As Jimmy had heard one pilot say bitterly into his drink one night,

"We're going to prove the daylight bombing concept even if every one of us has to die doing it."

General Willie Canfield had told Jimmy confidentially that there were many high-ranking American officials who were beginning to question the concept. But they weren't quite ready to back out yet and thereby lose face.

"Yeah, well, I can certainly understand that," Jimmy had replied. "Better we lose our ass than they lose their face."

Jimmy thought about that conversation as he started toward the briefing shack. He saw hundreds of shadows moving silently through the early-morning darkness, the pilots, navigators, and bombardiers. The others would be individually briefed by their officers when the crews assembled at the aircraft.

The briefing room was already full by the time Jimmy got there, but because he was the squadron commander, he didn't have to worry about looking for a place to sit, for a seat in the very first row was always reserved for him. He quickly made his way to the vacant chair and sat down, and Major Don Petrey, commander of the *Truculent Turtle*, who was sitting in the second row, leaned forward to speak to him. Like Jimmy, Don Petrey had been an airline pilot before the war; in fact, they had once shared a house in Manila. Like Jimmy, Petrey had volunteered to go beyond the required twenty-five missions. This would be his thirty-first.

"You should have gone with me yesterday," Petrey said.

"Yeah, I heard you went into London," Jimmy said. "Did you have a good time?"

Petrey smiled crookedly. "I must have. I can't remember a damned thing that I did."

Jimmy laughed. "Someone said you were going through all the bars in London, trying to drink the town dry."

"From the way my head feels, I must've made a pretty good run at it."

Further conversation was cut off when a lieutenant colonel stepped onto the briefing platform. The room grew very quiet, and a few people coughed nervously as the briefing officer pulled aside a black curtain, disclosing a large map of Europe. A black ribbon stretched from Waddlesfoot east across the channel, across France, and deep into Germany. When the men saw where the string ended, they groaned.

"Oh, no. I thought we took care of that place two months ago," someone said under his breath.

"Your target is Schweinfurt," the colonel said, and now those who hadn't been able to tell where the string ended, or who didn't want to admit that it ended where it did, groaned as well.

"Shit, we've already been there. Why are we going again?" someone asked.

"That place is a real ball buster," another added.

"If there was ever a case for nighttime bombing, this is it," another said.

"Yeah, let the damn Brits have it," another suggested.

"Please, gentlemen, please," the briefing officer said, holding out his hands. "Settle down."

"All right, men, let's give it a listen," Jimmy ordered, and the pilots grew quiet.

The briefing officer cleared his throat before he began again. "You are quite right," he agreed. "We did hit it last August. But we're going to hit it again." He pointed to the map with his pointer. "And contrary to what you're saying, this is *exactly* the kind of target we mean when we talk about precision bombing. You see, there's only one target in Schweinfurt worth hitting, and that's the ball-bearing factory. We must drop as many bombs as we can inside the factory itself. It's very important that we bomb accurately because we must destroy that factory. You can see how vital it is when you realize that everything in the German war machine depends on those ball bearings . . . from their fighter planes to their tanks, all the way down to the Führer's chair."

"Well, hell, by all means, let's take out Hitler's chair," someone shouted, and the others laughed.

The lights went out and some slides were projected onto a screen.

"Who's got the popcorn?" someone shouted, but since

someone always shouted this, it was answered not by laughter, but by long-suffering groans.

"Here is the primary target for today," the briefing officer began. "These are the buildings of FAG Kugelfischer. As you can see, they are in a large triangular configuration, about one mile west of this sports stadium. They'll be well camouflaged and screened with smoke. In the target area there are more than three hundred known flak batteries. However, we have routed you through the best possible channel so that only a minimum of their guns can come to bear at any given time."

"One damn eighty-eight is enough," someone shouted, and his statement was greeted with nervous laughter.

The briefing officer stared coldly. "You'll pick up FW-190's and ME-109's on the way in and on the way out," he continued. "They stay on station and will be radar-vectored to you by a central fighter control operation located somewhere else in Germany. You'll have P-47's at least halfway in. The rest you'll have to do by yourself. So keep your combat boxes tight. Now, if there are no questions, we'll get meteorology."

An overweight, bald-headed captain gave them a weather briefing. This was followed by an intelligence briefing given by a professorial-looking major in horn-rimmed glasses. The major discussed the underground organizations in France and how to contact them, should they get shot down. Finally, General Willie Canfield stepped up onto the stage.

"Gentlemen," Willie said, "I'm not going to lie to you. This mission today is going to be a rough one, the roughest you've been on . . . perhaps the roughest of the entire war. And there's a great deal riding on it. As you've heard, a really successful strike could do a lot of damage to Germany's war machine. I put in a request to go with you, but they've got Colonel Bud Peaslee set up to lead the strike, and they feel like it wouldn't be fair to him to have a general going along for a joy ride. So I'm going to stay back here and sweat this one out for you. But I promise you this: When you get back, the O-club and NCO-club bars will be open, and the drinks will be on me."

"How about one now, for the road, General?" someone shouted, and everyone, including Willie, laughed. Then he held up his hands for silence.

"I want to wish you fellas good shooting. And I'll see you all when you get back," he said and stepped down from the stage. His doing so signaled that the briefing was officially over. The chaplains took over then, among them Catholic, Protestants, and Jewish, and many of the men hurried to the corner of their particular faith to receive a prayer or blessing.

Willie invited Jimmy to have breakfast with him, and Jimmy agreed. He ate heartily of fresh eggs, bacon, potatoes, and creamed beef on toast. Willie drank a cup of coffee and ate a bowl of Corn Toasties.

Jimmy pointed to the cereal and laughed. "You know, I never knew if you really like that shit, or if you just eat it to be loyal to your old man."

"I like it, all right," Willie said. He chuckled. "But if you swear you'll never tell my dad or my brother, I have to admit that I like Rice Krispies better."

"They'll never hear it from me," Jimmy promised, grinning. He poured himself a second cup of coffee.

"I hear you took the new guy as your copilot," Willie said. "What's his name? Overstreet?"

"Yeah, well, there's no sense in passing him off to somebody else. Hell, some of my pilots don't have much more time than he does. They've got all they can handle just to keep themselves out of trouble, let alone trying to wet-nurse somebody new."

"Jimmy, listen, I don't have to tell you to be careful out there today, do I?" Willie asked.

"Don't worry about me, Willie. I'm not looking to be a hero," Jimmy said. He finished his coffee, then set the cup down and pushed away from the table. "By the way, were you serious about buying everyone a drink tonight?"

"Damned serious."

"I'm not trying to spend all your money or anything, but I hope you wind up with one hell of a bar bill."

Willie smiled. "The bigger the better."

All over England, in the farmhouses, homes, and small towns that were near American air bases, dishes began to rattle in the cupboards and windows began to shake in their frames as thousands of engines whined and coughed into life. Some of the good citizens cursed the noise, others had become so acclimated that they rolled over and went back to sleep, while still others mouthed a quick and desperate prayer for the safety of the aircrews.

At Waddlesfoot the bombers began to trundle awkwardly into position, for the aircraft, while things of beauty in flight, were most ungainly on the ground. Most of them sported flamboyant names and caricatures and had tiny bombs painted on the fuselage to indicate the number of previous missions flown. Under the name *Stand and Deliver* was a cartoonist's rendition of an Old West road agent, wearing a bandanna across the lower part of his face and holding a pair of pistols with unusually large bores.

Behind the name, cartoon, and painted bombs was more information:

A/C SERIAL NUMBER: 314389
FOR RESCUE CUT HERE
FIRE EXTINGUISHERS LOCATED AT STATIONS
115, 430, AND 610
SERVICE THIS AIRCRAFT WITH 115/145
FLIGHT ENGINEER: T/SGT JOHN L. POTTS
PILOT: LIEUT. COL. JAMES BLAKE

"There's the green light, Colonel," Jimmy's new co-pilot, Lieutenant Barry Overstreet, said. His voice cracked in nervous excitement.

"Okay," Jimmy said, shoving the throttles forward. "Here we go."

Jimmy could taste the rubber as he breathed the raw oxygen through his mask. The formation was at twenty-eight thousand feet as they crossed the coast of France. Up there the sky was a bright crystal blue, cloudless except for the vapor trails extending from each bomber. The planes were enveloped in an avalanche of sound from the pounding engines and beating propellers.

They had already rendezvoused with the fighter planes and crossed the channel. Now, far below them, the green and brown fields of rural France stretched from horizon to horizon. From here the scene was so pastoral that it was hard to believe there was a war on.

Since they hadn't yet reached the point of radio silence, there was an incessant chatter over the air as navigators coordinated checkpoints with each other and pilots exchanged power settings and fuel mixtures.

"Flight Commander, this is ten. Permission to check my guns now."

Jimmy keyed his mike. "Roger, this is Flight Commander. It's okay to check guns."

Throughout the formation gunners checked their weapons. On board the *Stand and Deliver*, guns exploded in staccato firing as they were cleared.

"Oops, sorry, Colonel," Barry Overstreet suddenly said, referring to a rather severe bounce the plane made.

Jimmy was letting Overstreet fly, and the young man was having a difficult time of it. So far Jimmy had said nothing and hadn't made any corrections. Overstreet was just now learning what all the experienced pilots knew: Trying to maintain position, heading, and altitude in a bomber stream was nearly impossible. The air that looked so clear and innocent and smooth was actually a boiling cauldron, storm-tossed by the tremendous forces of all the airplanes pushing through it. There were propeller washes, wingtip vortices, and turbulent wakes that rolled back with a hurricane force of two hundred miles per hour, and the bombers bobbed and bounced like corks on the wildest sea.

Jimmy knew that it wasn't fair to the other members of the crew to let Overstreet continue to slide all over the sky. Some of the men were already filling their air-sick bags, even the most seasoned veterans, and he could have prevented much of that simply by taking over the controls. But Jimmy also knew that Overstreet might have to bring the ship home alone. That wasn't a pleasant thought, but it was one that had to be faced, so it was better to let his copilot gain his experience now, with him here to act as a backup.

He turned his head to look at the leading edge of the left wing. Behind the blur of the spinning propellers he could see the lusterless glare-reducing paint on the inside of the engine nacelles, the black of the wing de-icing boot, and the red-and-yellow unit ID stripe at the wingtip.

"Colonel, I have a fix," the navigator said, cutting through the static of Jimmy's earphones to interrupt his thoughts.

"Go ahead, Paul," Jimmy said into his headset.

"We are one hundred eighty miles from our first check-point on a radial of oh-three-five. Our ground speed is one hundred eighty-five miles per hour."

"Okay, thanks."

One hundred eighty-five miles per hour, he thought. Anytime the public saw a picture of the B-17 in a magazine or in a newsreel, they were assured that the speed was "over three hundred miles per hour." Three hundred miles per hour might be possible in a very clean B-17 with no gun blisters of any kind, no crew except perhaps pilot, co-pilot, and flight engineer, and no bombs, no machine-gun bullets, no patched-over bullet holes, and fuel tanks that were only one quarter full. But the only way anyone would ever get *Stand and Deliver* to do three hundred miles per hour in its present configuration would be to point the nose straight down and shove all four throttles to full power.

"Left waist gunner to pilot. Bandits at one o'clock high! Looks like FW-190's."

"Check them over close, son," Jimmy said. "Don't forget, FW-190's and P-47's have the same profiles."

"Hold your fire, gunners," Sergeant John Potts shouted quickly. As flight engineer, Potts was also the top-turret gunner and as such had the best overall view of anyone in the ship. *"They're P-47's."*

"I'm sorry," the left waist gunner said.

"That's okay, Buck, this is your first time out," Jimmy said easily. "Most of us have made the same mistake once. Just take a real good look at them so you don't do it again."

"Yes, sir, I'll be more careful next time," Buck reported.

The ME-109's and the P-51's had very similar profiles, too, but Jimmy didn't say anything about it because there were no P-51's on escort duty today, and there was no sense in confusing the kid any more than he already was.

The P-47's stayed with them for a while; then, when their fuel ran low, they zipped through the formation from front to rear. The combined speeds of the bombers and fighters made them pass each other at almost six hundred miles an hour. They were little more than a blink of the eye, and then they were gone.

"Is that it?" Overstreet asked. "They're leaving now?"

"That's all the on-station time they have," Jimmy replied. "Their engines will be sucking air by the time they land."

"They sure didn't do anything, did they? I mean, they just sort of hung around for a while."

"When they don't do anything is when they do the most," Jimmy said.

"I don't get it."

"I used to know this man in Hong Kong who sold tiger powder to the local citizens. He promised them that if they just spread tiger powder around their houses, no tigers would ever come and bother them. He sold a lot of powder. None of the citizens were ever bothered by tigers."

"There aren't any tigers in Hong Kong, are there?" Overstreet asked.

"Pretty effective powder, huh?" Jimmy quipped.

"But the powder didn't have anything to do with it," Overstreet said in an exasperated tone of voice.

"How do you know? The powder is there. The tigers aren't."

"What does that have to do with the P-47's?"

"As long as they were here, the Germans weren't."

"Oh," Overstreet said, not certain if he was being kidded or not.

"*Left waist gunner to pilot. Bandits, nine o'clock high! I'm sure of them this time!*"

"Good job, Buck. Okay, guys, look alert. We've got company."

A moment later all the guns on the *Stand and Deliver* opened up, and the sky was suddenly filled with brightly glowing balls of fire. The first attack wave of ME-109's slammed through the formation, apparently with no hits scored by either side. The German fighters were so much faster than the bombers that they were able to regroup far in front, then come screaming back through in the opposite direction, closing on the bombers as fast as the American

P-47's had a short while earlier. The only difference was, the Germans were firing.

During such maneuvers there was a rather bizarre co-operation of sorts between the German fighters and the American bombers in order to avoid collisions. Since the fighter pilot was the only one who could manipulate his aircraft enough to prevent colliding, the B-17 pilots never took evasive action and so avoided inadvertently moving into the path of one of the wildly gyrating German planes.

As the fighters flashed back through the formation, the guns erupted again. Jimmy twisted around in his seat to follow a couple of the German fighters, and he saw the left wing break off one of the bombers, tumbling like a falling leaf. The B-17 continued to fly along for a second as if determined to cruise without a wing, but then it fell off into a sharp spin and began its five-mile fall to the ground, the propellers on its two engines continuing to spin futilely.

"*Colonel, that was the* Truculent Turtle. *That's Major Petrey's ship,*" Sergeant Potts reported.

"Yeah," Jimmy answered, thinking about the major with the hangover this morning, "I know."

Another B-17 was hit, and fire started streaming out from the wing root.

"There goes the *Lusty Virgin.*"

"*Get out! Get out, you guys!*" Potts shouted into his headset.

"There's one out, he went out the back," Jimmy said.

"*There's two more. They came out the bomb bay,*" reported Carson, the ball-turret gunner, situated underneath the plane just behind the wings.

Before anyone else could escape, the *Lusty Virgin* went up in a brilliant but seemingly silent explosion.

"*Shit,*" Potts breathed.

Suddenly, from beneath the airplane, a German fighter popped up, going away. The ball-turret gunner, the chin-turret gunner, and the upper-turret gunner were all able to track on target, and Jimmy watched all three guns hose into the ME-109. Smoke started streaming back from the German fighter's engine cowl, and suddenly the blur of what had been the propeller turned into black bars as it slowed to the point that Jimmy could actually count the revolutions. He knew then that the plane was fatally hit. The fighter rolled over onto its back, and the pilot fell clear, rolling himself into a ball for the plunge to the ground. Bailing out of his plane didn't mean that the German pilot was out of danger. He had to go through another bomber formation five thousand feet below, where more than one hundred spinning propellers were waiting for him. Jimmy idly wondered what the odds were of the pilot hitting one of the planes in his fall.

The fighters left suddenly, but another danger soon presented itself. The antiaircraft guns mentioned at the briefing abruptly opened up, and the sky ahead became a sickening mass of exploding flame and smoke and jagged chunks of metal. Flak was everywhere. It tore pieces off wings, smashed out engines, and exploded inside fuselages to rip airplanes—and crew—apart.

Jimmy's senses were being assaulted. Fire, smoke, and exploding airplanes were erupting before his eyes. He tried to blot out everything else and concentrate on flying. Finally they reached Schweinfurt. Smoke was already boiling up from the first wave of bombers that had gone in and scored hits when Jimmy turned the controls over to his bombardier.

"Okay, Danny boy, it's all yours," he said.

"I got it, Colonel," the bombardier answered.

The bombardier flew the plane with the bombing sight controls for a few moments until they crossed the release point. Then he called, "Bombs away!"

"Let's get the hell out of here!" Jimmy shouted.

The German fighters followed them off their target for another fifteen minutes, then mercifully pulled away.

"Is that it?" Overstreet asked. "Are they gone?"

Jimmy leaned his head back and took a deep breath. "Yeah," he said. "We've dropped our bombs; we can't do anything to them anymore. Now they're going after the third wave." He leaned forward and readjusted the trim to compensate for the empty bomb bay.

"I'm glad they're gone, but I hate to think about those poor guys in the third wave."

"Yeah? Well, better them than us," Jimmy said matter-of-factly.

BERGEDORF, GERMANY

Uta Tannenhower adjusted the mouthpiece on her collar as she prepared to make contact with the fighter squadron she'd be working today. Although she was the wife of one of the most powerful men in Germany, in that particular underground Luftwaffe Fighter Control Center she was just another one of the flight controllers.

Uta wasn't doing her job for show. She was serious about it and took a great deal of pride in her duties. From the very beginning of the war she had begged Karl to let her do something to help the war effort, but he had steadfastly refused. Then, one by one, German cities began to fall under heavy Allied bombardment. It reached its peak when Hamburg was firebombed and one hundred thousand of its citizens were killed. The Tannenhower home was among those burned to the ground, but the family escaped death because Karl had moved Uta and Liesl out of the city and into Bergedorf, a small town near Hamburg. During the week of the firebombing raids against Hamburg, all the residents of Bergedorf had stood outside their homes and watched as a huge, terrifying orange glow lit up the western sky. The continual bombing by the Americans by day and the British by night ignited a fire storm, a devastating phenomenon whereby superheated air in the center of the city created an artificial low-pressure area. That in turn sucking air in from outside the town to supply the flames with oxygen. Feeding itself, the cycle built up into a windstorm of two hundred miles per hour and two thousand degrees, turning the entire city into a blast furnace. The fire-fighting apparatus broke down, the river boiled, and the city had all its oxygen sucked away, suffocating thousands in the bomb shelters.

After Hamburg, Karl's resistance to Uta's "doing something useful" dissolved.

Uta briefly thought of this as she concentrated on the lights being projected onto the large frosted-glass map in front of her. Some of the lights represented the American bombers, some the German defenders.

"Falcon Leader, this is *M* for Magda," Uta said into

her microphone, establishing contact for the first time. "Falcon Leader, this is *M* for Magda. Are you there?"

"Ah, Magda, mein liebchen, yes, I am here with a flight of four," a voice replied in Uta's earphones. *"And may I tell you what a sexy voice you have?"*

Uta knew that the pilot was in a Messerschmitt, somewhere high over Germany in the cold upper reaches of sky. He was up there possibly facing a fiery death, and yet he was speaking to her exactly as if they were in a night club and he was trying to pick her up.

"Stand by, Falcon Leader, while we compute your heading."

"Falcon Leader, standing by. Tell me, do you live up to your sexy voice, M for Magda? What do you look like? Are you dark and sultry? Or are you blond and blue-eyed?"

Despite herself, Uta chuckled. She wondered what Falcon Leader would think if he knew how old she really was.

"Do you flirt so outrageously with all your controllers, Falcon Leader?" she asked, a smile tugging at one corner of her generous mouth.

"Only you, my love, only you," the pilot replied. *"Meet me somewhere, Magda. Meet me in the bar at the Adalon Hotel. Spend the night with me."*

"Falcon Leader, please, you cannot say such things over the radio!" Uta said in an exasperated voice. This was beginning to get out of hand. "Don't you realize we are being monitored?"

"Let the monitor get his own girlfriend. You belong to me," Falcon Leader replied with a laugh.

"I am too old for you," Uta said. She had to put a stop to this now.

"No one is too old for me," Falcon Leader replied easily. *"I may die today. You can't get any older than dead."*

"Please! Don't say such things, Falcon Leader," Uta gasped. "Oh, stand by now. Here is a position report on the bombers." She read the newly updated information. "They are heading for sector B-Four. We believe the target to be Würzburg, Nuremberg, or Schweinfurt. They are flying at nine thousand meters, speed three hundred fifty kilometers. There is a very large dispersion pattern."

"The Americans and their B-17's," Falcon Leader said. *"They come in the daytime and they dare us to shoot them down. Arrogant, yes, but I must tell you this, my sweet lovely: They are so beastly hard to shoot down that it is a challenge worthy of our best."*

"From your current position, steer one-seven-five true," Uta said.

"Vector one-seven-five true," the pilot repeated, and the tone of his voice showed that he was now ready for business.

Uta watched the light positions move on the large map in front of her. The light she was controlling was Falcon Leader and his flight. The large group of lights moving slowly, steadily across the map from west to east were the American bombers.

"You are ten minutes from intercept," Uta told Falcon Leader.

"Ten minutes," he acknowledged. *"We are forming into attack teams now and climbing to . . . please state again the bomber altitude."*

"Nine thousand meters," Uta replied.

"Thank you. We are climbing to ten thousand meters."

Uta could hear the roar of the engine over the voice of the pilot. Her stomach tensed, and she could almost believe that she was actually in there with him.

On the large frosted-glass map in front of her the light dots continued to move closer together.

"We have contact, Magda. It looks like a very large group of B-17's, perhaps as many as three hundred. We are starting the attack now."

Falcon Leader did not release the microphone key, and Uta could hear the high-pitched whine of the engine as his airplane started on its long dive.

"Magda? Magda, are you there?" Falcon Leader asked, his voice still incredibly calm.

"Yes, yes, I'm here," Uta answered, shocked to hear from him while he was actually carrying out an attack.

"I'm taking you on this one with me, my love. Will you give me a kiss for good luck?"

"Yes, yes!" Uta cried, feeling a fear unlike anything she had ever felt before. It was strange: She wasn't really in the airplane, she was here, safe, in an underground flight-control headquarters, and yet she could hear the roar of the plane's engine and even Falcon Leader's breathing as he started his run. It was simultaneously the most wonderful and the most terrifying thing she had ever experienced.

"I'm lined up on the lead plane now," the pilot said. *"They are firing at us. The Americans are so wasteful of ammunition . . . we are way out of range. Still, seeing all those glowing bullets coming toward you does give one pause."*

Suddenly there was a hammering noise in Uta's ears, so loud that she had to jerk the headset away. It lasted about two seconds; then it stopped.

"There's a bit of luck for you," Falcon Leader said. *"I've exploded his fuel tank."*

Uta knew then that she had been listening to Falcon Leader's machine guns.

"I've completed my first pass," he said. *"Now I must swing around for another go. Are you still with me, my love?"*

"Yes, yes! Oh, Falcon Leader, please! Please, be careful!"

"My name is Max. Are you worried about me?"

"Max?" Uta breathed in a choked voice. Max was the name of her son, killed in Poland during the first weeks of the war. Was this Max as young as her Max? "Yes, I'm worried about you," she admitted.

"Good, I rather like that. Well, here we go again. I've got another one lined up in my sights. Just be patient, American, and I'll shoot you down for my own sweet Magda."

Suddenly Uta heard a loud crashing sound that was different from any sound she had heard so far. It was followed by something that sounded like a terrible rushing wind.

"Max? Max?" Uta called. *"MAX!"* she screamed.

"Magda? I'm afraid I got a little careless that time," Max's voice said. No longer was it strong and relaxed. Now it was strained and labored.

"Max, what is it? What is that sound?"

"That . . . my sweet . . . is the sound of my plane breaking up. I'm going down."

"Max, jump out! Jump out of the plane! Use your parachute!"

"*Sorry, liebchen,*" Max replied. "*I'm afraid my back is broken. I am quite unable to move. Good-bye.*"

Max went off the air then, no doubt stopping transmission just before he crashed.

She couldn't go on after that, so she signaled for someone to take her place, and she left the plotting room. She went into the lounge, where she sat on a sofa and cried large, bitter tears—but she didn't know if she was crying for Max the pilot, Max her son, or herself. Finally she pulled herself together, washing her face and powdering her reddened nose, so that by the time the others came in, she was completely recovered.

"Ladies, you did a good job today," the chief controller told them. "Our brave fighter pilots shot down over one hundred enemy bombers."

The controllers cheered.

"Did the bombers get through to their target?" one of the women asked.

"They got through to Schweinfurt, yes," the chief controller admitted. "But I am absolutely assured that the damage they did on the ground was minimal."

"And our fighter losses?"

"Two or three only. They are of no consequence," the chief controller assured them.

"You are wrong," Uta said resolutely. "They *are* of consequence. Those brave fighter pilots that we control are more than voices in the void, they are flesh and blood human beings. My Max was of some consequence."

At that moment Uta wasn't sure which Max she was talking about, but it didn't really matter. They had somehow managed to become one and the same.

FIVE DAYS LATER, SCHWEINFURT, GERMANY

The director of FAG Kugelfischer, Schweinfurt's huge ball-bearing factory, conducted a tour through the grounds, showing the results of the American bombing raid the week before. It had rained earlier in the day, a cold, late-fall drizzle, and the several Nazi flags hanging above the entry-way that were meant to make a colorful display instead hung sodden and limp like so many rags.

There were eleven bomb craters in the ground inside the factory compound, all filled with muddy water. One of the main shop buildings was gutted and blackened by fire; another had a couple of holes in the roof and some damage to the walls.

Since Karl Tannenhower and Paul Maas were the highest-ranking members of the tour group, they were walking up front, receiving the personal attention of the factory director. Karl was wearing a long black leather coat, which he had drawn tightly around him. A red swastika armband was around his left sleeve, while his epaulets were covered with an impressive amount of gold braid. Paul was similarly dressed.

"As you can see, Herr Oberreichsleiter," the director was explaining, "only fourteen of the high-explosive bombs actually fell inside the compound. Eleven of them deto-nated harmlessly on the ground. Three obliquely struck the foundry."

"Did those three do much damage?" Paul asked.

"Very little," the director replied. "The machinery in the foundry is so solidly built that it would take a direct hit from a bomb to seriously damage anything."

"So you're saying that out of all that, the factory suf-fered no damage at all?" Karl asked.

"No, sir, I'm not saying that. The truth is, we did sus-tain some quite serious damage, but not in the way the Americans expected."

"What do you mean?"

"The Americans also dropped some incendiary bombs that they intended to be merely a nuisance. However, those bombs ignited the oil baths in some of our machines, warp-ing the rollers. Those machines can't be used now."

"How long will they be down?" Paul asked.

"A month. Maybe six weeks."

"So the American air raid *was* successful?"

"Only marginally successful," the director corrected. "And then, certainly, not in the way they thought."

"If only fourteen high-explosive bombs fell inside the

factory, what happened to all the others dropped by the Americans?"

"I'm afraid they fell on the city itself," the factory director said. "Have you been into town?"

"Not yet," Karl said. "I'll be visiting the downtown area after I finish here."

"You will find that the damage is quite severe and extensive. There are entire blocks where not a building is standing."

"And the loss of life?"

"Heavy," the director admitted. "But the American loss of life was also high. Nearly a thousand of their aviators were killed while making this attack. Surely they can't sustain such losses for too long a time."

"And yet we did not turn them back," Karl said. "Not once have we ever turned an American bombing attack away from their intended target."

"But they won't be able to keep that up much longer, Herr Oberreichsleiter," one of the accompanying military men said. "The Americans are expending all of their bombers."

"Yes, Oberst," Karl replied. "But the question is, what will be expended first? American bombers . . . or German cities?"

Later, after Karl had completed the inspection of the ball-bearing factory and the town, he and the rest of his party flew back to Berlin in a JU-52. Karl was working on a damage assessment report while Paul sat across from him, unobtrusively drinking a cup of coffee. It was now very late in the day, and the inspection team had departed early in the morning. Now, lulled by the monotonous drone of the three engines, several of the passengers were sleeping.

Paul was silent, waiting patiently until his old friend had finished his report and closed up the papers in his briefcase. Putting the case on the floor by his feet, Karl pinched the bridge of his nose and looked through the window. The cluster of small towns and villages below him were whole and undamaged.

"When I look at villages like that," Karl said in a quiet voice, "I can almost believe that there is no war. Look at them, how peaceful and undamaged they are."

"You must be growing very weary of visiting bombed-out cities, boosting the citizens' morale," Paul said.

"The task doesn't tire me. Although it does sadden me to see so many of our cities destroyed and our people made homeless, wounded, or killed."

"Why do you do it?"

"Someone must, and Hitler absolutely refuses to. Even on the train he will pull the shades so as not to see any demolished areas the train may pass through. And when some of the Hamburg fire fighters were being given medals for bravery, he wouldn't even see them."

"And so the task of boosting civilian morale has fallen entirely on your shoulders?"

"Yes," Karl answered. "I must say, however, that I am strengthened by the magnificent fighting spirit of the ordinary German citizen. Every tour I have made so far has uplifted me in one way or another."

"Karl, my friend, have you toured any of the relocation centers?" Paul asked.

"Relocation centers?"

"The concentration camps where we are shipping all the Jews."

"No," Karl replied. "No, I haven't seen any of them. Why do you ask?"

Paul took a sip of his coffee, then looked through the window of the plane at the deceptively peaceful farmland sliding by far below.

"Don't," he said softly.

"Don't? Don't what?"

"Don't visit any of them."

"Why not?" Karl asked. "Have you?"

"Yes. I had to see for myself why the trains were being tied up transporting Jews instead of war matériel."

"And?" Karl prodded, when Paul did not continue his thought. "What did you see?"

Paul's eyes grew flat and dead, chilling Karl. "I saw hell."

CHAPTER TWENTY-ONE

David Gelbman had no idea how long he had been a prisoner in this place. Time had lost any meaning. There was no past, no present, no future, no day, no date, no hour. There was only daylight and darkness.

David and Anna had managed to stay together throughout the grueling ten-day train trip that brought them across the border from Austria to a little village in Poland. But they had been separated upon arrival at Auschwitz's concentration camp. However, twice since then David had managed to get a glimpse of Anna. The first time he had seen her, she had been marching with a group of women. The second time she had been working on her hands and knees, pulling weeds near the fence that separated the men's camp from the women's. That time David had been pushing a wheelbarrow-load of recovered eyeglasses, and as he passed the fence he had managed to exchange a few words with her.

"I wonder how Miriam is," Anna had said.

"She is alive and well."

"How do you know?"

"She was alive and well when we saw her last. To me, that's how she will always be."

Though he had wanted desperately to hold Anna, or at least touch her, he wouldn't even look at his wife. Anna had concentrated on her weeding, and David had paid strict attention to his wheelbarrow. He couldn't have even slowed down as he passed by the fence, not for a heartbeat, for if the guards had seen that they were communicating, both would have been killed.

Because of the distortion of time, David had no idea how long ago that interchange had taken place. It could have been a few weeks, a few months, or a year or more. He had not seen Anna since that time, and he had no idea whether she was dead or alive.

David and Anna had arrived in the early days of the camp, before the gas chambers and ovens were operating at full capacity. Many of the hardier, earlier prisoners weren't sent immediately to their death, but were given jobs to perform. David was what was called a "Recovery Jew." He and the other Recovery Jews would gather, sort, bundle, and load onto trains all the clothes, eyeglasses, rings, and watches recovered from new arrivals who were immediately executed and longer-term prisoners who died as a result of unimaginable cruelty and deprivation. David was always amazed at how many rings and watches remained with the prisoners until the very end. Such things were, of course, the favorite targets of the guards in charge of rounding up the prisoners and transporting them to the concentration camp.

David's job was heart-wrenching. It was very hard to handle things that but a short time before had been someone's prized possessions. In David's early days as a recovery worker a child's sweater, perhaps with a monogram lovingly applied by the mother, would bring him to a halt and to tears. Now he knew better than to stop long enough to examine a single item of clothing. Thousands upon thousands of sweaters, shoes, dresses, trousers, shirts, rings, et cetera, tended, by their sheer numbers, to numb the senses. But a tiny dress could still fleetingly tug at his heartstrings.

After the clothes were gathered, they would be sorted by sex, size, and quality, then tied in bundles and loaded back onto the same train that had brought the Jews to Auschwitz. Loading the stuff into the cars was backbreaking work, for the bundles were quite heavy and had to be moved very quickly. The workers were constantly being prodded to hurry, and indeed the word most often heard at the depot was *"Schnell! Schnell!"*

But there were far worse jobs in the camp than working in recovery. Newly arriving prisoners were greeted with a sign rendered in iron over the portal gate proclaiming: WORK WILL MAKE YOU FREE. (The ghastly irony of the declaration was lost on the newcomers, but they learned it soon enough.) They were taken off the trains not by club-wielding guards, but by the "Camp Jews," who were prisoners like themselves. Camp Jews informed the new arrivals that they were going to be given the luxury of a shower. Small signs along the well-tended walkways pointed TO THE SHOWERS, and often the newcomers were serenaded by an orchestra playing light operas and show tunes.

Once inside the dressing room they would find numbered hooks for their clothing, along with signs that said: PLEASE REMEMBER YOUR NUMBER SO THAT YOU WILL HAVE NO DIFFICULTY IN RECLAIMING YOUR CLOTHES. There, the Camp Jews would help the new prisoners undress, then move them into the large community shower. It wasn't until the prisoners were inside and the doors were dogged tightly shut that they realized what was about to happen to them. Within a few moments it would be all over.

What made the Camp Jews' job worse than David's job, of course, was that they would have to look directly into the eyes of fellow Jews, knowing all along that these people were but minutes away from death. And they had to hide that fact from them.

David didn't generally come into personal contact with the new arrivals, but once an old woman managed to wander away from the group, all the way over to "Recovery Square," where David and other Recovery Jews were busily gathering clothes. David sensed the old woman's presence, and he glanced up from what he was working on to see her standing there, watching him. She was wearing a long dress that buttoned all the way down, solid black except for a pink rose made of silk sewn to the waist. The old woman's body was deformed by age, and her face had the slackness of desiccated flesh. Her eyes, however, were very much alive, and they were staring at David, boring into his soul.

"And so, we have come here to die?" she asked, not in fear or despair, but in resignation.

Though David couldn't answer the woman, she saw the truth in his eyes.

"But you and the others . . . you are spared?" she asked. The question wasn't condemning or even accusing. It was merely curious.

"I . . ." David couldn't finish his sentence, couldn't bring himself to talk.

"Never mind, you need not speak," the old woman said. "I feel pity for you. I know that for you it must be worse." She turned around and walked back to the others, then, pulling herself together with great dignity, joined the long line of people waiting patiently to get into the "showers." Later that same afternoon, David saw her dress, long, black, buttons all the way down, and with a pink silk rose sewn to the waist. And as he folded it tenderly, lovingly, he cried.

There were frequent discussions in the barracks at night as to whether or not it was proper to conceal the truth from the arriving Jews. Some people thought the new arrivals should not be told they were there to die. Others disagreed. After all, the second faction said, the SS guards wanted the truth concealed from the victims not from any sense of humanitarianism, but simply so they could maintain order, the rationale being that Jews who went meekly to their deaths would be much easier to handle than Jews who panicked. The Camp Jews who argued to tell the truth asserted that to conceal the truth was to collaborate with the SS guards.

"We should not hide from our people the fact that they

are condemned," one would say. "We should defy the Germans in any small way we can."

"And so to satisfy your own conscience that you are defying the Germans, you would cause our people to feel the anguish of knowing they are condemned?" another would counter.

"We are all condemned. It is just a matter of knowing when death is to be, that's all."

"It's better not to know."

In the end, the argument was always won by those who believed that it was more humane not to tell the arriving Jews that they were about to die. As a result, an unholy alliance was created between the Camp Jews and the SS guards, and the charade was carried off with remarkable effectiveness.

The worst job of all was that of the *Totenjuden,* the "Jews of Death," the ones who went into the gas chambers and removed the bodies. They did this by clamping ice tongs onto their heads, then dragging them outside where other Totenjuden armed with pliers would extract the gold teeth. Finally the bodies were taken to the crematorium, where they were dumped onto the conveyor belts that fed the huge ovens. The ovens operated twenty-four hours a day to accomplish their grisly task, and both the camp and the nearby town it was named after were continually saturated with the horrid, sickly sweet smell of burning flesh.

One day after the last car had been loaded and the door shut against the stack of clothes, David and the other prisoners who worked in recovery were marched back to an assembly area, where they were undressed. This was normal routine, done so the prisoners could be thoroughly searched to make certain no one was stealing gold, money, or other valuables.

The person in charge of the recovery team was SS Sergeant Heinrich Steiner. Steiner was tall, blond, and handsome, a walking poster for SS recruitment. He wasn't the highest-ranking SS guard over them, and as far as gratuitous cruelty went he wasn't even the worst. Like the other guards, Steiner had shot and beaten and hacked to death his share of prisoners, doing it matter-of-factly, taking no more notice of his victims than a factory worker on an assembly line would of an assembly part that passed before him.

But Steiner did seem to take an immense pleasure in devising irritants for those in his charge. Perhaps that was why David hated him more than any of the other guards. In a way it wasn't unlike the situation with the clothes: Just as thousands of articles of clothing could numb the senses while one sweater tugged at the heartstrings, the savage cruelty of all the dozens of guards numbed the senses while the individual guard who took perverse pleasure in devising humiliations could enflame hatred.

When the clothing and body search was completed, the prisoners started to put their clothes back on, but Steiner stopped them with a barked command.

"*I* am in charge here," he said. "*I* will tell you when you may put on your clothes. Stand at attention!"

The prisoners, still naked, stood at attention.

"Straighten up those ranks!" Steiner ordered.

Looking left and right, the prisoners aligned themselves into ranks and files. Then they stood there, unblinking and without the slightest muscle moving.

Steiner smiled at them. "You know, I think I have figured out what it is I don't like about you stinking Jews," he said. "You do not understand military precision. Therefore I have designed a drill for you. Put your hats on your head."

One of the prisoners in the front rank started to reach for his hat, but Steiner, who was carrying a policeman's night stick, cracked him over the head. The prisoner fell to his knees, blood streaming down his forehead.

"Get up!" Steiner ordered.

Slowly, unsteadily, the prisoner stood.

"When I say put your hat on your head, I mean do it in a prescribed manner. On the count of one, pick up your hat; on the count of two, straighten up; on the count of three, put it on your head; on the count of four, bring your hands down sharply by your side. Ready? Begin! One! Two! Three! Four!"

The prisoners tried to comply. In the beginning it was very sloppy, and Steiner sent his men around to "make corrections" by bashing the slow and inept over the head with their billy clubs. Two of the prisoners were corrected so severely that they were instantly killed. Finally, after nearly an hour, the prisoners were going through the drill with such military precision that their hands popped against their thighs in unison as they completed the last count.

"Ah, there, you see? You almost had it, but one of you was slightly off," Steiner said.

David knew damn well that nobody was off, but he knew, too, that it didn't make any difference. It would not be right until *Steiner* decided that it was right.

"Of course, you know there is always one stinking Jew who will foul up everything," Steiner said. "There is one among you who is not doing it correctly, and he is making it bad for all of you. But this is what I will do: I will turn my back and let you decide among yourselves who it is. Get rid of him, and you will be perfect. In fact, we probably won't even have to drill anymore. You could go right to your barracks."

Steiner turned his back for a few moments, then turned back around. "Well, who is it? Have you decided? No? You need a little more time? All right, to show you what a nice fellow I am, I will give you a little more time. But my patience isn't without limits. When I turn my back this time, you must choose from among yourselves who is to bear the guilt. If you do not choose, then I will select ten of your number. And their punishment will be . . . severe. Do you understand?"

You perverted bastard, David thought. *You are forcing us to make the decision as to who among us must die.*

After a few moments facing away from the prisoners, Steiner turned back around. "Now, what is it to be? One of you? Or ten?"

"One," someone said.

"Oh? Who?"

"It was . . . my son," the man said.

The others gasped.

"Your son?" Steiner replied.

"Yes."

Steiner stroked his chin as he studied the formation. "Oh," he finally said. "Oh, how wonderful. The sacrifice of

Abraham. I am touched. I am truly touched. And as the son of Abraham was spared, so now shall I spare your son. There now. Do you see how generous I can be? You are dismissed. All of you. Have a good night."

That night, in the darkness of the barracks, David could hear the father and the son speaking.

"Please forgive me," the father begged.

"There is nothing to forgive," the son replied. "Nothing happened."

"I betrayed you."

"Do not concern yourself."

"I knew God would not let you die," the father insisted.

"As God wouldn't let the son of Abraham die?" the son replied.

"Yes, as God would not let the son of Abraham die."

"There is no God."

"Oh, but there is, there is!"

"If there is a God, why does He let this happen? Why must we all suffer so?"

"It is a test, my son. It is a test to see if we, His chosen, are truly worthy."

"I don't want to be His chosen. I curse the fact that I was born a Jew."

"You mustn't think such things!" the father said in despair. "Don't you see, if you curse your own birth, then the evil ones will have truly won."

"They *have* won."

"No, you must not say that. You must not believe that."

"How can I *not* believe that?"

There was silence for a long moment; then the father spoke again. "There is one way to defeat them. If you want to do so badly enough."

"Yes," the son said. "I know the way. And I am willing."

"Are you sure it's what you want?"

"Yes."

"You are prepared to die?"

"Yes, Father, I am prepared to die. I cannot endure another day of this."

"Then come. We will help each other. We will die together."

"You need not die with me, Father."

"But I must, don't you see? I can't let you make the journey alone. You have lost your faith. Therefore, I must go with you so that I can personally take you into God's presence."

The son was quiet for a moment, then said, "All right, Father. We will go together."

David lay in the darkness, listening to the preparations as a box was moved into position and makeshift ropes—strips of cloth knotted together—were thrown over the rafters.

"Good-bye, my father," the son said.

"Until later," the father replied.

There was a scruffing sound, then the creak of the rafters as weights pulled against them. After that came a moment or two of death rattles, then silence. Other voices murmured in the darkness then, whispered prayers ending in "Amen."

It was two days after the suicides of the father and son when David saw Anna again. This time, miracle of miracles, she was working on the depot platform, helping to sort clothes. That meant he wouldn't have just a brief glimpse; he would get to see her all day!

"Anna," David whispered as he brought a bundle of clothes to be sorted to the table. "Are you all right?"

"Yes. How are you?"

"I'm fine. It is wonderful to see you."

"I am told I will be here every day for one week," Anna said.

"God has truly blessed us!" David whispered.

That night he could barely sleep, so excited was he over the prospect of seeing Anna again in the morning. When he arrived at the platform and saw her working with the other women, his heart leapt with joy, and he thought she was as beautiful then as she had been on that day, many years ago, when they stood together under the marriage canopy.

Once, while transferring a bundle of clothes, David's and Anna's hands managed to meet. It was for but the

briefest of moments, and David felt a charge of electricity
course through his body. That night, as they had been the
night before, his prayers were prayers of thanks.

And during the night David got the idea that he would
try to arrange an escape for himself and Anna. He knew
that escape was practically impossible and that in all probability they'd both be killed. But he decided he would rather
be killed trying to get away than wait around and die in the
prison.

David lay awake all night thinking about the escape,
and by morning he had devised a method. The most difficult part of the scheme lay in explaining the plan to Anna.
He'd only be able to do it a few words at a time, and she
had to be able to understand and react without question.

The key part of his plan was to find a way to get Anna
into one of the outgoing cars. Once she was on board, he
could then load the clothing bundles in such a way as to
leave a space for her to hide in.

"I have an escape plan," he whispered the first time he
passed by her with his wheelbarrow on the way to the
clothes bin.

"Do exactly as I say," he told her the next time. "Act
quickly and without hesitation."

It was almost an hour before he passed by her table
again.

"When you can do so without being seen, go to the bin
and hide under the clothes." This was a reference to the big
bin that held clothes already sorted and bundled and waiting to be loaded into the freight cars.

Half an hour later, one of the SS guards came over to
the table where the women were working. "You will come
with me," he said, pointing to three of the women. Then he
started in the direction of the clothes bin.

Anna put down the bundle of clothes she was working
with and started off as well, a step behind the others. Fortunately the guard stationed by the table hadn't been paying
strict attention to his duties. Having heard the other guard
summon some of the women, he didn't even question
Anna's leaving for he hadn't noticed that she wasn't among
those summoned. It was an audacious, risky move on
Anna's part; at any moment the summoning guard might

turn around and see her. Even if he didn't suspect that she was up to something, just disobeying orders could result in a brutal punishment.

Anna followed the guard and the other three women until they reached the clothes bin. Then, with a quick look around to make certain she wasn't being seen, she slipped into the bin and burrowed under the bundles.

David didn't actually see Anna leave, but he did find that she was gone the next time he passed the women's worktable. He could only hope that she'd been able to follow his instructions.

It was a full hour after he had found her gone before he was able to push his wheelbarrow over to the clothes bin.

"Anna, if you're in here, get into my wheelbarrow now!" he hissed sharply.

There was a movement underneath the clothes, then Anna crawled out. She climbed into the wheelbarrow and David covered her with several bundles. He started pushing her toward the railroad car, paying very close attention to the loaders and the carters coming from other sorting posts. He had to time it exactly right. His wheelbarrow had to be the last to arrive at that car, for the car door would be closed by whoever was last.

David watched the other carters, and he sped up or slowed down as was necessary, breathing a constant prayer that he would arrive at the car at the proper time.

"You!" the SS man in charge of loading shouted, pointing toward David. "Go to the next car!"

At first David thought the SS man was pointing at him; then he realized that he was pointing to the person just behind him. He had done it! He was going to be the last wheelbarrow at this car! David was so delirious with joy that he had a difficult time keeping his face impassive.

"When you have emptied your wheelbarrow, call me so that I may inspect the load before you close the door," the SS man instructed David—as if he hadn't heard the same order given hundreds of times over the last several months.

"*Jawohl,*" David replied.

The SS man then moved down to the next empty car

with the newly arriving wheelbarrow, leaving David to finish with that car.

"Anna, I will have to pick you up with the first bundle," David said under his breath. "I will put you on the car. When the train leaves the camp, wait for a while, then jump off."

"And you?"

"I will find a way."

He picked up a bundle and Anna at the same time. Like everyone else in the concentration camp, Anna was so thin as to be literally just skin and bones, so she didn't add that much weight to the bundle. But the bundle was heavy enough by itself, and David was as malnourished as everyone else, so it was very difficult for him to make the lift and do it easily and quickly, as if he were lifting only the bundle of clothes and nothing more.

He set Anna down inside the car, then turned away to grab the next bundle. Within a moment he had his wheelbarrow empty, Anna hidden, and the car ready to close.

"Anna. Can you hear me?"

"Yes."

"I am going to close the door, but I will not set the latch. You should be able to open it from inside."

"I love you," Anna said, her voice muffled by the clothes.

"Good-bye, my love," David said. He turned away from the car. "The car is full, sir!" he called. "It can now be closed."

The SS man walked back from the other car and looked inside. All he could see was a solid wall of clothing bundles. He nodded his head. "Close the door," he said.

David closed the door and turned the handle, making certain that the locking pins weren't really engaged. With the handle turned, however, only someone who paid particular attention to the actual pins would be able to tell that the door wasn't latched.

It was late afternoon by the time the train was fully loaded. Without someone to assist him as he had assisted Anna, David knew that he wouldn't be able to hide inside one of the cars for his own escape attempt. But after giving it some thought, he had come up with a much simpler—

and much more dangerous—plan: He would wait until the train was actually starting out of the yard, then scoot underneath between the wheels and hang on to the underside of the car. Success then would depend not only on whether or not he was seen, but whether or not he could hang in such a way as to keep from falling onto the track and being crushed by the train passing over him.

David knew it would be easier and less dangerous to get under the car while the train was standing still, but he figured that if he didn't make his move until the last moment, there'd be less opportunity for him to be caught. He waited until the train began rolling before he started toward the car, trying to work out the timing in his mind so he'd know just when to throw himself between the wheels and how to grab the undercarriage. He looked around to see if the coast was clear—and his heart almost stopped in fear.

About one hundred meters away from David, near the front of the train, SS Sergeant Heinrich Steiner was watching each of the cars pass—paying particular attention to the latches!

Why was he doing that? David wondered. For months now, trains had left here every day without anyone giving the latches a second thought. Why was Steiner doing it today of all days? Why this train of all trains?

David knew that if Steiner saw that the door on Anna's car wasn't actually locked, he'd have the train stopped and the car searched. And if he found Anna, which he was sure to do, he would have her hacked to pieces right in front of David's eyes.

David would not let that happen!

He started running toward Steiner without even considering what his next step might be. All he knew was that he had to reach the SS guard before Anna's car got to him, and that was going to be hard to do because already the train was picking up speed, gaining on him.

Forty years before David had won his letter as a runner on the college track team at Jefferson College. He was a damned good runner then, and he had derived great pleasure from the sport. Even the most grueling race had been a thing of joy to him. When he was twenty-one, he had been lean and muscular. But he was sixty-one, not twenty-one. He wasn't lean and muscular, he was weak and emaciated. And he wasn't running for the pure love of running, he was running to save Anna's life.

Every breath sent tongues of fire into his lungs, and with each step he felt as if someone were thrusting a knife into his side. Out of the corner of his eye he saw the train picking up still more speed. There was no way he was going to beat Anna's car to Steiner.

Suddenly, on either side of him, David saw two young, muscular men, running easily and smiling broadly. They were dressed exactly as he had once dressed, in green track uniforms with a diagonal red band and the red winged *J* on the front of the singlet. One was short and light-haired, the other was tall and dark.

"David," the short one said. "You can do it. Keep up with us."

"Terry? It can't be! You died in Panama forty years ago!"

"What do you mean I'm dead? You're the one who looks dead here. Come on. I can do better than this running backward!" To illustrate his point, Terry Perkins turned around.

"Come on, David," the tall dark one chided. "Terry never saw the day he could beat you. Run! Run, David, run!"

"J.P.! My God! I'm clearly hallucinating! You went down with the *Titanic*!"

"What difference does that make? All you have to do is run. Do it for good old Jefferson! Do it for the Quad Quad! Remember your kick, David? You had the best finishing kick of any of us."

David closed his eyes, took a deep breath, and went into his finishing kick. When he opened his eyes again he saw that he was gaining on the train.

"I'm doing it!" he gasped. "J.P! Terry! I'm doing it!"

But David was alone.

SS Sergeant Steiner had been paying such close attention to the latching mechanism on each car as it passed that he didn't see David running toward him, and the train was making so much noise that he didn't hear him, either. That allowed David to launch himself against Steiner, knocking him down, just before Anna's car passed by.

"*Oooff*," Steiner grunted, going down under the onslaught.

With the wind knocked out of him, the SS man was slow to get back up onto his hands and knees. When at last his wind returned and he looked around, he found David kneeling on the cinders alongside the track, breathing in deep, painful-sounding gasps.

"Why, you decrepit old son of a bitch! What the hell do you think you're doing? I'm going to kill you for this, you Jew bastard!" Steiner reached for the pistol he kept in a covered leather holster on his belt.

But David wasn't looking at the guard. He was watching the train going by behind him. When he saw that Anna's car had already passed safely, he smiled.

"What are you smiling at, you piece of Jewish filth?" Steiner demanded as he raised his weapon.

David hadn't played football when he was in college, but he had gone to many of the games, and he suddenly realized that he was in exactly the same position linemen assumed when they were going to make a block. With a loud scream of defiance, he charged straight into Steiner, driving his shoulder into the German's chest. Steiner fired his gun just as David hit him, but the bullet bounced off the rocks, then ricocheted harmlessly out over the compound area. By now other SS men were arriving, having been drawn to the scene by the commotion. They ran toward the two men with their own guns at the ready, but they were unable to fire because Steiner and David were too close together.

David kept his shoulder in Steiner's chest and continued to drive forward with his feet, thrusting both of them underneath the slow-moving train.

Steiner, a look of horror on his face, saw the rear set of boxcar wheels bearing down on them. He opened his mouth to scream, but the scream died in his throat as the steel wheels worked their terrible, bloody carnage.

David felt only exultation.

CHAPTER TWENTY-TWO

Of the one hundred twenty men who had embarked with Colonel Sir John Paul Chetwynd-Dunleigh on the long-range penetration behind Japanese lines, fewer than eighty remained. Many of those still with him were suffering from dysentery, and all were plagued by the relentless onslaught of jungle insects and other pests.

John Paul and his special task force were an independent operation that had been ongoing for nearly two months. It had been extremely successful in its mission of disrupting Japanese communications and supply lines, but the cost in suffering and human lives was growing daily. Cut off from their own lines for so long now that they had nearly exhausted their supplies, the men were now dependent for their sustenance on the very jungle that so ruthlessly plagued them.

John Paul had established his base camp along the bank of a river to prevent a surprise attack from one flank at least by the Japanese. The river offered the additional advantage of being a source of water, though they had long since run out of purification tablets. The handsome thirty-one-year-old aristocrat was at that moment in the base camp, sitting with his back to a tree, burning leeches off his body with a lighted cigarette while listening to a discourse by Captain Thomas Winston. Winston had started out as John Paul's adjutant, but John Paul's second-in-command and the next officer below him had been killed, which meant that Winston was now acting as John Paul's executive officer.

"How bad can monkey stew be?" Winston asked, continuing his argument. "I mean, after all, the bloody natives eat it all the time."

"I didn't say the men couldn't eat it," John Paul replied. "I just said *I* didn't want to try it."

"I really think you should, sir."

"Would you give me one reason why?"

"We're almost out of rations, aren't we? And if *you* won't eat the buggers, many of the men won't. Some of them will die if they go much longer with nothing to eat."

"But a *monkey,* Thomas. Isn't that a little like eating . . . I don't know . . . they're so humanlike that it's almost cannibalism."

"Ah, but you're wrong, Colonel," Winston replied. "There are no dangerous psychological problems caused by eating monkeys. I admit that there could be from cannibalism, but I must remind you that even that has been resorted to upon occasion."

"I certainly hope you aren't about to propose *that* action," John Paul muttered.

"Of course not," Winston said. "We have an ample source of food without resorting to that extreme. Provided, of course, you take advantage of it. What do you say? A little stewed monkey, simmered slowly in its own juices, flavored with a bit of wild pepper, jungle onion, bamboo shoots, mustard, and palm root? Sounds good, doesn't it?"

John Paul laughed. "If I ever open a restaurant or club anywhere, I want you writing my bills of fare. You make it sound quite tasty."

"Then you *will* try it?"

"Yes, damn you, I'll try it. I only ask one thing."

"What is that, Colonel?"

"I don't want to see the blighter before it's cooked."

Winston laughed. "Colonel, I promise you, it'll be simmering in the pot before you're even informed of its demise."

"Good," John Paul said. He started to put his shirt back on, but Winston stopped him.

"Wait a minute, sir. You have a couple on your back." Winston took the cigarette from John Paul and began taking care of the leeches.

"Damn this place," John Paul said. "How can humans live in this part of the world?"

"Oh, I actually enjoyed quite a lovely assignment," Winston said. "I mean, there I was, only a lieutenant in the Indian Army, and yet I daresay no one in England lived a better life. Granted, I wasn't camped out in a snake- and bug-infested jungle. I had a large house, a dozen servants, I belonged to a polo club. . . . I had everything a proper gentleman could ask for. Then the bloody war came along."

"Yes, I've heard that peacetime service in India was quite comfortable," John Paul said.

"What I don't understand, Colonel, is why *you* are down here."

"What do you mean?"

"Well, you hold your commission by title, don't you? You could be sitting back quite comfortably in England now. And yet here you are in what is arguably the most disagreeable theater of operations of the entire war."

"Yes, well, after we withdrew from France, I was given an indefinite furlough," John Paul said. "In theory I was still in active service. I think that somewhere on the manning charts I was carried as the commander to a battalion that didn't exist, of a regiment yet to be formed, in a division that hadn't even been drawn up. All this was for some proposed invasion of the continent that would occur sometime in the future. I just didn't want to sit back and wait the war out like that."

Thomas Winston grinned. "Give me half the chance and see what *I* would do. I mean, there you had a colonel's commission and a medal for already having done your bit. If it were me, I'd have been quite content to wait until they called on me again, even if they *never* called me. I certainly wouldn't have volunteered to go fight in the bloody jungles. Especially if I had a lady friend as attractive as the one whose picture you carry."

John Paul laughed. "Don't give me this 'reluctant hero' business, Thomas. You volunteered for this patrol just like everyone here."

"Well, perhaps so, but then, the life of ease I once knew was gone, wasn't it? What else was I to do?" The last leech withered under the heat of the cigarette tip and fell off John Paul's back. "Ah, there you go, sir. I do believe I have them all now."

"Thanks," John Paul replied. He stood up and put on his shirt, then reached for his Bren gun, which hung from a limb on the tree. "You will look out for things while I'm gone, won't you?" he asked. He checked the chamber of his weapon. "I'm going to take a patrol out to have a look around."

"Very good, sir. Your dinner, pipe, and slippers will be waiting for you when you return," Winston said, affecting the obsequious tone of a servant.

"Yes, well, if I'm not back in about three hours, do start without me, won't you?" John Paul rejoined. "I suppose I can always grab something at the club."

"Quite."

They both laughed, and then John Paul slung his weapon over his shoulder and sauntered through the camp. Five of the men stood up to join him, even though he didn't say a word. Despite the hardships the long-range patrol had endured, the morale of the men was still high, and nowhere was that better evidenced than by the fact that volunteers never had to be called for. When someone saw that a job needed doing, he did it without being asked.

John Paul and his patrol had been moving swiftly and silently through the jungle for nearly an hour before they heard Japanese voices. John Paul held up his hand and the patrol stopped. Silently he signaled for the others to get into place, and they slipped behind cover on either side of the trail. John Paul waited until the Japanese patrol was completely by them, then gave the signal. He and his men stepped out onto the trail behind the Japanese and opened fire. The British were armed with automatic weapons, whereas the Japanese were armed with rifles that had to be manually operated to rechamber a round after each shot, so even though the Japanese significantly outnumbered the British, they were badly outgunned and managed only a weak and ineffective response.

The automatic weapon recoiled roughly against John Paul's shoulder, and as the gun sprayed out the spent cartridges, hot little specks of gunpowder flew back in his face. Though his eyes and nose were burning from the spent gas, and his ears were ringing from the sound of the gunfire, he held the trigger down and hosed his fire into the group of enemy soldiers.

The British fire cut down palm leaves and splattered bark from the trees, but most of the bullets found their target, and after a short but furious fusillade, the last Japanese soldier fell.

"See if any of them are carrying food," John Paul said.

Two of the men went up to check the fallen soldiers and searched quickly and efficiently through their uniforms and rucksacks.

John Paul looked down at one of the dead Japanese soldiers. Alongside him lay the man's billfold, which had slipped out and flipped open, displaying a picture of a Japanese girl dressed in a kimono and holding an umbrella open before her. In the background was a *tori* gate. The girl was smiling shyly, as if embarrassed by the whole thing.

John Paul swore and kicked the billfold so that it sailed several feet before disappearing into the thick foliage. What was he doing looking at that picture? He knew better than that. He couldn't let himself think of the enemy as human beings, with girlfriends, wives, mothers, fathers, sisters, and brothers. He could go crazy doing that. But then, what did it matter? he thought. The whole bloody world was crazy anyway. Only crazy people would kill other people who carried pictures of loved ones in their wallets.

John Paul took out his own wallet and opened it to look at the pictures. One was of his mother, the other was of Shaylin McKay. He thought of the last time he had been with Shaylin, and he actually felt a stirring in the pit of his stomach. Shaylin was without doubt the sexiest, most inventive creature he had ever—

"Colonel, look out!"

The warning came too late. The Japanese soldier who had raised up from the bushes behind John Paul blew the back of John Paul's head away. Colonel Sir John Paul Chetwynd-Dunleigh was dead before he ever knew he was in danger.

JUNE 4, 1944, COMBINED FORCES HEADQUARTERS, ENGLAND

"Have you ever met Eisenhower?" Shaylin asked, as she and Eric Twainbough rode in a press-pool car toward their appointment.

"Yes, many years ago," Eric said. "Though I'm certain he won't remember."

"When was that?"

"During World War One. He and Loomis Booker shared an office in Washington. I stopped by to visit Loomis before I went overseas, and he introduced me to Ike."

"What did you think of him?"

"I wasn't with him long enough to form an opinion," Eric admitted.

"Well, I've met him several times now," Shaylin said. "And I find him most deceptive."

"Duplicitous?"

"No, I don't mean deceptive in a negative sense. It's just that he's not a man prone to vain affectations. He has a terribly engaging grin, but a rather low-key personality that makes you wonder at first how he ever made it so far. Your first impression of him is likely to be that he is a very *nice* man . . . too nice, in fact, to have any business conducting the affairs of war."

"But he's a man who gets beyond first impressions?"

"Absolutely," Shaylin replied. "Just when you've been lulled into thinking he doesn't quite have the picture, you suddenly discover that not only does he see what you can see, but also much more. It can be most disconcerting . . .

rather like playing a poker game to one deuce showing, then finding that there are three more deuces down."

Eric laughed. "Remind me not to get into any poker games with him."

"You'd be smart not to, as a matter of fact. I understand he's an excellent player."

Shaylin and Eric were to meet General Eisenhower at his personal quarters at SHAEF, Supreme Headquarters of the Allied Expeditionary Force. SHAEF was situated in a large camp at Busy Park by the Thames River in Middlesex, and Eisenhower's personal quarters were located in Telegraph House, a large, elegant house very near the park.

"Isn't this place beautiful?" Shaylin asked as they parked the car out front. "Except for the MPs, you'd think we were visiting the Duke of Marlboro or something."

"Well, you'd know more about that than I would," Eric replied. "Seeing as you're such a special friend of Sir John Paul Chetwynd-Dunleigh. Is his place like this?"

"Oh, much nicer," Shaylin replied. She affected an upper-class British accent. "It isn't all cloyed up with you disagreeable American chaps."

"My God, girl, would you be for listenin' to yourself now?" Eric replied in as equally affected an Irish brogue. "Sure an' himself, the Mr. McKay who's still buried in the old sod, would be spinnin' in his grave to think of a fair Irish lass like yourself talkin' with the accent of the oppressors."

Shaylin laughed. "Let's make a bargain, Eric. I won't try any more proper British accents if you'll promise no more brogue. You're absolutely terrible."

"Promise," Eric replied. "By the way, what do you hear from his lordship?"

"Nothing," Shaylin said, becoming solemn. "In fact, it's been nearly six weeks since I heard anything."

"Maybe he doesn't love you anymore."

"Not much chance of that. I have him eating out of my hand."

"Hmm, that sounds like fun. I haven't tried that yet," Eric teased.

They hopped out of the car and hurried into the house, where they stopped at the adjutant's desk and showed him written confirmation of their appointment with Eisenhower. The adjutant picked up the phone and made a call. A moment later he put the phone down and looked back up at them.

"The general will receive you now," he said.

Eric thanked him, and he and Shaylin walked into what had once been a dining room but was now General Eisenhower's office. The general was shuffling through some papers when they entered, and he stood and flashed his famous grin at them, taking Shaylin's hand when it was extended, then offering his to Eric.

"It's good of you to see us, General," Eric said.

"Well, it would be poor politics of me to refuse to see you, wouldn't it?" Eisenhower replied. "The two of you reach quite a formidable audience. If there must be press about me, I at least want to give it every chance of being good. By the way, Mr. Twainbough, what do you hear from Loomis Booker?"

Eric's eyes opened wide in surprise. "You remember that, General?"

"Why, of course I do. Loomis and I shared the same office for over a year. And he was arguably one of the most brilliant men I ever met."

"Yes, I agree, and it's no surprise that you remember him. I was just surprised that you connected *me* with him."

Eisenhower chuckled. "That isn't hard to do, either. Loomis used to talk about you quite a bit. He was convinced that you were going to be a great writer someday. I'm glad to see that you didn't let him down."

"Thank you."

"I've read several of your articles, Mr. Twainbough, and I have a great admiration for your perceptiveness. But I must confess that I haven't read any of your novels. For escapist reading, I tend to lean toward paperback westerns. My staff keeps me supplied with all the latest—though they do like to keep the books out of sight whenever we have important visitors. I'm afraid they think that reading westerns is beneath the dignity of a four-star general."

"I hope everybody doesn't feel that way. I *love* westerns," Eric said.

"And you, Miss McKay, have done some wonderful

stories. Your piece on the ground crews at Waddlesfoot was positively brilliant. The men who keep the bombers flying never get any of the glory, but they are the backbone of the entire air operation against Germany. By the way, how's your brother? He's in the Navy, isn't he? In the Pacific somewhere?"

"Yes, he is," Shaylin said. She laughed. "General, you are amazing."

Eisenhower grinned. "Well, when your brain isn't crowded with really brilliant concepts, you can hang on to the small things. Now, what can I do for you two?"

"We want to be in on the invasion," Eric said.

"Do you know when it's to be?"

"No, I'm sorry, we don't," Eric replied.

"Well, I'm not sorry," Eisenhower said. "If you did, I'd be furious and alarmed. That would mean our security's been breached."

After a lengthy pause, with Eisenhower seeming disinclined to say anything more, Eric prompted, "Well, what about it, General? Can we go along with the men?"

"You mean you want to be aboard one of the ships?"

"No," Eric replied. "I mean I want to go in with the first wave."

Eisenhower shook his head. "No, I'm afraid not. It would be too dangerous."

"No more dangerous for me than for the hundreds of thousands of boys who will be going," Eric countered. "How can you send them out to die while denying their families the right to know what's going on?"

Eisenhower folded his arms across his chest and cocked his head slightly as he studied the two journalists. "Are you making the same request, Miss McKay?"

"Heavens no," Shaylin replied, laughing. "I leave the heroics to Eric. I'll be content to watch the invasion from one of the ships . . . preferably a big ship with big guns. I'll go ashore later, when it's more secure."

"I'm glad to see that you, at least, are showing good sense." He addressed Eric again, asking, "But you want to go in with the first wave?"

"Yes. Actually, I initially wanted to go in on one of the gliders, but then I realized that I'd be taking up space that could be occupied by a fighting soldier, so I gave that idea up."

"You'll also be taking up space on one of the landing craft," Eisenhower reminded him.

"Yes, but on the landing craft space isn't as critical. And if you noticed, I didn't even try to talk you into letting me go in by parachute."

Eisenhower laughed out loud. "Why not? Were you afraid I might approve?"

"Something like that," Eric replied, joining in the laughter.

"I'm going to pay the airborne troops a little visit before nightfall. I'm glad I won't be having to foist you off on them. Okay, if you want to go in on the first wave, you'll get no objections from me. But it's up to you to find someone who'll take you along. I won't order anyone to do it."

"I'll get it taken care of, General; don't you worry about that," Eric said easily. "And thanks for the permission."

"Yes, well, I just hope we don't both regret it," Eisenhower said. "All right, as of now, you're both on restriction."

"Restriction?"

"Yes. I'll have someone take you down to the docks and put you aboard one of the ships."

Shaylin's eyes widened. "The invasion?"

"Tomorrow," Eisenhower replied, nodding. He flashed his big grin again. "That's why I can't let either one of you go. You are now entrusted with one of the biggest secrets of the war."

A lieutenant colonel came into Eisenhower's office at that moment and handed him a note. Eisenhower thanked him, then read it. The smile left his face.

"Something wrong, General?" Eric asked.

"Yes. I had hoped, as sort of a psychological boost to the morale of the British, to let the British officer who was the last to withdraw from the Continent to be the first to return."

"General, would that be Colonel Chetwynd-Dunleigh, by any chance?" Shaylin asked.

"Yes, as a matter of fact, it would be," Eisenhower

said. "That's right. You wrote a story about him, didn't you? Someone brought me a copy when we first conceived the idea of letting him go back first."

"What do you mean you had hoped?" Shaylin asked, tensing. "What's happened to change your mind?"

"He was on some long-range patrol mission, so we just got the word," Eisenhower replied. "I regret to say that Colonel Chetwynd-Dunleigh was killed a couple of weeks ago in Burma."

"Oh God!" Shaylin gasped, and she covered her face with her hands.

"What's wrong?" Eisenhower asked. He turned to the author. "Eric, did she know Chetwynd-Dunleigh? I mean, beyond the article?"

"Yes," Eric replied. "She knew him quite well, in fact."

"Oh," Eisenhower murmured. "Look, I'm terribly sorry. It was very insensitive of me to blurt it out like that, but I had no idea."

"Of course you didn't," Shaylin said, looking up and shaking her head. "Please, don't be angry with yourself. I'll be all right."

Eric put his arms around her, and she lay her head against his chest. He expected there to be heavy, raking sobs, but there were only a few silent tears.

"Poor John Paul," she whispered. "Poor, poor John Paul."

NORMANDY, FRANCE

Though the invasion had been scheduled for the fifth of June, weather conditions were such that the whole thing was called off. After much soul searching and weather prognostication, the invasion fleet put back to sea the very next night and, on the morning of June 6, at 0630 hours, the Americans landed on Utah and Omaha beaches. They were on the beaches one full hour before the British, who hit the beaches of Gold, Juno, and Sword at 0730. The difference in time was dictated by the different conditions the invaders faced.

The Americans chose 0630 because the tide would be at its lowest ebb, and the underwater invasion obstacles would be exposed. The British chose 0730 both to ensure a longer preinvasion bombardment and to enable the landing craft to ride in with the high tide that would place the men higher on the beach.

Eric stood on the deck of the ship in the predawn darkness, looking at the other men who had been shuffled up to their "station" while waiting for the word to go over. They had actually been brought up at 0100, and many of the men, including Eric, hadn't slept a wink the entire night.

Eric wasn't sleepy, though; his adrenaline was flowing too freely for that. He imagined that most of the others were just as excited as he was.

Suddenly the heavens were lit with brilliant flashes, and streaks of light sped through the night, heading toward the shoreline. A moment after the light came the roar of explosions.

"Well, there they go, fellas," one of the waiting soldiers said. "The Navy boys have opened the show for us."

The naval ships continued with their bombardment, and the sky all around took on the illusion of a horrendous thunderstorm, complete with brilliant flashes and stomach-shaking roars. Each time one of the Navy ships unleashed a salvo, Eric could see the silhouette of the hundreds of ships that lay quietly at anchor off the Normandy coast.

Shaylin was on one of those supporting ships, Eric knew, but he had no idea which one it might be. He didn't know exactly when he'd see her again, but they had made tentative plans to get together sometime after the invasion.

"Mr. Twainbough? Mr. Twainbough? Are you up here, sir?"

"Yes, I'm right here," Eric replied. "Who's calling me?"

"I am, sir," a young lieutenant said. "You've been assigned to my boat. Did you get any practice climbing down the nets before you came aboard?"

"I'm afraid not, Lieutenant. But what can there be to it? You just climb down, don't you?"

"No, sir," the young officer replied. "I'm afraid there's a bit more to it than that. If you don't mind, may I give you a bit of instruction?"

"Go right ahead," Eric said, his tone indulgent.

"Here," the lieutenant said, stepping over to a hatch bulkhead where a cargo net was being stored. He pulled out the net. "You can see that the net is composed of a series of squares formed by crossing ropes. Your feet go on the horizontal ropes, but your hands must grip the vertical ropes . . . like this." He demonstrated.

"Why's that?"

"To keep your hands from being stepped on by the fellow above you."

Eric smiled. "That does make sense."

"When you first go over the side, keep the upper part of your body leaning in toward the ship. Push out with your feet. If the upper part of your body should lean outward and your feet come in, you may find yourself parallel with the sea, and you'll have to hang on for dear life. Remember, the upper part of your body in."

"All right," Eric said, listening far more intently now.

"Be very methodical as you climb down. The ship is rolling, so you may take a step and find there's no rung there. Most of your weight should be borne by your hands. Your hands are for support, your feet for transportation. Don't look up and don't look down. If you look up, the upper part of your body will swing out. If you look down, you can become disoriented. Now, and this is very important, when you get to the bottom of the netting, there will be net holders . . . men assigned to keep the net away from the side of the ship. They'll tell you when to disengage. You must disengage the moment they tell you, for what with the rolling of the ship and the landing boat, the last step can sometimes be as much as ten feet. Don't go before they've given you the word, and don't hesitate once they do."

"Thanks, Lieutenant," Eric said. "I didn't realize it would be so complicated. I appreciate your advice."

"Now all troops to their disembarking stations! Now all troops to their disembarking stations!" a metallic voice said

over a loudspeaker, and there was a general shuffling movement among the men who'd been standing on deck.

"First serial into the boats . . . that is, first serial into the boats."

"Over here, Mr. Twainbough," the lieutenant said, leading Eric to his place.

Eric watched as the men began climbing over the nets. One of the men slipped just as he was going over. He let out a startled scream, which was cut off sharply as he hit the deck of the landing boat below.

"What happened?" someone shouted.

"Did you see that?" another asked.

"Who was it?" a third man said.

There was a rush to the railing. The loudspeaker ordered the men back to their proper places.

"He broke his back," someone said a moment later, and as the stretcher, suspended from a cargo winch, brought the hapless man back up, the others resumed their loading.

When Eric went over, the lieutenant was right by his side, solicitous for his safety. Eric was glad for the young officer's dedication and thankful when, at last, he was standing in the landing boat and waiting for the others.

Finally the boats pulled away from the ships, then started circling while waiting for the waves to form. The circling may have been the most difficult part, if only because many of the men became so desperately seasick. Even Eric, who had once been a seaman, was feeling pretty unsettled by the time the boat operator gunned the engine and pointed the craft toward shore.

After everything else, the actual landing was somewhat anticlimactic. The portion of the beach Eric landed on was relatively unchallenged, though he could tell from the gunfire and the explosions that others making the landing weren't so fortunate. He moved off the beach with the advancing forces, then took up a position with the rest of the men, waiting for the lines to stabilize.

JUNE 6, 1944, HITLER'S HEADQUARTERS, BERCHTESGADEN, GERMANY

Karl Tannenhower was sitting outside on the terrace of the Berghof, drinking coffee and reading the newspaper, when a lieutenant colonel approached him, clicked his heels, and waited to be addressed.

"Yes, what is it?" Karl asked, looking up from his paper.

"The Allies have begun their invasion," the officer said.

Karl slowly put the cup down and stared at the messenger.

"Where?" he finally asked.

"Along the beaches of Normandy."

"Has the Führer been informed?"

"No, Herr Oberreichsleiter. He is not yet awake, and he will hear no news until after he has had his breakfast."

"I think he should be informed," Karl said.

"Is the Oberreichsleiter ordering me to inform him?" the colonel asked.

"No," Karl said. "No, not yet. Where are the others?"

"In the drawing room, Herr Oberreichsleiter," the colonel said.

Karl put his newspaper on the small table, then started into the house toward the drawing room. He could hear voices, a low buzz, before he reached the room. When he got there, he found everyone silhouetted against the great picture window that looked out over Untersberg Peak. Only Göring was separated from the others. He was standing by the fireplace, where he had a plate of sausages and Brötchen on the mantle. He picked up a sausage with his fingers and shoved it in his mouth just as Karl came in.

"Ah, Tannenhower," Göring said. "Let's hear what you have to say about the situation."

"I don't know anything about it," Karl said. "I only just heard the news. But I think we should awaken the Führer and tell him."

"And why should we do that?" Goebbels asked. "The Führer is convinced that this is just a feint. The real attack will come at Calais. That's why all our defenses are located there."

"I would think, then, that that would be precisely the reason why the real attack *wouldn't* come there," Karl said irritably.

"Tannenhower, perhaps you should stick to bolstering the morale of the city officials after the Allied bombing attacks and leave matters of military strategy in the hands of the experts," Himmler suggested coolly.

"Yes, I can see the sense to that," Göring told Himmler snidely. "Tannenhower flew airships during the war, and you did . . . what? Raised chickens? I'm sure you are much more qualified to speak of military strategy than he."

"If I were you, Göring, I would see if I couldn't find a way to turn back the British and American bombers and stay out of discussions that don't concern you," Himmler countered.

Göring walked over to Himmler, dominating him with his bulk. "When the Führer isn't present, *I* am in command," he said. "It *is* my business when members of the Führer's staff begin bickering with each other. Now, if you don't like it, Himmler, you can always visit one of your concentration camps and watch your brave 'heroes' burn Jews."

"I make no apologies for the work my men do," Himmler said, taking out a handkerchief and wiping the sweat from his face.

"All right, Herr Reichsmarschall," Goebbels put in. "You are in charge; now, what do we do? Do we wake him and tell him? Or do we wait until he wakes on his own and tell him after breakfast?"

Göring thought about it for a moment, then walked back over to the mantle and picked up another sausage. He held the sausage for just a moment.

"We wait," he said finally. "As you know, we have built several V-One bomb launching sites near Calais. I am certain that the flying bomb sites are the real target of the Allied invasion. The landing at Normandy is only a feint, designed to draw our Army into a trap."

IN THE AIR OVER BERLIN

Going in on the bombing run, the flak defending Berlin had been incredibly heavy. Coming off the run, the flak was much lighter, for the German antiaircraft gun crews knew that an empty bomber couldn't hurt them. Nevertheless, there were always a few guns out of position, so instead of challenging incoming bombers, they sent up their best efforts against the planes coming *off* the bombing run. Jimmy saw a few light puffs dot the sky around him, but compared to the stuff they had just flown through, this flak hardly merited his attention.

With the bombs gone, the weight and balance configuration of the airplane had changed, so he started readjusting the elevator and aileron trim and setting the fuel mixture and propeller pitch for the long flight back to Waddlesfoot. He had just gotten everything set up the way he wanted and leaned back in his seat when he felt it . . . the slightest little tick, so small that he couldn't be sure he wasn't imagining it.

"Did you feel that, Overstreet?" he asked his copilot.

"Feel what, sir?"

Jimmy scanned the instrument panel and saw nothing out of the ordinary. He looked through his window at the left wing and its two engines. The nacelles were whole and the props were spinning blurs. When he leaned forward and looked at the two on the right, he saw the same thing. Everything looked normal. Still, he couldn't get rid of the disquieting feeling that something had just happened.

"Left waist gunner to pilot. We're trailing something from our left outboard."

"Smoke?" Jimmy asked into his headset.

"Yes, sir, I guess so," Buck said.

"Colonel, you want me to activate the fire bottle on number one?" Overstreet asked. He was a first lieutenant now, and considerably more seasoned that he had been during the Schweinfurt raid. Jimmy had no qualms about him now. If he had to, Overstreet was quite capable of bringing the *Stand and Deliver* home.

"Hold off," Jimmy said. "I don't want to use it unless

we're sure we have a fire. What about it, Buck? Do you see flames?"

"*No, sir,*" Buck answered. "*And hold it. It's not even smokin' anymore. Whatever it was has quit.*"

"Pilot to flight engineer. You're up there in your turret, Potts. Can you see any damage?"

"*No sir, not that I can . . . wait a minute, I do see something. There's a jagged exit hole, about the size of a quarter, in the cowling right on top of the engine,*" Potts replied.

"Carson, can you see anything from the ball turret?"

"*Yes, sir, I can see where it went in,*" Carson said. "*Damn if I know when that happened, though. And like Potts said, it ain't no bigger'n a quarter.*"

"It's big enough," Overstreet suddenly said. "Take a look at the RPM on number one, Colonel. It's running away."

"The propeller governor," Jimmy muttered. "Damn, that one little piece of flak took out the prop governor."

"It's up over twenty-five hundred RPM now," Overstreet said, his voice more urgent. "What are we going to do?"

Jimmy moved the prop lever back to decrease RPM, but it did nothing.

"That sure didn't help," he said. "I wonder if we can throttle back."

"That'll cause a lot of drag," Overstreet cautioned.

"Better to have a little drag than a runaway prop," Jimmy replied, coming back on the throttle.

"Shit, Colonel, look at the manifold pressure. It's forty inches."

"That was a busy little piece of flak, wasn't it?" Jimmy said. "It not only took out the governor, it took out all the control linkages. We can't do anything with that engine."

"We can't even shut it down?" Overstreet asked.

"I'm afraid not. The mixture and idle cutoff are out." He addressed his flight engineer again. "Potts, what about the cross feed? Is there anything we could do there?"

"*No, sir, all that does is select the tank. We can't isolate the engines.*"

"Twenty-eight hundred RPM," Overstreet said. "This son of a bitch is going crazy!"

"Colonel, the prop shaft is starting to smoke," Potts called. *"It's going to throw the prop."*

"Yeah, that's it!" Overstreet said. "We'll throw the prop!"

"Colonel, when it goes, there's no tellin' where it'll go," Potts warned. *"It could come right through the pilots' compartment."*

"Not if I turn this baby into a slingshot," Jimmy answered.

"A slingshot? What do you mean?"

"Can't tell you. I'm going to have to show you. You got your binoculars up there, Potts?" Jimmy asked.

"Yes, sir."

"Keep your eyes on that shaft, real close. When you think it's got less than a second before it lets go, give me a yell."

"Okay, Colonel," Potts said. *"I don't know what you got in mind, but I'll watch it."*

"The rest of you guys, don't worry about the prop," Jimmy said. "You keep your eyes open for bandits."

"Thirty-two hundred RPM!" Overstreet hollered.

By now the prop was screaming so loudly that it could be heard above the other three engines.

"Four thousand!"

"It's startin' to wobble," Potts called.

"Waist gunners, you better grab hold of something!" Jimmy shouted.

"Forty-five hundred RPM!"

"It's going . . . NOW!" Potts shouted.

At the precise moment Potts yelled, Jimmy hauled back on the wheel and whipped it over to the right, at the same time jamming the right rudder bar forward, putting the B-17 into a snap roll. The propeller popped off and went spinning in a high arc over the top of the ship. The B-17 was now flying straight and level, but with only three engines.

"Son of a bitch!" Potts shouted. *"Son of a bitch! That was better'n a ride at Coney Island!"*

"Everyone okay?" Jimmy asked.

"*We're okay back here, sir,*" Buck replied.

"How about up front?"

"*We're all okay, sir,*" the bombardier answered.

"Good. Then all we have to do is try to make it home on three engines. And, boys, that *ain't* gonna be easy."

Though Jimmy had all three engines on overboost, he was unable to keep up with the bomber stream, and within thirty minutes the *Stand and Deliver* found itself all alone.

"*Where'd everyone go?*" the bombardier asked.

"*Was it something we said?*" the navigator asked, and the others laughed nervously.

"Keep your eyes open," Jimmy warned. "The German fighter pilots really like stragglers."

"*They're not wastin' any time. Here they come!*" Buck responded. "*Three of them; nine o'clock high.*"

"*Three more at six o'clock!*" the tail gunner called.

The fighters bored in on the B-17, and all the gunners responded. The first one to come in from the six o'clock position was hit, and the other two broke off their attack. They re-formed into a queue from the nine o'clock position and started in again. The lead ME-109 was blown out of the air by the concentrated fire of the waist, dorsal, ball turret, and top turret guns. The second fighter broke off with its engine smoking, and that left three. They flew by the bomber with flashes of fire winking from their wing guns. Bullets pierced the skin of the B-17, but no vital parts of the plane were hit.

After all three of the remaining Germans completed their pass, they circled wide and formed up for another attack. The gunners returned fire. Again, several dozen bullets from the attacking Messerschmitts popped through the aluminum skin. This time they shot away an entire section of sheet metal, exposing the ribs and stringers of the bomber's fuselage, though again nothing vital was hit. They zipped on by, then wheeled around to start their third attack.

"*Colonel, when they come back this time, all I can do is make faces at them,*" Buck said. "*I'm out of ammo.*"

"*Me, too!*" Carson in the ball turret reported.

"Potts, how are you doing?"

"*I've got about five seconds left,*" Potts replied.

"Aren't *we* in a pretty spot?" Jimmy muttered.

"Yeah, and if that ain't enough, here comes another Messerschmitt," the bombardier said.

"Sure, why not. Get in on the fun," Jimmy snarled. "Hey, wait a minute! That's not a Messerschmitt! That's a Mustang! It's a P-51, one of *our* guys!"

"Yeah, but there's only one of him," Potts said. *"There are three Germans."*

"Maybe they don't see him," Jimmy suggested. "He's awfully far out."

Jimmy was right. The German fighter pilots, not expecting any company, were busy concentrating on the big, fat bomber that had fallen into their lap. As a result, the P-51 was able to shoot down the lead Messerschmitt before any of the Germans even knew he was there.

The P-51 pulled up through the debris of the exploding Messerschmitt, and the pilot hurled the plane around in a turn that was so tight Jimmy could almost feel the G's the guy was pulling from inside the B-17. The maneuver brought the Mustang around so that the pilot could bring his guns to bear on the second German plane, and a short burst had one more Messerschmitt going down.

"Look at that son of a bitch fly, will you?" Jimmy shouted. *"Whoowee! Am I glad that bastard's on *our* side!"*

The third German didn't want anything to do with the P-51; he turned his plane upside down, then let it fall. Contrails streamed out from his wingtips as he reached a speed of nearly six hundred miles per hour in the long power dive. He was thousands of feet below them before he flattened out, then beat a retreat toward Berlin.

"Hey, little friend, thanks for coming around," Jimmy said into his headset.

"Would you like some company on your way back?" the Mustang pilot asked.

"There's never been an ugly girl who wanted an escort more," Jimmy replied.

"I've been around the block a time or two, and I don't think I've ever seen an ugly girl," the P-51 pilot replied. The Mustang slid right up alongside the B-17 and tucked in close. The pilot was wearing an oxygen mask, goggles, and a leather flying helmet, so nothing could be seen of his

features, but Jimmy was certain the pilot was smiling. That was when Jimmy noticed the strange markings under the canopy, where pilots usually painted tiny swastikas to denote the number of enemy aircraft shot down. Whatever these marks were, there were nine of them.

"Hey, if you don't mind my asking, what the hell are those marks on your plane?" Jimmy asked.

"*Watermelons.*"

"Watermelons? What for?"

"*I'm going to paint two more on today,*" the pilot said. "*Does that answer your question?*"

"You paint on a watermelon every time you get a German plane? Why?"

"*Take a look over here,*" the pilot said.

Jimmy looked over into the cockpit of the Mustang, and the pilot pulled his goggles up and his oxygen mask down. Jimmy was right, the pilot *was* smiling. The white of his teeth could be seen quite clearly against the dark skin of his face. The pilot put the mask and goggles back on.

"*When I got my first kill, the white sergeant who was supposed to paint on the swastika thought he was being funny,*" the pilot explained. "*I started to take it off, then I thought, what the hell? A watermelon is as good a way to keep count as anything else, and I like 'em a hell of a lot more than I like swastikas. So I decided to keep it on. I plan to have quite a crop of them by the time this war's over.*"

"You look like you've got a good start," Jimmy said.

"*Now that you know the complexion of things around here, you want me to move to the back of the bus?*" the P-51 pilot asked.

"Are you kidding?" Jimmy replied. "If I had a sister I'd set you up with a date."

The pilot laughed. "*I'd settle for a bottle of bourbon. Send it to me at the Ninety-ninth Fighter Squadron. But make sure it's got my name on it. You know, we all look alike over there, and I'd hate to see it get lost in the confusion.*"

"What *is* your name?" Jimmy asked, laughing.

"*Jackson. Captain Travis Jackson,*" the pilot replied.

"To hell with a bottle, Captain," Jimmy said. "When we get back, I'm sending you a case."

CHAPTER TWENTY-THREE

DECEMBER 1944, THE ARDENNES

The Ardennes was covered with a mantle of snow, and within the American rest encampment brightly colored Christmas ornaments hung from every available append-age. Incongruously, also within the gaily decorated camp lay a number of burned-out half-tracks and jeeps. Supplies were scattered in disarray on the snow, and the soldiers who were picking through them were not American but German, members of the 5th Combat SS Panzer Battalion.

The German soldiers were there because three days earlier, on December 16, Hitler had ordered a massive counteroffensive against the Americans advancing toward the German West Wall. Four German armies, consisting of two hundred fifty thousand men, had been hurled into the attack against eighty-three thousand American troops de-ployed thinly across eighty-five miles of the Ardennes Front.

The Americans had been totally unprepared for the onslaught, and the Germans poured through with stunning success, recapturing in hours ground it had taken the Allies weeks to gain. Tons of equipment had been abandoned by the Americans as they retreated from the German advance.

Lieutenant Rudi Schultz, who reluctantly found himself acting as the executive officer in a *waffen*, or combat, SS unit, was one of the soldiers milling around the American rest camp. He drained some gasoline from an overturned American jeep, then put it into the small American field stove. He worked with it for a few minutes, then lit it, and was rewarded with a steady blue flame. He held his hands over the stove, grateful for the warmth.

SS Major Ebert, Rudi's commander, trudged through the snow to Rudi and then held out his hands over the stove as well.

"The Americans can come up with some wonderful inventions," Rudi said. "Do you see how small and simple this stove is? If we had possessed twenty-five thousand of these in Russia, we would have won the battle there."

"Stoves do not win a battle, troops win a battle. If the Waffen SS had been in Russia, we would have won," Major Ebert said. He sniffed loudly, and wiped his runny nose with the sleeve of his tunic. "Just as we have won here."

"The attack is but three days old," Rudi said. "I would suggest, Major, that it's too early to judge whether or not we have won."

"How can you question it?" Ebert asked. "Look around you. Do you see how the Americans have abandoned their equipment? Do you think any army that has lost so much can long survive?"

"You don't know the American Army," Rudi said. "They can leave everything here and still have anything they want. They have all the artillery in the world—and dry socks and hot coffee. They have bullets and toothpaste, gasoline and soap, tanks and ham. They have a supply system that is so untaxed that we have found homemade cookies and record players among the American dead. Could you see us using our transports to ship such nonessential goods?"

"No. And it is just such foolishness that makes me certain our victory is just around the corner," Ebert said. "Why, it's just like the days of the Blitzkrieg!"

"Were you a part of the Blitzkrieg, Major?" Rudi asked.

"Well, no, not exactly," Major Ebert hedged. "I had important duties in Germany at that time."

"I'm sure," Rudi said rather derisively. "If you had been a part of the Blitz, you would realize that we carried our own equipment and didn't have to rely upon captured goods to supply our Army. We are living on borrowed time now, Major."

"It is precisely that type of defeatist attitude that has kept you a lieutenant when officers junior to you have been promoted over you. You have no faith in the Führer or his plans. Well, the Führer has grown tired of such defeatist attitudes, and that is why he has given spearhead command to SS General Dietrich. In just three days the SS has put right all the wrong done by the Army."

"How privileged we of the Army are, to be in the company of the brilliant Waffen SS," Rudi sniped.

"There will be a reckoning," Major Ebert said, pointing an accusing finger at Rudi. "Do not think, Lieutenant, that people like you will escape reexamination for political reliability. Those who are found wanting will be dealt with most harshly. And don't think your Iron Cross First Class or your friendship with Oberreichsleiter Tannenhower will save you."

"I have no illusions, Major," Rudi replied, turning away.

"Lieutenant," one of the sergeants called from across the way, "would you like some of the American field rations for your lunch?"

"Is there any ham?" Rudi asked.

"I don't know. How do the Americans say ham?"

"It is spelled h-a-m," Rudi replied.

"There is something here called ham and beans," the sergeant said, pronouncing the last word with a long A so that it came out "bains."

"Bohnen," Rudi said. "Yes, that would be good. Perhaps we could heat it over this stove."

The sergeant brought the can over. "Look at this, at how ingenious it is." He demonstrated a small finger-held can opener. He opened the can, then held it over the stove.

Rudi chuckled. "We must thank the next American prisoner we see, not only for leaving us these fine tins of food, but also for providing us with the means to open them."

"I'm afraid that will be impossible," Major Ebert said.

Rudi turned back to him. "Impossible? What do you mean?"

"We will see no American prisoners because there are no American prisoners."

"But surely there are," Rudi said. "No one, not even the Americans, could so effectively withdraw their army that no prisoners are taken."

"Not even the Americans," Major Ebert repeated in a sarcastic, singsong voice. "Lieutenant, you seem to be obsessed with the greatness of the Americans."

"I have seen their capabilities."

"Well, what do you think of their capabilities now?" Major Ebert asked. "We have thoroughly routed them and killed thousands. That includes anyone who has tried to surrender . . . therefore, you will see no prisoners."

"Major, are you telling me we are murdering prisoners of war?" Rudi asked in shock.

"*Murder*, Lieutenant? We are at war. Killing during time of war is not murder."

"By all the rules of civilization it is, if you are killing prisoners," Rudi countered. "I will not be a party to such a crime."

"You are under my command, Lieutenant. You will do exactly what you are ordered to do. If you do not, I will have you shot."

"I have never failed to carry out my orders, Major," Rudi said coldly.

"Good, good," the major said. "Now, have you a map of this sector?"

"Yes, sir," Rudi replied, taking it out of the small leather map case he carried on his belt.

"Open it up and let us have a look," Ebert said. Like the others, he had been warming up a can of ham and beans, and now he began to eat them as he pointed to the map. "Here," he said, putting his finger on a road junction near the village of Baugnez, "I want you to take a platoon to this place. It is imperative that we hold the junction if our panzers are to continue to advance."

"*Jawohl!*" Rudi said sharply with a stiff salute. He folded the map and started off, leaving a half-eaten can of ham and beans sitting by the stove.

"What about the ham and beans?" Ebert asked, holding up his can. "Aren't you going to finish yours?"

"I don't think so, sir," Rudi said. "They tasted a bit odd to me. I'm afraid the Americans may have poisoned a few cans and left them for us to find."

With a choking cough, Ebert threw his can down. Since Rudi's back was to him, the major didn't notice his grin as he walked away.

THE AMERICAN SECTOR

"Captain Twainbough, the old man wants to talk to you," the radio operator said.

Ham walked over and picked up the headset. "Bulldog Six, this is Bulldog Two. Over."

"*Bulldog Two, this is Bulldog Six. Proceed to checkpoint Able-Charlie three. Take a look and see if there is anyone there, then get back. Over.*"

"Roger. Do you wish platoon strength or higher? Over."

"*Negative, Bulldog Two. All I want is a look-see. We've got to have some information. The Germans have broken through our lines, and they're pouring everything they've got through the Ardennes. Over.*"

"The Germans are attacking? I thought they were withdrawing. Over."

"*So did everyone else,*" Bulldog Six replied. "*But I guess no one told the Germans. Over.*"

"I'll get right on it," Ham said. "Over."

"*Out,*" Bulldog Six said.

Ham handed the receiver back to the operator, who asked, "Captain, you want the radio to go out with the patrol?"

"No, you stay here," Ham replied. "We'll take a walkie-talkie with us. It won't have the range to reach headquarters, but if we have anything, we can reach you here, and you can relay the information. Sergeant Pratt!" he called.

"Yes, sir," Bill Pratt replied. Like Ham, Pratt had been promoted, and he now wore the stripes of a first sergeant.

Ham got his map out and began looking at it. "The Germans have broken through," he said. "We've got orders to take a look around up at Able-Charlie three. That would be"—he studied the map for a second—"that would be right here, the road junction near Baugnez."

"I know the place," Pratt said. "There's a bombed-out church there. There's not much left to it."

"What about the steeple? You think I could get up into it? If so, I could have a good look around."

"You? What do you mean you? You aren't going, are you?"

"Yes."

"Captain Twainbough, if you don't mind my saying so, that's pretty dumb. I mean, what's the use of being an officer if you do everything yourself? That's what you've got sergeants for. I'll go."

"No, I want to see for myself what's going on."

"All right, if you want to come along, who am I to say no?"

Ham chuckled. "I'm not 'coming along,' Sergeant, I'm going. You're staying here."

"I'm staying? What the hell for?"

"I need somebody to keep an eye on the company," Ham said.

"Well, goddamn, Captain, you've got three lieutenants for that."

"Yes, and every one of them a ninety-day wonder, still wet behind the ears," Ham said scornfully.

Pratt chuckled. "Hell, Captain, *you* were a ninety-day wonder."

"Maybe so, but that was years ago," Ham said. "Now, pick out a patrol for me, will you?"

"Yes, sir," Pratt said. "You want to take Parker? He's a good man, and he's been around long enough to know what's going on."

"Uh-uh. Parker's a married man."

"So are you a married man, Captain," Pratt reminded him.

"Maybe so, but I don't have any kids. Parker does."

Five minutes later, with the patrol formed, Ham moved out. It wasn't until they had almost reached their destination that he realized Bill Pratt had come along on the patrol despite instructions to the contrary.

"Pratt, I thought I told you to stay back," Ham hissed angrily.

"Did you? I don't recall that."

"The hell you don't. You deliberately disobeyed my orders."

"So bust me," Pratt said. "You didn't think I was going to let you come out here with nobody but a bunch of sad sacks, did you?"

Ham glared at his sergeant; then the anger left, and he shook his head and smiled. "All right," he said. "I guess I'm glad to have you along. Come on, let's go."

"Hold it, Lieutenant!" Pratt warned. "Look down there!"

Ham looked where Pratt pointed and saw about twenty German soldiers coming up the road. The Germans were walking with their weapons slung over their shoulders as if totally unconcerned that they might encounter any Americans here.

"Quick, into the ditch!" Ham ordered, and the five Americans dived off the side of the road.

The Germans had seen them at about the same time, and they dived into the ditch on the opposite side of the road. The Germans started firing, and Ham and his men returned the fire.

"Call for help!" Ham ordered.

"Bulldog Two, Bulldog Two, do you read me? Over."

"*This is Bulldog Two,*" a voice came back over the walkie-talkie, and Ham grabbed it.

"We've run into Germans in platoon strength," he said quickly, ignoring radio procedure. "Get Lieutenant Hawkins's platoon up here now!"

"*Roger,*" the voice answered.

The Germans tried to advance across the road, but the five Americans who had the cover of the ditch were able to beat them back with deadly accurate fire. A second attack was beaten back as well, and Ham realized then that they were at a stalemate. The Germans couldn't advance on the Americans, but the Americans couldn't leave the ditch.

"Captain, maybe if I could get across the road down there, I could use the berm to come up behind them," Pratt suggested.

"They've got that part of the road covered," Ham said. "I don't think you could make it across."

"I could try," Pratt said, and before Ham could stop him, he was up and running. There was a short, furious burst of fire from the German side, and Pratt fell forward, facedown in the dirt.

"Pratt! Pratt!" Ham screamed. He started to climb out of the ditch, but a bullet hit right in front of his head and he had to slide back down.

"American commander, do not risk your life for your friend," a voice called from across the road. "He is dead."

"How do you know?" Ham called back in German, a language he had learned from his German-immigrant grandparents.

"I can see a bullet hole in his forehead," the German answered. "I am sorry."

"Yeah, I just bet you are."

"I *am* sorry," the German replied. "Already there has been too much killing in this war."

"Who are you?" Ham called.

"No, you do not want to know that," the German answered. "It is not good to know the name of the man you are trying to kill. I am in command here, as you are there."

"If you are tired of the killing, why don't you and your men surrender?" Ham called.

"I cannot do that," the German said.

"Why not? You know you have no hope of winning."

"I have no hope, that is correct. But I do have honor."

"Captain, here come our guys!" one of Ham's men shouted, and when Ham looked around, he saw Lieutenant Hawkins leading his platoon across a snow-covered field.

"German commander, this is your last chance to surrender," Ham called. "You are outnumbered now."

The Germans began firing again, and all conversation

stopped. In the meantime, in twos and threes, the men of Hawkins's platoon began infiltrating the ditch alongside Ham and his men so that the volume of fire being put out by the Americans increased dramatically.

After a few more minutes of firing Ham was surprised to see a white flag fluttering over the German position.

"Cease fire, cease firing!" Ham ordered. When the shooting stopped, he called across the road, again speaking in German. "Well, I see that you have decided to be reasonable. Come on out with your hands in the air."

Slowly, hesitantly, the Germans began to stand up on their side of the road, holding their hands in the air.

"Come out into the road," Ham demanded. The German soldiers complied, though there were only eleven now where there had been many more before. "All of you," he said.

"We are all that is left," one of the Germans said.

"Which of you is in commmand?" Ham asked. "Who was I talking to?"

"You were talking to Lieutenant Schultz," one of the Germans said. "But now he is dead."

Inexplicably, Ham felt a twinge of sadness. The German officer had warned him that it was not good to know the name of your enemy. He was right.

"Lieutenant Hawkins, get Sergeant Pratt's body and these prisoners back to our lines," Ham said. "I'm going to check their commander to see if he has any maps or papers on him that G-Two might want."

"Okay, Captain," Hawkins said. "Let's go, krauts," he growled. "*Raus, raus. Schnell!*"

Ham walked across the road and examined the bodies of the dead Germans until he found one in an officer's uniform. He turned the dead officer over and looked into his face. Though his eyes were open, they had already become opaque. The face was that of a comparatively young man, but it was drawn and haggard to the degree that Ham knew this wasn't one of Hitler's recent conscripts. This was a man who had been around for a while.

"Sorry I have to disturb you like this, Lieutenant Schultz," Ham said quietly. "But I have to see if you're carrying anything of interest."

Ham opened the small leather case on Schultz's belt and took out a map. Across the top of the map was written in ink LIEUTENANT RUDI SCHULTZ. Ham looked over the map to see if any of the German positions were marked, but even before he examined it, he was sure there wouldn't be. Lieutenant Schultz had obviously been around long enough to avoid making such a glaring error. Still, the G-2 people might be able to glean something from it, so he folded it up and put it in his pocket. That was when he saw the other item that was in the lieutenant's map case. It was a book, the jacket cover tattered and torn, the pages dog-eared and yellowed. The title was *Stille auf der Linie*— German for *Stillness in the Line*. It was one of his father's books!

Ham gasped in surprise, but when he opened the book and saw the inscription inside, he got an even greater surprise!

> To Karl Tannenhower. We share the brother-hood of war, albeit from different sides of the line.
> Eric Twainbough
> Wertheim, Germany
> October 1926

MARCH 1945, TOKYO

Saburo Amano sat on the ground with his back against the wall of the Home Defense Wing operations building. Though he was a naval aviator, he had yet to fly from the deck of a carrier—because most of the Japanese carriers had already been destroyed by the time he was a qualified aviator. He had been assigned to the Home Defense Wing with the mission of defending against the B-29's.

Saburo had been very proud to be picked for such an assignment. To shoot down a B-29 would be a victory beyond description, for there had never been a bomber like it. By comparison, the mighty B-17 paled into insignificance before the giant, high-flying, superfast B-29. Even its name, *Superfortress*, was formidable.

Many of Japan's cities had already felt the fury of B-29 bombing raids. All over the land, the beauty of what had been Japan lay in blackened heaps of rubble. Hiroshima, though, had been spared, and Saburo was very thankful. The last time he had seen his home city it was as beautiful as ever. He had gone from the railroad station to the house of his mother and sister, pleased to see that the fish vendors were still in place, still arguing with each other in their efforts to attract customers. The mist on the river was just as lovely, the smells just as enticing, the sounds just as comforting. Saburo had no idea why Hiroshima had been spared when so many other cities, many smaller and less important, had been destroyed, but he didn't care. He was glad that it had and that his mother and sister had thus far been spared the horrors that had visited so many other Japanese civilians.

The B-29's that brought such devastation to Japan had proven to be invulnerable to attack by the Zeros. Sitting there now, Saburo recalled the conversation he had had with his new commander when he had first reported for duty.

"The Zero is essentially worthless," Commander Takiyama said forcefully.

"Worthless?" Saburo replied in surprise. "But my father told me it was the best fighter plane in the world. With it he shot down twenty-one enemy airplanes, including a B-17."

"Your father was a brave and skilled airman," Saburo's commander said. "But not even he could shoot down a B-29 with a Zero. The Zero was a fine plane in its day, but its day has passed. Do you know how high the B-29 flies? Ten thousand meters. By the time we get a warning that the B-29's are approaching, it is too late for us to do anything. They fly even faster than the Zeros, and don't forget, we must climb to ten thousand meters to intercept them. The B-29's can come, deliver their bombs, and return, before the Zeros can even get up to their altitude. And if we do manage to get high enough, their guns are all controlled by a radar firing device. There is no skill to firing them; the gunners need only to push a button, and the guns aim themselves. Our planes are cut to shreds."

"I . . . I can't believe anyone could construct such a machine," Saburo said, stunned by the frank briefing of his commander.

"Believe it," his commander replied. He lit a cigarette and leaned back in his chair, letting the smoke escape slowly through his nose. "Do you still wish to attack the B-29?"

"Yes," Saburo said. "I have not lost my resolve."

The commander chuckled. "You have not lost your resolve, eh?" He took another deep puff on his cigarette. "Well, that is good, that is good. You are going to need all your"—he tapped his cigarette on the edge of the heavy glass ashtray—"resolve. But I do not intend to waste a new pilot or a Zero by letting you show your resolve. The Zeros are being readied for another purpose."

"What purpose would be better than to destroy the devil bombers?" Saburo asked.

"Soon the Americans will launch an invasion against Japan itself. They will bring an armada of one thousand ships. When they do, they will be in for a big surprise. We will go out to meet them, five thousand strong, and we will crash-dive into their ships, five to a ship if need be. They will not get through."

"Commander," Saburo asked, his heart beating wildly, "do you actually believe such a mission will save Japan?"

"There are four other waves of equal strength," Takiyama replied. "If the first Special Attack Wave is not successful, then perhaps the next will be. Or the next. Or the next. There is no way the Americans can escape the determined efforts of twenty-five thousand brave men ready and anxious to die to save their country. The plan has a new name: One Million Cherry Blossoms."

"Have you enough volunteers to man such a force?" Saburo asked.

"Pilots are volunteering from all over Japan," the commander assured Saburo. "When the time comes, we shall not lack for young men to die for the emperor."

Saburo's throat felt dry, his knees felt weak, and his head felt dizzy. He had long believed in the principle of

lying for his country, but only in the heat of battle. He had
never considered that he might calculatingly sacrifice his
life in a kamikaze mission, and he marveled at the courage
it would take to do such a thing.

"Suit up, Saburo," his commander called, coming out
of the operations building, breaking into Saburo's reverie.
"We have incoming B-29's. You will finally get your chance
to fly against them. And luckily for you, you will be doing it
in the new Raiden fighter planes, which just arrived this
morning, not the outmoded Zeros."

Though he tried to appear nonchalant, Saburo was
certain that his face reflected his excitement. This was what
he had been waiting for, dreaming of, for months. And to
get the chance to do battle in the new Raiden aircraft was
beyond anything he could have wished for. These aircraft
were supercharged for high-altitude flying and equipped
with a more powerful engine than the Zero. They flew at
more than four hundred miles per hour, faster even than
the B-29 and as fast as any fighter airplane anywhere in the
world. They were also equipped with rapid-firing cannon,
specially designed to attack the Superfortress.

Saburo got into his flight suit, got his orders, then ran
to his assigned plane and took off. He nearly lost control on
takeoff, however, because the plane developed so much
power that he wasn't prepared for the torque. But he was
able to hold it, and soon he was climbing with the other
fighter pilots, watching in amazement as the altimeter began to wind its way up.

The Raiden fighters leveled out at ten thousand meters, and for a moment Saburo could have forgotten why
they were there. A scattering of clouds hung several thousand feet below them, and they glistened bright silver under the full moon that hung cold and white in the night
velvet above them. The stars looked even closer than the
moon, and Saburo had an almost overwhelming sensation
that he could simply reach through the canopy and take
one of the brilliant orbs of light between his thumb and
forefinger. Never had he seen such beauty as was displayed

before him now. He wished there was some way he could
just stay there, almost two miles high, forever.

The city of Tokyo was below them, but it was totally
blacked out for the impending raid. A few dim glints of
reflected moonlight from tin roofs was the only indication
of the existence of a city of over four million souls. Saburo
thought of the people in the city. They were all in their
homes now, huddled around hibachi heaters or under padded comforters because it was early March and very cold.
They were totally dependent upon men like Saburo Amano
to protect them, and Saburo prayed that he would be worthy of their trust.

Suddenly he saw flashes of light and realized that it
was exhaust flames from engines—American B-29 engines.
There were hundreds of flames, seemingly more numerous
than the stars, and Saburo gasped at the number of B-29's
involved in the raid.

The Japanese fighter planes turned toward the approaching bombers, Saburo among them. The Superfor-
tresses were coming faster than anything he could imagine,
and as he got closer, he gasped at their size. How could
they hope to shoot down anything that large? How did
anything that large ever get into the air in the first place?

Saburo opened fire on one of the bombers, and he saw
his shells raking into the B-29's belly. The B-29 returned
fire. It was unbelievable! A solid stream of tracers zipped
toward him. He passed under the B-29, and the guns of the
giant bomber followed him so that he had to do a wingover
to avoid being hit.

The wingover spared Saburo, but it also took him so
far out of the bomber stream that, with their great speed,
he couldn't get back to them. He shoved the throttle to
overboost, and though he was somewhat faster than the
bombers while in level flight, he had lost several thousand
feet in altitude that he couldn't make up.

Then the B-29 he had attacked suddenly erupted with
a sheet of white-hot flame. The bomber was carrying incendiary bombs, and Saburo's cannon fire had apparently
started fires that had set off the bombs. A long jet of flame
spewed from beneath the bomber, then began wrapping
around the bomber, spreading rapidly. It became a brilliant

flare, lighting up the sky and disclosing a wave of B-29's that stretched back seemingly into infinity. Suddenly the flames reached the fuel tanks, and the giant bomber exploded. Saburo felt a tremendous thrill. His very first air victory was against a B-29!

His thrill was short-lived, however, because the bombs from the lead B-29's were already beginning to light up the city far below. There were scores of fires, then hundreds, then thousands, and before Saburo's shocked and disbelieving eyes, the city of Tokyo became a virtual ocean of fire.

Three more bombers were knocked down by the Raidens, but like Saburo, the other fighter pilots discovered that they could make only one pass, and then they were unable to recover their altitude. With their bomb loads gone, the B-29's were even faster, and Saburo and the others cursed in helpless rage as they watched the giant planes speeding back to their island base, easily outdistancing their pursuers. As Saburo looked down at the burning city below him, he felt bitter tears of frustration and anguish streaming down his face.

The next morning, Saburo learned that more than twenty square miles of Tokyo had been completely gutted and turned into a giant funeral pyre. More than 130,000 people had died in the air raid.

USS STARKE, OFF KERAMA-RETTO

Kerama-Retto, some six miles off the coast of Okinawa, had been secure for some time now, so the attack came as a complete surprise. There had been no aerial activity for several days, but Kevin McKay had the antiaircraft gun crews of tubs two and four at their stations, and their guns were loaded and ready. Nevertheless, the sight of a single airplane didn't arouse much interest until someone suddenly shouted, "Kamikaze off the starboard bow!"

"Holy shit!" Kevin yelled into his headset. "Tubs two and four, bring your guns to bear! Commence firing!"

Not only Kevin's guns, but every gun on the ship opened up on the incoming airplane. Blazing orange points raced up toward the plane, which was still quite a distance out and approaching them at full speed, already starting its shallow dive.

"Come on, come on!" Kevin screamed. "Take him out, take him out! Take the son of a bitch out!"

The tracer rounds continued to reach out toward the kamikaze, but none of them were finding their mark. Kevin leaned left and right, trying with body English to guide the rounds to their target. The airplane grew bigger and bigger as it approached . . . its big, fat, round nose looking, oddly enough, like the barrel of a gun.

"Shit! He's going to hit us!" one of the gunners yelled, and at the last minute Kevin dived for the deck. From his perspective he had a close-up, ringside view of the impact, and as he watched in gruesome fascination, Kevin had the bizarre sensation that all the action had been slowed down just for his benefit. First, the plane skimmed just over the top of the number-four tub, taking the quadmount with it. The loader in the tub managed to dive to the deck just before the plane hit, but the gunner stayed in his position, watching the plane approach as if mesmerized by it, as if he and the pilot had completed a mutual suicide pact. The propeller of the plane cut the gunner in two, throwing his torso back over the wing much as a bull would toss a toreador with his horns. The bottom of the gunner stayed in place, still standing, even as the plane continued on to impact with the number-one gun turret.

So detailed was Kevin's view of the crash that he even saw the Japanese pilot's body thrown forward at impact, a split second before the plane, the turret, and the front one-third of the ship erupted in a big ball of fire. Kevin buried his head in the crook of his arm and felt the pressure wave pass over him. A moment later, surprised that he was still alive, he managed to roll away from his position, then drop down onto the deck behind the forward part of the ship's superstructure, thus keeping a barrier between himself and the roaring inferno of the crashed plane.

Within seconds the clanging bell of General Quarters sounded throughout the ship, and someone made an announcement over the loudspeaker, his voice incredibly calm under the circumstances:

"*Now hear this. We have taken a kamikaze hit in number-one gun turret. Fire-fighting and damage-control parties, lay forward.*"

Kevin looked forward toward the number-one gun turret and saw a huge billowing cloud of smoke being fed by a roaring orange fire. Then he looked at his two antiaircraft gun tubs, saw what was left of his men, and turned and began throwing up.

"*Now hear this. All hands not engaged in rescue, fire fighting, or damage control, lay aft.*"

"Chief!" Kevin yelled, turning around as the fire-fighting party rushed forward. "What can I do?"

"Get this on," the chief called back, tossing a canvas bag toward him. Kevin knew that the bag contained an asbestos suit. "If there's anybody left alive up there, we're going to need to get them out."

"I'll be right with you," Kevin promised, pulling the suit out of the bag.

Moments later there was another explosion, much louder than the first, and this time Kevin was unable to avoid the pressure wave. One second he was standing on the deck, pulling the asbestos suit out of the canvas bag, the next second he was tumbling through space and splashing into the sea. When he popped back up to the surface a moment later, coughing and spitting salt water, he saw the *Starke* down by the bow and sinking fast. Sailors were jumping over the side as the ship was going down. He knew then that the magazine for number-one turret must have gone off, taking the bow of the ship with it and probably killing everyone in the fire-fighting and damage-control parties. He knew, also, that if he hadn't stopped to put on the asbestos suit, he would have been right up there with them. A large wooden hatch floated by, and Kevin swam over to it, then climbed on. When he looked around he saw half-a-dozen dinghies had already been put into the water from other ships close to them.

Kevin sat on the hatch, waiting to be rescued. He had survived the loss of another ship, but he was getting damned tired of having them sunk under him.

CHAPTER TWENTY-FOUR

Karl looked out the back window of the Stork, a little two-seater, high-wing airplane, as the pilot maneuvered it skillfully between the ruins of Berlin's bombed-out buildings.

"I see nothing but rubble down there. Are you sure you can find a place to land?" Karl asked apprehensively.

"Yes, sir," the pilot replied confidently. "Fräulein Reitsch has landed here several times already, and she has told me what I must do."

"Very well," Karl replied. "You're the expert. I'll leave this up to you."

The pilot pulled back on the throttle, and the engine noise lessened. He lowered the flaps, shoved the stick forward, then began dropping down onto the brick-strewn street. The plane hit fairly hard, bounced, came back down again, then taxied roughly, but safely and in one piece, across the rubble. Even as the propeller ticked to a stop there was an explosion less than a hundred meters away, an incoming artillery round from the Russian troops already at the outskirts of the city.

"You go on into the bunker, Herr Oberreichsleiter," the pilot said. "I will try to find a safe place for the plane."

"Yes, thank you," Karl replied. "Be very careful."

As he exited the plane, he heard the loud *whoomp*, like a railroad car coming down a track, of another incoming artillery shell. It hit slightly farther away than the other one had, though even this one was close enough for Karl to hear not only the initial explosion, but the follow-up rumble and clatter of debris tumbling back down after the blast. The smell of smoke and powder was so strong that his nostrils burned.

A German soldier picked his way through the smoking and blackened timbers to meet him. The soldier saluted, then guided Karl back through the rubble to the entrance of Adolf Hitler's bunker.

"Watch your head on that fallen beam, Herr Oberreichsleiter," the soldier warned. Karl ducked, then went down the stairs to the bunker entrance. The heavy steel door was opened, and he was met by Josef Goebbels.

"Ah, Tannenhower," Goebbels said, "how good of you to come. The Führer will be so pleased."

Karl thought that Goebbels made it sound as though he had been invited to afternoon tea on the terrace at the Berghof. "Do you have any idea why he has sent for me?"

"Uh, yes," Goebbels said. "But I would rather let him tell you himself."

There was a very loud explosion outside, so close that the bunker shook, and bits of plaster and masonry fell down, showering the small anteroom with a fine, white dust. Goebbels coughed and waved his hand back and forth in front of his face.

"They are getting closer all the time," he said. "You have no idea what the Führer and I have been through. But, of course, it is of vital importance that we stay here to provide the inspiration for our soldiers. It is too bad that Göring and Himmler couldn't understand that."

Karl had the strangest sensation at that moment, and one look at Goebbels's triumphant face confirmed what he was thinking: Germany was coming down in a heap around them, and Hitler's regime had but a few hours to live, but Goebbels was happier than Karl had ever seen him, having, at last, won the battle of the pecking order. Göring and Himmler were gone; Goebbels was still there.

"I cannot imagine what it must be like to have to live in this place," Karl said, looking around the close, stuffy quarters. "How is your wife coping?"

"She has taken ill, I'm afraid," Goebbels replied. "She is having difficulty with her heart."

"I'm sorry to hear that."

"It is all quite awful," Goebbels admitted. "But, thank heavens, it won't be much longer now."

"It won't? Why do you say that?"

Goebbels smiled. "You will soon find out. Come," he said, taking Karl by the elbow. "I'll tell the Führer you are here. I know he is most anxious to see you."

As they went deeper into the bunker, Karl found that it was staffed with a number of secretaries, valets, and soldiers.

An artillery round exploded outside. Throughout the whole time Karl was in the bunker, there was a constant *kerrumph!* sound, a background timpani-roll of exploding artillery shells, some close in, others far off. The secretaries, valets, and soldiers seemed to pay no attention at all to the explosions. Even the Goebbels children played with no apparent notice of the incoming artillery shells.

Karl turned to one of the secretaries. "I'm surprised to see the Goebbels's children here."

"Why, Herr Oberreichsleiter?"

"Why?" Karl couldn't believe he had been asked such a stupid question. "Because they have been subjected to terrible danger, that's why."

"What is the difference?" the secretary asked, shrugging. "They will soon die anyway. The children have been included in the suicide plans."

"The suicide plans? What suicide plans?"

"Haven't you heard? The Führer is planning to take his life, and he has given us all a fine gift." The secretary reached into the pocket of her dress and pulled out a small envelope. "This is a cyanide capsule," she explained. "One only has to bite down on it, and death is instantaneous."

She laughed a high, shrill laugh. "Isn't that a wonderful gift from our Führer?"

BOOM! That artillery round was a little closer than the one preceding, Karl thought.

Goebbels reappeared then. "Tannenhower, the Führer will see you now."

"Thank you," Karl replied.

Kerrumph! Far off.

Hitler was seated behind his desk in his office, which wasn't much larger than a cloak room. As Karl looked around it, he couldn't help but think of the oversized office Albert Speer had designed for Hitler in the new Chancellery. The desk in the Chancellery was nearly as big as this entire office.

"Ah, Tannenhower," Hitler said. "I knew you wouldn't desert me. You have been one of my truest and closest friends, loyal to me from the very beginning."

"I am saddened to see that it has come to this, my Führer," Karl said. "And I grieve for the plight of the poor German people."

Kerrumph! rumble, rumble.

"The plight of the poor German people?" Hitler repeated, sneering. "The poor German people, as you call them, do not deserve your grief." Hitler got up from his desk and began a diatribe, pacing back and forth, keeping time with his enmity. As he spoke, his eyes flashed, spittle flew from his lips, his hands alternately jabbed the air to make a point or brushed a wild shock of hair back from his forehead. "I tried to lead the German people to greatness. I tried to create a Reich that would last one thousand years, but the German people were not worthy of my efforts! What do I care now for the plight of the German people? Better that the fields be sown with salt and left permanently barren! Better that the rivers and streams be poisoned, the forests flattened, the cities laid waste, all schools, hospitals, and churches destroyed! It is better that no two bricks be left together in any home in the land!" Hitler returned to his desk and slammed his fist down. "They are all traitors and cowards, Tannenhower! This entire country is a nation of traitors and cowards!"

BOOM!

"Surely, my Führer, there are some Germans who are worthy of our pity," Karl suggested.

"Who? Who is worthy? My loyal friends? Have you heard? Göring and Himmler have both betrayed me. Even Obergruppenführer Fegelein, Eva's own brother-in-law, deserted his post. I had to have him shot."

Kerrumph!

"Now nothing remains for me. No allegiances have been kept, no honor lived up to. There are no disappointments that I have not suffered, no betrayals I have not experienced. Every wrong imaginable has been done me!"

"But Goebbels is here," Karl said. "And his wife and his children."

BOOM!

"Yes," Hitler said. "Yes, at least Goebbels has remained loyal. Did you know? He and Magda, even their children, will die with me. I couldn't be more touched. That is a magnificent gesture."

Kerrumph! rumble, rumble.

"Killing one's own children is somewhat more than a gesture, I would say," Karl replied coolly. "Perhaps you could persuade the Goebbelses to let the children live."

"Why should I?" Hitler asked.

"They are merely children, my Führer," Karl said. "You have always loved the children."

"It is precisely my love for them that prevents me from dissuading Goebbels from his plan," Hitler countered. "When I die, National Socialism will die with me. Goebbels would not want to live in a Germany without National Socialism, and neither would his children."

"How do we know that? Shouldn't they be allowed to make that decision for themselves?"

"They are too young to make that decision," Hitler said, waving his hands dismissively of the subject. "But that is of no importance. You are here; *that* is important to me. It is so good of you to come, Tannenhower. Did you have much difficulty?"

Kerrumph! Kerrumph! rumble, rumble.

"Some. The skies are controlled by the enemy, but I flew in with a fine pilot," Karl replied. "With skilled flying, there is still a way in and out. My Führer, let my pilot take you out of here before it's too late."

"No," Hitler replied. "My destiny is now quite clear. I must obey my own command to defend Berlin to the last. At first I believed firmly that Berlin would be saved on the banks of the Oder. Then when the encirclement of the city began, I thought that perhaps my staying on would inspire the Army to come to the rescue of the city. On the way in, Tannenhower, did you notice General Wenck's army? It is moving up from the south. Is there any hope it will be here in time?"

BOOM!

A moment before, Hitler had seemed resigned to his fate. Now he showed a forlorn glimmer of hope. It was all the more pathetic because Karl knew that rather than moving his army toward the defense of Berlin, Wenck was retreating west so that he could surrender to the Americans instead of the Russians. Nevertheless, Karl couldn't bring himself to tell Hitler the truth.

"We flew in from the west, my Führer. We wouldn't have been in a position to see Wenck's army."

"No," Hitler mused. "No, I guess not." Suddenly he smiled again. "But now, I'm sure you're wondering why I asked you here."

"Yes, I must confess that I am curious."

"I want you to stand by me at my wedding," Hitler said.

"I . . . I beg your pardon?"

Hitler laughed. "Yes, yes, I knew it would be a wonderful surprise to you," he said. "Even though you have long known of my relationship with the woman who is to be my wife."

BOOM! Crash, rumble. Close.

"Eva Braun?"

"Yes, of course, Eva. She has been steadfastly loyal to me and it is my desire to reward that loyalty by marrying her. And having made that decision, I started thinking about who I would want to stand by me."

My God, Karl thought. *He asked me here . . . had an innocent pilot risk his life to fly me through flak and enemy fighters . . . to come into a besieged city for this? No won-*

der Goebbels had sounded as though Karl's coming was for some festive occasion.

KaBOOM! CRASH! Rumble.

The last was an extremely heavy explosion, louder than any since Karl first came into the bunker. After the explosion, as in the one earlier, the air was filled with a fine white powder.

"You will do me the honor?" Hitler asked, as unmindful of that explosion as he had been of the others.

Karl sighed. He was here now. He might as well. "Yes, of course."

"Good, good. We will have the ceremony sometime tonight. I thought perhaps we would have a small celebration of sorts. Then Eva and I will retire to our apartment, and together, sometime before dawn, we will take the final, irrevocable step that will free us from this nightmare. I've given it a lot of thought. Eva wants to use poison, but I think I shall shoot myself. Poison doesn't seem to me to be the way a man of my stature should die."

"It was good enough for Socrates," Karl suggested, unable to keep the aspersion out of his voice.

"Yes, I suppose it was," Hitler responded, oblivious to the jab. "But then, he wasn't a military leader, was he? No, for me, a pistol shot is the only way my life can be ended. Afterward I intend to have my body cremated. I don't want to wind up like Mussolini and his mistress, hanging upside down in some service station somewhere, for the rabble to defile."

Kerrumph!

"Tell me, Tannenhower, have you made your own plans?"

"I have no plans to commit suicide," Karl replied.

"Why not? It would be so easy. One act and it's all over."

"Someone is going to have to give an accounting to the rest of the world for what we did," Karl said.

"Give an accounting?"

"Perhaps apology is a better word," Karl said. "Though a thousand years of apologies will not erase our sins."

Hitler's face stiffened. "I could have you shot for that kind of talk, Tannenhower," he said angrily.

"Yes, I suppose you could," Karl replied. "But you won't."

BOOM! Crash!

"And just why won't I?" Hitler demanded.

"Because that would provide the escape you are looking for, for yourself. On the other hand, if you let me live, you know that I will be one of those held responsible."

Hitler smiled evilly. "Yes," he said. "Yes, you are so right. Perhaps I will leave it to people like you, and to the traitors Göring and Himmler, to answer for the deaths of six million Jews."

"*Six million?*" Karl gasped. "My God, we killed that many?"

"I only wish we could have killed six million more," Hitler said flatly.

Kerrumph!

"I . . . I had no idea of the real magnitude of our crimes," Karl said, feeling sickened beyond words. "I closed my eyes to it. I didn't want to know."

Hitler sneered. "And so now you begin to use the defense that will be used by all our people. The same people who stood by the railroad tracks and watched train after train of human offal being taken to the concentration camps will claim they had no idea where those people were going. And in the towns near the camps, all the people who smelled the smoke from the crematoriums will say they didn't know what it was. One by one their neighbors and fellow townspeople disappeared until there were no more Jews in all of Germany, but the people will say they did not understand what was happening."

"You are right," Karl said. "The argument sounds weak, even to my own ears."

Kerrumph!

"Go, Tannenhower," Hitler said sharply. "Leave this bunker, return to the *poor German people*. I don't want you to stand beside me at my wedding. I don't want to look into your face ever again. Someday history will look back on the final hours in this bunker as a sterling example of loyalty and heroism. Those who are here with me now will be enshrined in glory. There is no place here for the faint-hearted or the faithless."

BOOM!

"Good-bye, Adi," Karl said, using the name Hitler' friends had used in the past.

Hitler said nothing. He simply turned his back as Kar Tannenhower—the man he had long admired as a true pa triot, the loyal soldier who had carried the Blood Flag o that cold November afternoon so many years ago—left th living symbol of the Thousand Year Reich.

JULY 16, 1945, ALAMOGORDO, NEW MEXICO

The testing ground was called Trinity Site, located i the middle of the desert in an area named *Jornada de Muerto*—Journey of Death. Fewer than fifty people wer present, including Dr. Sigmund Rosen, Dr. Dub Wilker son, and Dr. J. Robert Oppenheimer, the project director who was passing out very dark glasses to everyone. In th distance stood a hundred-foot-tall tower, but the tower wa so far away from where the observers had gathered that i was barely visible, despite its height.

"Do you think we're safe here?" Sigmund asked Dub

Dub looked at his friend. "I think we are," he said "No one can guarantee it, of course. But then, as far as tha goes, no one can guarantee that the world is safe. There's one-in-a-million chance that once the chain reaction be gins, it won't stop. It could split every atom on earth an turn this planet into so much cosmic dust."

"One in a million," Sigmund repeated slowly. "In th world of physics, one in a million may as well be ever odds."

"I know. It's like shooting craps with God," Dul agreed. "Let us just hope He grants us a pass."

"Gentlemen, we have one minute," General Leslie Groves announced, looking at his watch. "Everyone put on your goggles!"

Sigmund slipped the goggles on and turned to face the tower. The glasses were so dark that he felt as if he had been blindfolded, and he had a desire to slip them up. But his own calculations warned him that it would be extremely dangerous to do so.

"Ten seconds!"

Sigmund tensed as the seconds were counted down.

"Six . . . five . . . four . . . three . . . two . . . one . . . zero!"

At that instant a light—more brilliant than any light ever before seen on the face of the earth—turned the pre-dawn darkness into the sunniest afternoon, even through the dark glasses. Fed by a temperature of one hundred million degrees, it was a light that could have been seen from any planet within the earth's solar system.

After the light, a tremendous ball of fire began to grow, growing larger and larger until Sigmund thought that it would never stop. He began to fear that perhaps this really was the beginning of the chain reaction Dub had spoken of. Finally, mercifully, it stopped growing, and be-gan changing colors, going from white to yellow to orange to red to deep purple, until finally it subsided, leaving be-hind a tremendous black cloud that formed into a gigantic mushroom.

"You can take off your goggles now!" someone called, and everyone did, then stood there looking out toward the blast site in stunned silence. Even those who had worked on the project from the very beginning had had no idea of the power that would be unleashed, and they were shocked beyond any ability to express their feelings in words.

Sigmund couldn't get over the eerie silence, the long, long period of absolute . . . total . . . dead silence.

And then it hit, the shock wave and sound waves trav-eling together. The concussion, even this far away, nearly knocked Sigmund over, and a whistling hurricane came up, with sand thrown before a wind that had the searing heat of a blast furnace. There was a roar louder than any Sigmund could have imagined, and he closed his eyes and prayed in fear, for it seemed as if they had tapped straight into the forces of hell itself.

When the smoke finally cleared away and the scien-tists could go to the site for a closer examination, the awe-some power they had sensed earlier became even more graphic. The hundred-foot steel tower upon which the de-

vice had sat was gone, completely vaporized by the heat o
the explosion. The explosion had left a giant twelve-hun
dred-foot-wide dish in the desert floor, formed of jade
green glass from the action of the heat on the sand. Al
animal and plant life had been destroyed within a radius o
one mile.

"It is finished," Sigmund said solemnly. And he coul
not have said for certain if he meant their work there . .
or mankind itself.

ABOUT THE AUTHOR

Writing under his own name and 25 pen names, ROB-
ERT VAUGHAN has authored over 200 books in every genre
but Science Fiction. He won the 1977 Porgie Award (Best
Paperback Original) for *The Power and the Pride*. In 1973
The Valkyrie Mandate was nominated by its publisher, Si-
mon & Schuster, for the Pulitzer Prize.

Vaughan is a frequent speaker at seminars and at high
schools and colleges. He has also hosted three television
talk shows: *Eyewitness Magazine*, on WAVY TV in Ports-
mouth, Virginia, *Tidewater A.M.*, on WHBQ TV in Hamp-
ton, Virginia, and *This Week in Books* on the TEMPO
Cable Television Network. In addition, he hosted a cooking
show at *Phoenix at Mid-day* on KHPO TV in Phoenix, Arizona.

Vaughan is a retired Army Warrant Officer (CW-3)
with three tours in Vietnam where he was awarded the
Distinguished Flying Cross, the Air Medal with the V for
valor, the Bronze Star, the Distinguished Service Medal,
and the Purple Heart. He was a helicopter pilot and a
maintenance and supply officer. He was also an instructor
and Chief of the Aviation Maintenance Officers' Course at
Fort Eustis, Virginia. During his military career, Vaughan

was a participant in many of the 20th century's most significant events. For example, he served in Korea immediately after the armistice, he was involved in the Nevada Atomic Bomb tests, he was part of the operation which ensured that James Meredith could attend the University of Mississippi, he was alerted for the Cuban Missile Crisis, he served three years in Europe, and of course, the above-mentioned three tours in Vietnam.

The saga continues with

THE AMERICAN CHRONICLES

VOLUME SIX: 1945–1950

THE IRON CURTAIN

ROBERT VAUGHAN

Turn the page for an exciting preview of
THE IRON CURTAIN, on sale in April 1994
wherever Bantam Books are sold.

CHAPTER ONE

A sign just over the door of the flight operations building read: WELCOME TO NORTH FIELD, TINIAN, THE WORLD'S BUSIEST AIRPORT.

A sprawling complex of barracks and maintenance hangars, several hundred P-51's and B-29's, and four parallel ten-thousand-foot paved runways tended to support the sign's claim. At that very moment three of the runways were active with landing traffic.

On the remaining runway a B-29 was starting its takeoff roll, and the quartet of twenty-two-hundred-horsepower engines with their seventeen-foot, four-bladed props flailing at the warm Pacific air emitted a throaty roar. The glistening giant moved down the runway on its tricycle landing gear, gathering momentum as it passed row upon row of parked fighters, bombers, reconnaissance, and cargo planes until it was a speeding silver streak. As all men everywhere who love airplanes will do, several mechanics from the 315th Bomb Wing stopped their softball game long enough to watch the takeoff.

Three quarters of the way down the runway the

bomber rotated, and its nose came up as it broke free of the ground, a graceful bird in flight. But almost immediately a brilliant flash of light came from the left inboard engine, followed seconds later by a heavy, stomach-jarring explosion.

"*Oh, shit!*" one of the mechanics shouted. As everyone watched in dumbstruck horror, the plane nosed back to the ground, then erupted in a huge ball of fire.

General William Canfield, just deplaned and heading for the headquarters building at the far end of the field, ordered his driver back to the crash site. He braced himself against the sway of the vehicle as the driver turned sharply onto the runway, then accelerated to seventy. At the end of the runway thick, oily smoke roiled up from the gasoline-fed flames of the crashed B-29.

"There may be survivors," Willie shouted over the scream of the jeep's engine and the roar of the wind. "It was a maintenance test flight, so there were only three on board."

"Jesus, General, there's no way anyone coulda lived through that!" Willie's driver, Sergeant Grega, shouted back. "It's burnin' like all hell."

"But it wasn't carrying a bomb load. There's at least a chance that there were survivors."

"Not much of one," Grega insisted.

By the time they arrived at the crash site, the fire trucks and ambulances that were on permanent standby at each end of the runway were already at work. The foam generators of the fire engines were spraying frothy suds into the fire while two asbestos-suited rescue workers dashed into the flames. After what seemed an agonizingly long time they reemerged, carrying one of the bomber crewmen with them. A stream of water was directed toward them as they broke out of the wall of fire.

"Over here! Get him over here!" a medic shouted, holding open the back door of the olive-drab three-quarter-ton truck marked with red crosses.

Struggling with their burden, the two rescuers started toward the waiting ambulance. As the medics loaded the injured crewman, Willie jumped from his jeep and hurried over. He recognized the victim as the flight engineer. The man was conscious but obviously in shock.

"Good work, men," Willie shouted encouragingly to the rescue workers. "What about the pilot and copilot?"

One of the rescuers took off his helmet and shroud, and when he did, Willie was struck by how young he was. He couldn't have been over eighteen. The young man looked at Willie with sad eyes and shook his head.

"Sorry, General. The other two was dead."

"Are you sure?" the noncommissioned officer in charge of the fire detail asked. "How do you know they were dead?"

"One of 'em didn't have no head," the young man answered flatly. "The other one had less 'n that."

"Okay, let's go!" one of the medics shouted to the ambulance driver, slapping his hand on the side of the truck. "Get him out of here!"

The ambulance raced off with its siren screaming.

"Did you know the two officers, General?" the noncom in charge asked.

"Yes, I knew them," Willie answered. "The pilot was Major Whittaker, the copilot was Captain Carlisle. They served with me in Germany, and I had lunch with them just a short while ago when I stopped to refuel, as they had."

"I'm sorry," the NCOIC replied. "I knew 'em, too. They were fine men, both of them."

Willie sighed. "We've lost a lot of fine men in this war, Sergeant—so at least we know they're in good company."

"Yes, sir, that is a fact," the sergeant agreed. "That is truly a fact."

"General Canfield?" Sergeant Grega spoke up. "You ready to go back now? Don't forget, you got that meetin' with General LeMay."

"I haven't forgotten," Willie replied, walking back to the jeep. He sat in the right front seat with his foot propped up on the door sill and his arms folded across his chest. He stared at the fiery wreckage for a long moment, then said to his driver, "Okay, Sergeant, let's go."

As Grega put the jeep in gear and swung around, leaving the burning bomber behind them, Willie pulled his mind away from his dead comrades to his meeting with Curtis LeMay. He wondered what the general wanted to see him about—and whether his life would once again be irrevocably changed.

Though at five feet nine he was only of average height, Major General Willie Canfield was an imposing figure, a real man's man, with powerful shoulders and arms and a flat stomach, none of which he had to work at. His muscular conformation was just a part of him, like his hazel eyes, his auburn hair, and his stubborn determination. Thirty-seven and unmarried, he was the youngest son of Robert and Connie Canfield and the younger brother of John Canfield, once an adviser to President Franklin D. Roosevelt and now holding that same position of trust with President Harry S Truman.

Willie wasn't a career Army officer and held his rank by direct congressional appointment. Shortly after the war had begun, President Roosevelt had prevailed upon him to accept the commission so that the War Department could utilize Willie's experience as president of a major airline. In creating and building World Air Transport, Willie had set up maintenance support bases and airline terminals and established worldwide airline routes; his experience with the movement of equipment and personnel and the demands placed on the support system by a large fleet of planes flying an intense schedule was an invaluable asset in helping the United States establish a bomber command in Europe.

Willie's World Air Transport venture was far from the Canfield family's conservative business roots. The family had made its fortune through landholdings and Canfield-Puritex International, a multinational food company headquartered in St. Louis that processed such things as cereals, baking products, canned meats, and animal feeds. The Canfields still owned vast tracts of land, including several thousand acres of farmland in southeast Missouri, a big ranch in Texas, and timberland in Washington and Oregon. Before the war Willie's name had kept popping up on lists of "America's most eligible bachelors." One of the few benefits of being in a war was that such foolish fluff seemed to have stopped—or at least Willie was no longer aware of it if it continued.

The jeep pulled to a stop in front of the 21st Bomber Command Headquarters Building, and a lieutenant colonel hurried out to meet Willie. He saluted crisply.

"General Canfield, I'm Colonel Hathaway of General LeMay's staff. Welcome to Tinian."

"Thank you," Willie replied.

"General LeMay is expecting you and asks that you come right in."

"That's Curt LeMay for you," Willie said as he climbed out of the jeep. "He never was one for wasting time."

The staff in the anteroom stood respectfully as Willie passed by. Colonel Hathaway, who was walking ahead, opened the door to Curtis LeMay's office, then closed it behind Willie as he stepped inside.

General LeMay was a big, broad-shouldered man with a square jaw, dark hair, and dark bushy eyebrows. He tended to walk and stand slightly hunched forward, as if rushing to the next event. A cigar firmly clenched in his teeth, he hurried around from behind his desk with his hand extended.

"Hello, Willie," he greeted. "How was your trip out here?"

"Impressive," Willie replied. "Very impressive. I came from the States by B-29. It was my first experience with the airplane. We caught the jet stream at thirty thousand feet, and that gave us better than a four-hundred-fifty-mile-per-hour ground speed."

"The B-29 is a wonderful airplane, now that we have all the bugs worked out," LeMay said. He walked over to his window and looked out across the field in the direction of the crash. "Of course, we still have our unfortunate incidents, as you no doubt just witnessed." He nodded toward the column of smoke. "General Powers said you knew those boys?"

Willie nodded. "Not intimately, but they were with me in Germany."

"That's too bad," LeMay said. "Any loss is bad enough, but it seems particularly hard to take when it's an accident that serves no useful purpose." He turned back toward Willie and changed the subject. "So, how were things in the ETO when you left?"

"Busy," Willie answered. "Everyone in the European Theater is getting ready to shift to the Pacific."

"How was it that you beat everyone else over here? Are you so anxious to get back into the war that you couldn't wait for everyone else to come? You had to get the jump on them?" LeMay teased.

Willie laughed. "I don't know. I think I may have stood up when I should have *shut* up," he said. "But for some reason the War Department seems to think that my being here might make the transfer of the Eighth Aircorps go a little easier."

"They've got good reason to think that," LeMay said. "There are some, myself included, who still remember what a brilliant job you did in getting our bombers moved into England." Noticing that his cigar had gone out, LeMay walked back over to his desk, picked up a lighter, and relit it. He waited until the tip was a red ember before he continued, waving it like a baton as he spoke. "But if we're lucky, Willie, we won't be needing your services here. The war will be over in a matter of days."

"A matter of *days*?" Willie asked, astonished. "Why would you say that? The latest intelligence reports I've heard give the Japanese a home-defense army of more than two million . . . and a kamikaze fleet of ten thousand suicide planes."

"Pretty formidable odds, wouldn't you say?" LeMay asked through a puff of cigar smoke.

"Formidable enough that the casualty figure estimates are running at better than one hundred thousand American dead in the initial attack waves," Willie replied.

"Yes, well"—LeMay pulled the cigar from his mouth and studied the end of it—"don't worry about it. I give you my word, we won't have to invade Japan."

Willie looked at the general as if he were crazy. "Curt, do you know something that I don't know?" he asked.

LeMay smiled slyly. "As a matter of fact, I do."

"What?"

"I'm waiting right now for authorization to give you a full briefing. The problem is, it's the middle of the night in

Washington, and I haven't gotten the okay yet. But I'll get it soon, and as soon as I do, I'll tell you everything."

"It must be something big."

"Big? Willie, it's the biggest damn secret of war in the history of our country . . . hell, probably in the history of the world."

"If that's the case, I may not even get a clearance," Willie said. "Don't forget, I'm really a civilian at heart. I'm an airline president, remember? I'm not a military strategist."

"You'll get clearance," LeMay said. "If we have to wake up the President himself to get the okay, you'll get clearance."

"And you feel that this secret—whatever it is—will eliminate the need for us to invade Japan?"

"It'll put the finishing touches on it, yes. But the truth is, we've already come a long way toward that goal. I suppose you've heard that I abandoned daylight precision bombing."

"Oh, I've heard," Willie answered with a little chuckle. "Believe me, I've heard."

"I guess the boys back in the old Eighth Aircorps feel like I've turned my back on everything we worked for in Europe," LeMay said. "Well, in Germany I went along with the idea because it was a valid concept. Germany had specific targets . . . factories, fuel dumps, and industrial areas that called for precision bombing. But Japan is different. Japan has what they call a shadow industry, consisting of thousands of tiny backyard manufacturing plants. We can't pinpoint them well enough to take them out with rapierlike thrusts—so I'm going after them with a sledgehammer. What's more, I'm going after them under the protection of darkness. To do that, I've stripped the planes of all their guns except the tail gun. Without the weight of the guns and ammunition and with a smaller crew, the planes can carry more bombs. And since January we've dropped fifty thousand tons in high explosives and twice that tonnage in incendiaries. We have been particularly effective over Tokyo."

"Yes," Willie said. "I've seen the figures on the firebomb raids on Tokyo. So far, I understand, fifty-six square miles have been gutted."

"It doesn't end with Tokyo. We're going to go after every city in Japan, one by one, until the Japs realize they can no longer resist . . . or until the entire country is turned into a smoldering cinder, whichever comes first."

The phone on his desk rang, and he picked it up.

"LeMay," he grunted. He listened for a moment, said, "Good," then replaced the receiver and looked at Willie. "You've been cleared by the War Department. Come with me now. There's something I want you to see."

KANOYA, KYUSHU, THE JAPANESE HOME ISLANDS

Though twenty-one-year-old Ensign Saburo Amano, a Navy fighter pilot, had never taken off from an aircraft carrier, he had flown his Raiden airplane valiantly against the repeated B-29 raids over his homeland. The name *Raiden* meant "thunderbolt." In this new airplane, which was larger than the Zero and equipped with a turbocharged engine, more armor, and cannons instead of machine guns, Saburo had managed to shoot down two of the huge, swift American bombers. But there were far too few of the Raidens, and they had come much too late to turn the tide of war. As a result each B-29 raid was bigger and more devastating than the one before, and under the relentless firebombing more and more Japanese cities were being turned into burned-out wastelands.

Finally, in mid-July, Saburo had felt such impotent rage, coupled with burning hatred for the unreachable enemy who could attack with such impunity, that he had gone to see Vice-Admiral Matome Ugaki to volunteer for the Special Attack Corps.

The Special Attack Corps was the official name; most Japanese preferred to refer to it by the name the first attack group had taken: Kamikaze—"Divine Wind."

Vice-Admiral Ugaki had just been appointed commander of the final line of defense, a great kamikaze offensive code-named *Ten Go*, or "Heavenly Operation." This name, like Divine Wind, had been chosen to reflect the spiritual purity of those willing to make the supreme sacrifice.

"In order for Japan to survive," Vice-Admiral Ugaki told Saburo, looking up at the young officer from behind his desk, "we must depend upon the courage of our most courageous."

"I am honored to offer myself to such a glorious cause," Saburo replied, standing at rigid attention.

Vice-Admiral Ugaki got up and walked over to a beautifully lacquered cabinet. Taking out a bottle wrapped in red felt, he held it up for Saburo's inspection. "I was given this bottle of sake by Admiral Yamamoto," he explained. "I drink from it only on the most special occasions." He poured them each a glass. "And I would be deeply honored now," he continued, "if the son of an old friend would drink with me."

"Thank you, Admiral," Saburo said, accepting the glass, bowing, then drinking the liquor.

"I was, of course, extremely saddened to hear of the fate of your father, my good friend Hiroshi Amano," Ugaki said. "But I was filled with pride to learn that he was killed while flying Admiral Yamamoto. To die in such glorious company is indeed an honor."

"Yes. My mother and sister take great comfort in the glory of his death."

"Your mother and sister—they are still in Hiroshima?"

"Yes."

"Good, good. They are quite fortunate, you know. The bombers have not harmed Hiroshima, and the Americans have no intention of doing so."

"I am pleased that this is true," Saburo replied. "But I am puzzled as to why the Americans would spare the city."

Ugaki grunted contemptuously. "Well, of course, it is simply an example of the American arrogance. You see, they truly believe they can conquer Japan. And when they do, they will need an undamaged city from which to rule. They have chosen Hiroshima as that city."

"I would rather see Hiroshima destroyed than used in such a way!" Saburo said resolutely.

"Spoken like a true samurai," Ugaki responded with a chuckle. "But perhaps the Americans are a bit premature, eh? When they feel the full effects of our 'Heavenly Operation,' they will not think our homeland so easy to conquer."

"When I die," Saburo vowed, "I will take one thousand Americans with me."

Vice-Admiral Ugaki's eyes brimmed with tears, and he poured another glass of sake, then held it out in a stiff-armed salute toward Saburo. "I drink to you, Saburo, and one thousand like you. Together you will destroy one million Americans . . . and you *will* save Japan!"

As Saburo learned when he had reported to his barracks at the airfield near Kanoya, it hadn't been difficult to find volunteers for the Special Attack Corps. Like him, the other kamikaze pilots were convinced that they would not survive the war anyway and welcomed the opportunity for a patriotic suicide. They much preferred to die gloriously by crashing their bomb-laden planes into American ships than to bleed their lives away in some meaningless and obscure engagement.

Although Saburo had been under the impression that he'd be selected for the very next suicide mission, he soon found that wasn't the case. Each day when the rosters were posted, he hurried to the bulletin board with the other pilots to see if his name was there. Each day that it wasn't he turned away, deeply disappointed that his rendezvous with destiny was to be delayed a bit longer.

Those who did find their names on the board would laugh and pat each other on the back, proud of the selection that made them "Gods without earthly desires."

"We will wait for you," those who were chosen said to those who were left behind. "We will wait at the shrine of Yasukani until everyone else arrives."

Day after day Saburo would check the board looking for his name, only to come away disappointed that he hadn't yet been selected. Meanwhile, he settled into the routine of the Special Attack Corps.

To his surprise, the routine of the squadron was little different from that of any of the other units he had been assigned to. There was, however, a greater closeness among the men, with absolutely no bickering or jealousy or in-fighting. No brothers had ever been closer than these men were to each other, and Saburo's heart swelled with love and pride every time he passed his barracks' motto. One of the other pilots, skilled in the art of calligraphy, had made a beautiful brush-stroke rendering of the stirring words:

BORN APART, WE DIE TOGETHER

Neither Saburo nor the others appeared to show any anxiety over their appointment with eternity. They read or played cards, and when there was someone among them who could play the piano, they would sing, generally picking folk songs or songs from their youth. Saburo had a fine, clear tenor voice, and he was often called upon to sing his favorite song:

> *Sakura, Sakura*
> *Yayoi no sora wa*
> *Miwatasu Kagiri*
> *Kasumika kumo ka*
> *Nioizo izuro*
> *Izaya, izaya*
> *Miniyou—kan.*

The song was an ancient Japanese folk song celebrating blue skies, cherry blossoms, and young love. Saburo knew about blue skies and cherry blossoms, but knew nothing of young love, the love of a woman.

When Saburo told the others that he had never been with a woman and would die a virgin, he thought they might laugh at him. Instead they cried with him.

"It isn't fair. No one should be asked to sacrifice his life without having first known the pleasures of a woman," one of the others declared.

"I am prepared to give to the emperor whatever is asked of me," Saburo insisted.

"The emperor asks for your life and your soul. He does *not* demand that you die celibate."

That night as Saburo lay sleeping, a hand touched him lightly on the shoulder. He had been dreaming that there was no war, and he was home on his own sleeping mat. When he opened his eyes and saw it was a young woman who had awakened him, he thought it was his sister, Yukari, calling him to breakfast. Then he realized that he was not at home, and the young woman looking down at him was not his sister.

"Who are you?" he asked anxiously. "What do you want?"

"I am Sasi," the girl answered in a soft, lilting voice. "Your friends have brought me to you."

"My friends?" Saburo raised up on one elbow and looked around the barracks. To his surprise everyone was gone. He was alone with the girl. "Where is everyone?" he asked in alarm. He sat up quickly and reached for his clothes. "I must go!"

"No!" the girl cried. Gently but insistently, she pulled his hand back from his clothes. "Don't you understand? I am for you."

At first Saburo didn't understand. Then he realized what was happening. His friends, troubled by his confession that he had never known a woman, had arranged it so that he wouldn't have to die a virgin.

"What . . . what must I do?" he asked hesitantly.

Sasi smiled and brushed away a fall of hair. Her skin shone, and her eyes glistened in the ambient light coming through the barracks' door and windows. Saburo thought he had never seen a more beautiful woman.

"You don't have to do anything," Sasi said. Her voice was as musical as a wind chime. "I will do everything."

Her hands began their work then, gently massaging and kneading Saburo's body. He had never experienced anything like the sensations he was feeling now. He was hot and cold and shaky all at the same time, and he had a pounding erection. Sasi reached down to hold his penis, and he gasped in intense pleasure.

"Sasi," Saburo said, his voice breathless with passion. "Sasi, I love you."

Saburo knew that love was something that came later, after an arranged marriage and the long period of adjustment of a man and wife living together. It wasn't something one felt in the first few minutes of meeting someone, and certainly it wasn't something one felt for a comfort girl. But time and place had been altered for Saburo. This barracks, his sleeping mat, and Sasi made up his entire world, and time no longer had meaning. He was already standing at the portal of eternity; the few days he had left on earth were as decades; the hours, months. When he told Sasi he loved her, he meant it truly, and he gave her all that was his to give.

With a deft, lithe movement, Sasi threw one leg over Saburo's body, then very slowly made the connection. Saburo looked down at where they joined, watching in fascination as he disappeared inside her. She leaned forward across him and her breasts swung down, the nipples brushing across his chest. Her hair fell to either side of her face as she brought her own face down to his.

"And I love you, Saburo Amano-san," Sasi said, her sweet, minted breath caressing his lips. At that moment she meant it as much as he did.

The very next day, August 4, Saburo's name appeared on the roster.

The new novel of the American frontier from

Terry C. Johnston

WINTER RAIN

Three years have passed since the close of the bloody conflict between North and South—three years of bitterness, sorrow, and pain for Jonah Hook. He paid his debt for siding with the Confederacy—first in a Union prison and then serving on the frontier—only to return home to find an even more terrible loss: the abduction of his wife and children. Determined to save them and bring their brutal kidnappers to justice, Hook turns westward, setting out across the lawless territories of the Great Plains. The journey ahead will test Jonah's courage and endurance to the limit. On that bloody trail of rescue and revenge, nothing will stop him save success...or death.
